THE MAYA PROPHECY

THE MAYA PROPHECY

P. A. FABER

iUniverse, Inc.
Bloomington

The Maya Prophecy

This is a work of fiction. All of the characters, names, incidents, organizations, and dialogue in this novel are either the products of the author's imagination or are used fictitiously.

iUniverse books may be ordered through booksellers or by contacting:

iUniverse
1663 Liberty Drive
Bloomington, IN 47403
www.iuniverse.com
1-800-Authors (1-800-288-4677)

ISBN: 978-1-4697-9210-1 (sc)
ISBN: 978-1-4697-9212-5 (hc)
ISBN: 978-1-4697-9211-8 (ebk)

Printed in the United States of America

iUniverse rev. date: 03/21/2012

DEDICATION

This novel is dedicated to:

Edward Faber Jr. (December 28, 1954-Febuary 6, 1988), my brother, who first gave me the idea that writing a book was a life-long goal and a noble achievement.

Dianne Faber Stanley (October 6, 1946-May 26, 2009) my sister, who shared an intense love of books and reading with me all through her life.

Steven Mitchell (March 30, 1952-April 17, 2010) a friend who was as fascinated by the Maya and the Maya Prophecy as I. He shared in my initial research and encouraged my intention to write a novel about it.

ACKNOWLEDGEMENTS

This work would never have been begun, much less completed, if not for many, many good friends and family. These individuals supported me and what I was doing and encouraged me to begin and to continue. They listened to endless recitals: of Maya history and myth, of changing story lines, of complaints about plot confusion and the tedium of copy editing, and the disappointment of editorial reviews. They listened, they encouraged, and they held my hand; whatever was needed. They know who they are and they have my eternal gratitude.

Several special thanks are needed:

To Debbi Deats, who did the endless and tedious job of proof-reading. She tirelessly read and re-read the manuscript in all its phases and gave honest, helpful critiques. Thank you, Debbi.

To my family who put up with me through the frustration and the elation and never stopped believing in me and telling me so.

To my AAUW writers group, Martha Treichler and Gary Brown, who gave me invaluable constructive criticism and encouragement.

To all of the staff at the Steuben County Health Care Facility where the manuscript was finally completed while I mended from a fractured femur and wrist.

And most of all to my parents: My mother, Mildred V. Faber, who instilled in me belief that I could do anything and everything I set my mind to, and my father, Edward Faber Sr., who believed in hard work and perseverance and passed those traits on to me.

Author's Remarks

This novel is a work of fiction. No characters or organizations are based upon actual individuals or groups. Any similarities are coincidental and not intended. All actual locations are based on descriptions and characterizations accessible on the internet.

This novel is not meant to be a history of the ancient Maya civilization or the modern Maya people. Although based upon a civilization with a historical reality and a culture that has survived to the present, there is little written documentation of the people; nothing to tell us who the Maya were, how they lived and, most intriguing of all, why they disappeared over a thousand years ago. So the story of the Maya people in The Maya Prophecy is pure fabrication coming from my imagination. I took as my source material for what Mayan life might have been like the works of Michael Coe, Linda Schele, and John Major Jenkins but I embellished their descriptions of the civilization with my own imagination. Therefore this work is in no way a history or true picture of the Maya people.

Some of the myths retold here are based on recorded myths but they are derived from many different city-states and cultures over the 10 centuries that the civilization existed. The creation myth comes from an interweaving of the creation told in the Popol Vu attributed to the Mayan Quiché kingdom in the Guatemalan highlands and Mesoamerican creation myths from oral tradition. The rest of the myths that begin each chapter, especially the story of the Wise Women and the priest, are entirely my creation.

It is true that the Maya had vast knowledge of astronomy and the solar system. They seemed to have predicted the occurrence of the convergence that will occur sometime around 2012. It is also true that all of their calendars end on 12-21-12 and that this would indicate the end of the fifth creation and the beginning of the sixth. There is also a vague allusion to a cataclysm of some sort occurring at that time in the Dresden Codex, but only a fragment of the codex exists and what remains is incomplete.

Nothing that remains of the Maya written text says anything at all about that day being doomsday or predicting the end of the world.

Finally, there is no secret codex of Chan Bahlam II or any hidden codex written by a Maya priest. There were no historical figures to match the Wise Women or the Priest. And certainly the existence of a sacred tile meant to save the world is pure fiction. I wrote the book because of my fascination with the what ifs: what if the Maya Prophecy were to come true, what if the end of the world is coming on 12-21-12, and what if the Maya had discovered a way to prevent that destruction. Only time will tell.

List of Characters

Present day—2011-1012

Main characters

Kate O'Hara	Main character, anthropology professor at a New York University
Adam Mallory	Master student in anthropology
Brian Conway	Master student in archeology
Calvin Otis	Master student in archeology and IT
Carli Peters	University senior majoring in anthropology
Daniel Keith	Archeology professor at a New York University

Other characters:

Enrice` Sanchez	Mexican radio talk-show host
Jorges Casteo	Guide at Chichen Itza
Padre Alejandro Domingo	Catholic priest
Professor Robert Allen	Head of the Department of Archeology/anthropology at a New York University
Roberto Mateos	Head of the Department of Archeology/anthropology at a New York University
Senor Frederico Diego	Director of the Merida Nationale Museo
Shaman	Wise woman, fortune teller

Chichen Itza 933-944 CE

Main characters:

Ahkan	Ah Chinche K'an Kan, young Shaman wise woman, literally yellow butterfly
Took Pak	Chan Took Pakal—small flint shield, the young Mayan priest
Ko'lel ix K'aax	Shaman, wise woman of the forest
Nuxib Mak Lu'um	the gardener, literally old man of the earth

Other characters

Ah Kin Mai	the High Priest, Koloome Ek Suutz
Ah Tz'on K'an	Took Pak's second brother
Ahab Ch'e'en	Took Pak's father, literally lord keeper of the cave
Ajaw K'inich B'ox Kan	the fictional Maya king in 944 CE
Ajaw K'inich K'uk	the father of the present king
Ak'a ch'iick	Ahkan's mother
Cha Mach B'en Kan	the aged principle astronomer
Chaak Pul Aj k'uhm	Ahkan's father an Aj k'uhm, a scribe
Chak	the cook
Chan Bahlum II	(635-702) king of the city-state of Baakal(aka. Palenque)
Chawak K'ab'	Took Pak's eldest brother
Chich'en Itza	means "At the mouth of the well of the Itza (people)".
Cho Piintol aj Tzib	chief scribe
Diego de Landa Calderón	Spanish Bishop (1524-1579) of the Yucatán destroyed all of the written works of the Maya
Ek Chuk'in Och	Ahkan's brother
Halach Uinic	true human, the first man
ix Ajawb K'an B'al1	the fictional royal consort, Queen, in 944 CE
Janab ha'	Took Pak's oldest sister
Kay Nuuk yu Lu'um	a boy at the Temple school
Kiichpak pas	Took Pak's younger sister
Koloome Ek Suutz	Ah Kin Mai, the High Priest
Ku'kul'kan	the Plumed Serpent god
NaabYutzil	Took Pak's mother
Sajal Ch'itz'aat	the High Priest's undersecretary
Yax Ahk	young priest tutor at temple school, later novice master

Mayan gods:

Ah Uincir Dz'acab	the god of healing
Chaac	the god of rain
Chac Chel	the earth goddess, also of childbirth and fertility
Cisin and Xbalanque	gods of the underworld
Hun Bstz and Hun Chuen	the twin gods
K'u K'uk'Kan	Plumed serpent god, symbol of the sun
Quetzal	sacred bird revered by the Maya
Yumil Kaxob	the god of the Maize

THE MAYA[1]
PROPHECY[2]
PROLOGUE

June 25, 2011
12.19.19.17.7, 4 Manik, 10 Mac [*, 3]
Yucatán Península, México

I open my eyes, but can't see anything. I'm in total darkness. My head hurts. I feel groggy and sick to my stomach. I feel confused and frightened. I realize, with a start, that I don't know where I am and I can't remember how I got here.

I raise my hand and gingerly touch the side of my head. Something warm and sticky coats my fingers. I probe a lump the size of a golf ball at my temple. The area is very tender and obviously bleeding. That isn't the only thing that hurts. The simple effort of lifting my arm makes me aware that every inch of my body hurts. It seems to be covered with scrapes and bruises. What has happened to me?

My head begins to clear and I take stock of my surroundings. Wherever I am, it is dark and still. It smells of rock and earth, dry and dusty. I can't hear anything, no wind or bird or animal sounds, nothing beyond the sound of my own breathing. My eyes become accustomed to the dark and I can see a faint lightness directly above me. "I seem to be in a hole," I say outloud into the darkness. I stretch out my hand and encounter a wall to my left, only inches away. No, not a wall, but rough stone. Yes, I seem to be in a small, deep hole, a cave. I reach to my right and can feel nothing. I seem to be perched on a narrow ledge of some sort. A wave of nausea

---

* This is the Mayan date: 12.19.19.17.7 from the Long Count Calendar indicates 12 Baktun, 19 Katun, 19 Tun, 17 Winal, 7 Kin. And 4 Manik from the Tzolkin Calendar and 10 Mac from the Haab. For further explanation see readers notes.

comes over me making me unbalanced . . . I begin to slip sideways and grab out frantically, just managing to grasp hold of a small protrusion in the rock face beside me. My head swims and I feel faint. The confusion deepens and I'm on the brink of unconsciousness once again. As I begin to fade, I think, "Have I fallen down the rabbit hole?"

I become aware of my surroundings again sometime later and wonder how much time has elapsed. I still can't remember anything beyond waking here in the dark. "Okay," I think, "I don't know where I am or how I got here. That's what I don't know. What do I know? I'm alone, hurt and bleeding, and probably have a concussion. My name? Of course, I know that." It takes effort but the information comes to me slowly. "My name is Kate, Kate O'Hara," I say out loud, "and I'm a college professor, a college professor of anthropology." I think again. "I'm an American. Okay, so far." Some clarity comes rushing back. I'd been looking for something, hadn't I? But what? I shake my head as if that will clear the cobwebs, but it just makes my head throb. I still don't know where I am or how I got into this predicament, literally stuck at the bottom of a smelly hole.

I rest from thinking for a moment. It's too hard. I close my eyes, but the possible consequence of my situation nags at me. I am alone and hurt. There doesn't seem to be anyone else around, no sounds of activity. What if I can't get out? What if no one finds me? What if I die here? Panic sets in and quickly takes over. I do the only thing I can think of doing. I scream. "HELP ME!"

No response. The only result of my efforts is another wave of nausea and pain in my temple. I'm shaky and sweating from the exertion. I need to get out of here. My heart is pounding, my breath short and rapid. The awkward position I'm lying in only makes everything worse. I gingerly test the movement of my limbs. Nothing seems to be broken, at least. I move cautiously in an attempt to sit more securely on the narrow shelf. I feel something, the impression of something hard underneath me. My cell phone, I realize. My cell phone in my back pocket. I reach my hand back to extract the phone, but in my excitement, I move too fast and nearly fall again. I regain my balance with effort, but in the process dislodge a piece of rock from the cave's wall. The stone falls into the crevasse and I wait to hear it hit the bottom to see just how far down it goes. I wait. I'm surprised. I hear nothing. My first thought is that the cave has no bottom, a bottomless pit. "Ridiculous," I chide myself. "No, the more logical explanation has to be that the stone has landed on something soft, probably soil or vegetation that has fallen into the hole and accumulated in the bottom.

I return to the chore of getting at my phone without following the stone into the pit. I work very slowly this time and finally remove it from the pocket of my jeans. I hit the connect button and the phone lights up. The screen tells me it is June 25, 2011, 7 PM. Okay. I look closer at the phone and my spirits plummet. No bars, meaning no service here. So much for summoning help that way. I feel the panic rise again and I do what comes naturally, I scream. "Help. Somebody help me!"

Again, there's no answer.

Suddenly my attention is caught by a sound. Is that someone or something outside? The sound comes again and I realize it's coming from below me, not from above. It's coming from within the cave, not outside. I think shakily, "Something is here, in the cave with me, but what?" I don't want to think about the possibilities, none of them good. A wild cat or a bear come immediately to mind and then, even worse, the thought of a giant snake or lizard grips me. A feeling of terror returns, but this time I don't dare scream out for fear of alerting whatever shares my cave. I hold my breath and listen.

Nothing! And then another sound, this time a moan, definitely a moan, a very human sound. Someone else has fallen into this hole with me. I am not alone. Then the sense of the situation comes to me fully. I am not alone, but my companion is hurt, hurt worse than I am, probably severely injured and possibly dying. I need to think. I need to come up with a plan to get both of us out of here, and soon.

I try to think and slowly the fog in my brain seems to clear a little. Who can the other person be? The thinking makes me dizzy, makes my head hurt, makes me tired. I close my eyes again and drift.

A woman approaches me, a girl really. A girl dressed in a bright, yellow skirt and loose fitting blouse, both ornately embroidered with designs I recognize as those of the Maya. The figure shimmers in the darkness, ethereal, ghostly. Seated on her shoulder is a large emerald and gold bird, with a long plumed tail and brilliant scarlet beak. The girl comes closer, reaching out her hand to me, in comfort or in supplication? I do not know. She smiles at me and I feel calm and safe.

I start awake. A dream? A hallucination? An omen? Suddenly, memory floods back to me. "Eduardo," the name comes unbidden. And I remember. "Eduardo is missing. We were looking for him." The pieces fall into place, one after another. I am in the Yucatan, in Mexico. I came to an archeological dig of an ancient Mayan village and a colleague, Eduardo, had gone missing. I . . . we, others had been with me, had been searching for him. I had gone off by myself. I was on a hill and had been startled by a shriek and I had fallen. There was a bird, I think, a huge green and gold bird, whose harsh cry had frightened me and I had fallen. I can remember nothing after that. Is the other occupant of the cave Eduardo? I reach my hand down into the hole but cannot feel anything. "Eduardo, I'm here, hang in there. They'll find us," I say into the darkness. Only a moan comes in response.

My head is clearing slowly. So there are others. Daniel and the rest, I remember, are out there, somewhere, looking for Eduardo and, probably by now, looking for me, too. "I need to attract their attention if . . . when . . . they come close enough to hear," I tell myself. So I call out loudly, not in panic but with purpose. "Help. Help. Over here, down here. Help." I repeat the call over and over again, for what seems an eternity, without results. My voice grows hoarse. "I don't know how much longer I can continue," I whisper. Then I hear another noise, a sound from outside this time, not the moaning. I wait, breath held, for the sound to repeat. Minutes pass. Was I dreaming again? Then I hear it once more.

"Kate," comes a voice from a distance. "Kate."

"I'm here," I croak, and then louder, "Over here. Over here."

CHAPTER ONE

I

December 28, 1987
12.18.14.11.13, 3 Ben, 1 K'ankin
Yucatan Peninsula, Mexico

Mayan Myth

In the Ninth Baktun of the Fifth Creation,
In the great city-state of Baakal,
Ajaw K'inich Chan Bahlum II[4] sat upon the throne.
A great king, son of the mighty Ajaw K'inich Pakal,
He was a seer and a prophet
One who could read the stars and foretell the days.

He foretold the fortunes of the Maya
Far into the future.
Chan Bahlum foretold the end of creation,
When the will of the gods would destroy the world.
For the fifth time the world would come to an end,
This time by water.

He foretold the exact day, the exact hour.
13.0.0.0.0, 4 Ahau, 3 Kankin,[5]
As the sun reaches its zenith

Chan Bahlum looked to the stars
And in the Heavens he saw the answer,
And so devised the means to thwart the will of the gods.
This he wrote within a secret Codex
Which he hid, for future generations
To discover when the time was right.

Many Baktun passed,
The Maya people were still strong
And the Temple still held sway.
In a city far to the North
Lived a nina chinca, a young girl.
She was wise, a Shaman, and a seer.

She learned the shaman ways
And was a great healer to the people.
She was called Ko'lel ix K'aax,
Wise woman of the forest.
And so she has been known
Through the intervening ages.

Then too lived an Aj k'uhm,
A priestly scribe,
His name, Piedra Escudo,
Meant stone shield.
The wise woman loved him
And he loved her.

The priest was a wise and learned man.
He knew the movements of the stars
And of the planets.
How they guided the fortunes of the people.
He knew the history
And the legends of the Maya.

One night, the great Ajaw Bahlum
Came to Piedra Escudo in a dream.
The King told him of a time in the far future
When the gods, angry with humankind,
Would align the stars
To set in motion the end of creation.

And the mighty king whispered
In the priest's ear the secret,
Of how men might outwit the gods.
He gave to Piedra Escudo a holy shield
To protect mankind from the wrath of the gods.
And a book to instruct them in its use.

These he must pass on
Through the generations.
Piedra Escudo gave
The holy shield and sacred book
To the Wise Woman,
Ko'lel ix K'aax.

She hid the sacred book
In a cave far to the north,
The shield she placed in sacred ground
At the center of the earth.
And so they remain
To be found when they are needed.

The gods were angry.,
And so they demanded
Piedra Escudo's sacrifice
Upon the high altar,
To appease their anger.
And this was done.

Ko'lel ix K'aax mourned his death,
Living many, many years in the forest.
There she ministered to the people
And told them of the future.
When she left this world
Her waay remained.

Her spirit haunts the warab'alja still.
And the legend says,
When the end of this creation is near,
Ko'lel ix K'aax will return
As the sacred Quetzal,
To guide the way.

II

June 23, 2011
12.19.18.8.13, 3 Ben, 11 Zec
Kennedy Airport to Mexico City

I get through airport security with no difficulty and head to the departure gate with plenty of time to spare. I drag my rolling carry-on, and with an overstuffed book bag and my purse over my shoulder, hurry through the crowded terminal. I hate airports, the rushing and the scores of people. I always feel compelled to arrive early for fear of missing my flight, only to wait an interminable amount of time for a flight that inevitably boards late.

I am early today as usual, but there are a dozen or so passengers already assembled at the gate. Among the usual assortment of businessmen, college students and senior citizens, there is a group of five individuals standing off to one side. Despite their varied appearances they are, to my eyes anyway, obviously academics. Dressed in attire from casual sportswear, to blue jeans and T-shirts, to one in safari garb, they, nonetheless, all looked cerebral. I know right away that this is my group.

I slow and take a moment to observe them from a distance. I know a couple of them, old colleagues if not old friends. I decide to postpone joining them and slip into line at the coffee bar. A latte is just the thing.

While waiting I watch them surreptitiously. There are four men and one woman, a girl really. The information I had received regarding the summer archeology course said there would be three master's students and an undergrad, as well as myself and a fellow doctoral candidate. Dr. Robert Allen, the director of the project, is to meet us in Mexico City.

I know two of them. Neither of them is a 'friend' of mine and, sorry to say, they don't have a personality between them. Daniel Keith, PhD candidate in archeology, is an insufferable know-it-all. Daniel and I teach together at the University and had spent the last four summers with Professor Allen at the Yucatan site. We get along, but barely. Daniel is good looking, and knows it; five ten or eleven, black hair, emerald green eyes, and a perpetual smirk, all this, a testament to his elitist, wealthy, Boston Irish heritage.

And Calvin Otis, a master student in archeology and an astonishing math wizard. Calvin had been a student of mine as an undergrad and he had joined us last summer in the Yucatan. We've had little contact since then. I don't dislike him, but he's such a nerd. He's not bad looking though, if you can get past his insipid character. He's of medium height, well built, with slicked back brown hair on the longish side. He is dressed today, as usual, in black: black jeans and black tee. He is standing slightly apart from the group in his usual slouch.

The female member of the group has to be the undergrad. She looks all of about sixteen, blond, thin and leggy. She is probably part of the group only because her father is rich and can therefore pay her way. But she's another pair of hands at the dig and cash to the University too. I just hope she isn't as dumb as she looks.

That leaves the other two guys as the other two master students. One is drop dead gorgeous: tall, blond and bronzed. I assume he's the guy from California, got his undergrad from Cal Tech. The last is a scrawny, bespectacled, geeky guy. He has to be the one from the mid-west, somewhere in corn country. He's wearing a wrinkled khaki safari outfit: shorts and open shirt over a white t-shirt. All he's missing is the pith helmet. Maybe he checked that through.

My turn at the coffee counter: an extra-large mocha latte with extra whipped cream. I'll be doing heavy manual labor for the next three months, so to Hell with the calories. Can't put it off any longer as they'll be calling our flight shortly, so I grab my bags and make my ungainly way over to join the group.

Daniel is the first to note my approach. "Well, Kate, it's about time," he says with his usual smirk, a hint of amusement, and, yes, condescension. "Thought you were going to miss the flight or had just decided to forgo our little expedition this summer. More pressing engagements, perhaps?" He grins broadly. "That would have been such a shame as you are one of the highlights of this dreary adventure." And he grins even more broadly.

I feel like hitting him. He invariably elicits this response in me, but I just smile sweetly and say, "Hello, Daniel."

He puts his hand on my shoulder condescendingly and turns to the others. "This little lady" and he smiles down at me.

"Little lady my sweet ass," I think but hold my peace, don't want to make that kind of impression on the others, at least not yet. I grit my teeth and smile up at his near six feet height from my near five feet and say nothing.

". . . is Kate O'Hara, doctoral fellow in anthropology," he continues, "and a four year," he looks at me questioningly and I nod grudgingly, "veteran of the Yucatan." He bows slightly, as if taking credit for my very existence, the insufferable bore. "She has a bit of a temper, takes a bit of getting used to, but she's good at her job." And he laughs.

Okay, so I'm barely five feet and have bright red, auburn, hair and I'm pushing forty. And okay, I'm small, small framed, but I'm strong with good muscle tone and can take care of myself. And yeah, I have a temper. As a result of these failing, or attributes, I need all the authority with these younger, untrained students that my experience and credentials can give me. And here he is undermining me from the get go. Damn him.

The surfer dude steps forward, takes my hand in both of his and smiles at me warmly. "I'm Adam Mallory," he says in a deep, melodious baritone and he smiles at me again. He has deep, blue eyes and dimples, yes dimples. He's so good looking it must be illegal. He brings me back to the present by continuing, "I'm also an anthropology student." He says this as if it gives us a special bond. I almost swoon, but catch Daniel's smirk out of the corner of my eye and get myself under control. Adam is still speaking, "Got my undergrad at the U of Wisconsin, Madison." I react with a surprised grunt and he laughs richly. "Took me for a city slicker, did you? Nope. Born and bred in the mid-west. A hick if there ever was one. But I have learned to wear shoes," he says looking down at a shiny pair of leather boots that must have set him back half my weekly paycheck. So not from California. Do they surf in the Wisconsin Dells?

10

Our intimate little tete-te-tete is abruptly interrupted by Little Miss Cheerleader. "My name is Carli, Carli Peters," she chirps. "I'm a senior in anthropology too." She smiles over her shoulder at Adam while she grabs my hand. "This is my first dig and I'm so excited, and so excited to be working with you, Professor O'Hara," she burbles. Of course you are, I think. A brownnoser, for sure.

She turns expectantly to Calvin, who looks at her dully. After a protracted pause, he says sullenly, "Calvin Otis. Archeology and IT. Second season in the Yucatan." He doesn't smile, just seems relieved to be done with a tedious chore.

Carli turns to the last member of the group expectantly, obviously reveling in her cheerleader role. The other student looks at his feet. "B . . . B . . . Brian C . . . Conway." he stammers, and I do believe he is blushing. And this is the Californian, graduate of Cal Tech. Well, so much for stereotypes.

When he doesn't continue, Carli whispers, "What discipline?" as if encouraging a young child.

He finally looks up at her, gives a weak smile, and blushes even more. "Ar . . . ar . . . cheol . . . logy," he manages to blurt out. "First t . . . time on a d . . . dig." And he smiles timidly at Carli again. She has made an easy conquest. Daniel breaks in, "Hate to break up this love fest, but I do believe our plane is about to board."

We all scramble to get our belongings together and proceed to board the flight to Mexico City. Our seats are scattered throughout the plane, as we had purchased our tickets separately, and so I have several hours of blessed solitude to look forward to. The last hours of real privacy for the next few months; as an archeological dig affords one little privacy. You work, eat, live, and sleep (oh, you know what I mean) with your fellow academics, 24/7. I start out leafing through some journal articles, but soon nod off into an uncomfortable nap. Halfway through the flight my arm is jostled and I'm startled awake, as Daniel settles into the seat next to me. Obviously, he has changed places with the older gentleman who had been sitting there quietly leaving me alone.

"Catching up on your reading, I see," he chuckles. I ignore him, or try to. "Looking forward to another exciting summer?" I don't answer. "Nothing of any interest at the dig, obviously . . . or they wouldn't let the likes of us mucking about. Anything of any interest long gone, bound to be." I hate his superior attitude, even if he is right, especially, when he is

11

right. He pauses for a moment, then resumes, "How is your dissertation progressing?" He doesn't wait for me to answer but bludgeons on. "Of course, the summer dig might yield something useful for your area of interest, something about Maya cultural practices?"

"Women's roles in the Maya Post-Classic period," I can't help retorting.

"Well, yes, just so. Digging about in people's ancient garbage in the bottom of a rural village cenote might give you something useful. But there's little doubt it won't hold anything for me. A waste of my time, really."

Irritated, and unable to help myself, I grumble, "Then why did you come?"

"It's part of my job, just as it is yours. Besides, this way I get to spend the summer with you." And he laughs. I sniff but don't say anything. "Wonder why Professor Allen is meeting us in Mexico City rather than flying down with us, as he usually does?"

I hadn't thought much about the change in routine. Why is Daniel, I wonder? "Professor Allen has lots of friends in Mexico. He could be meeting someone, or he has a meeting at the Museum or the Office of Antiquities. There are loads of reasons why he went to Mexico City ahead of us."

"I suppose you are right," Daniel says off handedly. He is quiet for only a few minutes. I think my contradicting him might have conveyed the message that I really want to be left alone. But he doesn't get the hint. "What do you think of this year's crew of Indiana Jones wannabe's?" Then he continues without giving me a chance to respond, not that I want to. "Not an ounce of experience among them. Well, yes," he says as if I had made some incisive comment. "Calvin was at the dig last year, but he has no archeological talent or insight. Good at numbers and computer craft though, I'll give him that."

What is this? I have never heard Daniel talk so much in all the time I've known him and here he is talking my ear off, despite the fact that I barely say a word. He continues his soliloquy, "Now the other two chaps, I don't know much about." How pretentious can you get? "They obviously haven't any experience. The kid from California can't even string two words together. But you know some of those brainiacs aren't much in the communication department but do have flights of genius."

He pauses shortly, more to catch his breath than to wait for any response from me. "Lover-boy on the other hand," he says with a sneer, "hasn't a grey cell to work with." He pauses again, this time waiting for a response from me. I don't agree with him, of course. How can he make that kind of assessment on five minutes conversation? He expects me to argue and I'm not going to give him the satisfaction.

Failing to get a rise out of me, he continues, "And as for Little Miss Sunshine, it's apparent why she is here. Daddy has big pockets and has promised a large endowment to the University in exchange for whatever his little girl wants. Not much brain power there either. I wonder how long before the heat and the dirt gets to her and she packs up and runs back to Daddy?"

This is too much. I can't let him get away with such arrogance, even if I do agree with him about the cheerleader. I lose my cool. "You insufferable, pompous ass," I say in a hissing stage whisper. "You don't know anything about the young woman. Of course, she doesn't know anything. I mean, is inexperienced," I stammered on.

He laughs and interjects snidely, "I didn't say anything about her being inexperienced."

I ignore this last remark and rant on. "She's only a college senior. Give her a break. We were all there at one time." I humph and fall silent.

"Yes we were all there once upon a time," he chuckles and is finally quiet. When he doesn't resume the conversation, I realize he has gotten what he wants, a rise out of me.

For the rest of the flight he leaves me in peace and we arrive in Mexico City with plenty of time to make our connecting flight to Merida. We are to meet Professor Allen at the gate, but by the time our plane is called and we have boarded, he still hasn't shown. Just before takeoff the attendant brings a note and hands it to Daniel. He reads it, grunts and shows the note to me.

I read: "Something came up. Had to take an earlier flight. Will meet you at the airport in Merida. Allen" This year's dig isn't starting off well at all.

III

August 10, 933 CE
10.5.4.16.10, 12 Oc, 13 Ceh
Chechen Itza[6], Yucatan Peninsula

The sun was bright, the air hot and dry. It felt warm upon her bronzed skin. Ahkan paused in the center of the courtyard and turned her face to the midday sun. She drew energy from its radiance and inhaled deeply of the warm fragrance of summer flowers and aromatic herbs. A beautiful yellow butterfly flew past her raised head and landed on one of the coral blooms in the nearby flower garden. It was from the yellow butterfly that she derived her name, Ah Chinche K'an.[7]

She laughed with delight and resumed her skipping across the open patio. The little girl glanced over her shoulder at the boy sitting on the stone wall edging the herb garden along the south wall of the enclosure. She danced closer to him and laughed again. The boy kept his head down, apparently absorbed in the slate balanced upon his knees. He ignored her, but Ahkan saw the hint of a smile upon his lips. The dark haired, dark eyed little girl laughed merrily and skipped around the outer edge of the courtyard. She scuffed her bare feet in the dry sand, raising a fine cloud of dust into the still, hot air. She danced close to the boy, the only other occupant of the patio.

"Ahkan, go away. I am busy. Can you not see?" the boy complained. He leaned closer to the slate he held in his lap. She laughed gaily and skipped away across the courtyard, but was quickly back again, dancing close to him, swishing the bright orange material of her beautifully embroidered skirt. She flicked her long, straight hair at him, catching him across his cheek and bare chest. He absent-mindedly brushed it away with his hand as he would a fly, but did not take his eyes from the slate in his hands. She laughed and flicked her hair at him again.

"You are such an insect," he said irritably, still not raising his eyes from his work. "Always buzzing about."

She laughed again, leaned close to him and whispered in his ear, "Not an insect, a butterfly," she said, and she tickled him again with her hair.

"Humph," he growled, trying to hide the grin that threatened to break through, despite the growl. "You are a pesky fly and I am the spider," he said, trying to make his voice scary, but laughing instead. He put down his slate and grabbed her about the shoulders. "And I am going to tie you up so you cannot fly away." He took her long, black hair and proceeded to tie it into a large knot. Ahkan giggled, wiggled out of his grasp, and shook the knot out of her hair. She danced out of his reach.

"Ahkan, leave your cousin, Chan Took Pakal[8], alone with his work," came a voice from the kitchen end of the courtyard. Her mother appeared in the archway. Ak'a ch'iick was an older version of her daughter, dark hair and dark eyes, but with skin coarsened by the sun. "I need herbs and vegetables from the garden, hun p'iit (little one)[9]. Ahkan, go pick them for me and bring them to the kitchen hut. I need pungent bulbs, herb grass, and green onion tops, too. And sweet lavender for the linen chests and bedrooms." She headed out through the archway again, adding over her shoulder, "And I will need ilk, (chili peppers), sweet and spicy, for today's cooking."

Ahkan picked up a small xu'ul (woven basket) from the corner of the yard and went to the raised beds that circled the courtyard. She closed her eyes and breathed in the pungent fragrance of the herbs and flowers that she gathered from the various beds. Ahkan knew a great deal about the plants and bulbs that grew in the kitchen gardens, for a girl of nine. She spent much of her time working with Nuxib Mak Lu'um, the elderly gardener of the household. This accounted for her often disheveled appearance; bare dusty feet and free flowing hair. Ahkan carried her nearly full basket out the doorway to the kitchens, singing softly to herself.

The household compound was typical of the homes of Maya noblemen, Ahab. It was larger than most, as befitted a family of considerable wealth. It was constructed around a large open courtyard, partially shaded with thatched rafters. In the center of the courtyard was the household pwes, well. The patio was surrounded by the family living quarters to the north and south. The east side contained the archway to the kitchen gardens and the outbuildings that housed the kitchens and the pottery and bake ovens. To the west were the public sitting room and dining room, and the offices and custom house.

The south wall held a small doorway leading to the private rooms of the main family: Took Pak, his parents, brothers, and sisters. These rooms included a sitting room, a sewing room, and small windowless bed chambers for each of the family members. The doorway on the north wall led to the small sleep chambers of the lesser family members and staff: Ahkan, her mother, father, and brother, the cook and the seamstress. The

15

gardener had a hut on the far side of the gardens. The slave quarters were out beyond the gardens near the family fields. The main public entrance was on the west side of the compound adjoining the city plaza.

Took Pak watched Ahkan as she left the patio, a smile upon his face. Though left to his studies in peace, it was a few minutes before he returned to the figures on the slate. He was studying the rudimentary pictographs taught to beginning scribes. It was a simple form of Maya writing, taught to all the sons of the nobility from an early age. Took Pak had taken to it easily and, at the age of 12 years, was beginning the more complex glyphs and mathematics used in the custom houses and in the Temple.

Chan Took Pakal, his name meaning small flint shield, was the third son and the youngest of five children of the noble house of Ahab Ch'e'en. His father and his father's father before him were wealthy merchants, who traded with neighboring city-states near and far. They traded local goods: maize, vegetables and fruits, pelts and furs, and the local crafts of pottery and tools. They dealt in the fine cloth and fabrics for which the region was particularly known; richly colored cottons and linens in brilliant oranges and saffron, beautifully embroidered by the women of the community. Took Pak's great, great grandfather had come from the south and had started the family fortunes by mining jade in the distant mountains. Took Pak's great grandfather had been raised to the class of noble as a result of the financial assistance he had given to the former king, Ajaw K'inich K'uk, the father of the present king. The family had continued in favor from that time. The family's wealth and friendship with the royal family gave them influence in the community and power within the political structure.

Took Pak's eldest brother, Chawak K'ab', being the first son, would take over the family business and his father's place in the royal court. Chawak was currently traveling widely to learn the skills of trade and commerce. Took Pak's second brother, Ah Tz'on K'an was destined for the military. He would serve the city-state and king, by protecting the community from the ever increasing enemies from without. This was the Maya custom: the first son for the family and the court, the second son for the state and its defense.

Chan Took Pakal, as the third son, was promised to the Temple. Took Pak accepted this without question. This was the way it was to be. He had known his path since he was small and had first attended the ceremonies at the Temple. Entering the priesthood meant much study and initiation into the mysteries of mathematics and astronomy. His father often said that the gods had chosen wisely, as Took Pak was surely the brightest of his sons. His intelligence would serve him well and assure his rise within the Temple hierarchy. Took Pak enjoyed studying and, therefore, was content with his lot.

Ahkan came skipping back into the courtyard, still singing quietly to herself. Her voice was as sweet as that of the morning dove. "We are to have venison, b'ak' keeh, for the evening meal tonight as Ah Tz'on K'an will be coming," she told Took Pak. "His division is home and he will have a few days of rest." Ah Tz'on K'an was currently on maneuvers, serving his apprenticeship with a unit of his father's legions. Ahkan's brother, Ek Chuk'in Och, was with him serving as his military aide. They had been gone for many months and Ahkan missed them both. Her brother, Ek Chuk'in Och, six years her elder, was her favorite, except for Took Pak, of course. Ek Chuk'in Och was dashing and daring. He was well liked by everyone, but reckless and often in trouble. His sparkling personality, good looks, and the intercession of their uncle, Took Pak's father, had so far prevented severe consequences.

Ahkan and Took Pak were cousins, as Ahkan's mother and Took Pak's mother were cousins. Their grandfathers were brothers. Took Pak's mother, Naab Yutzil, was from the wealthy branch of the family and had married well, very well indeed. Ahkan's mother, Ak'a Ch'iich, was from the poorer side of the family. She had married well also, but not as well as her cousin. Ahkan's father, Chaak Pul, was an Aj k'uhm, a scribe. He was an educated man who knew the written language and mathematics. He was employed as a scribe within Took Pak's family's business. The mothers, Ak'a Ch'iich and Naab Yutzil, had been childhood friends. With their marriages, Ak'a Ch'iich and her family became part of the Ch'e'en household and so Ahkan had grown up with Took Pak and his siblings. She was one of the family.

Ahkan's mother ran the household. She managed the kitchens and the gardens, and supervised the servants: the maids, the gardener, the cook, and the slaves. Hers was no easy task with such a very large household and as the home of an Ahau, there were many servants and slaves.

Naab Yutzil, Took Pak's mother, oversaw the sewing rooms and the pottery shed, where fine cloth, embroidery and pottery were produced for the household and for trade. She was also responsible for entertaining the many guests that visited the Ch'e'en otoch (home). This was an arduous job for there was much coming and going, many guests and much entertaining, as demanded by their position in the community.

Ahkan was busying herself in the far corner of the courtyard, picking a large bouquet of flowers for the evening table. She continued to sing softly. Although she left him to his studies, Took Pak could not concentrate. Her mere presence distracted him. Her sunny nature drew him out of himself as no one else could.

The sound of voices and giggling came from the house behind him and two young girls entered the courtyard from the archway to the south. The girls were in their early teens, dark haired and bronzed skinned. They chattered merrily as they entered.

Ahkan looked up and the older of the two girls said petulantly to her, "Where have you been? I thought you were to join us in the sewing room this morning. Instead, you have been playing indolently in the sunshine, while we have been slaving away in the shadows, wearing our fingers down with our needles and thread."

"Oh, Janab Ha', you know the seamstress would rather Ahkan not join us," tittered her sister, the younger of the two. "She is so inept with her needle that she causes the seamstress to cry into her linens. Everything Ahkan does, I have to unpick and rework," she continued sourly. "Anyway, she just makes more work for all of us."

"You are right, Kiichpak Pas. I am useless in the sewing room," Ahkan replied. "But I have not been idle. I was up long before either of you, long before daybreak, out in the gardens helping Nuxib Mak pick the vegetables and the herbs for market."

"So that explains your dirty feet," Janahb Ha' said as she looked down at Ahkan's bare and muddy feet.

"And your tangled hair and the dust that covers your face and skirt," Kiichpak Pas laughed, not unkindly.

"And you smell decidedly like the fields and the gardens," added her sister.

"How lovely," smiled Ahkan. "What better things could I smell like, but the fields and the flowers and the gardens?" she said.

"Not very ladylike." said Janahb Ha'.

"Who wants to be a lady?" quipped Ahkan with a haughty look over her shoulder at the two sisters. She continued to fill her already full arms with bright fragrant blossoms.

Took Pak observed the easy interchange between the three girls. They were obviously friends, as well as cousins, and enjoyed each other's company. Took Pak thought to himself, "I do not have any such easy friends, except perhaps Ahkan." This was true. Took Pak was quiet and withdrawn, much more at ease with his studies and hieroglyphs than with his fellow creatures.

Janahb Ha' and Kiichpak Pas left through the archway toward the kitchens without further comment. Took Pak watched as Ahkan filled several pottery vases with water from the pwes. She arranged her flowers in them to place on the tables at dinner that night. She moved in and out of shade to full sunshine. The sun made her ebony hair glisten as if with diamonds. Her sweet face concentrated on her task. She looked much like the butterfly she would like to be.

Finished with her job, Ahkan came over to where Took Pak sat and perched herself on the wall beside him. She rested her chin on his shoulder and gazed at the slate in his hands. She pointed to one of the glyphs. "K'in," she said "the designation for the sun and this, K'u ix tz'it, the god of the maize."

Took Pak looked over at her, astonished. "How do you know that?" he asked.

"Well," she said, as if it was self-evident. "I could not sit with you and the tutor, day after day, and not learn something."

"But you do not seem to pay any attention to what we are talking about," he replied.

"That is all you know. You are always so involved with your work, that it is you who pay no attention to me. But I do pay attention to you and to the tutor. It is interesting."

"The writing and the mathematics are not for women," Took Pak said severely, "especially not for xchuu paal (little girls)."

"I am not a xchuu paal," she protested angrily. "I am finish line smart," she argued, "and I can understand these things. At least, some of it, anyway. And it has nothing to do with whether I am a girl or a boy," she asserted stubbornly. She paused, pondering something. "Took Pak, do you think the tutor would let me study with you? I mean, really study with you, not just listen in?"

"No, I do not think so," he said in horror. "It is unheard of for a girl! It would get the tutor into trouble. It is not proper and completely against the dictates of the community, of the priests, and of the gods."

Took Pak was far too conservative for her taste. He was not daring like her brother, or progressive like she was. "You men want to keep it for yourself, you mean," she countered.

"Shush," he said only half in jest, looking around as if someone might be listening. "You should not talk like that. The priests will not like it. You might get into trouble and so might I. The priests are quick-tempered right now, with the drought that has gone on so long."

She laughed. "As if the High Priest would pay any attention to me, just a xchuu paal." She pulled the slate from his hands and drew several glyphs. He looked over at the slate. "My name," she said, proudly pointing to a glyph. "I like the mathematics best of all," she added, "and the stars and planets."

"Better that you stick to your pottery and herbs, or even better, learn to sew," he laughed. "Learning mathematics and astronomy will not get you a good husband," he told her.

"I do not want a husband," she said firmly.

He looked at her in surprise. "You do not want a husband? But every girl needs a husband," he stammered.

"I do not," she told him, "unless you want to marry me?" She looked coyly up at him through her thick, black eyelashes. She laughed and went on. "No, I plan to become a wise woman, a shaman, a Ko'lel ah Waay (medicine woman). I will sell my herbs and charms and live by myself in the forest like the wise woman, Ko'lel ix K'aax." She referred to the old woman of the forest, who was called upon by the peasant farmers to attend the women in childbirth, the children in sickness, and the men with wounds from hunting or from war.

Took Pak was horrified. "Do not even joke about that," he said.

She laughed again and skipped out of the courtyard, calling, "See you at dinner," over her shoulder.

Took Pak watched her disappear from sight, shaking his head. He did not understand the wild, rebellious streak in her, and in her brother as well, so unlike their parents or any of his family.

As he watched her leave the courtyard he saw a flash of green and gold in the sunlit sky. Then he heard a shrill cry. A large brightly plumed bird soared overhead. Took Pak gasped. It was a Quetzal, the sacred bird of the Maya. This was an omen, Took Pak was sure. But was it an omen of good fortune or of ill?

IV

June 22, 2011,
12.19.18.8.12, 2 Eb, 0 Zec
Midnight: A cellar somewhere in Mexico

Down the darkened stairway came a slow procession of hooded figures, clothed in coarse, dark brown robes, their faces hidden. One by one they reached the foot of the stairs and in silence formed a circle against the dank walls of the subterranean chamber. In the center of the room, raised on a rectangular wooden platform, stood an altar covered by a cloth of red, the color of blood. Upon the altar cloth stood a bowl carved from stone of the deepest ebony.

The last to descend the stairs was a figure, with regal bearing, garbed in white. Rather than joining the circle he mounted the platform and approached the altar. The celebrant placed his hands around the carved bowl and intoned a lilting chant in some forgotten language. The others echoed the cadence.

The white clad figure raised a hand. A second figure came forward; a sack twisted and squirmed from an outstretched arm. Mounting to the altar the supplicant presented this as an offering. When the sack was opened, a pure white cockerel was extracted. The bird struggled but in vain and in silence, for its feet and beak were bound with scarlet cords.

The chanting continued in a slowly rising crescendo. The cock was raised over the obsidian bowl. The figure in white reached inside his coarse robe and withdrew a gleaming, black blade.

The chanting reached its climax and stopped abruptly. At that exact moment the knife was raised and in one swift motion, struck. The rooster's struggle ceased and from the severed neck a stream of bright, red blood ran. As the stream slowed, the chanting began again, slower and more somber. The high priest, for so the central supplicant must be, dipped his fingers into the bowl and with the scarlet liquid, streaked the forehead of the other supplicant and then his own.

Thin strips of parchment, adorned with strange symbols and ciphers, were placed into the bowl and lit with a long taper. The flame burned bright blue and emerald and sent a tendril of grey smoke toward the ceiling. The white robed figure leaned forward and breathed in the acrid smoke. With a gasp he fell back, falling to his knees behind the altar, his head bent to the floor, mumbling incoherently. No one approached him. No one offered help. The murmuring and muttering continued for some time, accompanied by the rhythmic rocking of the figure on the floor. Gradually the rocking slowed and finally ceased and so did the muttering. All was silent.

The outer circle slowly converged upon the center, mounted the platform, and assisted the High Priest to his feet. The procession then filed back up the stairs, in abject silence.

CHAPTER TWO

August 11, 3113 BCE,
0.0.0.0.0, 4 Ahaw, 8 Kumk'u

I

Mayan Myth

And so began the 5th creation of the world.[10]
On 0.0.0.0.0, 4 Ahaw, 8 Kumk' the world began again.
On that day Quetzalcoatl and Ah Puch created the universe.
The gods created the earth to lie between the 13 layers of heaven
And the 9 layers of the underworld.

Upon that which lay between,
They planted Yax-Cheel-Cab,
The first tree of this world, the Tree of Life.
The gods filled the earth with a multitude;
Plants and trees, reptiles and animals,
Birds and fishes.

The gods bade the plants and creatures of the earth
To pay them homage.
But the plants and the trees were mute.
And the animals and the fishes were dumb.
These creations could not worship the gods as they wished.
And the gods were angry.

And Quetzalcoatl and Ah Puch called upon Chac Chel,
Goddess of the earth, goddess of childbirth,
Divine midwife and guardian of fertility.
And they said to her, "Fashion for us a creature
Who will bow down to worship us
And do homage to us, as is our due."

And Chac Chel took the soil of the earth,
Mixed it with the rain from the sky.
And from the mud,
She formed a creature
In the image of the gods.
And she placed the creature upon the earth.

But the sun came with its blistering heat
And dried the creature
And the mud turned to dust.
And the winds came
And blew the dust away
And the gods were angry.

And Chac Chel, goddess of the earth,
Took wood from the Ceiba tree,
The Tree of Life.
And she fashioned a creature
In the image of the gods
And she placed the creature upon the earth.

But the rains came
And covered the creature.
And the creature became sodden
And the wood rotted
And sank back into the earth.
And the gods were angry.

Then the goddess of the earth, Chac Chel
Took maize from the fields
And she fashioned a creature
In the image of the gods.
And she placed the creature
Upon the earth.

And she turned to the gods,
Quetzalcoat and Ah Puch, and said,
"Give to me a portion of your blood."
And this they did.
And Chac Chel took the blood of the gods
And placed it in the sacred bowl of blackest obsidian.

Then Chac Chel poured the blood of the gods
Over the head of the maize creature.
And the creature, Halach Uinic, true human,
Breathed with life, rose,
Opened its eyes,
And beheld the world.

And the man, Halach Uinic,
Knelt down and worshiped
The gods in thanks.
And the gods were pleased.
And the gods called the man, Maya.

II

June 24, 2011
12.19.18.8.14, 4 Ix, 2 Zec
The airport, Merida, Yucatán Península, México

We touch down at the airport in Merida at about 3:20 PM. Without the Professor, I have no idea how we are going to get to the site.

"Isn't this a bitch," growls Calvin. "How does the high and mighty Professor Allen expect us to get to the dig, out in the middle of nowhere, without any transportation? Just like the old fool. Never is organized. Never knows what he's going to do next. Absentminded professor, my ass. So much for tenure in all its glorious wisdom."

I'm not entirely in disagreement with his assessment of the Professor. Professor Allen isn't the most organized of individuals. But, I am disgusted with Calvin for voicing his opinion, so blatantly, in front of the other students. They don't know the Professor and have to work with him for the rest of the summer. Calvin is self-centered and arrogant, and a pain in the posterior. He had been a grouch all of last season. I don't expect he has changed in the interim, but I am sick of it already.

"Really, Calvin," I say in exasperation. "I'm sure some kind of emergency has come up that took the Professor to the site earlier than planned. We don't know what arrangements he has made for our transportation, so before you get all hot and bothered, let's wait and see, shall we?" I say peevishly. I can hear the irritation in my voice. I'm behaving as childishly as Calvin and am ashamed of it.

"Come on," says Daniel as if he is talking to a pair of children, "first things first. Let's get our luggage and then we can search out whether a driver has been arranged for us."

Calvin mutters something under his breath that I can't hear, but can imagine. Since this is a new experience for the other three, they look more than a bit confused and willing for anyone to take the lead. Daniel is more than willing to do so, as usual. We all docilely pick up our carry-ons and follow Daniel through the nearly empty airport to the baggage claim area.

Our luggage is already on the carousel. We quickly claim our odd assortment of bags, boxes, crates and other paraphernalia. Brian sheepishly stammers his offer to carry Carli's two oversized bags: an offer she eagerly accepts with a girlish giggle and a nod. She is obviously used to having someone carry her bags for her. None of the men offer to carry my bags for me, but then the only things I have, besides my carry-on, are three large boxes of equipment and documents I've brought from the University for the Professor. Those we will need help with, a red cap and a luggage cart, at least. I wrestle them from the carousel. Adam comes to my assistance after I drop the first of them on my foot. Thank God for heavy boots. Just as we are finishing, I feel a tap on my shoulder and turn to see a short, middle-aged Mexican looking at me apologetically. He is crumpling his hat nervously in his hands.

"Senorita Professora," he says timidly. "The Professor Allen asked that I come to collect you here at the aeropueto."

"Buenos dios, Miguel," I say with a smile that I hope will put him at his ease. I recognize him as the senior overseer from the dig last year. He looks at me contritely, waiting for me to tell him what to do next. This is not a chore he normally undertakes. "Where is Eduardo?" I ask. Dr. Eduardo Gomez, Professor Allen's counterpart from the university in Mexico City, usually makes the airport run. "And more to the point, where is the Professor?" I think, but don't say out loud.

Miguel crushes his hat even more, clearly at a loss for what to say. At this point, Daniel breaks in, silencing whatever it is the older man is attempting to tell me. "You've come to get us, Miguel? Good." And pointing to the large pile of boxes and luggage stacked nearby, "Those are ours. We'll need a luggage cart." With a frightened look, Miguel nods and turns to comply with what was obviously an order.

I know that something else is going on. Something is wrong, and Miguel hasn't been given the chance to tell me what it is. I reach out and gently catch the overseer's arm. "What's wrong, Miguel? Where is Eduardo? Where is the Professor?"

Daniel starts to interrupt again. "We can get to that later. But first . . ."

But I hold on to Miguel's arm and look into his face. "Something is wrong," I repeat, not a question this time, but a statement of certainty. Something is definitely wrong, as Miguel is near to tears by this time.

"Eduardo," he stammers. "Eduardo is missing."

"Missing?" Daniel and I say together. This finally gets Daniel's attention.

"Si," Miguel says. "Two days ago . . . when we got to the dig, he is not there, though we expect him to be. Then we see his car is parked behind the office and his apparatus is in his tent. We did not worry at first. We think he just went off for a hike, as is often what he does. It is his . . ." and here he stumbles over the right word.

"His routine?" I offer.

"Si. His routine. But he did not return that night. And he did not come all the next day. When it began to get dark again last night, and he still had not returned, we got worried. We then got in touch with the Professor, Professor Allen, to report Eduardo is missing."

"So that's why the Professor took the earlier flight," says Daniel, now obviously concerned.

The others, having finally collected all of their belongings, notice us talking to Miguel. They come over to join us. "So what's up?" says Adam, curious, but not seeming to pick up on our alarm.

"W . . . what's the problem?" says Brian, as he joins our group, mirroring our concerned faces.

Carli and Calvin sidle up as well, Carli smiling cheerfully, Calvin still muttering to himself, something about getting "this f* * *n circus on the road." They seem totally unaware of the tension in the group.

"Eduardo, Professor Gomez, is missing," says Daniel. "His belongings and his car are at the site, but he has been missing for two days." He repeats the information succinctly for the others. "That's why Professor Allen left Mexico City early." He turns back to Miguel. "There is nothing we can do from here, obviously, so let's get our belongings together and get out to the site where we might be able to do some good." He promptly takes command of the situation as he always does. I must say, however, before getting into action, he takes Miguel aside, puts his arm around the other man's shoulders and says something to him quietly. Miguel's look of near terror changes to one of gratitude and he moves off quickly to get the needed luggage cart. I have no idea what Daniel said to him, but it seems to calm the man.

Eventually, we get the old, rusty, grey van loaded with all the luggage and ourselves. A tight fit, but we just make it. The ride, in this ancient vehicle which lacks any form of suspension, is in the best of times uncomfortable. But this time I have to put up with Carli's incessant chattering about how terrible this all is and what can possibly have happened to the poor man. I think I might be sick, for sure. Her fussing just makes everyone else uncomfortable and Miguel feel worse. I could choke her with my bare hands. Finally Adam nudges her with his elbow and whispers, "Carli, I think you should be quiet. You're just making Miguel feel bad." I give Adam a grateful smile and Carli is blessedly quiet for the rest of the trip. What a way to start the summer.

An hour later, the last half hour over a narrow, ill-repaired, back country road, we reach a wide, open flatland. The landscape is studded with corn fields interspersed with sugarcane, and occasionally fields of squash or beans. The camp itself stands in the middle of these planted fields. In the center of camp is an ancient well or cenote, dry and abandoned for centuries. This well had once supported a thriving village. With the disappearance of the water, the village disappeared as well.

The archaeological excavation of the area had begun 25 years ago. We are here to excavate the cenote and the surrounding area, looking for what might remain of the ancient village. This is the source that we archaeologists mine in order to learn about how people lived hundreds or thousands of years ago.

The camp itself is an accumulation of ten or so, semi-permanent tents, canvas buildings supported by a variety of metal or wooden frames. All is sepia colored, like an old photograph, bleached by the accumulation of dust and from exposure to the intense, tropical sun. This color scheme is contrasted, here and there, by the brilliant, tropical green of the foliage and bright reds, oranges, and yellows of flowering plants. Our little complex looks like an old woman bedecked in the flamboyant attire of youth.

As the van clatters into the clearing, the camp is bustling with restless activity. The laborers, natives of the area for the most part, are dressed in faded jeans and dusty white T-shirts with brightly colored bandannas tied around their foreheads or about their necks. Some are emptying boxes of foodstuffs and other supplies from a large truck. Others are mending the canvas tents that have become dog-eared over the long off-season. Still others are moving mattresses and bed frames back into the tents after they have aired in the dry sunlight.

I am glad to be back. I find the work we do here, though hard and sometimes tedious, still enjoyable, at times even exhilarating. The exhilarating times come when we find something: a piece of bone, a shard of pottery or a bead. These moments are well worth the discomforts and privations of living so far from everything and in such close quarters with virtual strangers.

As the van comes to a stop, two men approach Miguel. One of them speaks rapidly in Yucatec, the native language of the area and a descendent of the ancient Mayan language. I do not speak the language, but can make out an occasional word or two. The men are saying something about Eduardo and pointing off to the east. Miguel nods and turns to us. "They tell me they have not yet found Eduardo. Professor Allen has gone off there," and he too points east. "It is there that Eduardo often walks, to the ancient mound. The Professor asks that you get settled. I leave you to do so, on your own, as I must rejoin the search."

"Miguel," says Daniel, "I am going with you." He turns to me and I know he's about to tell me to stay in camp and look after the others. I'm having none of that. He sees the look of defiance on my face and with resignation adds, "We need to start out immediately." And without another word to me, he hurries off with Miguel to where the other camp vehicles are parked

I look over at the others huddled together near the van. They look completely confused, all except for Calvin. He is pulling his paraphernalia from the vehicle, oblivious to whatever else is going on. I call out to him, "Calvin, you know the lay of the land. Show the others where they can stow their gear. You know where to put them. Carli goes in my tent and Adam and Brian bunk with you. Daniel and I are going to help in the search." And I walk off without giving him time to argue. As I run after Daniel, I turn back and see that he is grudgingly directing them to get their things and follow him. He is muttering angrily to himself all the while.

I catch up with the two men in the parking lot, as they load an assortment of gear into the back of an old, rather battered jeep. Finished, Miguel climbs behind the wheel, Daniel jumps in the passenger seat, leaving the rear of the vehicle for me, among shovels, tarps and a cooler. I make no complaint for fear they might object to my coming along. We drive east out of camp along a narrow trail through the cornfields, out to where the cultivated land meets the tropical forest. The path here joins a dirt road heading south, edging the forest. The road is not much bigger than the path and just as rocky.

As we jostle along the rutted track, Miguel tells us about the area we are entering. "The jungle here is not so thick," he says. "It has been burned and planted as recent as my grandfather's time. It has been left for the jungle to reclaim. Not enough men and boys to keep it clear. They go to the cities now." He pauses, sighing deeply. "My people have been here for a thousand years and more, but the land and the forest was here before."

We are quiet for a time. I watch the landscape pass on either side of the jeep. On my right, the thigh-high corn, evidence of man's domination. On my left, the thick untamed vegetation of the rain forest comes right up to the edge of the narrow road. So close that the jeep brushes against the foliage as we drive.

After several miles, Miguel breaks the silence again. "The Professor thinks that Eduardo has gone to the mound, as he often does."

"A mound, you mean a burial mound?" I ask. "I'd not realized there was one so close."

"I've never taken the time to visit it," adds Daniel. "The excavation there is out of bounds to us as Americans. It is the purview of the Mexican Office of Antiquities, but I think they abandoned it some years ago. They had not found much of interest."

"That is so," replies Miguel. "They do not take kindly to interference from outside. But they no longer dig because the local peoples drove them out. The land there is sacred and should not be defiled." His voice is harsh with conviction. I can see that he is on the side of his people. He continues in his usual, quiet tone. "But Eduardo, he goes there often. The mound, it is a man-made hill, constructed thousands of years ago by the Maya. It is not known if these constructions were early burial mounds or religious sites, predecessors to the giant pyramids that come later. For whatever reason, they were long since reclaimed by the forest. Eduardo feels its pull. He often says he feels the call of our forefathers there. He goes there every summer, alone. I fear he has had an accident. The terrain is rough and deserted. And the Waay inhabited it."

"Waay, ghosts, you mean?" I ask incredulously.

"Si," Miguel whispers as if afraid he will be overheard, "the spirits of the dead, si." And we are all quiet again.

Ten minutes later, Miguel brings the jeep to a halt and I can see three other vehicles parked at the edge of the cornfield, two old pickup trucks and a newer silver land-rover. Two locals are standing next to one of the trucks, smoking and drinking from bottles of water. Miguel joins them. They carry on a brisk conversation, pointing repeatedly toward the jungle, first north and then toward the south.

Miguel returns to us. "They say that the Professor and the others started out far to the north of here at midday. These men have searched this area and have found nothing. The Professor is to meet them here, soon they think, and then they will move off to the south. I have told them we will start south from here, on the west side of the mound. When the Professor comes, they can move to the east side and search south also." He looks at his watch. "It is 5:45 now. It will be light until after nine tonight, but we must be out of the forest before then."

Daniel hands me a small rucksack from the back of the jeep, puts two bottles of water into it along with two energy bars. "You need to keep hydrated in this heat." I am surprised by the note of concern in his voice, but then he adds more gruffly, "And make sure you stay close, don't want to lose you, too."

"Patronizing old creep," I mutter under my breath, and move over to the other side of the road. I can see there is a well worn path parallel to the road just on the other side of the first line of trees. The two men join me and we head south on the path. The vegetation here, though thin, still encroaches onto the path and we must push it out of our way as we walk. Several minutes later we come to a branch in the path. The primary path continues to follow the more southerly course. A second path branches off to the east. This path is less worn, less used, and to me almost invisible.

Miguel pauses here and turns to Daniel and me. "We need to cover a large area. To do so we must separate." Daniel starts to object, but Miguel stops him. "It is the only way if we are to find Eduardo . . . in time. Professor Daniel, you search here, along the main trail. Cover a wide area, as high up the hill as you can. I will cover the middle of the mound as that is the most densely forested and the roughest. Senorita O'Hara, you climb to the top of the mound, the vegetation clears there and is easier walking. Stay to the crest and look for any signs that Eduardo has been there. Stay within ear shot. Call out frequently."

Daniel doesn't look at all pleased with the plan, but he complies grudgingly.

Miguel and I take the less worn path and very soon it becomes steeper, more rugged, and strewn with rocks and fallen trees. I realize that we are now climbing the side of the mound. Midway Miguel stops me with a hand on my arm. "I will leave you here. Continue up the path and you will soon reach the top." And he turns without another word and moves off into the thick foliage and is immediately lost from sight.

I turn back to the path and resignedly continue up the hill. My breathing is labored and I'm sweating like a pig. The tree branches and thick vines are constantly grabbing at my jeans, shirt, and hair, making the going even more difficult.

Finally I come to the crest of the mound, short of breath and exhausted from the effort of the climb. Here the trees and the vegetation thin and the sun shines brightly, still high in the western sky. A clear, blue sky opens above me. I stand here for a moment, turn my face to the sky, and relish in the feel of the sun on my face.

I take a few moments to catch my breath and drink some of the water, then I head off south along the top of the mound. It is flat here, hard earth and rock, along the summit. The trees start again where the mound begins its rather precipitous descent. I keep to the open area, wandering back and forth from one edge to the other. I take my time looking intently into the forest for any sign of disturbance, any sign that anyone may have been there. The afternoon wears on. I am growing hotter and more tired.

A feeling of futility begins to overwhelm me and I sit down on a fallen tree at the edge of the clearing. I can hear Miguel trampling through the undergrowth somewhere below me, as I have all afternoon. He is south of where I am sitting and moving further away as I rest. "I'll catch up in a minute," I think to myself, not really afraid of being left behind.

Then off to my right, half way down the side of the mound, I see something. I glimpse a small object that is bright red in color. In an attempt to get a better look I venture out to the very edge of the clearing where a ledge of rock overlooks a sharp descent. Leaning over I try to make out what the object is. A piece of cloth, perhaps. There seems to be an area on the hillside that has been disturbed, as if something or someone slid down the embankment. Eduardo?

I am about to call out to Miguel when an awful shriek suddenly breaks the silence and I jump in alarm. I step back from the precipice. "A wild cat?" I think in terror. I look around to see what it might be, but see nothing. The shriek comes again. It's blood curdling. I feel like running, but where? At least here I'm in the open and can see anything coming at me. This thought gives me no comfort at all.

The shriek comes again, this time from overhead and looking up I catch a flash of green and gold. A bird, a huge bird, soars over my head and with another shriek passes out of sight behind the trees to the west. I am mesmerized by the spectacle. As I swing around to keep the bird in view, I catch my foot on a loose rock and my ankle twists under me, throwing me off balance. I try to right myself, but my left leg gives way and I fall. There's nothing for me to grab onto and I tumble down the decline, gathering momentum as I fall. I reach out my hand and just catch the edge of a piece of limestone protruding from the ground and hold on. It slows my descent, momentarily. I take a deep breath of relief and attempt to get up, only to feel the slab of stone suddenly give way. I begin to slide again, this time more slowly, but still I am unable to stop the fall. I slide another twenty feet before coming to a stop again. Before I can reach out and grab the surrounding vegetation I feel the earth beneath me disappear. I fall again, but not over the earth this time, but into it, as if the earth has opened up and swallowed me whole. I fall, hitting every outcropping of rock on the way down, scraping my body on the sharp protrusions. My head hits the bottom and everything goes black.

III

August 10, 935 BCE
10.5.6.17. 0, 1 Ahau, 13 Ceh
Chechen Itza, Yucatan Peninsula

The house was filled with the sounds of conversation and laughter. The dining-room was lit by a myriad of torches in sconces that circled the room. The flicker of softer candle light came from kib', candles made of bee's wax, on the table. The men were seated on backless, wooden benches around a long plank table in a room off the courtyard. There were thirteen men and adolescent boys, garbed in rich, magnificently embroidered, garments: brightly colored skirts and cloaks of reds, oranges and yellows. Some wore turbans to match their garments. Others wore the traditional headbands and hair cords that held back their long black hair. Each of the men wore ornate jewelry of intricately carved jade, obsidian, wood, and shell; each according to his age and his station among the Ahauob, noble class.

Took Pak's father, Ahab Ch'e'en, sat at the head of the table, as he was the host. Took Pak sat at his father's right hand, as this was the cha'ah, celebration, of his coming of age. It was the 14th anniversary of Took Pak's birth. He had been born on 10.4.12.13.7, 10 Manik, 10 Ceh (August 10, 921 CE), one of the Wayeb, the five nameless days before the beginning of the next cycle. An auspicious day, but whether of good or ill was debated. The priests assured Ahab Ch'e'en that it portended only good things for his son and that it guaranteed Took Pak's place in the Temple.

The table was laden with an overabundance of food, a feast that befitted such an occasion. There were b'ak' keeh (roast venison), kutz (wild turkey), and ix lu (fish), all fragrant with the many herbs that grew in the kitchen garden. There were kamul (sweet potatoes) and b'u'ul (beans) cooked with lik (peppers, sweet and hot). And, of course, there were platters of xiim (corn) and warm wah (flat bread made of corn) drizzled with fresh kab (honey). The addition of meat to the table made the meal special, indeed.

This fare was accompanied by cups of the bitter drink brewed from the seeds of the cacao. This beverage was reserved for special occasions and was thought to heighten one's awareness and increase one's perception of pleasure. Took Pak and the other young boys had theirs liberally watered and sweetened with kab.

The meal was nearly over. The women and girls were clearing the table. They were anticipating their own celebration, which would begin in the kitchen when the men were through. There was plenty left over, including a good portion of the cacao. The men would retire to the plaza outside for some of the stronger, more intoxicating beverage, ul atole, made of fermented corn and honey.

Took Pak had enough celebration. He was overly full and was anticipating only his bed or a quiet walk in the night air. While he mused over this, trying to decide bed or a garden stroll, Ahkan leaned over his shoulder in a pretense of clearing his wooden trencher. He could smell the sweet, pungent odor of lavender that clung to her. She whispered softly in his ear, "Meet me in the courtyard when the others leave the table." She did not wait for his reply. She knew he would be there. He watched her supple figure as she exited the room gracefully, although laden with heavy wooden luuch (serving bowls) and trenchers.

The courtyard was empty and dark when Took Pak entered it a short time later. A sliver of moon lit the enclosure only dimly, leaving much of it in deep shadow. Took Pak had grown taller. He was five feet four inches, nearly as tall as his father. The people of the Maya were not tall, but were ordinarily broad shouldered and stocky. Took Pak, however, was lean and narrow of hip and shoulder. He was as graceful as a keel (white tailed deer) in his movements and as agile as the sturdy mountain goat.

Took Pak was grateful for this moment of solitude, a moment to take leave of his childhood. Today he had turned fourteen and was, therefore, considered a man. He had removed the white, carved bead he had worn on a cord about his waist since birth, and had donned the ornately, embroidered headband that pulled back his long black hair. His hair now fell in a thick braid down his back.

He sat upon the wall of the pwes (well) and stared up at the stars. He would be entering the Temple school tomorrow to join the other sons of the Ahaob. He was excited and eager to start this new phase of his life, but he was also sad for the changes it would bring. He would live in the boys' dormitory and study with the Ah Kin, priests. Although the Temple was only a short distance from his otoch (home), and he could come home on holy days and special occasions; it would not be the same. He would not be privy to the daily comings and goings of the household. Family members would grow and change, have secrets and lives of which he would not be a part. And he would change, as well, becoming a wholly different person. He would become a priest with the knowledge and the responsibilities that would entail. And he would lose Ahkan, whom he had shared his life with and seen every day since she was born.

He sensed, rather than saw, her enter the courtyard from the eastern archway. It was as if he had conjured her appearance with his thoughts. She appeared as a ghost in the pale moonlight. Her thin, strong body was clothed in soft, ivory linen, bound at the waist with a scarlet cord that held the red sea shell that all young girls wore. Her skirt swayed gracefully as she walked slowly toward him. Her straight, black hair hung unbound, framing her golden, oval face. Her hair reflected the moonlight and seemed to form a halo about her head. She wore soft, deer skin sandals on her usually bare feet. Ahkan had grown over the last two years as well. She was not much taller, but her shoulders and hips had broadened and there was just a hint of breasts showing beneath her dress.

Ahkan came into the courtyard quietly and sat next to him on the wall. She was silent so long, he became uneasy. "You look very pretty tonight, hun p'iit," he said, merely to break the silence. She leaned her head on his shoulder. Her hair smelled of the yucca plant she used to wash it and the scent made him light-headed.

"I do not want you to go," she sighed.

"I will not be far away," he said. "I will be just down the street in the center of the city. I will be home every few days. I must come home for your mother's cooking. Rumor has it that the food at the Temple, at least for the initiates, is vile," he laughed quietly, trying to lighten the mood.

"But it will not be the same," she said in a whisper.

"No," he agreed. "Not the same." And he sighed too. There was a short pause in the conversation as they both contemplated the vast expanse of starry sky.

"I will miss you," she said, so softly he had to bend his head down closer to catch her words. He took her hand in his and could feel her warm tears on his hand. "You are my best friend, Took Pak. What will I do without you?"

"What you always do," he replied. "You always manage to keep yourself busy. You have your gardens and the pottery. Your herbs and your potions," he smiled, teasing her. "You still plan to become a wise woman, do you not? Not much time for me or anything else in that busy schedule."

"Yes" she said with a smile in her voice as well, "but what of my mathematics and astronomy lessons? You will be learning so much more than I will," she added with a pout.

"What I will be learning from now on is not for those like you, xchuu paal, little girls. The rest of my studies are just for those entering the priesthood. The mysteries are not for you, hun p'iit."

"I am not an xchuu paal," she began to protest, but stopped without continuing, because she liked him calling her his hun p'iit. They gazed at the stars and the planets circling overhead and took pleasure in their time together. "What do the stars hold for us?" said Ahkan after a long silence.

"Do you mean for us, you and me, personally? The usual I would think. Are we so special that the gods should take special notice?" he answered.

"I did not mean just you and me," she replied. "I meant all of us. Times are difficult and getting harder all the time. The drought has gone on so long. I do not remember the last time the rains were sufficient and the crops were good. The Ah Kin tell us that the gods are angry, but what have we done to anger them?"

"This is for the priests to worry about," he said dismissively, but he was troubled by what she had said.

"Ko'lel ix K'aax, the wise woman of the forest, says that our lives are ruled by the planets and the stars. Ko'lel says that, just as the heavenly bodies move in cycles, always returning to the place where they began, so our lives and the lives of our people move in circles. She says that just as a man is born and lives, and then dies to make room for the next generation, so too the world was born, lives for a time, and then dies to be reborn in the next cycle. She says that the Ah Kin know how to read the stars and the days, and to foretell what will happen and when. But they keep these secrets to themselves, not telling the people. Are these the secrets you will learn, I wonder?" she said to him. He did not answer. He had no answer to give. "I have a feeling," she continued, "Ko' lel calls it a premonition," and here her voice got even softer. "I have a feeling that something bad is going to happen, something evil, and you and I will be in the center of it. You must take care," she whispered. "You must take care in that place of secrets."

"Do not be silly. You are just letting the sorrow of our parting, and the fear of the changes that will come, color your emotions. Omens, premonitions, these things are the grist for the stories that the shamans tell to scare little children, xchuu paal." But he was chilled by her words and her conviction.

He felt her tremble. "Here, you are cold and it is very late. I must rise very early. I cannot be late my first morning at the Temple. Off to bed with you." He kissed her on the forehead and, without another word, Ahkan rose and left the courtyard through the doorway into the north wing and her bed chamber. Took Pak sat for a few moments longer brooding over what she had said.

IV

June 25, 2011
12.19.18.8.13, 3 Ben, 1 Sek
A basement, somewhere in Mexico

The room was damp and cool. It was dark, lit only by tapers burning in sconces adorning the walls. In the middle of the room was a long plank table of heavy teak, flanked by two wooden benches. On these sat six figures, robed in floor-length garments of coarse dark brown sacking. The long, full sleeves and oversized hoods covered every inch of them. At the head of the table sat another figure, similarly robed but this time in red, the color of blood.

The figure in scarlet seemed to be holding court, carrying on a long monologue, his voice cold and unemotional. "The time is drawing near and we must be prepared. It falls upon our shoulders to ensure that the will of the gods comes to pass and so ushers in the new creation of the universe. Many laugh at us. Others will put obstacles in our way. We are the direct descendents of the Ah Kin, the order of priests from the time of the ancients. We have survived. We hold power and influence in all segments of society. This will be our finest hour. This is the reason why we have survived."

The others were silent and he continued, "The day is coming. On the winter solstice next year, December 21, 2012, the Maya prophecy will be fulfilled. On that day the fifth creation of the world will come to an end, as it should, and the sixth creation will be ushered in. Toward that end we must dedicate ourselves and bring about the will of the gods."

CHAPTER THREE

I

1000 BCE
5.7.3.11.8

Mayan Myth

Halach Uinic was born under the glow
Of Noh Ek', the morning star.
He looked upon the world around him
And asked questions:
How did the world come to be?
What was his place within it?

The elders listened to his questions,
But they had no answers.
They told him, "Why do do ask?"
And he answered, "I wish to know."
And the elders said,
"Seek the answers from the gods."

Halach Uinic watched
The changing of the seasons.
He watched the movement of the stars.
He watched the animals and the plants
That grew upon the land.
He watched the birds in the air and the fishes in the sea.

He saw what the others did not see.
He saw an order to the universe.
He saw the cycles of the days,
The years, the ages.
He thought about what he saw
And answered the questions that he had.

The elders asked, "How do you know these things?"
And he said, "I read them in the stars.
I hear them in the wind.
I see them in my dreams."
The elders laughed and called him crazy:
'He who sees it in the smoke'

Halach Uinic continued
To watch the world around him.
He hunted in the forests
And he gathered in the fields.
And he watched,
And he thought.

He knew where and when the herds ran.
He knew what fruits and nuts
And berries were edible,
And where and when they could be found.
He told this to the Maya,
And the Maya heeded what he said.

And the Maya prospered.

The Maya asked Halach Uinic,
"How is it you are so wise?"
And he told them,
"The gods have given me the knowledge.
They placed it before my eyes,
They whispered in my ear."

The Maya came to him
For his knowledge
And his advice on everything.
And the Maya honored him
For his wisdom.
And they called him 'Wise Man.'

Time passed and still the Wise Man watched.
One day, he saw a grain growing along the stream.
Halach Uinic tasted the new fruit
And found the yellow kernels sweet.
He gathered what he could and gave it to his wife, ix Chel,
Saying, "See what the gods have given us."

The Wise Man shared the yellow grain with his family
And with his neighbors.
And they found it good and plentiful
And the Maya called it 'Maize.'
They honored the Wise Man who brought it to them.
And they thanked the gods for this good fortune.

And the gods were pleased.
And the Maya prospered.

The Maya gathered much more than they could eat.
The Wise Man's wife saw that the grain,
Left in the sun, became dry and did not rot.
She took the hard dry kernels and crushed them,
And made a thick porridge.
And she called it 'Sa.'

In the winter months, when food was scarce,
The Maya were sustained
By the maize they had harvested in the fall.
And the Maya were thankful to the gods.
And the Maya were thankful to the Wise Man.
And they called him 'Shaman,' 'He who speaks to the gods.'

And still Halach Uinic watched
And he saw that from Maize buried in the Earth
In the spring, a new plant would grow.
The Shaman showed the Maya how to till the fields,
And how to sow the seeds
And when to harvest the grain.

And the Maya came to the Shaman.
They came for advice in all matters,
As he was the one who knew.
And the Shaman passed his knowledge to his sons,
And they to their sons, and they to theirs.
And so the knowledge of the Maya
Was preserved through the generations.

The Maya paid homage to the Shaman,
And to the gods
From whom the knowledge came.
And the gods were pleased
And they blessed the Maya,
And the Maya prospered.

II

June 25, 2011
12.19.18.8.13, 3 Ben, 1 Sek
Yucatan Peninsula, the dig.

This time I wake to bright sunlight. It is streaming through the open doorway of a canvas tent. I realize I am back at camp, in my own tent, on my own cot. Had I been dreaming? The pain in my head and the aches from every other part of my body lead me to think I haven't been dreaming. I don't know how I got back here. The last thing I remember is being in the bottom of a hole. Then with a start, I remember, someone else was in there with me. I need answers.

I start to get off the cot, but stop as a wave of nausea sweeps over me.

"You're not to get up, at least not yet. The doctor said so. You have a concussion and have been out of it all night," comes a voice from across the room. "I've had to wake you every few hours to make sure you were alright. You grunted at me each time so I supposed you were." Then a face swims into view, a sweet, smiling face.

"I know that face," I think, but I can't quite put a name to it. "I'll think about that later." And I fall back to sleep.

I'm awakened again, this time by singing. Someone is singing "Amazing Grace", not quite on key. I open my eyes, not sure why someone would be in my apartment, much less singing. Then I realize where I am. Of course, the person who is singing is Carli. I like hymns as well as the next person, don't get me wrong, but not when I'm sleeping, and not when I have a headache and definitely not off key. I groan and sit up. The headache is better and there is no nausea accompanying the movement. I climb regretfully from my cot and stand shakily on my feet.

Carli stops singing and chirps, "Oh, you're up. Are you sure you should? I mean, maybe you should wait for the doctor. He said he would come back to check on you this evening. We were all so worried, you know. More worried about Eduardo, of course, but worried about you too. Taking such a fall and all."

I sit back down on the cot. "Eduardo? It was Eduardo in the cave with me?"

"Why yes," she says in surprise. "You found him. I mean, if you hadn't found him and fallen in after, I don't think he would have ever been found. Not alive anyway."

"How is he?" I break in. "Is he alright?"

"Well, he was in bad shape when they got him out. Broke his leg in the fall. Was burning up with fever and dehydration. They brought him back here and then took him to the hospital in a helicopter. All very exciting I tell you. But the poor man."

"Do you know how he is now?" My head throbs with her chatter, but I have to know about Eduardo.

"No. The Professor is at the hospital in Merida with him now. He had to have surgery, but we've heard nothing since then."

I get to my feet again and totter to the door.

"Where are you going?" asks Carli, as she tries to block my way.

"I have to go pee and you're not going to stop me."

She laughs. "At least put your shoes and pants on."

I have on only an over large tee shirt. I see a pair of sweat pants folded neatly at the bottom of my cot and a pair of sandals under it. I grudgingly sit back down and allow Carli to help me into them. How humiliating. She then insists on accompanying me to the latrine, though I put my foot down when she tries to follow me into the stall.

After a blessedly hot shower, I realize that I am enormously hungry. The nausea has gone and my head is much clearer. Carli is still hovering like a mother hen, babbling on and on about nothing. Anyway I'm not listening.

"I need a cup of coffee and a bacon sandwich, right now," I say vehemently. "What time is it, by the way?"

"Half past six. But I don't think either the coffee or the bacon is the best thing for you right now. I mean, coffee after a concussion can't be good, all the caffeine and all. And well, bacon is never a good thing, now is it. Cholesterol, you know."

"I don't need you to tell me what I should or shouldn't eat," I growl and head resolutely out the door.

As I enter the dining room, I am immediately bombarded with the wonderful aromas of baking cornbread, stewing meat, and hot peppers. It reminds me that I haven't eaten since a quick snack in the Mexico City airport, while we waited for our flight to Merida. I am starving. My mouth waters at the memory of the magnificent meals of last summer.

The mess tent is a single, large room with two long refractory tables running its length. Each table has rows of folding chairs drawn up to it. The kitchen is attached through a canvas flap door at the rear of the room. Everyone eats here: day laborers, staff, kitchen help, students and professionals. Everyone eats at the same time, family-style. Large platters of stewed meat and fresh vegetables, baskets of flat corn cakes, and bowls of fresh fruits, grace the tables.

We seem to be the last to arrive. Most of the seats are already taken. Everyone is eating and talking. Daniel has saved a seat next to him for me, and he pulls it out as I approach. The others that arrived with us yesterday are sitting with him.

"Kate, how are you feeling?" Daniel asks. I am grateful for his solicitude, but he ruins the effect by adding, "You certainly look much better than you did the last time I saw you. A bit of a mess, I'd say. Thought we'd never get you extricated from that hole, tight fit you know." I don't remember any of this, thank goodness, and am about to say so, when he continues,

"Of course, it is a good thing that you found the cave. Don't know that we would have ever found Eduardo, otherwise. Good job."

I don't know how to take this. Is he actually praising me or making fun of me? I can't tell. "It was pure luck, I guess. I really don't remember much. Something scared me, and I saw something red partway down the side of the mound, and then I fell," I say in explanation. Though why I think I have to explain myself, I don't know. Daniel always seems to have that effect on me. "Have you heard anything further from the Professor about Eduardo? How is he?" I ask anxiously.

Daniel finishes chewing, swallows, and finally answers, "I spoke with Professor Allen an hour or so ago. He told me Eduardo is still in surgery. They think they can save his foot, but it is in bad shape. He broke his ankle badly in the fall. The infection is severe, from the open fracture, and gangrene had begun because of the lack of circulation. He was seriously dehydrated, as well as toxic from the infection. He'll live, but it will take a long time for full recovery."

"How awful," says Carli. "Does he have any family? Have they been contacted? Will they be coming to the hospital? Is there something that we can do?"

"I haven't thought," I say with alarm, for I really hadn't. "He has a wife and two boys. They live in Mexico City. Has Professor Allen contacted them?" I ask Daniel. "Do you think she needs help getting here?" I felt terrible. I know Maria, have met the boys, and I hadn't even thought that they would need to be informed. I hadn't even considered what Eduardo's injury would mean to them.

"Professor Allen contacted her as soon as he got to the hospital," Daniel replies. "And I made arrangements for her flight from Mexico City. She and the two children should arrive late tonight. The Professor will meet them at the airport and has made arrangements for their accommodations."

I feel guilty. Daniel has shown more concern and responsibility then I have. And he did it so matter-of-factly, not gloating or expecting any praise. "A good man to have in a crisis," I think.

"How did the accident happen, anyway?" I ask.

"From what Professor Allen told me and from the look of where it happened, it seems that Eduardo tripped and fell from the top of the mound, down the embankment," Daniel tells all of us. "Just the way you did. This all seems fairly clear cut. Where it gets confusing is in his ranting. He talked about a giant bird that pushed him or caused him to fall down the side of the hill. Something about a bird god or sacred bird of the Maya. I guess he means a Quetzal, but I don't think they range this far north anymore."

I catch my breath. I remember the bird I had seen, that inadvertently caused my accident as well. I don't share my thoughts, as they sound as crazy and preposterous as Eduardo's.

Daniel looks at me quizzically but doesn't ask me what's the matter. He continues, "However, we saw a very, large bird, I don't know what kind, when we found you. In fact, we might not have found you if we hadn't been looking at the bird." He pauses, shaking his head. "Eduardo was saying something else, something about omens and students finding his bones. He was out of his mind with the fever, so I doubt any of this has any relevance," he concludes with another shake of his head.

"He was ranting about finding something, too," says Calvin, without any sign of real interest. "What was that all about?"

"What's that?" says Adam curiously. "He found something?"

"Well, yes," replies Daniel reluctantly. "Actually he left a note. He attached it to a button on his shirt. Very ingenious, really. You have to admire Eduardo's clear headedness and tenacity in an extremely precarious situation like that," Daniel says admiringly. He pauses, takes a sip of coffee, and then continues, turning again to me. "You never would have found him, I think, if he hadn't thrown his knapsack out of the cave to attract your attention. It was bright red."

"Oh, it was his knapsack I saw?" I muse.

"What is it that he said he found?" Adam asks again.

"He said he found an ancient Mayan manuscript," replies Daniel.

"A what?" says Calvin in surprise.

"The note said something like: 'Mayan book . . . in the box," says Daniel.

"Mayan? Highly unlikely," scoffs Calvin.

"Yes," agrees Daniel, "highly unlikely. But there is an area in the side of the cave that appears to have been chiseled from the rock. A container of some sort. I took a look before we brought Eduardo out."

"A container?" says Calvin.

"How interesting." chirps Carli.

"What was in it?" asks Adam.

"I don't know," says Daniel. "I didn't look inside, but I plan to go back tomorrow to get a better look. I asked the Professor. He won't be back tomorrow, and possibly not the next day. We can't start here at the excavation until he gets back, so he said we can make the trek to see what it is Eduardo thinks he found." Daniel looks at all of us questioningly. "Who's going with me? Could be a good learning experience, even if there's nothing to find."

"I'll go. I'll go," says Carli, leaping up from her chair and waving her hand like a fourth grader.

"So will I. Sounds Interesting," says Adam.

"Oh, I'll come as well,' Calvin adds without much enthusiasm, but any that was needed had already been supplied by Adam and Carli.

"What about you, Kate?" asks Daniel turning to me. "Are you up to it?"

"I wouldn't miss it." I say. Really I wouldn't miss it for the world. "What about you, Brian?"

"S . . . s . . . sure," he stammers.

"All right then," says Daniel "full house. We'll leave early, just after daybreak, so we can get a good start before the day gets too hot. I'll let Teo, the cook, know to pack a lunch and fluids to take with us. And I'll have Miguel pack the equipment we might need into the Land Rover tonight." Daniel has taken full command again, but I don't have the energy to protest. Let him play captain of the fleet. What do I care? "Better make it an early night," he adds.

The others leave for their tents. Daniel and I are the only ones left at the tables. I can see Teo peering through the kitchen flap. He obviously wants us to leave so he can finish closing up for the night. He is temperamental, as most chefs are, and it doesn't take anyone coming to the camp long to learn, if you piss off Teo you will regret it. There may be many privations at an archaeological dig, but here these do not extend to the food. Today's meal was not the exception but the norm. Daniel and I pick up the remaining dirty dishes and rubbish from the tables and carry them back to the kitchen.

"Excellent meal as usual," Daniel tells Teo.

"Yes," I add, "It was all great. I'll be gaining weight again this summer, despite the hard work, with you feeding me like this," I say smiling broadly at the man.

He is short, round, and dark skinned, with a perpetual smile on his face. He gives me an even broader smile and responds. "Gracias, Señorita. It is always a pleasure to cook for you." He is a bit of a flirt, but never steps over the line of propriety. He can flirt all he wants if he continues to feed me this way.

"Buenas Noches," I say as I leave the tent.

"Buenas Noches, Señorita," he replies.

"How about a nightcap?" Daniel asks, touching my arm. "I have a perfectly good bottle of scotch in my tent."

I look at him in absolute surprise. What is this? "No. No, I don't think so, Daniel," I respond, shocked at the offer. "Don't think I should drink so soon after a concussion anyway." I'm dead tired and scotch really isn't my drink. "And neither are you," I think, but don't add.

Daniel looks at me speculatively, probably wondering if I am being rude or just honest. "You are probably right," he says, "some other evening, perhaps."

I don't care what he thinks. Having a drink with him isn't high on my to-do list, even if I hadn't had a concussion.

I am not the only one who is exhausted by the overlong day. By the time I reach our tent, Carli is in her cot, breathing deeply, obviously sound asleep. Thank God. The last thing I need right now is to have a conversation with Ms. Goody Two Shoes. I crawl into my sleeping bag and am fast asleep before I can count to 10.

III

October 5, 935 CE,
10.5.7.1.16, 5 Cib, 9 Muan
Several months later: Chichen Itza, outside the Temple of
Ku'kul'Kan

A group of 15 young boys were seated on rough, wooden benches around a plank table. The outdoor classroom was placed under a tall, spreading ceiba tree on the lawn outside the Temple. Two robed priests, one in green and one in scarlet, paced back and forth along the row of boys, glancing periodically at the slates in the boys' hands. The boys were busy with their numbers; scribbling hurriedly upon their slates. Some wrote with confidence; others haltingly, frequently rubbing out what they had written. Took Pak wrote with confidence.

Kay Nuuk, sitting next to him, was a boy several years older than Took Pak. He leaned over to glance at the younger boy's slate. "I do not understand this," he whispered. "The mathematics are beyond me. Even all the time we spent on it last evening is of no use. I think I comprehend the theory. I do comprehend it when you explain it to me. But when Yax Ahk," he nodded his head toward the younger priest, robed in green, "adds the next step, I cannot grasp the connection. Why is it you understand it so easily? You are the youngest of us and you are doing work even the oldest of us is not ready for."

"I had a good tutor," responded Took Pak, though he knew this was not the full answer. Yes, his tutor had been good and they had worked hard since Took Pak was a little child, but the truth was that the learning came easy for him. He enjoyed it and he seemed to have a talent for it as well. He just seemed to understand it without trying.

"Well, Yax Ahk is impressed with you and, I think, even Sajal Ch'itz'aat, the High Priest's undersecretary, has his eye on you," said Kay Nuuk. Took Pak shook his head but said nothing. He suspected that his friend was right, but he did not wish to appear immodest by admitting it.

"That will be enough Scholar Kay Nuuk yu ne Ahab Lu'um." The acolyte, Yax Ahk, had come up behind the two boys without their being aware, and rapped Kay Nuuk on the shoulder with a slender ceiba switch. Kay Nuuk flinched at the strike, but was glad that it was Yax Ahk and not Sajal Ch'itz'aat, who had wielded the rod. "You would do better to spend this time working on your lessons, than disturbing Took Pak with your chattering." He walked away, down the row of benches, tapping his hand with the rod and smiling to himself. He liked the boy. True, Kay Nuuk was not much of a scholar. The boy had great difficulty keeping up, until the talented scholar, Took Pak, had taken him under his wing. But Kay Nuuk was a personable boy, always pleasant and cheerful, witty if not book smart

Kay Nuuk rubbed his shoulder and bent his head over his slate again. When the teacher had moved out of ear shot, he whispered with good humor, "Teacher's pet, he did not take the switch to you, I see," and he laughed quietly.

Sajal Ch'itz'aat beckoned to Yax Ahk and moved away from the classroom area. Yax Ahk followed, respectively. When out of the hearing of the boys, the Sajal stopped. He waited for the young priest to join him, and then said softly, "The Ahab Ch'e'en's son, he is progressing well?"

"Very well," responded Yax Ahk. "He is exceptional, very bright. He knows more than all the others, though he is the youngest of the group and last to join the school."

"Yes, yes," replied Sajal Ch'itz'aat. "He has been well taught. His tutor was obviously a good one, but is there more?" He looked at Yax Ahk with intensity. He had a feeling about the boy. Here possibly was a true prodigy. Those with true talent, smiled on by the gods, were rare.

Yax Ahk paused before answering, unsure what his superior wanted him to say. He was astonished that Sajal Ch'itz'aat, a priest of the Inner Circle, was asking him, a mere acolyte, for an opinion. "Well," he finally stammered. "The boy enjoys learning and puts a lot of thought into it. He teaches the other boys, especially Kay Nuuk. He has an ability for mathematics, particularly. He is special."

"Yes, Yax Ahk. I see that you like him and he is easily taught," said Sajal Ch'itz'aat irritably, "but why is this so? Why do you say he is special, except for his good humor and pleasant appearance and manners? Why is he special?" He paused and then continued, without waiting for the other priest to respond. "What are the omens, the circumstances of his birth that have the gods smiling upon him?"

"I do not know," replied Yax Ahk. "He was born during the days of Wayeb. This could be a good omen or ill, one cannot tell. He is of a rich and well positioned family. His father is a counsel to the Ajaw.

"Yes, yes," Sajal Ch'itz'aat said again. "All this I know, but I feel there is more. Something about the boy interests and attracts me. I have a feeling he will go far in the Order. He will have an impact but of what kind, I wonder?" He shook his head then reverted to the aloofness that befitted his stature and the lack of stature of the acolyte. "Keep me informed of his progress," he said and walked away.

Yax Ahk was astonished. Never had Sajal Ch'itz'aat, or any of the ordained priests, shown such an interest in any of the boys, much less the youngest. True, Took Pak was unusual, but this interest was even more unusual. He would have to keep his eyes on the boy, he thought. Perhaps he should ingratiate himself with Took Pak? It could not do any harm.

Having been left alone for such a long time the boys had slipped from their usual decorum. Yax Ahk hurried back to the table to restore what order he could, and recoup what little authority he had over his pupils, when the watchful eyes of his superior were no longer present.

At the same time: in the kitchen gardens of the Ch'e'en household

Ahkan was involved in her own schooling, of a sort. She was happily assisting Nuxib Mak, the elderly gardener, in the afternoon harvesting of herbs and medicinal plants needed for the household.

"Ko'lel ix K'aax has requested that I bring to her additional herbs and plants to stock her larder for the coming winter," she told the old man. "She requires Chaya to help heal broken bones, and the resin of the Ek' Balam shrub, to stop bleeding. Also corn silk flowers to mix with cacao for fever, and kalawala for infection. I could use Aloe and lavender for the household as well," Ahkan added.

"You be careful what you let that old woman teach you," remonstrated Nuxib Mak. "She is a powerful shaman, but not all of her potions and spells are holy. Some say she is ah waay, a witch. They say she has powers that she learned from Cisin and Xbalanque, the gods of the underworld. These are of a dark nature and will serve you ill."

"I do not believe that of her. Ko'lel has power, that is true, but her power comes from her knowledge of the herbs and plants of the forest and the earth. It does not come from any evil god or goddess," Ahkan replied solemnly.

"I am not so sure of that, hun p'iit," said Nuxib Mak, shaking his head sadly. "True, she does much good for the poor folk. Look what she did for my sister's girl, Chan K'iin, when she was in childbirth. She would have surely died if not for the wise woman. And Ak'ta Ahk's boy, when he broke his leg and it festered. Without the old woman, he too would have sickened and died."

"You see," said Ahkan, seriously, "what would we do without her? Even the priests and the Ahau of the court call upon Ko'lel when all else fails."

"To be sure, to be sure. As I said, she has her uses, but there are those that say she has other talents as well; other talents not so pure. Some say that she can cast spells and has potions that have great power over a man."

"Love potions?" Ahkan laughed. "And curses too, perhaps?"

"Yes curses, dark magic," Nuxib Mak replied.

"Well," Ahkan said, "I have no use for love potions and dark curses. And I have no belief in them either."

"Just remember," the old man warned, "other folk do. So stay away from the dark arts," he cautioned, as he returned to the tasks he had interrupted.

Anyone who knew him would have been astonished to hear Nuxib Mak in such a long conversation. With everyone else, he was taciturn and spoke little, answering the questions put to him in monosyllables. With everyone, but this smiling, inquisitive child, that is. Ahkan, in her turn, loved the old man. She felt relaxed in his company, relaxed enough to speak to him about her dreams and aspirations.

She had told him she planned to become a wise woman like Ko'lel. She had learned a great deal from him, but at the age of 11 years now, she had learned all that he could teach her. So she now had turned to Ko'lel for what she wanted and needed to learn. Nuxib Mak had doubts about the wisdom of this. Ahkan's mother was ignorant, as yet, of the time Ahkan spent with the old woman and of the little girl's plans for the future. She would not be pleased and Nuxib Mak debated whether he should inform her of Ahkan's activities. But he could not break the child's confidence and risk losing her friendship. Her daily trips to the forest would not stay a secret for long. Ak'a Ch'iich would hear of it before long. Ahkan would have to face that, when the time came. He was sure she would not be deterred by her mother or anyone. The only other person who knew of her dreams was Took Pak and he did not take her seriously.

Ahkan gathered her herbs and plants into her large woven xu'ul. She added others to a xu'ul Nuxib Mak was filling for the household. She turned to the gardener and said, "Take these to the kitchen for me. I will be home before dark." She smiled sweetly at him, picked up her heavily laden xu'ul and headed toward the forest, singing to herself.

The hut of Ko'lel was hidden deep in the forest, several miles outside the city. It was no more than a hovel, a one room shack made of roughly hewn logs and thatch, with only a tanned deer hide covering the doorway. Ahkan called out to the old woman as she entered the small clearing. "Ko'lel, it is Ahkan. Are you to home?"

A tiny, stooped figure lifted the door flap and stood in the doorway. "Ahkan, my dear child," said the wizened old woman. Ko'lel had long white hair that haloed her head in a tangled thatch. "I was hoping you would come today. I have just returned with a fresh assortment of the bark of the bakalche' tree and of the cacao. I could use an extra set of hands to help in preparing it."

"I promised you I would be here today. I try hard to keep my promises," said the girl. "Look what I have for you from the household gardens. Nuxib Mak sends his regards."

The old woman laughed, "I am sure that he did and called upon the gods, at the same time, to ward off the black magic. I know very well he considers me ah waay and is afraid of me, as all the people are. It is a wonder that he does not try to keep you away, or even tell your mother of your frequent visits here to me."

"Oh, he would never do that," laughed Ahkan. "Not so much in fear of you, however, but rather for fear that I would be so angry I would never speak to him again. He dotes on me," added the girl, with more than a little pride in her voice.

"Yes, xchuu paal, you do have a power about you that mesmerizes those around you, old men and old women at least. Just be careful how you wield it, for it can be used for good or ill," warned the old woman.

"Nuxib Mak says the same thing of your gifts, Ko'lel," replied the girl seriously.

Ko'lel reentered the hut and Ahkan followed, carrying her laden xu'ul. The room itself held little: a single coarse mattress stuffed with corn husks, a long wooden bench, and a plank table. There were crowded wooden shelves lining the far walls. These were overflowing with pottery jars and woven baskets containing dried plants, bulbs, and other indistinguishable contents. The room had an odd fragrance, a combination of the unpleasant, pungent smells of fungus and rotting vegetation, and the sweet aromatic odors of flowers and spices. In the hearth in the corner of the room, a fire burned in the center of the traditional, three sided fireplace. On the fire, a large paayla (pottery vessel) boiled, giving off noxious vapors that filled the shack with acrid fumes. These made it difficult to breathe. The table was covered with a vast assortment of baskets and crates containing what had been harvested from the forest. These were all collected by the old woman to be used in the creation of her medicinal brews, salves, and concoctions.

Ko'lel busied herself, emptying the basket that Ahkan had brought. She smiled over some of its contents, clicked her tongue in disappointment at others. "Not a very good year for Aloe, not enough rain," she said. "But this Ek' Balam shrub is lovely and I am all out of corn silk flowers. This kalawala comes just in time, as well. Chaya is excellent for the aches that come to us old ones, as the nights get cooler. Thank you, Hun P'iit, and make sure you thank Nuxib Mak as well. And be sure to take a jar of the aloe and kib' (bees wax) salve for the cracking and sores of his hands."

Ahkan looked at her in surprise, "But how did you know he was suffering from that complaint?"

"It is not magic or witchcraft," chuckled the old woman. "I know because he suffers with that complaint every year at this time. It does not require magic, just careful observation and a good memory."

The two worked, side by side, through the morning and into the early afternoon. They talked occasionally, but much of the time was spent in companionable silence. Ko'lel broke the silence, from time to time, to give gentle instructions or explanation. She taught Ahkan the process of preserving the plants, and the uses to which they could be put. Or Ahkan would ask occasional questions regarding the properties of this or that ingredient. And so the day passed pleasantly.

As the sun began its slow descent, Ko'lel raised her eyes to the girl and, wiping her hands on the cloth she had tied about her waist, said, "It is getting late. It is dark so early this time of year. You had best start out for home if you are to get home before dark, hun p'iit."

Ahkan shook her long black hair out of her eyes. "So soon?" she asked. "It seems as if I just got here."

"Time goes by quickly, that is true," replied Ko'lel, "whether it is a busy morning, or the season, or the year, or a life time. Time passes for me. I have grown old and my life passes rapidly."

"Do not say that," said Ahkan in a frightened voice. "You are not so very old." But she knew that her friend was old, older than anyone else that she knew.

"Do not worry, Hun P'iit. I do not plan to pass into Xibalba, into the underworld, any time soon. But I find that I cannot do all that I once could. I am in need of an assistant." Seeing that Ahkan was about to say something, Ko'lel stayed her with a movement of her hand. "You are a great help to me here. But what I need is an apprentice, someone to learn all that I know, someone to take over for me when I am gone."

"But that is what I have always wanted," cried Ahkan. "That is why I am here." She looked down at her hands and said weakly, "Do you think I am not good enough? Do you think I am not smart enough?" She was almost in tears, an unusual thing for Ahkan, who did not cry.

"No. No," said the old women seriously. She put her hands on the young girl's shoulders and said to her earnestly, "It is you who I have chosen to succeed me. Rather, it is you that the gods have chosen. You have a gift, Hun P'iit. You have an understanding of and a feeling for nature and the earth that cannot be taught. It is a gift given by the gods. I am sure it is you who is meant to carry on my work. But from now on your education will require a great deal of time and dedication. It is not something that can be continued in secret. If it is truly what you want, if it is truly what you were meant for, then it must be done openly." She paused to allow Ahkan to absorb what this meant. "This means," she continued, "that you must tell your parents and get their blessing."

Ahkan stared at Ko'lel in surprise. "But what if they say no?" said Ahkan in a frightened voice, tears starting in her eyes again. "What if they will not give their blessing?" she added in a whisper.

"Then it was not meant to be," replied Ko'lel gently, putting the jar of ointment for Nuxib Mak into Ahkan's hand and pushed her gently out of the door. "Come back when you have your parent's permission."

Ahkan walked slowly toward home. She knew that her mother would not be pleased, and that her father would be shocked. Her mother would argue, at first. Her father would refuse to believe that she was serious. But Ahkan had faith in Ko'lel. If she said that it was meant to be, then Ahkan was sure that it would come to pass, whatever the obstacles.

IV

June 25, 2011
12.19.18.8.15, 5 Men, 3 Zec
An office somewhere in Mexico

The office is large and dimly lit. Heavy, mahogany furnishings upon a thick maroon and gold carpet decorate the room. The walls are lined, floor to ceiling, with glass fronted book cases filled with expensive looking, leather bound volumes. The centerpiece of the room is a broad, ornate desk, at which is seated a man. He is dressed in a dark, obviously expensive, well-tailored suit, well manicured hands are clasped, immobile, on the desk in front of him. He is talking quietly, but with authority to another man seated across from him.

"Am I to understand that this is just a rumor that you have brought me? A rumor from the Yucatán?"

"Si, Monsignor," the man facing the desk said shakily. He was a man of about the same age and size as his companion, but he appeared smaller as he sat hunched in a low, straight backed chair. He too wore a dark suit, but not as expensive or well tailored.

There was a pause, and then the first man continued, "And these rumors, their source?"

"From the peasants, laborers at an archaeological site run by North Americans, a small, insignificant site about an ancient dry well. Rumor, only rumor, so far." He answered apologetically, wringing his hands.

"Probably nothing," the other man said dismissively. "But we must ignore nothing, with the time so short." His voice grew hard and menacing, and the man facing him shook visibly in response. "Make inquiries into the matter. Find out the details from a reliable source." This was a command, not a request. The other man recognized this. "Keep me informed." The man behind the desk waved the other man away and the subordinate backed out of the room, mumbling his acquiescence.

CHAPTER FOUR

I

400 BCE,
7.2.13.14.19

Mayan Myth

Then the gods told the Maya to build shelters
Close to their fields and orchards.
And the Maya did as the gods bid them.
The Maya stopped their wandering
And built their dwellings
Beside the fields they planted.

The gods told the Maya
To work their fields together.
And the Maya worked their fields together,
So that where once ten farmers sowed and gathered
Grain from the fields, each for his own family,
Now five could do the same for the whole community.

And where it had required ten men
To hunt game for their own families
And ten women to provide vegetables
For their own tables,
Now five might do the work
For the whole village.

The Maya did as the gods told them
And their bounty increased tenfold.
And the Maya were thankful
And they worshipped the gods
And their tribute
They increased tenfold.

And the gods told the Maya to
Gather cotton from the fields,
And taught them to weave it into fine cloth
With which to clothe themselves.
And showed them how to take the mud from the earth,
To fashion it into pots and vessels to store their surplus.

And the gods told the Maya to
Gather the stalks of the maize
To weave into baskets to carry their goods.
And the Maya did as they were told.
And they worshipped the gods
And paid tribute to them.

The Maya paid tribute to the gods
With bright, colored cloth,
Finely woven baskets,
And beautifully crafted pottery
They burned their offerings, as instructed by the gods,
In a place set aside for this purpose.

The Maya gave a portion of their wares in tribute.
And the gods were pleased
And they blessed the Maya.
And the Maya prospered.

II

June 26, 2011,
12.19.18.8.14, 4 Ix, 2 Sek
Yucatán Península, México, the dig

I wake to the incessant ringing of an alarm clock. I groan, stretch, and then climb regretfully from my cot. It's still dark outside, much too early to be up after the last few grueling days. I grab a quick cup of coffee, an orange and a banana from the mess tent on my way through. By the time I get to the center of camp, everyone else is already there. Daniel and Calvin are squabbling over who will drive. Daniel wins out, as usual, pulling rank on the younger man. Calvin really hasn't put up much of a fight. He doesn't seem to have much of a real passion for anything. The Land Rover is packed with our equipment, a box of food, and an ice chest, leaving barely enough room for the six of us. I climb into the passenger seat next to Daniel, pulling a little rank of my own. Brian, Calvin, and Carli squeeze into the back seat and Adam, without any sign of resentment, climbs into the back of the vehicle with the equipment and provisions. The sun is just rising above the forest on the horizon as we set off.

We drive out of camp and down the same dusty, one lane road as we had done the other day. Daniel is quiet, concentrating intently on navigating the bumpy dirt track. Carli, on the other hand, chatters merrily to anyone who will listen. Calvin ignores her. Brian listens avidly without saying a word. Adam, in the far back, is ignoring everyone, playing with his Blackberry and whistling to himself.

Calvin rouses himself enough to holler back at him, "Stop that damn whistling. You're driving me bonkers. Don't you know any other tune? What are you doing anyway?"

"Just fiddling with my GPS. Pretty good reception out here," Adam answers jauntily. "Don't want to get lost or anything. With this, we'll be able to get back no matter what." He smiles good-naturedly and returns to whistling what sounds vaguely like "Yankee Doodle."

It takes us about 45 minutes to reach the point where the trail branches off from the road, headed into the thicker jungle toward the mound. This is as far as we can take the car, so we unpack what we can carry, what is essential, leaving the food and the ice chest for later. The hike up the side of the mound is worse than it was the other day. My head is throbbing again and I am soon out of breath. Adam, Calvin, and Carli get to the summit without breaking a sweat. Brian and Daniel bring up the rear, panting and gasping, so it appears I'm not in such bad shape.

We come out into the clearing at the top. The sun is bright in a cloudless sky and it has gotten very warm. I sink gratefully to the ground to catch my breath. We all pull our water bottles from our backpacks to quench our thirsts.

After he regains his wind, Daniel again assumes command. He starts lecturing, giving the neophytes a quick tutorial on how to conduct an archaeological excavation. "What is of central importance is protecting the site and maintaining the integrity of any evidence it might hold," he begins, in true professorial style, pacing across the clearing as he speaks. I can see Calvin smirking behind his back and Adam still playing with his Blackberry. Brian and Carli, of course, give Daniel their rapt attention . . . "Don't make assumptions," he tells us fifteen minutes later. "Even if what you find is a candy wrapper thrown down two days ago, don't assume that is the case. Collect and categorize, make determinations later."

Back on our feet, we walk for another hour along the ridge of the mound, finally coming to an area I find all too familiar. Daniel leads us to the hillside where I had fallen. He points down to where the entrance to the cave is now clearly visible. We climb down the hillside some distance from the site, to prevent any further disturbance of the area. I think this is unnecessary as the area had been disrupted completely by the rescuers two days ago.

"Stakeout an area 6 feet from the cave entrance in all directions," Daniel instructs us. "We will consider that our archaeological site. Then, we will work our way from the outer circle toward the middle, where the cave is. Photograph and record everything that you find within that circle."

"Isn't that a bit of overkill?" remarks Calvin. "I mean, we haven't a clue whether there's anything to find here, only the ranting of a man half out of his mind."

"You may be entirely right," Daniel replies. "But the Professor said to treat this as a training exercise, and so we will do it just right, to the letter. Anyway," he adds, "if we do find something of importance, we can then assure ourselves, and everyone else, that we didn't compromise the find in any way."

"B . . . b . . . but," stutters Bryan, "hasn't the site already been c . . . compromised? Has . . . hasn't it?" He stops, embarrassed at having contradicted Daniel.

Carli comes to his rescue. "I think he means, with all that coming and going involved in finding and getting Professor Gomez and Professor O'Hara out of here, the site has been pretty well trampled over."

"That is true," Daniel concedes, "but we can do our best to prevent any further contamination. And as I said, this is a training exercise as well."

Without any further comments we get to work. Working in twos and threes, we set up the grid, resulting in 1 foot by 1 foot squares, demarcated with intersecting lines of twine. When it is time to begin photographing the sections, Daniel asks if anyone has any experience with camera work.

Carli raises her hand and says timidly, "I have some experience, nothing technical, but I dabble a bit, as a hobby."

Daniel looks at her speculatively. "Well, alright. Eduardo generally does most of the photographic work. Kate, you've done some as well, right? Show her the equipment and give her a hand."

I could spit. He knows, full well, that I helped Eduardo with the photography last year, and, if I say so myself, I'm pretty good at it. If he just wants to give Carli a chance and see if she can do it, why doesn't he just say so? But instead he has to make me out as a novice at it as well.

It takes Carli and me several hours to photograph every square within the grid, whether or not it contains anything. The others follow behind, cataloging and recording the various objects found in the area. They then collect them, tag them, place them in envelopes, and pack them in crates.

We stop for lunch just after midday. Brian and Calvin returned to the car with the packed boxes and brought back the cooler and the food basket. The lunch of corn tortillas, marinated meat, and vegetables is delicious. After I eat my fill, I feel like taking a nap; however, we are ready now to enter the cave. My excitement and energy return at the prospect.

Eduardo and I had fallen through the roof of the cave. The entrance to the cave is actually ten feet, or so, further down the hillside and it is through this opening that the rescuers had extracted Eduardo. It is here that we will enter the cave. We approach the cave entrance as a group, all of us eager to get our first glimpse of what might be inside. We brought portable, high-intensity lights with us, which Calvin and Adam set up just inside the cave entrance. Carli then takes photographs of every inch of the cave's interior. I must say that Carli is doing a good job.

I'm surprised at how small and narrow the cave is, only 5 feet wide at its widest. "How in the world did Eduardo fit in here?" I remark.

"N . . . not very comfortable," says Brian. "Not c . . . comfortable at all."

"No, not very comfortable at all," agrees Daniel. "When we found him, he had slid down into the central hole, there, in a jackknife position. Though he told us, as we were getting him out, he had managed to get himself up to the edge somehow." He points to the area above the cave. "You can see where he and Kate" he smiles at me, "fell through the upper part of the cave, increasing the fall by twenty feet. It's a wonder he wasn't killed."

"Just lucky," says Adam sardonically.

"That's just what he said," Daniel rejoins. "He was ranting when we found him, of course, saying something about it being his fate, that he was meant to find the cave, and about the bird, the Quetzal. He claims it led him to the spot, caused him to fall by distracting his attention, and so leading him to find the book, the Codex."

"His fate?" remarks Carli, in astonishment. "It was meant to be?"

"Nonsense," say Adam and Calvin together. They look at each other, surprised that they agreed with each other on anything

"I don't agree," says Carli, apparently ready to argue the point.

Brian jumps to her defense. "It . . . it depends on your w . . . world view. Yes, on your world view. How you s . . . see the world."

"Sure. Sure," Calvin says with a laugh.

Daniel brings us back to the present, as he points to the rim of the cave. "Here," he leans closer, "do you see this area?" We all take turns putting our heads into the crevice and looking to where he pointed.

Sure enough, I can make out a flat surface and what is obviously a lid to something chiseled into the rock wall. I run my fingers over the groove and can feel my excitement rise. "So how do we proceed?" I ask, turning to Daniel for advice. After all, he has the most expertise, of the six of us, in excavating historical sites.

"The next step is to open it," he says smiling. "Calvin, give me a hand. We must be very careful not to drop the lid into the cave. We want it intact. After all, it's an artifact in its own right. It has been hand chiseled, made by man, no matter when." The two of them kneel on either side of the cave opening and reach in. Each grasps an edge of the stone and lifts carefully, bumping heads in the process.

"Careful. Careful. Careful," Daniel keeps repeating as if it's a mantra. They get the lid up to the rim of the enclosure and slide it carefully on to the ground outside the cave. Adam quickly lifts it into a padded crate brought for that purpose.

Daniel leans into the cave once more and I can hear him catch his breath. Whatever he might say to the contrary, he is as excited as the rest of us. He comes away, saying under his breath, "Remarkable." Then he motions the rest of us forward. "Take a look, Kate." I do. There in the side of the cave is a stone coffer chiseled into the limestone. The chamber that had been made measures approximately 10 x 12 inches and is about 12 inches in depth. Within it is a light brown bundle of what appears to be some sort of animal hide.

"Wow" is all I can say. It's weird, but I feel an energy emanating from the stone chamber. I back out to let each of the others, in turn, take my place. Each comes away with a look of incredulity on their face.

Daniel asks Carli to photograph the object as it lay in its sarcophagus. This she does eagerly. The preliminaries complete, Daniel dons latex gloves, leans once more into the cave, and slowly removes the leather wrapped bundle. As he brings it out into the sunlight, I wonder how long it's been since it has seen the light of day. Daniel places it gently into a waiting crate and hammers the lid into place. I feel a moment of disappointment. I want to see what the bundle contains. I want to see it right now, not wait until we get it back to camp. But, of course, we can't do that. Procedure is procedure, and procedure must be followed. Science before curiosity.

We secure the site, covering both the stone casket and the walls of the cave with heavy tarps, firmly securing them at the corners. Then we put a final tarp over the entire cave entrance and secured it as well. It takes us two trips to get all our paraphernalia back to the Land Rover and, by this time, the sun is already low in the western sky.

We are hot and tired by the time we get back to camp, hungry too. But I can't contain my eagerness to get a look at what we have found. Daniel, however, isn't going to let me get a look at the bundle, now. "Let's leave the unpacking for a bit. As for me, I need a shower and something to eat, right now," he commands.

"But what about the artifact?" I stutter. "Don't you want to see what it is?"

"It's waited this long. It can wait a little longer," says Calvin, on Daniel's side for once. "I'm for the showers, too." He saunters off without another word.

Daniel smiles, "See you in the mess in an hour or so." And he too walks off toward his tent."

"Well, I think a s . . . s . . . shower is a good idea," stammers Brian.

"I'm filthy and can't wait for a hot shower," Carli sings. "Wasn't this just the most exciting day?" she asks, tapping my arm. "I just can't wait to see what can possibly be in that bundle we found, but I need a shower first." Then turning to Brian, she takes his arm and leads him off toward the tents, still chattering on about the day and how wonderful it has been.

I look over at Adam. He smiles and says, "Looks like we've been outvoted. Guess the great disclosure will have to wait."

But I'm not ready to give up quite yet. "Don't you think . . . ?" I start, and then stall, not knowing what it is I think. I start again, "What if the bundle is what Eduardo says it is? What if it is a real artifact?" I stumble on, feeling more and more ridiculous. Adam smiles at me quizzically. "I mean," I continue "should we leave it just sitting in the Land Rover like this? What if something were to happen to it?" I feel idiotic. I know how absurd this all sounds. I actually feel myself blush, like an adolescent. Yes, I'm blushing.

Adam laughs. "You mean, like someone stealing it or something?"

"Well . . . yes." I can feel my face getting hotter and hotter. Finally I laugh out loud at myself. "Or it suddenly catches fire or a flood washes it away." I say in self-ridicule. Adam laughs too, a deep, rich laugh. "Okay, so nothing's going to happen to it while we get cleaned up," I concede, and turn to follow the others.

"Wait," says Adam. "If it will make you feel better," and he moves back toward the Land Rover. "Where do you want to put it?"

Now that someone is listening to me, I don't know what I want to do. "I feel so stupid," I admit. "It's just that there's something about Eduardo's story and how the artifact, or whatever it is, was hidden, that makes me think it's important. I know that's illogical, since we haven't even seen it yet. It's just a feeling I've had since I first saw it in that stone box."

"Okay," Adam says, "nothing stupid about it. It'll take only a minute. Where do you intend to put it?"

"Let's just put it in the office, for now." I don't know why this insistence on my part for what is essentially illogical. Not my usual style, but I am grateful to Adam for acceding to my wishes. We take the crate containing the object from the Land Rover. Adam carries it into the office, placing it on the corner of the table. "Thanks," I say, really meaning it.

He smiles again, dimples and all. "No problem. Think I'll get my shower now. Meet you at dinner." And he leaves.

Being left alone only makes me feel more ridiculous. I look at the crate as it sits on the table. I feel better with it here, safer because it is safe. I feel linked to whatever rests in the box, as if I am responsible for it in some way. Creepy, I know, but that's the way I feel. I leave it there, reluctantly. I am trained so that I cannot, will not, open it without all the safeguards that are necessary, but I want to. I go to take my shower, but not before locking the office door which is always kept unlocked.

We return, as a group, later in the evening, after getting a bit of rest and enjoying another fabulous meal. Even Calvin, who had not exhibited any interest in the object so far, is not going to be left out of its unveiling. When I pull the office key from my pocket and insert it in the lock, Daniel looks at me with amusement and shakes his head. Adam smiles and laughs softly to himself. But neither says a word.

"Well, let's just see what we might have in this interesting package," says Daniel, in command as usual.

"Probably just some trash hidden there by some 14 year olds in the 1950's. A cigar box full of rocks, bird nests, and girlie magazines," Calvin mutters. But he is there with the rest of us, crowding eagerly around the table.

"Probably," agrees Daniel. "But just in case it is something of interest," he adds, "Let's do it right." He looks around at each of us in turn. "Carli?"

"Yes?" She answers, eagerly stepping forward.

"You handled that camera pretty well today. Here, we need to record each step, each layer, meticulously. The camera is over there. See if you can find the flash equipment and that you have enough film." Carli is ecstatic.

"We'll need an exact written record of each step," I break in. I'm not about to let Daniel take over the whole show. "Brian, why don't you take notes? The pen and paper are over on the desk." I point off to the far side of the room.

"S . . . sure," Brian replies, totally taken aback at being asked to take part. "I can do that. Yes, I can do that." And he rushes to get the notepad from the desk.

Daniel takes over again. "Calvin, can you get the lid off this crate?"

"Sure thing," grunts Calvin, magically taking a screwdriver from his back pocket. Daniel is pointedly ignoring Adam actually almost pushes him out of the way to help Calvin with the crate.

I step forward, about to demand that I have a part in opening the discovery, when Daniel surprises me by waving me over and saying, "Kate, why don't you do the honors?" I hesitate a moment in my surprise, and am about to thank him, when he ruins the gesture by adding, snidely, "After all, you seem to be the only one who believes in Eduardo's fantastic fairytale."

Of course, he has to make fun of me, but to hell with him. I feel like something wonderful is about to be revealed. Both Daniel and I put on surgical gloves to handle the artifact. I step to the crate, reach over the edge, and gingerly place my hands about the object inside. I'm surprised to find that my hands are shaking and that I have been holding my breath for so long, I felt lightheaded.

"Come on," grumbles Calvin. "Let's get on with it already."

I take the bundle out of the crate. It is heavier than I expect. Adam removes the crate and I place the object on the table. Daniel moves forward again and begins to examine it carefully. "The object is wrapped in what appears to be animal hide, probably deer skin, but that we can determine later," he says. I can see Brian scribbling furiously onto his notepad, recording every word Daniel says.

"The covering is in very good condition considering where it was found. Some minor tearing at the edges, but otherwise intact," he continues. He then asks for a tape measure. Adam quickly finds one and hands it to him. "The object measures 12 inches long by 8 inches wide by 3.4 inches in depth." He then steps back and asks Carli to take pictures of the object as it lies on the table. This she does with unexpected expertise.

Daniel returns and turns the object over, repeating his inspection of the other side, reporting his observations aloud, as before. Brian records them.

When he is finished, Daniel steps back again and says, "Kate." He indicates that I should continue to open the bundle. I do so. The deerhide wrap is thin and slightly oily, but intact and sturdy. I fold each corner back while Carli photographs the object at each step. Under the leather wrapping is a second layer, this one an off-white fabric, linen-like in appearance. It, too, is in remarkably good condition.

Daniel comes forward again and makes his meticulous observations. Brian records as he speaks. When he has finished, Daniel again steps away and motions me forward. With great care I fold back the last of the linen wrappings to reveal a wooden object inside. There's a moment of silence, almost reverence, as we all gaze in awe at what is revealed. I look down at the object. It is a book made in the style of the ancient Mayan codices[11]; two flat pieces of wood tied together with rawhide laces, holding multiple pages between them. I touch the object gently and feel a warmth in the palms of my hands. The warmth seems to be emanating from the book itself.

I look at the object closely and realize that it has carving on the surface. I trace the outline with my finger. "These are hieroglyphics," I say in wonder. "Classical Mayan hieroglyphs." I place my hands flat on the surface of the wooden cover and close my eyes for a moment. I can feel a strange sensation, a throbbing, as if it is a heart beating, as if the book is alive. Or perhaps, the sensation is just my own heart beating wildly, as the realization comes to me of just how important a find this truly is.

Daniel pushes me aside, not roughly, but with authority. He looks closely at the carving. "Yes, pictographs, or hieroglyphics of some sort. Whether or not they are Mayan, we'll have to see. Even if they are Mayan glyphs, no way of telling when they were written. Carbon dating will be needed to determine that. Carli, take detailed photos of this," he says. There is an odd note in his voice that I cannot identify. Is it excitement at the possible import of the find, or irritation that it cannot possibly be an ancient manuscript?

Carli takes pictures, then Calvin steps forward drawing on a pair of gloves. He touches the wooden cover, an intensely thoughtful expression on his face. "I am not so savvy about hieroglyphs, but I do know the Mayan number system pretty well. These are numbers," he says as he runs his fingers down the sides of the Codex cover, "dates, to be more exact. These in this column, on the left side," he runs his fingers down that column, "read 9.12.16.2.16. If I'm not mistaken, have to double-check, but I'm pretty sure, this Mayan date is equivalent to 688 C.E. Gregorian. And these," he points to two sets of symbols at the bottom of the column, "I'll have to calculate it, but they indicate a particular day in the Mayan calendars."

I am impressed and, by the look on his face, so is Daniel.

I look again at the cover of the manuscript, this time more closely at the central glyphs. "This one," I point to a recognizable glyph at the top of the cover. "This symbol is the symbol usually used to indicate K'inich Chan Balham II.[(3)]"

"That fits," says Carli excitedly, and we all look at her in surprise. She blushes and continues, "Chan Bahlum II, son of Pakal, the Great. K'inich Chan Bahlum II was the king of the Maya city-state of Baakal, now known as Palenque, from 684 CE to 702 CE. So that fits with the date on the Codex." Then she adds, more tentatively, "That is, if we are correct with our translation." And she giggles nervously. I am again impressed with her. She has obviously done her homework.

"We will have to verify the translation, of course," Daniel interrupts. "Even if the glyphs are Mayan, authenticity is not assured. It may be just a very recent copy or even a forgery," he says pompously. "But whatever it is, we need to be meticulous in our handling of it. Slow and steady in the interest of its potential historical value. I recommend we stop here for tonight. It's getting late. We'll put it away and continue with our examination when we are all fresh." He says this as a command, not a suggestion.

I don't want to stop. I want to continue, to find out all the mysteries the book contains. But I know Daniel is right, damn him. "You're right, of course," I concede. "But before we put it away, I'd like to copy the glyphs so I can study them closer without interruption."

"So would I.," adds Calvin. And Daniel gives way. Calvin and I each grab sheets of paper and pens from the desk and carefully copy from the cover of the Codex.

"I'll download the pictures into the computer tonight," Carli says, "so you will have a backup copy too."

"Good girl," I say and I mean it. Calvin and I finish our copying, I then carefully rewrap the artifact. "Do we have a smaller box to put it in?" I ask Daniel.

"I believe so." He goes over to a box of supplies, finds a box of file folders, empties it, and brings the empty box back to the table. The manuscript just fits.

"Now lock it in the safe," I say and hand it to him. It is a demand, not a request. He complies without argument. I lock the office, as well, as we leave.

III

December 21, 936 CE
10.5.8.5.19, 6 Cauac, 2 Pop
Eighteen months later, the courtyard of the Ch'e'en household

The day was overcast and the air cool, for the winter season had descended upon the city. Ahkan and Took Pak sat in the courtyard, enjoying each other's company but saying little. Took Pak was home for only the second time since his last birthday. He was here for the two day festival celebrating the winter solstice, the shortest day of the year and a high holy day. He had arrived for the evening meal the night before. That morning the entire household had attended the ritual and sacrifice on the high altar of the Temple of Ku'kul'kan.

Ahkan enjoyed the celebration. She liked the crowds and the noise, the music and the festivity. She enjoyed shopping in the hectic bazaar that was set up in the central plaza during the holy days. All the local craftsmen sold their wares, farmers from the surrounding countryside brought their surplus crops, and traders from faraway city-states brought their foreign trinkets. She liked to stroll amid the stalls and to talk with friends and neighbors. But she disliked the ceremony and found the rituals disturbing.

The ceremony this morning was impressive and the crowd was large and excited. The ritual began with a grand procession. The priests, Ah Kin, robed in flowing green, saffron, and red garments, were led by the Ah Kin Mai (high priest), Koloome Ek Suutz, in his scarlet vestments. The Ah Kin Mai and the rest of the Inner Circle, also in blood red robes, were bejeweled with fabulous ornaments of jade and obsidian. Their tall aj k'uh hun, headdresses, were plumed with the green and gold feathers of the revered Quetzal. They carried in their right hands the sacred rods denoting their power. In their left, they carried a symbol of their place within the Temple hierarchy. The Ah Kin Mai carried a staff with the carved head of a Chan (serpent) in his left hand. The pelt of a Bahlum (jaguar) adorned his aj k'uh hun. The priestly assembly entered the plaza from the south gate.

The procession of priests was followed by the King, Ajaw K'inich B'ox Kan and his royal consort, ix Ajawb K'an B'al. The King was clad in a loin cloth and skirt with a cape of emerald green and gold like the Quetzal. Upon his head he wore a tall aj k'uh hun in the form of Bahlum, the jaguar. The queen wore a long, richly brocaded gown of dark, forest green, in honor of Chac Chel, the earth goddess. Braided in her dark tresses were polished shells and a woven crown of vines and flowers. At the end of the line came the temple school boys and the initiates, Took Pak among them. They were clad in plain brown robes and were unadorned. The column reached the foot of the Temple pyramid and began to mount the western staircase.

Once the King reached the top of the pyramid, he turned to the crowd amassed in the plaza below. He raised his arms, the scepter of his dynasty in his right hand and the rod of war in his left. He was tall for a Maya, broad of shoulder and muscular. He was glorious to behold as the rising sun wreathed him in a halo of golden light. The crowd below cheered and roared their appreciation and faith in their Ajaw. The King accepted the accolades of his people with a nod of his head and turned to sit upon the tunich tzam, a stone throne placed to the right of the altar.

The altar was a thick highly polished slab of stone mounted upon a tapered plinth. The Ah Kin Mai took center stage and intoned the proscribed ritual orosion (prayer), calling upon the gods and goddesses of the heavens and the underworld. He entreated them to show favor toward the Maya people. He prayed particularly to Chac, the god of the rain, requesting that there be an end to the drought that had distressed the land of the Maya for many seasons.

As the initial invocations were concluded, four old men, the executioners, robed in black, brought forward a gigantic Keeh, white-tailed stag, the sacrificial offering. They placed the offering upon the high altar. The animal was obviously drugged or stunned for it did not protest. A fifth old man, the High Executioner, also in black, came forward. He drew a knife of gleaming black obsidian and handed it to the Ah Kin Mai. The High Executioner stretched out the stag's head to expose its slender, graceful neck. Sajal Ch'itz'aat, secretary to the Ah Kin Mai, held the K'ubul Luuch, the sacred bowl of carved obsidian, in readiness. The Ah Kin Mai raised the knife and, with one swift stroke, opened the large vessels of the animal's neck. The stag gave one shuttering spasm. Its liquid life drained out and the precious K'ubul K'ik' (blood) was caught in the hallowed bowl.

The Ah Kin Mai dipped his fingers into the blessed liquid then raised his bloodied fingers to his lips. He dipped his fingers once more and sketched three chevrons on each of his cheeks and a circle upon his forehead. He placed within the bowl sheets of parchment on which were written sacred prayers and supplications to the gods. The papers soaked up the blood and turned a rusty red. Sajal Ch'itz'aat came forward and with a lighted taper set the papers aflame. To the bowl he added a handful of herbs, spices and wild flowers.

Smoke rose into the windless air, wafting toward the heavens. The Ah Kin Mai leaned forward. He plunged his face into the blue grey smoke emanating from the smoldering scriptures. He breathed in the acrid fumes, shuttered and fell back, dropping to his knees. The High Priest moaned loudly, his head swam and his vision clouded. He lost consciousness and all awareness of his surroundings.

He was carried away by a vision to a far plain, where the mists swirled around him. As his vision cleared he saw before him a dry and empty landscape. The carcasses of dead animals and men littered the scene. He could hear the lamentations of his dying people.

He prostrated himself before the altar, shaking all over. The crowd was silent. The Ah Kin did not approach their leader, but left him to his vision.

Gradually the Ah Kin Mai's vision faded and he returned to himself. He shook off the dream as best he could and, regaining his composure, rose shakily to his feet. His face was pale. The sacrificial blood, mixed with his tears, was smeared across his visage. He turned to face the crowd which was hushed and confused by the spectacle. He steadied himself with his staff and, in an attempt to return the scene to normality, lifted his head and addressed the heavens. He asked the gods to accept the sacrifice and thanked them for their continued blessings. He then dismissed the crowd, telling them to return to their homes and continue the celebration.

Took Pak was fascinated by the ceremony and the dignity and authority of the Ah Kin Mai. He was swept up in the spectacle and was awed by the ritual. He felt that something special and unusual had occurred here. Something had happened to him as well. He had caught a glimpse of the Ah Kin Mai's vision, had seen a small part of the whole. He had seen, for a moment, his own face, in the swirling smoke. He felt, somehow, his fate was linked to the Temple and to the ritual.

Ahkan was shaken by the sacrifice. She was nauseated by the slaughter of the beautiful animal in homage to the gods, gods in which she was not sure she believed. She could condone the slaughter of animals to nourish the body or even to provide hides to clothe the body or bone and sinew to make weapons and tools. But to kill purely to provide entertainment and spectacle was something she could not condone.

Now it was evening and the family meal was over. Ahkan's mother had excused Ahkan from helping the other women with the clean-up in the kitchen, so that she and Took Pak could have a short time together. And so they had met here and were sitting in the cooling air, enjoying each other's company. But they were uncomfortable after such a long separation.

Took Pak was unsure of how to begin the conversation. So much had changed in his life. He had learned so much. His world had expanded and no longer was encompassed by the family and the household, and Ahkan. Yes, Ahkan most of all. Where once he had shared his whole world with her, now their lives were worlds apart. She could not begin to understand what his world had become.

Ahkan was thinking much the same thing. Her world and her interests had changed so much in a few short months. She felt this, especially, after watching the ceremonies at the Temple this morning. She felt that her life and Took Pak's were moving in opposite and possibly conflicting directions. She knew that she could not possibly comprehend the mathematics, the astronomy and the mysteries that he was learning. He had moved miles beyond the simple writing and numbers that they had learned together in this very courtyard. She was sure that he thought that she was still the same xchuu paal he had left behind such a short time ago. He must think that she would still only be interested in what was going on in the household and the gardens. He could not know all that she had learned from Ko'lel and how her world too had changed.

Finally she could stand the silence no longer. "I hear that you are the star of the Temple school. That you excel in all your studies and have attracted the attention of Sajal Ch'itz'aat himself," she began quietly.

He was startled by the broken silence and surprised that she had heard anything about what went on at the Temple. "How is it that you have heard such exaggerations?" he replied.

"Your father has many contacts in the court and in the Temple," she laughed. "You do not think that anything that concerns his son would evade his notice? Or that anyone in that group, wishing to curry his favor, would miss a chance to be the first to let him know how well his son is doing. And I am quite sure none of the praise is an exaggeration, more likely the opposite. Word has it that they are considering advancing you to a senior level already, earlier than has ever been done before." She could not keep the pride out of her voice.

"Now I know this is pure exaggeration," he said with embarrassment.

'That I do not believe," she said. "I know you are doing as well as rumor has said." She leaned toward him, a look of intense interest on her beautiful face. "Tell me what you are studying and all about your fellow students, and the priests, and the Temple. Tell me what they feed you and where you sleep." She paused to catch her breath.

"Wait a minute," he laughed. "Slow down. Let me answer one question before you ask the next dozen."

"But I want to know it all," she said excitedly. Then suddenly turning serious, "I have missed you so much," she added with a catch in her voice, "But most of all, I what to know, I need to know, if you are happy?" She looked up at him expectantly through teary eyes.

He smiled down at her sweet face. "I have missed you too, Hun P'iit, but I have been too busy to be unhappy. And I have learned so much." He went on to tell her all about his new life. He told her stories about the other students and about the acolyte, Yax Ahk. He had her laughing at their antics and astonished at the amount of work they had to do. He told her how beyond their studies they had other duties. She was particularly interested to hear that they were expected to spend several hours a day working in the Temple gardens and kitchens. This, they were told, was as much part of their education as their slates and parchments. Ahkan thought that this was very logical, more than she had expected from the priests.

Ahkan then asked him tentatively what he had learned of the dogma and the mysteries of the Temple. He laughed and told her that he and his fellow students were much too green and too far down in the Temple hierarchy to be entrusted with any secrets, as yet. He added that the only pieces of dogma they had as yet been given were recitations of prayers to the gods and the creation story which every Maya child learned from the cradle. He knew her reservations regarding religion and the holiness of the Temple and the priests. He did not want to take any of the short time they had together to argue over subjects they could not agree upon. So he brushed these questions away with a wave of his hand. He changed the conversation from his life to hers. "And so what is new with you, butterfly?"

She looked at him speculatively. How much should she tell him? He would not be pleased, this she knew. But they had never kept secrets from one another and she really did not want to start doing so now. So with trepidation, she hesitantly told him all that had happened since she had seen him last. She told him of her visits to Ko'lel in the forest and of her confrontation with her mother and father over her intention to learn the shaman craft from the old woman.

Took Pak looked at her with horror. "How can you think of doing such a thing?" he said aghast. "And how could your parents think of letting you?"

"My parents came to understand that they could not stop me," she said quietly. "They came to believe that it was the will of the gods." He started to interrupt again, but she stopped him. "I told you of my intentions long ago," she continued. "But you did not believe that I was serious. No, it is true, you laughed at me, at the pretentions of a xchuu paal. You did not, and still do not, believe that my aspirations can be as noble and important as yours. But they are. I am learning as much as you are. And what I am learning is as important as what you are learning." She could see his skepticism but continued valiantly. "I am learning the healing powers," she said. "I am learning how to make salves and cordials that can help cure the ailments of the people, to reduce their suffering. And yes, even to keep them from death, when I have learned enough."

"And incantations and potions to assure them love or to curse their neighbors, I suppose," he scoffed and was immediately sorry.

75

She got hastily to her feet and stomped away from him to the other side of the courtyard. "See, you are still laughing at me," she said angrily. "But what I am doing is as important as what you are doing." She turned and returned to where he was sitting. She stood before him, her arms folded across her chest. "Maybe what I am doing is even more important, because it at least gets results," she said haughtily, "which is more than I can say for the weak prayers of your priests, who have been praying for rain for the last five years and we still have drought."

He was shocked by her outburst and then ashamed at himself for mocking her. He realized that she was in earnest and that nothing he said would change how she felt. "You are right," he said sheepishly. "I should not have made fun of your intentions. But," he continued with great seriousness, "I am fearful for you. The old woman, Ko'lel, although called upon by the poor folk in their extremity, is also mocked and laughed at. She is held in little regard and in some fear by the nobles of the court and by the priests of the Temple. If things were to continue to go wrong, I would not be at all surprised if your wise woman were not held responsible in some way and, by extension, you as well."

"I think that the Temple priests will be held responsible long before Ko'lel and me. For the people know Ko'lel and seek her help. She knows what she can help them with and she tells them when she cannot. She does not tax them and ask for tribute that they cannot afford. And she does not promise them what she cannot deliver, as your priests do." He was surprised by her vehemence and saw some logic in what she said. He did not want to argue with her. "I worry more for you," she said letting her anger go, for she did not want to argue with him either. "I feel that the people will not stand for the continuous raising of the tribute the priests demand for the gods, with no results. They will begin to blame the priests and," she paused for effect, "by extension, you."

"Let us not argue, Hun P'iit," he said warmly. "Let us just take pleasure in each other's company. I do not know how long it will be before we see each other again." She slipped her hand in his and they sat in companionable silence, listening to the familiar night sounds. They sat that way for a long time. Then Ahkan shivered with the increasing chill. Took Pak put his arm around her. "It is much too late in the season to sit out so late," he said. "You are getting cold and I must get up very early in the morning or I will be late for my lessons."

"I do not want to say good night," she whispered. "As you said, we do not know when we will see each other again." And the tears began again.

"Wait," said Took Pak, "I have an idea. You know how I told you I spend time working in the Temple gardens? Well, Nuxib Mak is often there as well. I have not spoken to him as yet, just nodded and he nods back. But I think I could approach him and speak to him without anyone thinking it amiss."

Ahkan looked at him excitedly, getting the import of what he was suggesting. "We could send messages to one another," she said smiling happily "Nuxib Mak would be glad to do that for us." But then her face clouded over and she added, "But I do not think the priests would approve. You might get into trouble."

"They need not know to whom I am sending a message," he said with a wink. "I would just be passing the time of day with an old friend and a servant in my father's house. How could they disapprove of that?"

"I think it is an ingenious idea," she said and was much more content to say goodnight and goodbye for the time being. Took Pak rose and she with him. Before leaving the courtyard she put her hand on his arm to stay him and said, "I have something for you." From her skirt pocket she pulled a bright green and gold feather and placed it in his hand.

He looked down at it smiling. "And what is this, butterfly?"

"It is a feather from the sacred Quetzal. I found it in the garden where the bird left it for me. And can you see? I have sharpened it to form a quill that you can use to write upon your parchment. Every time you use it you can think of me."

He looked down at the pen in his hand and then up at her. "I do not need anything to remind me of you," he said fondly. "But the others will be consumed with envy over such a magnificent quill." He bid her goodnight and watched after her sadly as she left the courtyard by the western doorway.

IV

June 28, 2011
12.19.18.8.18, 8 Etznab, 6 Zec
A room somewhere in Mexico

The room is the same. Nothing has changed in it from three days before, including its occupants. The dark, powerful man sits behind his ornate desk and the same weaker man sits before him. The conversation has been going on for some time and the subordinate has just stumbled through a rather long explanation.

"So if I understand you correctly, this unexceptional, unknown university professor has stumbled upon what he and his colleagues believe is an ancient Maya artifact, a Codex of some sort. And how did you come upon this information?" The man's voice was hard.

The second man's voice shook as he replied. "From the hospital staff: attendants in the emergency room, and nurses in intensive care. They all report that he arrived ranting about a giant bird that had led him to a cave and then, something about a sacred Mayan manuscript. They say he was in a bad condition, out of his head with the pain and fever. He is still in intensive care, doing better. He almost lost his leg. None of them give much credit to the story, just the rantings of a very ill man."

The other man pondered his hands folded on the top of the desk. "You were not conspicuous with your questioning? You did not display too much interest, I hope?"

The other man looked frightened. "No, no Monsignor. I was very circumspect. I posed as a member of the press requesting information about the accident."

There was another pause, then the man behind the desk mused, "And where is this artifact now?"

The other man looked even more frightened, finally stammered a reply, "I, I don't know exactly. I assume it is still at the dig site. The director of the excavation team, an American, Dr. Robert Allen from the University in New York, made the proper notification to the Oficina de Antiguedad, I understand, but that is all."

"Where, exactly, is this site?" The first man's voice was steely.

"A place called Sero Pazo, about 35 miles south east of Merida, in the middle of nowhere." The subordinate's voice trembled.

The man behind the desk looked up and stared, his black eyes cold. "You will find out exactly where the object is. Am I understood?" His voice held a clear threat. "Send in some of our associates. You know who I mean. Have them keep an eye on the archaeological site and those involved. I want to know exactly where in the camp they are keeping the artifact." He smiled cruelly. "Can you do that for me?"

The audience was over and the sycophant left the room gratefully.

CHAPTER FIVE

I

50 BCE
7.15.9.8.8

Mayan Myth

Halach Uinic gave knowledge to the Maya
As it was needed.
When to plant and when to harvest,
When to marry, when to give birth, when to go to war.
And when to honor the gods for their bounty,
The Shaman grew in wealth, in power, and in honor.

The Shaman studied the movement of the stars
And the changing of the seasons.
He saw that the seasons and the stars
Returned in an orderly fashion
Fall followed summer, winter followed by spring,
He understood the cycles of the universe and the circles of time

The Shaman knew what happened in this cycle,
Would occur in the next and the next,
Until the end of the universe.
He could predict what the future would bring.
When the rains would come and when they would not.
He knew the fortunes of the Maya.

The gods managed the order of the days
And of the ages.
The Shaman divined their meaning.
And he gave this knowledge to the Maya.
Nothing was done that he did not condone.
Through his intercession, the pleasure of the gods was assured.

And the gods were pleased and they blessed the Maya
And the Maya prospered.

The Shaman was given a dream.
In that dream the gods gave to him
Symbols to record the number of stars.
Symbols to record their names and the names of the gods.
And the gods gave the Shaman three calendars
To record the passage of the days, and the seasons, and the generations.

The Tzoln counted the sacred days,
Reminded the Maya of the times to honor the gods.
The Hun marked the seasons,
The time for planting and for tilling and for harvesting.
He The Long Count marked the passage of the years and the
generations.
To record the creations and the destructions of the universe.

The Shaman was the keeper of the calendars,
'The Keeper of Time.'
He was given this knowledge by the gods.
They gave time into his keeping.
The Maya honored the Shaman for his knowledge
They gave tribute to him and through him to the gods.

And the Shaman passed the knowledge on to his sons,
And they to their sons, and so on through the generations.

II

June 27, 2011
12.19.18.8.15, 5 Men, 3 Se
The dig, Yucatan Peninsula

The Professor returns the next day, leaving Eduardo in the loving care of his wife and family. Eduardo is out of the woods, but still very ill and recuperating slowly. We tell the Professor about the artifact. He is interested but unconvinced as to its authenticity. He cautions us, "The original dig site is our first priority. It is this for which we have approval. The finding of the Codex was an accident and we have no official authorization to dig or explore the mound. As a result, the Office of Antiquities will take possession of the artifact. Any further exploration of the site will be done through them. We will have no part in it. The Codex will stay here at the dig site until Eduardo is well enough to return and get a look at it. It was his discovery after all."

We all realize that what he says is true. But as long as the Codex is in our possession I, for one, have every intention of continuing my examination of it. I think all the others feel the same.

The Professor then tells us Eduardo sent him back to the dig to "get on with it". So that's what we do. "You will spend your time here at the well site," he says. "Any spare time you have can be spent on the Codex while it is here, but not at the expense of your primary duties." We all agree. What else can we do? Our time spent working at the dig sometimes means 10 to 12 hours a day. Not much time left for extraneous activities.

I pick up where I left off last summer, excavating an area that had been used over time as a garbage dump for the village. Professor Allen assigns Carli and Adam to help me. A 3 foot deep trench takes us back in history, the lowest layer yields debris from 5 to 6 centuries ago: pieces of bone, pottery shards, and stones used as tools or weapons, small finds and few in number. Commonplace finds that tell something of the everyday life of the village people over the ages. These are of particular interest to me because they tell primarily of the life of the women of the village. They tell us about what the ancient Maya ate, wore, and the implements they used. Carli is enthusiastic and eager to learn. If only she didn't talk incessantly, I wouldn't mind her help. Adam, on the other hand, lacks her enthusiasm but is cautious and careful in his work. He speaks little but always brings a hint of humor to what can be a tedious task.

Daniel, Calvin, and Brian are working at the excavation of a site of an ancient dwelling. They are working on what they expect will turn out to be the family hearth, a traditional three sided fireplace, in the corner of the structure.

The Professor spends his time between the two sites, giving rambling lectures about the history of the dig and archaeology, in general, to all of us. The information is interesting but often long-winded and difficult to follow. His appearance at the site tends to slow the work significantly.

We usually turn in early, as we are up with the sun and work hard until sundown. Most evenings are spent going through and cataloging the finds of the day. Rainy days, and there are many rainy days as this is the rainy season in this region, are spent the same way. This leaves little time for other pursuits, including work on the Codex. Anyway, before in-depth study of the manuscript can begin we need to document and photograph it completely. This means photographing each individual page, from every possible angle, and downloading the photographs into the computer. This Carli and I do in our 'spare time'

July 13, 2011
12.19.18.9.13, 10 Ben, 1 Xul
The dig, Yucatán Península, México

Time passes quickly and it is mid-July before we have any break to speak of. Then, a tropical storm hits the coast and comes inland far enough to deluge the camp for days. We catch up on our cataloging of articles from the well site quickly. This leaves some spare time for us. Not surprisingly, it seems that most of us turn our thoughts back to the Codex.

Carli and I have finally completed the photographing of the 24 closely written pages of the manuscript. The sheets of parchment are made from thinly hammered wood. The Codex itself is formed by folding long single sheets of parchment accordion fashion into multiple pages. These pages are covered in a thin layer of gesso and bound within the carved wooden covers. The gesso, if truly Mayan, will prove to be made of crushed limestone mixed with ashes and the parchment from the wood of the fig tree.

As for the translation of the manuscript, we haven't gotten any further than the front cover. Calvin continues to work at the numbers in columns. I am struggling with the rest of the hieroglyphs on the cover. They refer to Chan Bahlum II, once King of Palenque. He was noted for his writings and prophecies. The Maya Doomsday Prophecy, in particular, is attributed to him. I need to make a trip to the library or the museum in Merida for some research about him.

The rest of what is written on the front cover is even more difficult to interpret. I cannot tell if Chan Bahlum II is the author or not, for there is a second name on the Codex. Someone referred to as 'small stone or flint shield,' Chan Took Pakal, il Ahab Ch'e'en, son of the Lord of the cave. Can this refer somehow to the cave in which the Codex was found? The hieroglyphs also seem to describe the second person as Aj K'uhn, meaning a priestly scribe. Did this indicate that the manuscript is merely a copy of what had originally been written for or by Chan Bahlum II; that it had been copied by this priestly scribe? The monks of the dark ages had transcribed the great works of the preceding eras, thereby preserving the wisdom of the ages. So too did the scribes of the ancient Maya preserve their wisdom. Unfortunately all but four of the Mayan books were destroyed when the Spanish conquistadors invaded the area. What was left of the Mayan civilization's written works, Father Landa had burned in 1566. What a find this Codex will be, even if only a late copy of an earlier work. One of only five extant works. A big 'if" but still a possibility.

When it is still raining on the fifth day, I can stand it no longer. I make a suggestion at breakfast. "I'm going to go insane if I have to spend another day in my tent," I say, speaking particularly to the Professor. "Are you going into the hospital today to see Eduardo?" I ask.

"Yes, I had planned on it," he replies. He picks up on my intention before I can make the request. "Would you like to go along? If we take the van, we can all go into Merida."

"Just what I'd been about to suggest," I jump at the offer. "I'd love to see Eduardo, if he's up for visitors, and I would like to see Maria, as well," I say with enthusiasm. Then I add, "And I need to get to the museum or library. Some research I need to do."

"Research related to our artifact, I'll bet," says Daniel with a smirk. Then turning to Professor Allen he says, "I'd like to go as well. I'd like to pay my respects to Eduardo and his family."

"I think I'll stay here," says Carli. "Teo promised to teach me how to make that fabulous Posole, pork stew, we had the other night." Brian rapidly says that he prefers to stay in camp as well. No surprise there.

Adam thinks for a moment and then says he'll join us. "I'd like to take a look at the city, didn't get to see much on our way from the airport. I hear there are some beautiful 16th-century architectures in the old city."

Calvin says nothing. He has not been involved in the conversation at all. Finally Daniel asks him directly, "Are you planning on going to Merida with us, Calvin?"

"What?" Calvin looks up as if noticing for the first time that there is anyone else in the room.

"We are going into Merida this morning," Daniel repeats in obvious exasperation. "Would you like to go with us?"

"Oh," Calvin mumbles and then finally, as if he suddenly understands what Daniel has said to him, "No, I don't think so. I'm in the middle of some interesting calculations. Found some more dates and numbers in this lost Codex of ours." I am surprised at his expression of joint ownership of the Codex. I thought he had dismissed the whole thing, after his initial interest, but it seems he has been working on it all along.

"What have you found?" I ask.

"Well, further along in the manuscript," he says vaguely, "are a great many numbers, most of them are related to what I think are astrological signs. Then come pages and pages of dates: years, eons, and individual days. Don't know what that's all about. All very interesting, anyway. I'm right in the middle of some calculations and want to spend the day here working on it. Very interesting," he murmurs again, clearly off somewhere in his head, not sitting at the table with us. It must be very interesting indeed to capture Calvin's attention so completely.

When we get to Merida several hours later, we drop Adam in the middle of the city, then Daniel, the Professor, and I head to the hospital. I am shocked by what I see as I walk into the hospital room. If I did not know it was Eduardo lying in the bed I would not have recognized him. He must have lost 20 or 30 pounds and looks like he has aged 10 years. He is propped up in bed on several pillows and his left leg is suspended in a contraction of pulleys and ropes. It is encased in a heavy plaster cast. His once bronze complexion is sallow and gray. Maria sits at his bedside. She looks incredibly tired and almost as ill as her husband. Professor Allen had told us that their two teenage sons returned to Mexico City and are staying with Maria's mother. Maria had insisted on staying here with Eduardo until he is well enough to make the trip home.

As we enter, Eduardo smiles broadly and I see a glimmer of the man I know. His eyes sparkle with delight at seeing us. "Buenos dios, mi amigos. I am so glad to see you. Roberto has told me that you retrieved my little artifact, but he could not, or would not, tell me anything further. Now you can give me the . . . what do you say, the low down?" And he laughs.

The Professor makes a sign cautioning us not to get Eduardo excited, but Maria, getting to her feet, says, "No, no, Professor, let him talk and ask his questions. It is all he thinks about anyway. But for me, I will go out for a walk and get some air while you talk. I've heard all I can stand about his great find." She laughs too, but ruefully. She kisses her husband on the cheek and whispers in his ear. "Don't tire yourself." And she leaves the room.

"She worries about me," says Eduardo, smiling sweetly. "Now tell me all about it."

Daniel and I, between us, tell him step-by-step how we found and retrieved the artifact. Eduardo then demands an exact description of how we had opened and first examined it, with all our precautions and safeguards. He then asks us for our observations, descriptions, and conclusions about what it is we, or rather he, had found. We tell him everything we can, concluding with Calvin's current line of investigation.

"Fascinating," he says repeatedly. "Fascinating." And then he adds, "I knew it, I knew it."

When we finish and he seems satisfied, I add, "Now that we've told you all that we can, I'd like to hear your story." I sit in the chair Maria had vacated and take his hand.

He looks at me closely, gazing deeply into my eyes and whispers, "You have felt it too." I don't answer for I don't know what to say. What is it that I had felt? I can't describe it. If I try to, it will sound crazy.

"Felt what?" Daniel says, into the silence.

Eduardo looks up at him but Daniel doesn't seem to hold any interest for him. His eyes come back to me. "You have felt its pull, have you not? You have felt that it is alive, somehow, and speaking to you. So have I." There is a profound silence in the room. I nod slowly. Yes, that was what I had felt. "Me, also," he says again quietly, speaking only to me. "It was the bird, the giant Quetzal, the symbol of my ancestors, which showed me where the Codex was hidden. I was meant to find it. Meant to, for some reason I do not know as yet. It is important in some way that I do know." And he pauses.

No one says anything. What is there to say? He clearly believes in what he is telling us. "Maria says I am crazy. No, not crazy. She thinks that these ideas are the result of the fever and the near-death experience I had." Eduardo looks over his shoulder at the Professor and addresses him. "That is what you think as well, is it not, my friend?" He smiles up at him. "No matter, I know what I know, or rather, I believe what I believe," and he chuckles to himself. He looks back at me, "You felt it, that much I can see. You do not yet believe it, however." He rests back on his pillows, tired by all the talking. Maria returns and soon after, we make our goodbyes. "Keep me informed," Eduardo calls as we walk out the door.

"What was all that," asks Daniel, shaking his head. "What was he talking about your feeling, too?"

"I haven't a clue," I say flippantly, not wanting to talk about it with anyone, least of all, Daniel.

I spent the rest of the day at the museum library going through their large collection of Maya history. Most are in Spanish. My comprehension of the written language far surpasses my skill in the spoken language, but it is still not great. Luckily, they also have a collection of English publications and translations. I stick mainly to these.

I've been here several hours, seated at a desk in the stacks with a number of volumes scattered around me. A shadow suddenly obscures what I am reading. A gentle voice says something to me in rapid Spanish that I don't catch. I look up to see a pair of brown eyes smiling down at me from a round, kindly face. The man who belongs to the face is wearing a cassock and clerical collar.

"Indultar, Padre. My Spanish is not good enough to understand what you just said. Do you speak English?" I ask contritely.

"Disculpeme," he replies. "But I knew you were American from your dress and the books you are reading. I should have spoken in English from the start. Forgive me." He speaks in excellent, though heavily accented, English. He points to the pile of books on the table and continues conversationally. "I see you have an interest in Chan Bahlum II. He is an interest of mine as well. Are you interested in his role as an important

Mayan King and the history of Palenque, or is your interest more in his role as a prophet and his prophecies??

"A little of both, I suppose," I answer. I introduce myself and explain how I come to be here in Merida, in the museum library."

"I am Padre Alejandro Domingo, a Catholic priest, obviously. I am also a visitor here in Merida. I am from Pachuca in the state of Hidalgo, just north of Mexico City. So I am a tourist, as you are, and also have an interest in the prophecies of Chan Bahlum II. It seems we have two things in common and therefore are simpatico. Si?"

"Si," I laugh. I then think that he might be an alternative to pouring over these heavy books for the rest of the day. "There is a lot written about Palenque and its dynasty of Kings, Chan Bahlum and his father Pacal, but I can find little about the prophecies, other than that he was known as the King Prophet. What can you tell me?"

Padre Domingo smiles at me beatifically. "There is nothing I like more than to talk about my . . . what you might call, my hobbies; unless it is to talk about them to an intelligent and beautiful woman." He chuckles and seats his not inconsiderable bulk, on the edge of the desk, pushing some of the many books aside. "You are correct, there is little written about Chan Bahlum II as prophet. Of course, you know there are few authentic Maya writings left in existence, largely due, I am sorry to say, to the actions of my Church.[12]" He pauses here with a look of melancholy. "There are," he continues, "small portions of the Dresden and Paris Codices that refer to prophecies, but these are fragmented and incomplete. No, not much in the way of written verification. Most of what is known or assumed comes from the oral traditions, from the Maya people themselves, and from the shamans who still hold sway in the very rural areas of our country."

"And these traditions, do you know them?" I break in eagerly.

"Yes," he nods. "My brothers in faith call me crazy, those who are kind, that is. Others call me a bit of a heretic." He laughs, obviously unconcerned by these epitaphs. "I go out into the countryside and talk to my parishioners, most of the population is Roman Catholic. They tell me the stories because I am interested and will listen without rebuking them. They tell me the legends."

And the good Father tells me stories handed down through the generations of a mighty King who could read the stars and foretell the future.

I am fascinated by the Padre's stories and hate to leave. But 5 o'clock comes too soon. I have to leave in order to be on time to meet the others for our trip back to the dig. I say goodbye reluctantly. We exchange business cards and promise to keep in touch by e-mail. "On Facebook," the Father adds impishly, and asks that I let him know the next time I might be in Mexico.

When the men pick me up for the ride home, Adam is sleeping in the back seat. Daniel and the Professor are discussing their meetings at the Merida Nationale Museo and the Oficina de Antiguedad. I surmise from their tones that it had not gone well. They report that the officials at the Merida Nationale Museo demanded the artifact be turned over to them immediately. Daniel and the Professor met with the Director of the Museum, Senor Frederico Diego He had been irate with Professor Allen for not informing the museum as soon as Eduardo told him about the find. His position was that we should not have touched the site; that the retrieval should have been conducted by museum staff under the guidance of the Oficina de Antiguedad. The Professor evidently stood his ground, told the Director that the artifact would be surrendered to the museum at the end of the archaeological season. "I told him Eduardo would bring it to the museum personally. Eduardo is a member of the Universidad de Ciudad Mexico_and an adviser to the Museo Mexicana de Arqueologia in Mexico City. After all, it is his find." The Professor relates indignantly. "Senor Diego was not happy with this. He fussed and fumed but seemed unwilling or unable to force the issue."

"He is a rabbity sort of man," Daniel interjects, "rushing about all over the place but getting nowhere, like the White Rabbit in *Alice in Wonderland.*

"The museum director finally told us he had no recourse but to report the infraction and my refusal to comply with the Museum's request to the Oficina de Antiguedad; directly to the director, Senor Menos Tierro," the Professor snorts. "And this he did, right there and then. We were given an appointment with Senor Tierro within the hour.

"Senor Tierro met us in the lobby of the Oficina de Antiguedad." Daniel takes up the tale. "Obviously on his way out."

He greeted us graciously, almost warmly. A very pleasant man," the Professor says. "He knew our names and the history of the site. Said he knew of Eduardo's accident and asked after his progress. A very dignified and intelligent man."

"A typical bureaucrat," breaks in Daniel, "reminded me of a used car salesman. Thought he was going to go ballistic on us when Professor Allen first said we were not going to give up the Codex until the end of the summer. Then all of a sudden he is all 'hail fellow, well met' again."

The Professor seems not to take in what Daniel says, as he continues. "He understood entirely my feelings about Eduardo getting a chance to see his amazing find, that it would go a long way to helping him heal. The Director's only requests of us are: that we leave the artifact as untouched as possible, that we secure the cave site, and that we do no more excavation there until the Museum staff arrives. I gave him my assurance on this." I see a grimace on Daniel's face as the Professor makes this pronouncement.

Once they have related their experiences of the day, Daniel turns to me and says "That was our day. I hope your day went a bit better." He smiles and waits for my response.

"My day went well, very well," I reply. "Nice to be back among books. Libraries have always been one of my favorite places. Whether I was successful with my research, I'm not sure yet"

"What is it you were researching?" asks the Professor. I tell them about the hieroglyphs I've deciphered on the cover of the Codex, and that I wanted more about Chan Bahlum II. "If I remember correctly," the Professor muses; "Chan Bahlum II was a king of Palenque, son of Pacal the Great. He was also known as a prophet, a great seer. How does this link him to a manuscript found in an obscure cave 300 miles from Palenque?"

"That I don't know. My assumption is that this is a copy of a work of Chan Bahlum II. That's why I wanted to learn what I could about him and what writings may be attributed to him," I explain.

"An inquisitive mind. Information, the facts, can never be amiss," quips Daniel, his face serious, but I feel he might be mocking me again. I feel I need to defend my actions, but why that's so, I don't know. Or rather, I do know. It is just my reaction to Daniel, damn him.

"As to the connection of the manuscript to Chan Bahlum II and why it was hidden where it was, I think the rest of the Codex might answer that," I continue ignoring Daniel. "There is a second name on the cover." I tell them of the scribe described as the son of the keeper of the cave.

The Professor looks thoughtful. "Having the scribe's name on the cover of the manuscript is unusual. It may indicate that it is a copy completed by the scribe, but it was unusual for a scribe to affix his name to what he copied. Curious," he remarks.

"Yes, I think so too. What is even more curious to me is that on a subsequent page there are repeated hieroglyphics that seem to be those indicating Chichen Itza, not Palenque. Of course, Chichen Itza is the nearest Mayan city to where the Codex was found," I explain.

But Chichen Itza postdated Chan Bahlum II by 200 or so years," blurts out Adam from the back seat. Obviously he is awake and has been following the discussion.

"That's exactly right. That's why the research," I interject. "This may have been a recopying of a more ancient Codex, but why the inclusion of names and places that could not have been part of the original?"

"I have to say, without further research and study of the manuscript, that this is probably a fake, a fabrication of an artifact," asserts the Professor.

"I have to agree," says Daniel. "It just doesn't fit together. Did you find out anything else that might help?" he asks without any sign of ridicule this time.

"Not really," I say slowly and then add. "But I met the most amazing man, or rather, Priest." I tell them about my chance encounter with Padre Domingo. "There was not a lot about Chan Bahlum II's prophecies. The Priest, however, was able to fill in with some of the legends surrounding him. It is believed he predicted what would occur centuries into the future. He had predictions that identified what days, months, and years would be lucky and which unlucky. His prophecies were linked closely to the Mayan calendars. And, what is most interesting, is that in linking his predictions to the calendars, what is called the Mayan Doomsday Prophecy[13] is, by some, attributed to him. Some link it to the writings in the Dresden Codex, one of only four Mayan manuscripts that survived destruction."

"The end of the world prophecy?" queries Adam. "That is fast approaching." And he laughs.

Well, yes," I say sheepishly.

"A cult of sorts seems to have grown up around the idea," adds the Professor. "Highly unlikely."

"Unlikely, yes," agrees Daniel. "But it is gaining a significant following as the date approaches. December 21, 2012, I believe. A mass hysteria seems to be building, much like the one that built up over the millennium scare. And that came to nothing in the end," he says with disdain.

"More than just the Maya have pointed to that date," argues Adam. "Unlikely, but interesting nonetheless."

"The Mayan Doomsday Prophecy comes out of the fact that all the Mayan calendars end on that date. But what the Mayan mythology actually indicated was that it is the end of a cycle, the end of the long count and the beginning of a new age equaling 5213 years or 52 cycles,[(2)]" lectures the Professor.

"That's what I've found," I agree. "But there is also an astrological connection. According to some astronomers, some with good reputations, there will be an astrological convergence on that date as well," I say.

"There is disagreement as to the exact date, I believe," Daniel argues. "The alignment of the planets and the center of our galaxy is said to occur only every 5000 years or so. It, therefore, seems to coincide with the Mayan calendars. It will occur over a number of years, not just on one day." I am surprised at his knowledge of the subject.

The four of us are quiet for a time, each seemingly lost in his own thoughts. Then the Professor says, ending the discussion for the time being, "I would think that if this so-called Codex mentions the Doomsday Prophecy, it is a clear hoax. The whole thing is preposterous."

I don't agree. I don't know why, but I just feel there is more to the manuscript than some sort of shabby hoax. But, since I don't have any proof of any sort, I keep my peace.

III

August 10, 939 CE
10.5.11.0.1, 6 Imix, 14 Ceh
Chechen Itza

Took Pak woke early, before the sun had risen, before the others in the boys' dormitory were awake. This was his usual routine. He woke each morning before daybreak, washed in the attached outbuilding, dressed in his rough brown robe, and made his way to the gardens that surrounded the Temple. He walked here each morning before his Temple tasks and lessons began, before his time and attention were taken up by his fellow students and teachers. It was practically the only time he had to himself. Dawn was rapidly approaching, the sun just piercing the horizon. He breathed in the morning air, dry and dusty even this early in the day, portending a very hot and even drier day to come.

Although this day began as every other day had begun in the last four years, today was different, momentous. Last night had been the last night he would spend in the communal quarters of the Temple boys' school. Yesterday was the last day he would spend in community with his fellow students and friends of the last four years. Yesterday had been the last time he would sit at the plank table, on the wooden bench, under the ceiba trees in the Temple courtyard.

Tomorrow, he would turn 18 and the next phase of his life and his education would begin. Tonight he would go home to celebrate his birthday with his family, as he had celebrated every special day of his life. But this would be the last time he would celebrate with his family. The last time he would be going home for many years. Tonight, he would spend the night with his family, sleep for the last time in the room he still felt was his room and that his mother still kept as he had left it four years ago.

Tomorrow, Took Pak would officially enter the priesthood as a novitiate. As he took his first vows and began to learn the mysteries of the priesthood, he would be sequestered in the Temple. He would spend all his days and all his nights within the Temple grounds. The only people he would see and speak to would be the priests of the Temple, his fellow novitiates, and the few civilian workers and Temple slaves that entered the temple grounds to work daily. Contact with his family and with acquaintances outside the Temple would end tomorrow. Only formal correspondence to commemorate family anniversaries would be allowed and those addressed only to his father, as head of the household. Took Pak was eager to take the next step in his education and was committed, more than ever, to the Temple and his vocation in the priesthood. Still, the thought of the break with his past life, the isolation from his family and, especially from Ahkan, was almost more than he could bear.

As Took Pak walked slowly through the temple garden, he breathed in the sweet and pungent fragrances of the herbs and flowers that grew there. Their familiar aroma brought Ahkan to mind. Took Pak remembered her sweet scent and her sweet voice and ready laugh. How could he give her up? How could he promise never again to sit with her and talk with her; to bask in the warmth and vitality of her personality? But this is what he was about to do.

As Took Pak turned and headed back toward the Temple, a figure appeared at the edge of the garden. The man wore the saffron robes of the Ah Kin. As Took Pak drew closer, he saw that it was Sajal Yax Ahk, now master of the novices. The Ah Kin stopped and waited, impassively, until Took Pak reached him. He nodded and beckoned Took Pak to follow him, then turned abruptly and walked briskly back to the Temple. He entered a small door in the side of the north wall of the Temple of Kukulkan and Took Pak followed.

Took Pak was not surprised by Sajal Yax Ahk's arrival. In fact, he had expected him, but not quite this early. He followed the older priest through the door, into a dark and narrow corridor. They advanced slowly into the interior of the Temple and down a stone stairway. They descended two levels and into another narrow hallway. It was lit by flaming tapers ranged widely along the corridor, leaving much of it in deep shadow. The hallway was silent. Their sandaled feet did not make any sound. They came to the end of the corridor and entered a small, dimly lit room. At the far end of the room was a solitary stone bench in the shape of a Jaguar, painted red and with spots made of inlaid jade.

On this *chum tuun* sat another priest, garbed in a scarlet robe. Took Pak recognized the Ah Kin Mai. This was completely unexpected. Took Pak had only seen Kaloome Ek Suutz, the Ah Kin Mai, from a distance before. Up until now Took Pak had felt calm and eagerly expectant; suddenly he felt terrified. He had thought he knew what to expect, but an audience with an Ah Kin Mai was beyond any expectation he might have had.

Kaloome Ek Suutz did not look up as Took Pak and Sajal Yax Ahk entered the room. Took Pak glanced quickly at Sajal Yax Ahk. The novice master nodded, his face impassive. He indicated that Took Pak should approach the Ah Kin Mai. Took Pak did so with trepidation. As he moved toward the silent figure, the High Priest slowly raised his head and stared at the boy. Took Pak had the urge to look away, to avert his face, to do anything but look into the cold black eyes that regarded him. But he gathered all the courage and determination that he could muster and gazed back at the man before him. This man was the most powerful man in the city-state. More powerful even than the King himself. Took Pak had no idea what the Ah Kin Mai wanted of him.

Kaloome Ek Suutz stared at him for a long time without moving, without blinking. It seemed to Took Pak the High Priest did so without breathing and he held his breath as well. Finally, Kaloome Ek Suutz spoke. His voice was deep, rich, and cold. Though he did not speak above a whisper, his voice filled the room and filled Took Pak with terror. The boy felt like running from the room but could not move a muscle.

"Chan Took Pakal, il Ahab Ch'e'en, you will reach your majority tomorrow, is that not correct?" Though this was said as a question, it was not; it was a statement. "You have done well in the temple school in the last four years. I have been told that you are bright and have advanced rapidly in your studies. You are ahead of your peers, even though you are younger than many." Took Pak started with surprise. He was astonished that the Ah Kin Mai should know his name, much less know how he had progressed in his education. The hollow voice continued, "You are surprised? But why should you be? I know everything that goes on in the Temple, even what goes on in the Temple school and the Temple gardens." Took Pak was shaken. What did the great man mean? For the first time Kaloome Ek Suutz's face showed some expression, just the smallest hint of a smile. But it was quickly gone.

"You have shown diligence and promise. Therefore, I formally invite you into the novitiate of the Ah Kin Order of Temple of Kukulkan of Chechen Itza." As Took Pak was about to speak, Kaloome Ek Suutz held up his hand to stop him, and the Ah Kin Mai continued, "You will go home tonight. You will spend time with your family and loved ones, and you will contemplate the sacrifice that acceptance of this invitation will mean. Think of what you will be giving up and the responsibilities you will assume. You will return here tomorrow evening, at sunset, and give me your answer."

Took Pak would again have spoken, but Kaloome Ek Suutz shook his head. The High Priest turned and, without a sound, left the room. Took Pak was made aware that Sajal Yax Ahk was still in the room, when he felt a hand upon his shoulder. Without a sound the priest too left the room with Took Pak following closely behind.

The next day: The Ch'e'en compound

Four years have passed and again there is a celebration in the Ahab Ch'e'en's household, this time in commemoration of Took Pak's 18th birthday. Dinner was over, not a great feast this time with many nobles and acquaintances. Only the immediate family and a few friends were present. The men are now seated on the front veranda, talking quietly: Took Pak's father, his two brothers, and Ahkan's brother Ek Chuck'in Och. The women would join them shortly.

Took Pak has matured and is now a handsome young man. He is quiet and serious. He takes part in the conversation as an equal with the older men and the others listen to him with respect. The talk is of religion and politics, and of the increasing unrest among the peasants and the younger nobles. They speak of the problems caused by the continuing, debilitating drought that grips the countryside. As the women join them, the talk turns to lighter matters.

Ahkan enters with the other women: her mother, Took Pak's mother, and his two sisters. Ahkan avoids any eye contact with Took Pak as she enters, but Took Pak cannot keep his gaze from her. She too has matured. She is now 15 years old and her body shows the curves of a woman through the folds of her dress. She has the calm poise and the solemnity of a woman now, and has lost the bright effervescence that had made her who she was as a child.

Took Pak's mother smiles sadly at her youngest son and places her hand upon his head. "You are a man today, and I have no children left. You will be leaving home today." They all could hear the tears in her voice.

"You didn't make such a fuss when I left home four years ago," said Ah T'z'on K'an, her second son, in mock outrage. "But then, Took Pak always was the favorite."

"Truth be told," Chawak K'ab, his older brother, chimed in, "we are all glad to see you go." And he smiled broadly at his little brother. "Took Pak has always been greatly favored by both our parents. Now that he is going off to the great Temple, perhaps you and I will have a chance. Though from what I have heard, he has become a favorite there as well."

Took Pak made as if to protest, but was not given the chance to get a word into the conversation, as his sister Kiichpan Pas said, "Oh, everyone thinks he is so perfect, but I remember the day he let the turkey out of the pen and then climbed on the roof to get it back?"

"And fell and broke his leg," added her older sister, Janahb Ha', with a laugh.

"Oh, but that was terrible," cried their mother. "That was the day we had to call for Ko'lel, the wise woman, to come and set his leg. I was so afraid he would never walk again. But she did a good job," she continued, wringing her hands at the memory of it.

"That was the first time I saw her," said Ahkan quietly. "And that was when I first knew that was what I wanted to do."

Took Pak's mother reached out and patted Ahkan on the arm. "And you will make just as good a shaman as Ko'lel, but I fear it will be our loss."

Ahkan looked away embarrassed. Took Pak, not wanting to see Ahkan in any distress, quickly changed the subject. "Now wait a minute. That story is all wrong. I did not let the turkey out, our cousin, Ek Chuk'in Och, did. And he shot it with his new bow. The poor thing flew up on the roof of the kitchen out-building and I climbed up to save it."

"Ah, see," laughed Ek Chuk'in Och loudly, "always the precious boy. And, of course, I am cast as the villain, as always."

The others joined in his laughter and Janahb Ha' added merrily, "I am not saying Took Pak was always in the right, but his version of the story certainly rings true. It seems that you were always getting into trouble, Ek Och." She called him by his diminutive, Ek Och, Black Fox. "And little has changed in that regard even today."

"Now, now, now, little cousin, no need to bring up any unpleasantness," interjected Ek Och. "But what is this I hear in the marketplace, that a certain wealthy, young man has requested the hand of a certain young woman of this household in matrimony?"

Janahb Ha' blushed prettily and the conversation quickly turned to plans for an upcoming wedding. Took Pak withdrew his attention from the conversation, watching his family with fondness and not a little regret. He would not be there to celebrate his sister's wedding.

The rest of the evening was spent in enjoyable community. As the sun sank slowly toward the western horizon, Took Pak stretched and rose to his feet. "I must go. I must return to the Temple before sunset."

He went to his father, grasping him by the elbow and forearm as was the Maya custom. He looked at the older man, not saying a word, afraid that he would be unable to keep his composure. His father looked into his eyes and said, "Bring honor to your family and our house." Took Pak merely bowed his head in assent, still unable to speak.

He then went to each of his brothers, grasped each by the arm in a gesture of farewell. He advanced to his sisters and embraced each in turn.

Then he came to his mother. She embraced him tightly, not wanting to let him go. After a moment he broke the embrace and turned from her.

With a breaking heart he turned to Ahkan. He could not speak. She smiled sweetly, took his hand and said, "I will walk out with you." Without another word, he left his family home for the last time.

When they reached the street, Ahkan stopped. She reached up and lightly touched his face, and without a word turned and went back to the house. Took Pak watched her go and then crossed the plaza, turned north along the sacbeob back to the Temple.

He again entered through the north portal of the Temple. Sajal Yax Ahk was waiting there for him. As they had earlier, they descended the two flights of stone stairs to the same small, underground chamber. This time, however, the room was full to overflowing. All of the ordained priests and novices of the Temple Order were there. In the center of the room, standing before the chum tuun, stood the Ah Kin Mai, Kaloome Ek Suutz. Behind him stood the thirteen members of the Inner Circle, all of them robed in scarlet. In front of them, to the right and left, in saffron robes were the ordained priests, the Ah Kin; with them stood the novices in dark forest green. All of the assemblage turned to watch, as Took Pak and Sajal Yax Ahk entered the room. The novice master took his place among the Ah Kin and indicated that Took Pak should take his place before them facing the Ah Kin Mai. Took Pak did so. Sajal Yax Ahk, with a hand gesture, indicated that he should kneel, and Took Pak complied.

Kaloome Ek Suutz, the Ah Kin Mai, looked down at him and said, "You have been invited for acceptance into the novitiate of the Ah Kin Order of Temple of Kukulkan of Chechen Itza. What is your answer?"

"I accept with great humility and so, too, ask that I might have the honor," replied Took Pak.

Kaloome Ek Suutz's sonorous voice filled the chamber. "You enter into our Order as a novice, knowing full well the sacrifices and the responsibilities that this will entail?" He stayed Took Pak from replying with a gesture of his hand and continued. "You will enter the community of the Temple, severing all contact with your family and acquaintances. You will relinquish all personal possessions or property. You will have no contact with the outside world. You will dedicate yourself to the will and the service of the gods. You will commit yourself to the study of the mysteries of the Temple and you will place yourself as an intermediary between the gods and the Maya people. Understanding all that," he continued, "are you now willing to take your place within the Temple?" He waited for Took Pak to answer.

Took Pak raised his eyes to the Ah Kin Mai and said in a loud, clear voice, "I accept."

Kaloome Ek Suutz gestured to several of the priests standing to his right and they came forward with the green robes of a novice. They removed Took Pak's brown robe he had worn for the last four years, and replaced it with the new attire that befitted his new stature in the Temple hierarchy.

Took Pak again knelt before the Ah Kin Mai. "As the gods gave their blood to create the Maya, so we, as the servants of the gods, are asked to do the same. A blood sacrifice to honor the gods and gain their favor is required," Kaloome Ek Suutz intoned solemnly.

Took Pak had no idea what to expect at this point. This was obviously part of the Temple ritual that he knew nothing of, and the first of the mysteries that he would learn. And so with trepidation he began his education. Kaloome Ek Suutz reached out for his hand and turning it palm upward, looked again deeply into Took Pak's eyes. A knife, a gleaming, black, sacrificial knife, was placed in the Ah Kin Mai's outstretched hand. Sajal Yax Ahk came and stood behind Took Pak. He placed his hands upon the boy's shoulders. Took Pak did not know if this was to give him support or to prevent him from running away. Though he was frightened, Took Pak had no intention of running. This was his destiny. Kaloome Ek Suutz brought the blade forward and, with a rapid stroke, drew the blade across Took Pak's extended forearm.[14] Took Pak watched as his blood began to flow. He was surprised that he felt nothing, no pain. One of the priests of the Inner Circle placed the sacred bowl beneath Took Pak's arm to catch the bright, red blood that flowed from the cut. The blood flowed rapidly and all Took Pak could do was to watch in fascination. He heard, almost subliminally, the chanting of all those assembled, the slow rhythmic incantation of ritual supplication to the gods. He became aware of the sweet aroma of the Temple incense as it swirled about his head. Took Pak lost awareness of his surroundings. He became lightheaded and the room and all its inhabitants receded.

Suddenly, he was somewhere else, caught in an increasing fog. Through the mist he could make out a stark landscape, an empty, barren landscape.

99

He was there alone. He looked from side to side, seeking something, what he did not know. Gradually, he could make out, upon the dry karst plain, what appeared to be the carcasses of dead and rotting animals. He could no longer smell the sweet incense, but rather the fetid odor of decaying flesh.

High above soared a bright green and gold bird, but not a bird. This creature had the head of a mighty jaguar and the tail of the serpent. This was surely the god, Ku'kul'kan, himself. This was truly an omen, but not a good one. Took Pak swayed and the mists grew denser and darker. All turned black and the vision vanished. Took Pak knew no more.

Several of the priests rushed forward, staunching the flow of blood from Took Pak's arm with the resin of the Ek' Balam shrub. They raised him gently from the floor and carried him from the room. All the others followed them out of the chamber except for the Ah Kin Mai and his Inner Circle.

Kaloome Ek Suutz looked thoughtful as he listened to the murmuring of the other priests around him. They were saying: "Unusual," "Remarkable," "For one so young," "At the first bloodletting," "He obviously had a vision," "He must be interrogated," "What was it that he saw?" "I do not think that it was a good omen." The Ah Kin Mai agreed with all of them, but he made no comment. He must ponder this and then he would speak with the boy. Sajal Yax Ahk was obviously right, there was something special about this boy. He would have to keep his eyes upon Took Pakal il Ahab Ch'e'en. He must keep a close watch and a closer hand.

The Ch'e'en household; that same night

Ahkan ran back to the house, avoiding the others. She skirted the compound to the south and entered the courtyard through the eastern portico. The courtyard was empty and she entered her room without being seen. Her room was a small windowless cell with barely any furnishings: only a wooden cot with a coarse mattress stuffed with the husks of the maize, a sturdy wooden chest to hold her clothes, and a few personal belongings. Beside the cot was a small bedside table that held a kib', a candle made of bee's wax. Ahkan sat herself upon the bed, bent her knees up, buried her face in her folded arms, and wept. She had known all her life that this day would come, but that did not make it any easier. Although Took Pak had been gone from the house to the Temple school for the last four years, still she had seen him frequently. He had returned home for high holy days and family anniversaries. Now he was lost to her, for she could have no contact with him at all.

IV

July 14, 2011
12.19.18.9.14, 11 Ix, 2 Xul
A familiar room somewhere in Mexico

There were three men in the room this time. The owner of the room, the man behind the desk, is in control as usual; the subordinate in his chair across the desk from the great man. He appears even more frightened than usual. He'd just completed a rather lengthy report on the archaeological site, the participants in the dig, and the probable whereabouts of the Codex. He reported everything that had gone on in the last two weeks regarding the artifact. The man behind the desk seems impatient and indicates that all of this information is already known to him.

A third man, shabbily dressed, broad shouldered, and shorter than the other two, sits in a second chair facing the desk. He appears relaxed and unimpressed by what the man sitting next to him had to say. The man behind the desk forestalls any further explanation by his subordinate and, pointing to the third man, introduces him.

"This is Carlos. He is an associate of ours and has some specialized skills." He nods toward the third man but without warmth. Looking back at the other man, he continues, "Your informants, if I understand you correctly, believe that the article is still at the archaeological camp. In all probability, it is in the camp office, somewhere. The office contains a safe, an old rather simple one, I understand. Carlos here has experience with safes and feels that this one will be no obstacle to our acquiring the artifact."

The third man rose from his chair. He nodded to the man behind the desk, gave a fleeting glance at the second man, and left the room.

"I have set this in motion because Dr. Allen is being very obstinate about turning over the Codex to the proper authorities. Some sentimental excuse insisting that Professor Gomez should have an opportunity to examine it before it is surrendered." A look of anger, almost rage, crosses the man's face. His voice rises a few decibels as he continues. "I must see and examine the manuscript before anyone else does so. It may contain information that it would be inadvisable to make public." He looked up, his eyes blazing, at the other man who cowered in his chair and seemed to shrink in stature at his gaze. "Keep your spies at work near the site. Increase their number if necessary. Am I understood?"

His subordinate nodded rapidly in agreement.

CHAPTER SIX

I

50 CE
8.5.10.7.2

Mayan Myth

The villages grew in number and in size.
And the gods said to the Maya,
"Build for us a sanctuary."
The Maya built an altar
Upon a raised platform
And here they gathered to worship.

Here they brought their tribute,
Fruits of the orchards and the fields,
Pottery, ornaments, and fine linens.
And here they lit their sacrificial fires.
And the gods were pleased.
And the Maya prospered.

And the gods said to the Maya,
"Build for us a house, a sanctuary,
A place of worship worthy of our stature."
So the Maya built a roof over the altar,
And raised it high
Here they worshipped the gods.

And the gods were pleased.
And the Maya prospered.

And the gods said to the Maya,
"Build for us a Temple
Worthy of our power and our greatness."
So the Maya cleared the forest
And with stone from the mountains
Built a mighty Temple.

At the top they built their altar.
And here they worshipped the gods.
Here they lit the sacrificial fire
And here they paid tribute to the gods
For the bounty they had been given.
And a great city grew up around the temple.

And the gods were pleased
And they blessed the Maya.
And the Maya prospered.

The Maya tilled the fields and planted the seed.
The sun shone on the earth and the rains came.
And the crops grew,
The maize and the squash, and the beans,
The figs and the papaya were plentiful.
And the Maya prospered.

And the Maya attributed
Their prosperity to the Shaman.
For he knew when to plant and when to reap.

And the Maya honored him
And brought to him
A portion of their bounty.

For the Shaman spoke with the gods,
Knowing the proper words
And correct ritual.
He appeased the gods

And garnered their favor.
And the Maya called him Ah Kin, Priest.

The Ah Kin consulted with the gods,
And so ordained that the Maya worship
In a prescribed manner.
The rites must follow the design given by the gods.
With the exact words and precise ritual.
That only the Ah Kin had been given

The Ah Kin taught those who followed.
Taught them the proper words and the rituals
That they might converse with the gods.
And so the rites and rituals were
Preserved through the generations.
And he was called Ah Kin Mai, High Priest.

The gods said to the High Priest,
"Bring tribute to us, to honor us as is our due."
And the Maya gave a portion of their wealth
To the Temple and to the priests.
And the Ah Kin Mai placed the offerings upon the altar
With the proper words and ritual.

And the gods were pleased
And they blessed the people.
And the Maya prospered.

To the Ah Kin Mai the gods said,
"Build an altar in the center of the city.
Raise it above the heads of the people
To give honor to the gods as they deserve.
And the Ah Kin Mai built the Temple higher.
Here he performed the rituals as the gods decreed.

The Ah Kin Mai and the priesthood grew in power
For only they could speak with the gods.
Only they could make the will of the gods known

To the people through the generations.
Only they knew the correct rituals and the proper words
To appease and satisfy the gods.

And the gods were pleased
And they blessed the Maya.
And the Maya prospered.

II

August 4, 2011
12.19.18.10.15, 6 Men, 3 Yaxkin
The dig, Yucatan Peninsula, Mexico

It is incredibly hot through the end of July and into the beginning of August. Long days spent at the dig, added to the heat, exhaust everyone and cause tempers to be short. I find I have no energy at the end of the day for anything, including work at deciphering the Codex. Even though I am worn out at day's end, I find that in the heat I can't sleep at night. Even with fans going full blast in my tent, it is sweltering and claustrophobic. Most nights I escape out into the night air, to sit by a low smoldering campfire. We burn damp, green wood to produce a smoky haze that keeps the insects away. I enjoy the solitude. Much of each night I spend studying the stars that can be seen in such abundance in the sky. Here the stars are not blurred by the artificial light of civilization.

I am not the only person in camp to forgo my bed for the outdoors. There are always others about. Sometimes I share my fire with one or more of the others, but more often I have it all to myself.

The native laborers have their own fire at the other end of the camp. Every night I can hear their murmuring conversations from a distance. What words I can make out come in a variety of languages: Spanish, English, and most predominantly, the local dialect, Yucatec. Some nights I can see Miguel talking with the workers. Most nights, though, he goes home to his family in the nearby village of Tolecheo Pueblo.

I often see Adam sitting, talking, and laughing with the laborers around their campfire. He seems to be on very good terms with them. They welcome him into their group as a friend. One night, as I return from the latrine, I pass by the workmen's fire and see Adam sitting among them. They don't seem to notice me as they are engaged in animated conversation. There is much laughing and patting of each other on the back. As I get back to my campfire, I realize something rather strange. The group had been speaking Yucatec. That in itself isn't surprising. What is strange is that Adam seemed to understand what they were saying and, in fact, was responding in their language. He had never said that he knew the language, in fact, quite the opposite.

The next morning at breakfast I confront him. His reply is unsatisfactory. "Oh, that. I've picked up a little of the local language, I guess. Enough to make idle chat around the campfire. Can understand more than I can speak, but I get by." He walks away, dismissing me with a laugh.

As the summer progresses, I begin to see more and more men gathered around the far campfire. Some are men that I do not recognize as working on the dig with us. At first I don't take much notice, but as the numbers seems to grow, I become curious and then concerned. One night in early August, I hear loud voices and shouting coming from across camp. I look in that direction and see a group of a dozen or so men standing around the fire. There appears to be two groups facing each other. Miguel is standing in the middle talking and gesturing, first to one group and then to the other. Obviously he is trying to keep the yelling from breaking into a physical confrontation. I cannot make out what is being said for he is talking quietly. I cannot understand what the others are screaming, as they are speaking Yucatec. Gradually, Miguel's words seem to calm them and, finally, four of the men leave the circle. These four men I don't recognize. They walk away toward the edge of the tents and out of camp. The others settle back down around the fire, speaking, quietly now, to Miguel and among themselves. The confrontation over, Miguel too leaves, disappearing behind the office toward the parking area in the rear. All of this I find very odd and somewhat disturbing. Who are those men? Why are they hanging around camp? And what were they all arguing about?

The next morning, I meet Miguel outside the mess tent and I bring my concerns to his attention. "Buenos dios, Miguel."

"Buenos dios, Señorita Professora," he replies.

"I have a question, or rather a concern," I say.

"Si?" He looks at me questioningly, waiting for me to continue.

I hesitate, not knowing where to begin, then say, "I haven't been sleeping well, with this heat." I pause and he nods. "I've been up most nights sitting by the fire." Miguel nods again, obviously impatient for me to continue, but is too well mannered to tell me so. "What I mean is, since I have been up at night, I have noticed a large number of men gathered near the workmen's tents. More men than work here, it seems, and faces that I haven't seen around the dig." I pause again and Miguel nods again. "Last night I was sitting by the fire, over there," and I point to the central fire pit. "An argument broke out over there," and I point towards the laborers' tents. I stop, not knowing how to continue.

Miguel nods again and seems reluctant to explain what had gone on. When I don't continue he says, "Si, there was a . . ." he pauses, "a disagreement," he finally adds. He pauses again and then continues. "The Professor always allows the farmers from the villages to pitch their tents near the camp during the harvest season. He lets them use our facilities, latrines and showers and such. This way they do not have to make the long trip back to their homes each night." He pauses again. "It has always worked out well. The farmers are grateful and supply fresh produce to us: corn, beans, and squash. We have always gotten along." He pauses again, looking quizzically at me. I can see he is wondering just how much he should tell me. I remain quiet, not pushing him, and he continues. "This year in the last two or three weeks, things are different. Strangers have been seen around the camp. Each group, our laborers and the farmers, thought these men belonged to the other group. But then questions were asked and it became clear that neither group would claim then." He took a deep breath. "So our men and the farmers brought it to me. Last night we confronted these men. There were four of them at the campfire last night and it got . . ." he searches for a word, "caliente. Si, caliente, hot."

"Yes," I reply. "It sounded very caliente."

"Si. These men would not say who they were or why they were here. They tried to say they were looking for work, but they had not approached anyone asking for work. We told them to be gone and that is when the shouting started." He stops here, shaking his head and shrugging.

"They left without it coming to blows though," I say.

"Si, they left, but I still do not know who they were and why they were here. Jobs are plentiful right now. They could have gotten work in the fields, but they did not even ask. So, what is it that they want? And I fear they will come back." He turns to me. "If you see them again, let me know. If you see anything extrano, strange, let me know as well." He looks at me intently. "I do not think you should be sitting out at night. It may not be safe."

"I think I'll be perfectly safe here in camp. There is always a group of our workers just over there." I smile at him. "I'll let you know if I see anything."

I take Miguel's advice and spend less time at the campfire by myself. I return to my cot as soon as the night begins to cool. I don't see any more strange faces. There are still men I cannot identify as dig workers, but they are the farmers harvesting the fields. After the altercation I witnessed, they keep to themselves, building their fire outside the camp's circle of tents.

August 25, 2011
12.19.18.11.16, 1 Cib,4 Mol
The dig, Yucatan Peninsula, Mexico

Several weeks pass quietly, then one night in mid-August, after I return to my tent, I am awakened from a fitful sleep by a loud sound. It takes me a moment to wake sufficiently, to make out what it is. It is someone yelling. I jump out of bed, pull a jacket over my PJs and head for the door.

"What was that?" asks Carli, only one step behind me.

"Someone's shouting." And then the sound stops. Everything is quiet for a few seconds and then the sounds change. The single shouting voice is replaced by many voices, asking questions and calling for help. Carli and I rush across camp and come upon a group of men congregated outside the camp office. Daniel and Adam are there, bending over a figure lying on the ground. As we reach the group, I see that the figure on the ground is Calvin. He stirs, reaches up, and rubs the back of his head.

"There were two of them. Two," he says groggily. "Two."

"Who?" asks Adam.

"Are you all right?" asks Daniel with concern. "Do you know where you are? Is your vision blurred?" Then he looks at the back of Calvin's head where he's rubbing it. "Looks like he was hit over the head. He may have a concussion."

"I'm alright," Calvin mutters. "I'm alright," he says almost angrily and he struggles to get to his feet. "We need to check to see what they were after. If they took anything." He begins walking toward the office. When he does so, I notice for the first time that the office door is open and the lights are on. Calvin stumbles to the door and peers inside, all of us following. The room is a shambles. Boxes and crates are overturned and papers are scattered everywhere.

Daniel takes Calvin by the shoulders as the man appears ready to fall. He propels him into the room and sits him in the chair by the desk. Daniel looks closely at Calvin and seems to be reassured by what he sees. "Now tell me exactly what happened."

Calvin looks up at him and then at the condition of the room. "I was coming back from the latrine, almost back to our tent, when I heard something. I don't know what it was, but it was coming from this direction. So I came over to check it out. When I came around the corner, I saw that there were lights on in the office. I could see someone moving in here. I called out and someone came out of the door. He moved around back, toward the parking lot. I shouted at him and he ran. I started to run after him, shouting for him to stop." Here Calvin pauses and rubs the back of his head again." And then the lights went out."

"Did you see who it was?" asks Adam anxiously.

"No," replies Calvin. "I don't know who the runner was. Didn't see who hit me."

I look around at the mess that had been made of the office and am about to ask the obvious question, when Carli asks it for me. "What could anyone have wanted in here?" She looks around the office too, shaking her head.

"We've never had any trouble like this before," said Daniel, clearly concerned. "The only thing in here, of any value, is our petty cash, which doesn't add up to much. But to someone desperate for money, well . . . maybe . . ." He turns to the desk and opens the bottom drawer, removes a small metal box and opens it. It isn't even locked. Inside I can see some bills and a few coins. "Twenty pesos and 40 centime," Daniel counts. "I don't know how much should be in here exactly, but that seems about right. Anyway, if they were here to steal this, they would have taken it all. Nothing else of any value kept in here," he says again.

I look at him in consternation. "What do you mean? What about the Codex?" I say angrily.

"The Codex?" Adam breaks in. "We don't even know for sure that it is of any value. What's more, no one else knows about it yet."

"Yes, they do," I snap sharply, rounding on him. "Everyone here knows about it, as well as those at the Office of Antiquities and the museum

"I'm sure no one from the Office of Antiquities would come out here to steal an artifact that hasn't yet been authenticated. And why would anyone else want to steal it?" he persists. "It's not as if you could just go out and sell it. If you tried to sell it, everyone would know that it was stolen. No, I'm sure they must have been looking for whatever cash might be around and were interrupted before they could find it."

"I have to agree with Adam," Daniel comments. "Besides, the Codex is in the safe. Safely in the safe," he quips, looking at me. He crosses the room to the safe in the far corner and tests the handle, showing me it is securely locked.

"Check it anyway," I say quietly. He looks amused, but proceeds to turn the dial and open the safe. Inside is the small box into which we had put the manuscript.

Daniel looks to me, but it is Carli who says, "Open it just to make sure." Daniel does so. The Codex lays inside wrapped in its protective coverings.

"There," Daniel says. "Are you satisfied now?" He looks from me to Carli and back again. We both nod. "We better get back to bed and get what little sleep we can. We can clean this mess up in the morning, or rather later this morning," concludes Daniel as he replaces the Codex in the safe. As we leave the office, the first signs of daybreak can be seen over the forest to the east. "I'll tell the Professor later. No use waking him at this hour, as there is nothing he can do now anyway," Daniel adds and we all make our way back to bed.

Carli catches my arm as we walk. "Who do you think they were? What do you think they were after? Do you think they were after the Codex? Or was it just some vagrants looking for money and for anything else they could sell?" Carli chatters all the way back to our tent. I don't say anything. I don't have to. What's more, I don't have answers to any of her questions or to any of my own.

August 30, 2011
12.19.18.12.1, 6 Imix, 9 Mol
Yucatan Peninsula, Mexico, the dig

August comes to a close without any further incidents. The Professor is shocked and completely mystified by the break-in. He repeats, over and over, Daniel's comment: that nothing like this had ever happened before. The Professor is of the opinion that it is the work of vagrants looking for money. With the influx of strangers in camp over the last month or so, that may be the truth. But I don't think so.

The summer archaeological season is coming to an end. We begin preparing the site for the off-season; marking areas so we can pick up next year where we leave off, protecting individual sites for when we are gone, completing the final cataloging of what has been found, and packing them into crates for shipment back to the University.

Eduardo comes back to camp the last day of August. His left leg is still in a plaster cast and he is navigating awkwardly on crutches. He's regained some of the weight he lost, but is still pale and drawn. Everyone, especially the laborers, are happy to see him and greet him warmly. He seems glad to see all of us, too. After he makes the rounds, the Professor takes him into the office. There they remain for several hours. I can only assume they spend that time studying the Codex.

After lunch, as I pass by the office on my way back to my tent, I hear angry voices coming from the office. I recognize Eduardo's and the Professor's voices. They are speaking loudly in a jumbled mixture of English and Spanish.

"I found the Codex. I do not intend to give it up, so that the damn paper pushers at the Office of Antiquities get all the glory," Eduardo yells.

The Professor retorts just as loudly, but without anger, "We have no recourse. Excavation of archaeological sites is strictly controlled here in Mexico and for good reason. Without that control, the treasures of your country would be looted and stolen, as they were in the past."

Eduardo breaks in before the Professor can finish. "I do not plan to steal anything; to the contrary, it is being stolen from me. Why should the bureaucrats have the power over the scientists? The Museo Mexicana de Arqueologia in Mexico City has the reputation and personnel, of which I am one, to handle this, the find of the century. And it is that museum, not this one in Merida, which should have that honor."

"I know. I see your point, but . . ." the Professor tries to get his point across.

Eduardo interrupts again. "I found it. I should have a voice in where it will go."

"Yes, yes you should in all fairness, but that is not the reality," placates the Professor.

"I will not submit to them," shouts Eduardo.

"Wait. Wait. We do have an option," says the Professor, still having to shout to be heard over Eduardo's bellowing.

"What kind of an option? Saying to them, here you take this fantastic prize and I kiss your humoristico?" yells Eduardo.

"No, not quite that," laughs the Professor. His voice returns to a more normal tone, so that I have to strain to hear. It makes me feel like an eavesdropper, which actually I am. The Professor continues, "Daniel tells me they have documented the manuscript meticulously: photographing every inch of it, taking samples, and recording the process all the time. Highly unethical and, perhaps, even illegal, but I don't intend to report them. Do you?" And again the Professor laughs. "All the photographs are in the computer. Daniel also tells me Kate and Calvin have been working on deciphering the text. They are making some progress, slow progress, but progress all the same."

Eduardo mumbles something I cannot hear, then the Professor adds, "We are ahead of them, far, far ahead. We may not have the physical artifact, but we have all the relevant information."

Just then Daniel comes up behind me and I jump when he says, "What are you doing standing here in the middle of the camp? Stargazing at noon?"

"You scared the bejesus out of me," I complain.

"Guilty conscience?" he chuckles.

"Humph," I respond then say sweetly, "Good afternoon." And I walk back to my tent.

The next morning, Eduardo and the Professor leave for Merida with the Codex. Eduardo looks unhappy, but resigned. They are to surrender the Codex to Senior Diego, the curator of the Merida Nationale Museo, and Senor Tierro, the Director of the Office of Antiquities, at noon.

Before he leaves, Eduardo approachs me and grasps my arm, pulling me away from the others.

"Señorita Kate, the Professor has told me that you have documented the manuscript and are at this moment working at its translation. Gracias mucho. I will contact you soon at the University. Is that alright with you? But we must keep this information quiet for now. Those in the government will not like that we are doing this without permission. We will work together, si?"

I nod and would have said more, but we are interrupted by the Professor. He hurries Eduardo away, saying, "We must leave at once or we will be late and that will not do."

I watch them leave and wonder if what we are doing will get us in as much trouble as Eduardo and the Professor seem to think it will.

The Professor returns late that evening, having delivered the Codex to the museum. Then he dropped Eduardo at the airport to catch his plane to Mexico City.

The rest of us leave early the next morning. We promise to keep in touch and to keep each other apprised of our progress on the Codex. Just before climbing into the van for the ride to the airport, Brian approaches me.

"I've . . . I've found a program, c . . . computer, you know," he stammers.

"Excuse me," I say confused. "I don't know what you're talking about."

"A pro . . . program to translate ancient Mayan hieroglyphs," he finally gets out.

"You what?" I blurt out, surprised.

"I . . . I found," he is having more trouble getting out what he wants to say as I question him.

"Yes, I heard that," I say impatiently. "Do you think it will work on our manuscript?" I pause, then add. "Why didn't you say something sooner?"

"I've been l . . . looking since we found it. I . . . I knew there had to be p . . . programs out there, but just found one. I . . . I think it will work." He shook his head. "It will n . . . need some reworking. B . . . but I . . . I think it will work." He gives a great sigh of relief that he is finished with what he has to say.

I grab him around the shoulders and give him a big kiss on the cheek. I am so excited. He turns bright red and gapes at me, totally losing his capacity to speak. "You keep working on it and e-mail me as soon as you get something workable," I say and give him a big hug. He shambled away without another word.

III

December 13, 939
10.5.11.6.6, 1 Kimi, 19 Cumku
Four months later: the Temple of Kukulkan Chechen Itza

Took Pak wandered back toward the Temple proper after spending the afternoon working in the Temple gardens. His last four months as a novice here in the Temple had been an exciting and exacting experience. Sajal Yax Ahk had continued his interest in Took Pak and had undertaken his education himself. Took Pak had little contact with the other novices or, in fact, with anyone else within the Temple Order. Along with his studies he continued to spend several hours a day either working in the Temple gardens or in the kitchens. He particularly liked to work in the gardens, where he could enjoy the sunshine. It brought memories of home and Ahkan.

Today his routine would change. Yesterday, Sajal Yax Ahk had informed him that he would begin study with the venerable Cha Mach B'en Kan, the aged principle astronomer of the Order. This Took Pak knew was a great honor. Few, if any, of the fully ordained priests were asked to study with this learned man and certainly none of the novices had been invited to do so before.

Took Pak was excited and had difficulty keeping his mind on his tasks in the garden this afternoon. He was to meet Cha Mach B'en Kan on the platform atop the Observatory, just before sunset. Though he had time to stop in the kitchens for something to eat, his stomach was too nervous for him to make the attempt.

Took Pak mounted the inner staircase leading to the pinnacle of the Observatory Temple. This was his first time upon the high platform. He looked around and was awed by the sight. The sun was just setting to the west behind him and the sky was deep pink and purple. The last rays of the sun reflected off the smooth surface of the structure and the stone glistened. As his eyes adjusted to the glare, Took Pak could make out a small figure dressed in bright red robes.

Took Pak approached warily and came to stand at the old man's shoulder. Cha Mach B'en Kan did not move. Took Pak was unsure if the astronomer had heard him or not. He did not know whether to speak and call attention to himself, or to remain silent until the old man recognized his presence. The decision was made by the astronomer, for he raised his head slowly and looked deeply into Took Pak face. He was a small man, short and thin with watery, pale amber eyes and a balding head. He stood only as tall as Took Pak's shoulder.

"Good evening, young man. You are Took Pak, son of the Ahab Ch'e'en, are you not?" said the old man, smiling benignly up at the novice. Took Pak nodded and his fear disappeared in the warmth of the smiling eyes. "So you have come to me to learn of the stars and the planets and all of the wonders of the universe?" He placed his hand on Took Pak's arm and drew him to the eastern edge of the Observatory platform. Here was a low, stone bench. "So you wish to learn the secrets of the heavens, do you?" And he chuckled softly. Took Pak, still in awe of this great man, did not reply nor did he think the old man expected him to. After a pause Cha Mach B'en Kan continued. "I will tell you the secret," he said conspiratorially. "The secret . . ." and he paused for effect, and then continued in a whisper. "The secret is . . . patience." He looked over at Took Pak, noted his surprise, and chuckled again. "Yes, yes, patience is the key. The way that I, and all of those before me, have been able to decipher what is written in the stars is patience. Patience and long hours of doing nothing."

Took Pak started in surprise, and spoke for the first time. "Doing nothing?"

Cha Mach B'en Kan chuckled again. "Well, not quite nothing, but spending long hours sitting, right here, watching the stars. Watching, watching, and watching. And finally, after all these hours of watching, to put down carefully upon my slate what it was that I had seen." He paused again, whether to collect his thoughts or for effect, Took Pak did not know. He was beginning to think that this old man really liked an audience. When Cha Mach B'en Kan finally continued, he said, "And then I would go back to watching again." And he chuckled. "And after many more, long hours of watching, I would note again upon my slate what it was that I had seen. I record the movement of the stars and of the moon and of the sun. And after many years, yes years, I would go back and look at what it was I had recorded. Along with the movements of the heavenly objects, I would note the hour, and the day, and the season on which the movement had occurred. I noted the time and the position of the rising and the setting of the sun for every season. I noted the day and the time and the position of the rising and setting of the Morning Star and the Evening star, that we call Ek'. And I noted the day and the time and the phases of the moon. And do you know what I discovered?" He turned questioningly to Took Pak and this time he waited for an answer.

Took Pak did not know what to say, and so that is what he said. "I do not know."

"What I realized," said the old man, obviously warming to his story, "was that the movements repeated. What had happened last year had happened the year before, and the year before that. The movements recurred in exactly the same way, at exactly the same time, in exactly the same manner. This was true on every occasion that I had recorded upon my slate. And gifted astronomer that I am, I concluded that they would occur in just this way the next year, and the next and the next." The old man folded his hands in his lap and was quiet; contemplating what it was he saw in the night sky. Took Pak was quiet as well, not wishing to interrupt his contemplation.

It was dark, the sun having completely set. Cha Mach B'en Kan pointed toward the heavens. "That, of course you know, is Chac Chel. She is the old moon goddess tonight, for she is thin and has aged over the last 20 nights. She is the earth goddess, as well as goddess of women and children, and of birth and death. Like a woman she changes her dress from night to night. The changing of her garb follows the repeating pattern of the Hun calendar. She is constant and reliable, and by noting her changing appearance we can mark the changing fortunes and destiny of the Maya people."

He paused again as if to collect his thoughts. When he continued, he pointed out to Took Pak all of the many objects that adorned the midwinter sky. He told the boy briefly of their movements. He told him what they were harbingers of and where they fit within the calendars of the Maya. And then he said, "And now young man if you wish to study with me, what do you think you must do?"

Took Pak was beginning to understand this old priest, and so he answered, "I must watch and do nothing."

Cha Mach laughed out loud, pleased with Took Pak's response. "And what is it that you must have?"

"Patience." and Took Pak laughed as well. He knew that he was going to enjoy the study of astronomy with this quaint, old man. He was sure that he would learn much. What he didn't know was if he had enough patience to learn all the secrets that this old man held.

The forest north of the city, that same day

Ahkan had left the family home before sunrise as she did most every day. She headed out through the forest toward the hut where Ko'lel lived. She had learned much, over the last four months, working daily with the old one. Ko'lel trusted her now, to gather the herbs and plants from the forest on her own. The old woman complained that her old bones protested when she bent to gather from the forest floor.

Ahkan kept herself busy from early morning until late evening. This helped to keep her mind away from the sadness and emptiness that she felt with Took Pak gone. She had other worries as well. Her brother, Ek Och, had been in trouble repeatedly since the last time she had seen him. Word had reached the family that he was speaking out among his fellow soldiers, against the higher taxes imposed by the Temple. These were needed, they were told, to intervene with the gods in order to end the terrible drought. Ahkan was sure that this would only lead her brother to further troubles and she worried.

The drought had been devastating the land of the Maya for many years. The priests of the Temple prayed to the god of rain and they burned the offerings atop the Temple pyramid, to no avail. The drought continued. The Ah Kin asked for larger and larger tribute from the people and from the Army. But the crops had failed and the wild game became scarce. The Army did not have enough to eat. They were weak and stayed camped at the edge of the territory. When they did not advance against the enemy, there was no plunder and there were no slaves, with which to pay the tribute. Many of the men deserted to return to help their families who were starving. The legions were close to rebelling and Ahkan feared that her brother had become a leader in the movement.

Ahkan came out of the forest into the clearing where Ko'lel's small hut stood. The old woman was sitting on the wooden bench outside her door, sorting the dried leaves and seeds that they had collected the day before.

Ahkan sat down beside her and immediately began to help her with the task. "Something is wrong with you Hun P'iit," Ko'lel said, giving her a shrewd look. Ko'lel always knew just how she was feeling.

"I fear for the future," she said.

After a pause, the old woman replied, "The omens are not good. The drought has gone on so long and the people are starving. They have lost faith in the Maya relationship with their gods. I hear, from all the people that I care for, that they are sure that the gods have forsaken them." She gave a deep sigh and returned to her work.

"And the priests? What do they do? They ask for more and more from the people, who have less and less," Ahkan said angrily. "They take the maize, and the game, and the fruits of the fields, and they burn them upon their high altar, rather than giving it all to the people who are starving. And what good are their silly rituals? The people are beginning to see that the priests do not have any closer connection to the gods than the people do themselves." She shook her head in disgust.

Ko'lel agreed. "I fear that you are right and that the people will not stand for this much longer. But the rains will come, when it is time."

"What can we do in the meantime?" said Ahkan in frustration.

"We can do what we have always done. We can care for our own. And we can wait," said the old woman.

"I do not believe I have the patience," the girl said petulantly.

"No, I do not believe you do," the wise woman laughed.

Ahkan spent the rest of the day mixing the salves and ointments they used to treat sores and rashes. Ko'lel had, on occasion, sent her out to the farms and villages, to treat minor illnesses and injuries. The people were beginning to trust her, as her powers of healing were quickly developing. Since she was such a young girl, they did not hold any fear of her, as they still harbored for the old woman. Some felt Ko'lel was a witch.

Ahkan was concerned about Ko'lel, as well. She loved the old woman, but she feared that as the bad times continued, the people might very well turn against her, their shaman, as they were turning against their priests. Ahkan was sure that Ko'lel felt this as well, for she was a wise woman. Ahkan worried as her mentor aged before her eyes. Ko'lel no longer took to the forests as she had always done, but left these tasks to Ahkan. Ahkan felt as if she were carrying the world upon her shoulders. If truth be told, if she had looked into a mirror, she would have seen that she had aged as well.

IV

August 30, 2011
12. 19. 18. 12. 1, 6 Imix, 9 Mol
The familiar room, somewhere in Mexico

The two men are again sitting across from each other. Neither is speaking. Each seems to be lost in his own thoughts. The man in the chair across from the desk seems to be more relaxed and in control of the situation than before. On the other hand, the man behind the desk seems a bit more agitated. His hands, usually crossed and immobile on the desk in front of him, are today in motion, drumming lightly on the shiny surface. As if suddenly becoming aware of his tapping, he stops and folds his hands in their usual position.

He says, with a note of ill-controlled anger, "It seems our plans have not been successful. Carlos failed to secure the artifact. Also, your spies were detected and run out of the camp." Here the other man grimaced and actually moved reflexively, as if expecting a blow. The man behind the desk seemed to get himself under control and a sneer crossed his face. "The Codex has been delivered to the authorities at the Museum in Merida and is, therefore to all intent, in our control. I have plans in the works to prevent anyone from inspecting the artifact, before I have the opportunity of doing so. And this time, the plan will work."

He paused for a significant amount of time, so long that the subordinate was unsure if the audience was over or not. He was about to rise from his chair, when the other man began to speak again. "The question is, how much investigation did those fool Americans do on the Codex, while it was in their possession? Correct me if I am wrong, but I believe you said there were six Americans at the dig this summer: Dr. Allen, Professor Keith, Professor O'Hara, and three students." He looked over at the other man expectantly.

"Si Monsignor, that is correct," he replied tremulously.

"And they are all associated with the same university, I believe," the other man said.

"That is correct," said the subordinate.

"And we have ties to that university?" asked the man behind the desk, but he did not wait for an answer. "We need to put some pressure on all of them, and on the University in America. We need to put particular pressure on Dr. Gomez and his University in Mexico City." He paused, looking down at his well manicured hands. Then added, "And we need an informant within their ranks. Do you understand me? Do you know what you are to do?"

"Si, Monsignor," replied the other man.

"Then do so," his master said.

Chapter Seven

I

250 CE
8.10.12.0.9

Mayan Myth

The craftsman of the city grew in numbers.
They produced great quantities of fine linen
In brilliant colors, richly embroidered.
They fashioned intricate jewelry
Of obsidian and polished stone, carved wood and shell,
And brightly colored feathers.

They crafted ornate pottery vessels
To store their grain and maize,
Their herbs and potions and potent brews.
They wove beautiful baskets of thatch and reed.
Made spears, clubs, and lethal weapons,
Stone tools and implements of every sort.

And the merchants accrued great wealth and great power.
They brought a portion of their profits to the temple.
And the priests broke the pottery upon the high altar,
Burned the fine linens and baskets upon the sacred fire,
Saying the proper words
They performed the rituals as the gods ordained.

And the gods were pleased
And they blessed the people.
And the Maya prospered.

And the Mayan domain expanded far and wide.
The threat from outside increased as well.
And the gods told the Maya
"Build a strong and powerful army."
The warriors protected the people in the city,
And they protected the Temple.

This army invaded villages
And city-states across the land,
Plundered and brought back their wealth.
Brought back jewels and finery of every sort.
Brought back slaves, slaves to work the fields
And slaves to build the Temples.

The military grew strong,
And their campaigns were victorious.
The military gained wealth and gained power.
And they attributed their success
To the will of the gods,
And the intercession of the priests.

And they brought to the priests of the Temple
A portion of their plunder.
The priest laid the tribute before the gods
With the appropriate words and ritual.
They burned the offerings and slew the slaves
Upon the high altar, atop the Temple pyramid.

And the gods were pleased
And they blessed the people.
And the Maya prospered.

II

September 20, 2011
12.19.18.13.0, 12 Ahaw, 8 Ch'en
Archeology/Anthropology Department at the University

Once back at school, there is little time for worrying about the legalities or illegalities of absconding with copies of an ancient Mayan artifact. Instead, there is the rush that always attends the beginning of each semester: faculty meetings, student advising, scheduling problems, lecture and course syllabi, delayed book orders, and finally my own doctoral classes. My evenings are dedicated to recuperating from the chaos of my days. Weekends are spent reconnecting with family and friends.

I don't think much about the Codex and its still undeciphered hieroglyphics until mid-October. Then two things occur almost simultaneously. First, I get a cryptic message in my faculty mailbox from Brian. Why a computer geek like Brian sent me a handwritten note, rather than an email, I have no idea, but there it is one morning.

It reads: "Making some headway. Language doesn't match time difference from source material." I figure, after considerable thought, that what he means is, he has a translation program, but is having difficulty translating our manuscript. And the reason he is having difficulty is because our hieroglyphics are not consistent with those used in the extant codices: the Dresden, Paris, Madrid, and Grolier codices.

I have already determined that. This leads me to believe that our manuscript had been written at a different time than these other codices. The Dresden Codex was dated to the 13th or 14th century, long after the fall of the Mayan civilization. Either they were a historic retelling of the myths and stories of an earlier age, or they were copies, replicas, of earlier manuscripts. Over time the written language, as well as the spoken language, of the Maya has evolved. That the hieroglyphics in our manuscript differed, not greatly but consistently, from those found in the other manuscripts, indicates that ours must have been written at a different time. From where it was found, my best guess is that it dates from the 9th or 10th century, sometime between 900 and 1000 C.E., when Chichen Itza was at its height. I e-mail Brian, thanking him for his continued efforts and ask that he keep at it. I also ask that he keep me informed of his progress.

The second communication I receive is an e-mail from Eduardo. It is a rambling complaint about the Office of Antiquities and the Museo Nationale de Merida. Evidently they are not cooperating, not allowing him access to the Codex. They gave him the excuse that the manuscript must first be authenticated and that this they are in the process of doing. He is indignant, saying that they are dragging their feet. He says that their reluctance to let him examine "his" find is due to politics and professional rivalry between the museums. He requests that I have a word with the Professor and convince him to exert his influence. He adds that the University should get the museum to open its doors to him.

I e-mail back saying I will talk to Professor Allen. I don't think the Professor or the University has any power, at all, over the Mexican Office of Antiquities or the museum, but I don't tell him that.

I approach the Professor, but his response is exactly what I expected. "These things take time. Authentication of an artifact, of this sort, may take months, if not years. Interference from an outside institution, much less an American university and a virtually unknown professor of archaeology," and here he laughs at himself, "will only make them more resistant. Eduardo will just have to wait, like the rest of the world."

I e-mail a watered down version of the Professor's comments to Eduardo. I try to soften the blow by telling him of the work Brian is doing. I include my conclusions about the dating of the Codex, as well. He e-mails back, thanking me, but I can tell from his clipped response, he is disappointed.

December 5, 2011
12.19.18.16.18, 12 Etznab, 6 Mac
Two months later, the University

The semester progresses with all the usual problems and frustrations. My dissertation committee is finalized and, after much rescheduling, meets. As expected each member has his own take and suggestions on my proposal, projected hypothesis and methods of data collection. The result is my going back to the drawing board, yet again.

I see Brian, from time to time, on campus. Usually, he just waves timidly from a distance. Occasionally we literally run into each other, forcing him to actually talk to me. His response to my questions about the Codex is, invariably, "I . . . it's coming along, s . . . slowly. Still working on it, but m . . . my studies take most of m . . . my time." This I know and, of course, they should take priority, so I don't push him. After all, I am spending little of my time on the Codex myself, with all my other duties.

Carli and I see each other much more often. She has adopted me as a mentor of sorts, a role I am surprised I enjoy. She comes to my office every few days to 'hang out', as she calls it. I find her company still irritating at times, but I also find it invigorating. Her enthusiasm is contagious. It reminds me of the enthusiasm I had at her age and lost, somewhere along the way. Our relationship has developed to the point where, when her energy and incessant chattering become just too much, I can tell her to get out without her taking offense.

Adam I see regularly, as he is a student in my 'Women's Issues in Anthropology' course. We seldom speak, both of us maintaining the faculty-student distance required for me to remain impartial. He is a good student, but an unimaginative one.

Daniel and I see each other in the course of our daily routines, faculty department meetings and university social functions. He goes out of his way to greet me warmly, but I always feel a hint of amusement in his approach to me. I feel as if he is laughing at me, that I am part of a private joke he is having with himself, and that I am not privy to. As a result, any interaction with him leaves me unreasonably angry. Even so I find myself seeking him out, working my way into his vicinity at any function we both attend, and entering into conversations in which he is engaged.

I find I have developed a craving for the salty peanuts that only the vending machine in the east wing of the anthropology/archaeology building stocks. It isn't my fault that this machine is located just outside Daniel's office. But I'm not stalking him or anything. Adolescent behavior, I know, but I just want to know what the joke is.

Eduardo continues to e-mail me frequently, two or three messages a week, all of them essentially the same. "The museum still will not let me have access to the Codex. They keep putting me off with excuses," he writes. "First they tell me that the manuscript is being evaluated by outside authorities. Then they say it has been sent off to the Museo de Arqueologica in Mexico City. This is my museum. I have asked everyone I know; no one seems to know anything about it here. Lies, all lies." I e-mail back what I hope are calming comments, but I really don't have time for his paranoia.

At the end of December the tone of Eduardo's communications seem to change. The change is subtle at first, then more evident. He begins telling me about complaints made to his superiors, both at the University and at the museum. The complaints are about his making a nuisance of himself and making unreasonable demands about the Codex. The head of his department spoke to him kindly and with understanding at first, he admits. But of late his boss has become more insistent that Eduardo desist in his assault on the museum.

Eduardo also tells me that he is receiving phone calls, both at the office and at home. He writes that when he answers the phone, no one is on the line. His next e-mail tells me that he is receiving anonymous e-mails as well and that the calls have changed. Now, a voice he does not recognize says, "Leave it alone." When he asks what the person is talking about, the voice responds, "You know," and the line goes dead. I try to reassure him as best I can, but I'm not sure if any of this is real or not.

It's a few days before Christmas. I wake from a sound sleep to the incessant ringing of my telephone. I reach groggily over to my bedside table to pick it up and glanced at my alarm clock, as I do so. It reads 1:25 AM. Who, in the name of all that is holy, would be calling me at this time of the morning?

"Yes," I say, not even trying to keep the irritation out of my voice.

There's a moment of silence, then an embarrassed clearing of a throat . . . . "Professora O'Hara," says a voice I immediately recognize.

"Eduardo," I say in astonishment, my surprise giving way to fear. "Why are you calling me at one in the morning?"

"Oh, I am so sorry, forgive me," he murmurs apologetically. "I forgot the time." And he stops. The silence goes on so long, I'm afraid he's going to hang up.

I'm fully awake now. Might as well find out what he wants. If I don't, I will not be able to get back to sleep with wondering. "What is it, Eduardo?" I say finally, in what I hope is a calmer voice.

"So sorry, Señorita. So sorry to wake you," he stammers. "But I do not know who else to call. I do not know what else to do."

"What is it, Eduardo?" now I am scared. I realize he wouldn't have called me at all, much less in the middle of the night, if it hadn't been something very important. "Eduardo, are you alright?"

"Si, I am alright," a pause, "or maybe not so alright," he adds.

"What's happened?" I bark impatiently, really alarmed by this time. "Maria? The boys?"

Another moment of silence. "They say they will kill me," he finally says in a whisper, as if 'they' were there to overhear him.

"They?" I say stupidly. "Who are they, and why would they want to kill you?"

"The voices, the voices on the phone. Never the same voice. And e-mail messages, too. They say . . . they say," and he stops again, out of breath with the anxiety. I wait, and he finally continues. "They say if I do not stop making trouble, they will kill me. They say if I continue to ask questions, they will kill me."

I gasp. "My God," I say. "My God." I am at a loss for what else to say or what to do. Then, grasping at straws, I say, "Could it be a mistake?" I ask. "Could they have the wrong person?"

There is a silence on the other end of the phone and then, "You do not believe me." He says sadly, "I know it sounds loco, crazy. I know, but it is real." And then another spell of silence, neither of us knowing what to say.

"I believe you," I finally say, though I'm not sure I do. It just doesn't make any kind of sense. "What is it they don't want you to do?" I ask, but of course I already know.

"They want me to forget about the Codex, to stop asking about it," he says forlornly.

"But why?" I ask.

"I do not know," he whines.

There's silence again for a few minutes. I try to make some sense of it. Then I ask what I should have asked sooner. "Have you notified the police?"

"The policia?" he asks, as if it is the first time it had occurred to him. "But what can they do? I do not know who these people are. I do not know why they do not want the questions asked."

"Maybe the police can put a tap on your phone, trace the calls. Trace the e-mails," I say in desperation. What can I do from 2000 miles away, anyway?

"Perhaps they will not do this." He takes a deep breath. "If they do not believe me," he adds in resignation.

"Promise me," I beg. "Promise me you will go to the police, tomorrow. And that you will do what they, the voices, say, that you will stop asking questions."

"But that will mean that they have won and we will never know why this is so important to them," anger now replacing the panic in his voice.

"Promise me," I insist. "At least until we can figure this out."

"Si, Si, I promise," he says reluctantly.

"And tell the head of your department all about this tomorrow," I add as an afterthought. At least someone on the scene will know of the threats.

"No!" He says vehemently. "No, this I will not do. Dr. Ortega already thinks I am crazy. This will only convince him of the fact. It will cost me my job." And again there is silence.

I realize I'm not going to convince him of this, so I change the subject. "Remember, Eduardo, Brian and I are working on the translation. Remember we have photographic copies to work with. You don't need to see the real Codex. If we can translate the manuscript, perhaps that will tell us why the threats." Though I don't really see how. "Call me at my office every day to let me know how you are," I add. "You have that number too, don't you?"

"Si," he says, sounding tired and despondent now. "That I will do. Pardon me again, for calling so late. Buenos noches, Señorita Kate. Thank you." And he hangs up before I can say another word.

I sit there, on the edge of my bed, staring blankly at the phone, knowing I am not going to get any more sleep tonight.

Bleary-eyed from lack of sleep and wound up with anxiety, I manage to make it through my early morning classes. When I return to my office at 11 AM, Carli is there waiting for me.

"Man, you look like shit. Are you sick or something?" she asks me.

"No, I'm not sick, just didn't get much sleep last night," I drawl tiredly. "Come on in," I say, opening my office door. "There's something I want to run by you." I sit my briefcase down, motion her to a chair, and close the door behind us.

"What's going on?" she asks, a note of concern in her voice. I tell her of the early morning phone call from Eduardo and all that he told me. She stares at me, openmouthed, through the entire recitation. It is probably the longest time I have seen her keep quiet since I've known her. When I finish, she just shakes her head, still not saying anything.

After a few seconds she says quietly and slowly, "This will take some thought. Do you believe him?" She pauses, staring out the window. Then she continues in her usual rapid-fire manner. "Or is he having some sort of mental breakdown, paranoid delusions, or something? Wouldn't blame him if he is, I mean with the accident, nearly dying and all. And then that old museum practically stealing the Codex from him. Who wouldn't be on the verge? I know I would be." And she stops to breathe.

I take the opportunity to answer her many questions. "Yes, I think I do believe him. I didn't, not completely, at first. But, once he calmed down, he was quite convincing."

"So, what are we going to do?" she asks enthusiastically. I note her use of the word 'we.'

"I haven't the foggiest," I reply in all honesty. "Have you any ideas?" Not expecting her to have any.

She sits for a moment, clearly taking me seriously. "There are two things we need to do," she says earnestly. I am surprised. She has two ideas and I haven't a one. "First," she explains, "we have to translate that manuscript. I think you are right. The answer to the whole thing is in the manuscript." She says this as if it is the easiest thing in the world to do. She says it with complete certainty that when we do, if we do, it will solve everything, crazy madmen making threats to kill people and all. "Second," she goes on, not noting my look of incredulity, "We need to go down there and investigate."

"What!" I shout. "Are you crazy?"

"Well, no, I don't think so," she says, a little hurt. "We need to find out who wants Eduardo to be quiet about the Codex and, more importantly, why?" She makes this pronouncement with a look that asks why I hadn't thought of that myself.

I hadn't thought of it because it is insane. "First of all, a trip to Mexico won't get us anywhere. We aren't private eyes or superspies. What's more, it might be dangerous and could get us killed, if what Eduardo told me is true." I tell her all this, but she doesn't seem convinced and we leave it at that.

Next, I go to see Professor Allen. His take on the whole thing is that, clearly Eduardo is having a nervous breakdown. "Eduardo's department head contacted me with concerns regarding Eduardo's behavior. Dr. Ortega wanted more information about what had happened to Eduardo over the summer. He asked for any advice I might be able to give him." Professor Allen continues superciliously, "I gave him what information I could, which wasn't much. I suggested that they lighten Eduardo's workload at the University, as much as possible, but that forcing him to take a leave of absence might only make things worse." The Professor tells me to just reassure Eduardo but, not in any way, encourage him in his delusions.

My consultations, with both Carli and Professor Allen, haven't gotten me anywhere. I am still at a loss as to what to do.

Eduardo calls me at my office at 3 PM. He sounds less panicked and says he has not heard from 'them' so far today. He also tells me he has not contacted the police, as yet. I make him promise again that he will. His call does not reassure me at all. I doubt Eduardo intends to contact the police. I am not convinced that the Professor is right, either, about the threats just being the delusion of an overstressed mind. Now what should I do? Who is there who might be able to give me advice, good advice? And I think of Daniel.

I make a total of three trips to the vending machines at the other end of the building. Three bags of salted peanuts are all I have to show for the effort. Daniel's door is closed each time and I cannot summon the courage to knock to see if he is there. I don't want it to look as if I am looking for him. I want him to think it is just a chance meeting.

I go home disappointed and still no closer to a solution to my problem. Over a glass of wine and a dinner of whatever leftovers I can find in the fridge, I mull over my options. I decide I will talk to Daniel tomorrow, even if I have to show up on his doorstep, hat in hand, asking for his help.

As soon as my early classes are finished the next morning, I head for his office. This time his door is open, but a look inside shows me that it is empty. I am surprised by what I see. I expect Daniel's office to reflect his personality, ordered and controlled. Instead, the room is a chaos of books and papers stacked on every available surface. Rocks and stone implements clutter the bookshelves. Most surprising of all, rather than traditional office chairs, the office contains one overstuffed armchair, circa 1940, and a rocking chair complete with patch work cushions. Obviously Daniel is a more complex and eclectic man than I had imagined.

With my head still stuck into the room, I am startled by a voice behind me. "Are you here to see me, or should I call the campus cops and report a break-in?" Daniel laughs.

Being caught with my head in his door is more embarrassing than knocking at his door as a supplicant would have been. I preserve at least part of my dignity by matching my response to his bantering. "Caught in the act," I say, smiling broadly. "Your door was open and . . . well . . . I must say your office is interesting." Honesty is the best policy, at least when you can't come up with something better.

"I see," he says, smiling back with a touch of his usual mockery. "You've been frequenting our hallway a lot of late." And he looks at me quizzically.

"I've developed a penchant for the salted peanuts only your vending machine carries," I respond, ridiculously. Even to me that sounds lame.

"I see," he repeats, but by his smile, I can tell he doesn't believe a word.

I decide to come clean, despite what it will do to my self esteem. "As a matter of fact, there is something I want to speak to you about," I begin.

"Really," he says, any evidence of the smirk and the amusement gone. "Come in, please." He ushers me into the office, points me to the armchair while he sits in the rocker. "You look disturbed. Is something the matter? Can I help?" He leans toward me, a look of real concern on his handsome face. This look and his general manner, remind me of his manner toward Miguel at the airport in Merida, when the older man was so worried over Eduardo.

His solicitude, and yes, kindness, dispels the last of my reserve. I tell him the whole story: my growing concerns about Eduardo, the museum's refusal to let him see the Codex, the threats, what I advised Eduardo to do, and his reluctance to comply. I then go on and tell him Professor Allen's suggestions. Finally, I confide my dilemma over what to do next. I leave out Carli's suggestions, anticipating his ridicule. He says little during my rather protracted diatribe, nodding frequently and occasionally asking for clarification. When I have finished, I am nearly at the point of tears, but I am determined not to break down.

He then says quietly, looking directly into my eyes with his startlingly green ones, "You have had quite a trying few months, haven't you? So hard to hear that a friend is in trouble and be so far away, not able to help." He is so kind, none of the usual mockery. So kind that I feel the tears coming, impossible to stop. He changes his approach, probably seeing my distress and wanting to stave off a flood of tears. "So, what is your take on Eduardo's state of mind? Do you think that the Professor is right, and Eduardo is having some sort of mental break?" He waits as I compose myself.

"That's what I thought at first. I mean, it sounds completely preposterous. Threats? Death threats? Really, that's only for the movies, isn't it? That kind of thing doesn't happen to college professors . . . . Then I listened more closely to Eduardo. If you take away the indications of panic, which under the circumstances are perfectly reasonable, his story is consistent, coherent, detailed, and clear. Not the rambling and inconsistency of a delusional mind. Then I thought about who Eduardo is and what I know of him. He is an educated man, a scientist, dedicated to reason, clear thinking, and rational investigation. Nothing that I know of him would lead me to think he would suddenly lose his mind." I pause.

Daniel remarks into the void, "But on the other side of the equation, as a rational thinker yourself, you must look at both sides, all the evidence, before coming to a conclusion."

I nod. "On the other side, Eduardo's behavior regarding the Codex has been out of character from the beginning. His insistence that he should have the artifact, his anger at the Office of Antiquities and the Museo Nationale de Merida, insisting that they are thieves, and then that they are hiding the Codex from him. All of this brings his stability into question." I pause again, suddenly remembering something I had forgotten. I look up at Daniel. "Do you remember, in the hospital, his insistence that he had found the Codex for a purpose? He said it was his fate, that the Quetzal had led him to it." Then I pause again, unsure if I want to repeat the next part of the delusion, if it is a delusion, for I am part of it.

Daniel taps my arm, bringing me back to the present. "And?" he says knowing, somehow, that I am hiding something.

I continue tenuously. "He spoke as if it, the Codex, was alive and speaking to him." I shake my head, banishing the memory of what I had felt and brought the conversation back to reality. "That would indicate some imbalance on Eduardo's part. Add this to the whole idea of some kind of conspiracy and unknown men threatening to kill someone, merely because he is asking questions about an unauthenticated old book, is ridiculous," I finish.

"So, taking all these facts or assumptions into consideration, what are your reasonable conclusions?" And, to my surprise, Daniel poses this in all seriousness, no hint of his usual disdain.

I answer him truthfully. "The balance seems to fall on the side of logic, that this is a delusion of Eduardo's, prompted by some sort of mental break." I stop and look up at him. "But, though logically arrived at, it somehow doesn't feel right," I conclude.

"So, if the facts don't fully support any clear conclusion, what must we do?" He says like a true educator.

"We must gather more information," I answer, as a good student.

"Yes," he muses. "But how do we do that?" Here he is talking more to himself than to me.

"First, we examine the manuscript more closely, to see if there is anything in it to give us an idea of why it has stirred up such a ruckus." I say

"Okay," Daniel agrees.

"Second, we get more information about Eduardo's condition." I think for a moment. "The Professor has already spoken to his department head and Dr. Ortega thinks Eduardo is crazy." I think for another minute. "I can call Maria, Eduardo's wife. I know her, not well, but we have met several times over the years. The tricky part of that is to get information without alarming her." Daniel nods his agreement. "Eduardo is calling me every day to check in. I can monitor his condition somewhat, that way, but it really isn't adequate. The only way to really get an idea of his condition is to go down there and see him for myself." I say this last in surprise, for this was exactly what Carli had suggested. What has taken me days to come up with, had taken Carli only minutes of consideration. There is obviously much more to that girl than meets the eye.

"It may come to that," Daniel is saying. To my surprise he is agreeing with me, not calling a trip to Mexico City a ridiculous suggestion, which had been my first reaction. "But for the time being, I think we should stick to a more conservative line of inquiry. Definitely continue with the Codex. I doubt it will be of much help, but any information is good. And by all means, keep in close contact with Eduardo. Do you think I should contact him?" He considers this, then adds, "No, I think not. He contacted you initially, rather than the Professor or me. He evidently has built up trust in you. No reason to muck that up." He smiles, and then turns serious again. "And it's very important that you continue to urge him to contact the police. If there is any truth to the threats at all, we need to get the police involved." He thinks for a moment and then adds, "What I might be able to do is to make some discreet inquiries in archaeological circles. See if there are any rumors about the Codex out there. There should be. I mean, a find like this, even if not authentic, can't be kept quiet for long. If no word has leaked out, then Eduardo's assumptions of some sort of cover-up are, to some extent, supported." He looks up at me. "I think that's all we can do for now." And he pats my hand and says softly, "You did all that you could."

Nothing is settled, but somehow I feel better.

III

June 16, 941 CE
10.5.12.15.17, 6 Caban, 0 Yax
18 months later; the Temple of Ku'kul'kan, Chechen Itza

Time had passed quickly for Took Pak. He was kept busy with a multitude of varied tasks. First and foremost were his studies. He was required to learn all of the rites and rituals with which the priesthood paid homage to the Mayan gods. The incantations were involved and the rituals long and cumbersome, requiring memorization of intricate and complex gestures, words, and chants. Took Pak had a good memory and though this study involved time and effort, it came easily for him. Second, Took Pak was required to learn the intricacies of the many Mayan calendars. There was the Hun, the Tzol, and the Long Count,[3] each of which varied in length and in function. These calendars, interconnected cycles, guided the daily lives of the Maya: of the common people, of the nobles, and even of the priests. They pinpointed the most auspicious day for such things as weddings, births, contracts, and even war. Took Pak was fascinated by the calendars and their uses in predicting the future.

Took Pak's favorite subject was his study with Cha Mach B'en Kan, the elderly astronomer, at the top of the mighty Observatory. He enjoyed gazing at the stars and marking their paths. Took Pak spent almost every night gazing at the night sky, recording his observations. He had, as the old man had requested of him, developed some patience. After a year and a half, he was beginning to see the patterns in the movement of the celestial objects and to coordinate these with the Mayan calendars.

The life that he led in the temple was a busy one and time moved quickly. He had little time to miss what he had left behind. He filled his mind with all the new things that he was learning and experiencing.

Took Pak had spent the night before atop the pyramid as was his custom. He had taken the morning repast in the Temple kitchens. Then, though weary, he made his way to the Temple gardens. As he entered the gardens he met Nuxib Mak Lu'um, the servant from his father's house. Nuxib Mak was just returning to the kitchen with a heaping basket of fresh produce: onions, beans, yams, and other vegetables and herbs. Nuxib Mak nodded deferentially and would have continued on without speaking, but Took Pak halted and hailed the old man. "Good morning, Nuxib Mak. How are you this fine morning?"

Nuxib Mak was a bit surprised as they seldom spoke this close to the Temple proper. He looked around, to make sure none of the priests were close at hand, and then smiling, looked up at Took Pak. He said, "I am very well, Ahab. Thank you so much for asking. And how are things with you?"

"I am busy. Busy every minute of the day, and the night for that matter." He paused and then came to the matter that he most wanted to broach with the old gardener. Following the culturally correct order of the inquiry he said, "And how is my father?"

"The Ahab, your father is well," replied the old man.

"And how are my mother and my sisters?" Took Pak continued.

"The honored lady, your mother, and your sister, Kiichpan Pas, are well. Your sister, Janahb Ha', is not often at the family home for she lives now with her husband's family. I have heard from the other servants of the household that she is with child." Nuxib Mak told him with a large smile. "So it seems that congratulations are in order as you are about to become an uncle."

Took Pak gasped in surprise. This was something that he had never thought of. He was going to be an uncle. And then a wave of sadness hit him, for he realized he would never see the child. He paused and then shaking off the melancholy, he asked again, "And the rest of the household?"

Nuxib Mak knew what Took Pak wanted to hear, but answered the question in the way it was asked. "Your honored aunt and uncle are well, although they are growing older, as we all are." Nuxib Mak smiled as he saw a look of impatience cross Took Pak's face. "And your cousin, Ahkan, she is well also. She is gone from the house from early morning until late evening, every day. So we see less of her then we would want. She has grown to be a beautiful woman and a wise one as well. She ministers to the peasant folk. They trust her with their lives. She is a good shaman." A look of sadness crossed the old man's face.

"She . . . is she happy, Nuxib Mak?" Took Pak did not know what answer he wished the old man to give. He wished her happiness, of that he was sure, but a part of him was not sure that he wanted her to be happy without him. For if he admitted the truth to himself, although he enjoyed and was excited by all he was learning, he was not happy.

Turning to the old man again, he said, "Thank you for the news of my family. Tell them that I asked of them. Good day and good fortune to you, my friend." And he turned to make his way out into the garden.

Nuxib Mak bowed, shaking his head sadly for the unhappy man whom he had known as a child.

Shortly after Nuxib Mak went into the kitchen with his laden basket, one of the other novices came out of the temple. He looked toward the gardens. When he saw Took Pak, he hurried toward him.

"Brother," he called out, and as Took Pak turned, the other young man approached him. "Your presence is requested in the chambers of the Ah Kin Mai. Took Pak was surprised, for this was an occurrence totally out of the routine. But he knew better than to ask why the summons, for a novice would not have been given this kind of information.

Took Pak had no contact with the Ah Kim Mai since his entrance into the novitiate. He could not imagine what the High Priest might what of him. He was a little nervous but did not feel that he had done anything wrong. All of his teachers had praised his progress.

Took Pak followed the novice toward the Temple and they mounted the stairs that led to the Ah Kin Mai's chambers. They continued along a narrow hallway and stopped outside a heavy, ornately carved wooden door. His fellow novice knocked softly. The door was opened immediately. Sajal Ch'itz'aat, the High Priest's undersecretary, stood on the other side, as if he had been waiting there with his hand on the door in anticipation of the knock. Sajal Ch'itz'aat motioned for Took Pak to enter.

The room was lit by sunlight entering through several narrow windows on either side of the room. It held few furnishings: a long refractory table, with wooden benches on either side, and a small private altar in the corner. At the head of the table was a large, intricately carved chum tuun. The Ah Kin Mai sat on this stone throne. Kaloome Ek Suutz looked up as Took Pak entered the room. Took Pak advanced to stand at the foot of the table and waited to be recognized. Kaloome Ek Suutz did not immediately speak, but sat studying the young man, his face expressionless. Took Pak was unable to gauge his mood.

When he finally spoke, it was quietly, not the deep sonorous voice Took Pak was used to hearing during Temple ceremonies. "You have done well here in your first two years, Took Pak il Ahab?Ch'e'en. Cha Mach B'en Kan, in particular, says that you have a real aptitude for the study of astronomy. Sajal Yax Ahk finds that you are doing well in your other studies. He says that you have a fine hand and a particular gift in the art of the scribes." The high priest paused and looked speculatively at Took Pak. "Our chief scribe, Cho Piintol aj Tzib, is growing old and his hands have begun to shake with the effort of transcribing our sacred documents. He is in need of an apprentice and since you seem to have such a gift, I am placing you in that position."

Took Pak was obviously surprised and, although he tried to hide it, he was disappointed. Kaloome Ek Suutz's expression changed for the first time, as his lips formed a barely discernible, snide smile. "You are not pleased?" And there was menace in his remark.

Took Pak took a breath, steeled himself, and started to answer. "Very pleased at the honor, your Holiness," he replied. "I am just astonished. I have only begun my studies with Cha Mach Ben Kan and would wish to continue with these."

The smile on Kaloome Ek Suutz's face disappeared, as quickly as it had come. A look of displeasure crossed his face briefly and was as quickly gone. His face was again impassive. He stared at Took Pak stonily and after what seemed to Took Pak an interminable amount of time, the High Priest continued. "You as a novitiate do not have a choice in the tasks you are asked to perform." There was an even longer pause. Took Pak felt an increasing trepidation. Had he gone too far? "You will continue your education with Cha Mach Ben Kan, for now," Kaloome Ek Suutz added with an almost sinister note, "You will also continue your usual studies with Sajal Yax Ahk. Your new duties will be in addition to these." He saw the start of surprise that Took Pak was unable to hide and the high priest's smile returned. Took Pak did not know how he could possibly add any more duties to his already full schedule. "Your tasks in the temple gardens and in the kitchens will end, to be replaced by those as apprentice to the chief scribe."

Took Pak was disappointed but managed with great effort to not allow any of this disappointment to show on his face or in his bearing. Kaloome Ek Suutz looked down, with great contemplation, at his hands folded on the table before him, an obvious sign of dismissal and of how little importance he accorded the interview. Sajal Ch'itz'aat placed a hand on Took Pak's shoulder and nodded to him as an indication that he was dismissed. Took Pak left the room without another word.

Once Took Pak had left and the door closed behind him, Sajal Ch'itz'aat sat down at the table with a short laugh. Kaloome Ek Suutz lifted his head and looked up at his friend and said with a smile. "He was not pleased with his new apprenticeship and was unable to hide that disappointment."

"He is young and has little guile. For that we should be thankful. But he is very bright and he will age and, I expect, he will grow wiser. He will do as he is told, for now, and he will do it well." Sajal Ch'itz'aat replied, thoughtfully.

"Perhaps he is too bright. He has made many accomplishments in such a short span of time. And he seems to do each of them well," mused the Ah Kin Mai.

"Yes, he almost learns faster than we can teach him. He does everything he is asked to do and yes does it well. But I fear he has a spark of rebellion in his makeup," Sajal Ch'itz'aat added with a note of concern.

Kaloome Ek Suutz nodded sagely. "Yes, I see that in him. And that is why I have said from the beginning we must keep our eyes on him and keep him isolated." He paused briefly and then said, "He continues to make contact with the old gardener, against our strict edict that novices renounce the outside world and their past lives."

Sajal Ch'itz'aat nodded in agreement. "Should I confront him and put an end to it or should we banish the old man from the Temple grounds?"

The high priest shook his head. "No, I do not think that we should do anything so overt, yet. Took Pak's banishment to the library to work with the old fool, Cho Piintol, will keep him out of the gardens. That will make the continued communication impossible, without making an issue of it."

"Cho Piintol is expecting him this afternoon. I cannot think of any more boring and unfulfilling a task than hour after hour meticulously copying from one moldy codex to the next." And Sajal Ch'itz'aat laughed again. He waited for a few moments, but when Kaloome Ek Suutz made no further comment and seemed to be lost in his own thoughts, he rose and silently left the room.

In the gardens of the Ch'e'en compound later that same day

The sun was still high in the sky. It was near the summer solstice and the days were at their longest. Ahkan entered the garden from the nearby forest, carrying two heavy baskets on a pole balanced across her shoulders. She appeared weary and Nuxib Mak hurried to relieve her of her burdens. "What is all this baggage you are carrying, hun p'iit?" the old man said with concern.

She looked up at him, smiling her thanks for his help and concern. "These are just some potions and ointments for those of our household, and for some folk on the other side of the city that I plan to visit tomorrow. In fact," she continued, "I have something here that Ko'lel sent for you." She indicated that he should set down the xu'ul. When he did so, she dug in one of the xu'ul and came up with a small paayla, pottery container, and handed it to him. "This is a salve that the wise woman has sent for you. She says that it will help with the aches that come with age and with hard work. She uses it herself."

Nuxib Mak took the jar gratefully, smiling at the girl. "And it works wonderfully," he said. "You look tired and I fear you are working much too hard. She sends you from one end of the city to the other, ministering to all the poor folk."

"She does not send me anywhere," Ahkan said with annoyance in her voice. "It is what I choose to do. It is what I was meant to do. Ko'lel is growing older and is no longer strong enough to do it all herself. I worry for her, Nuxib Mak. What she has done all her life is so important. What would all of the people do without her? I must do what I can to ease her burden and prolong her life as long as I can."

The old gardener nodded sadly, "How old she is no one knows. But she is older than I am and I am quite old," he laughed. "But you must protect your own health," he said, "for we will have need of you when she is gone." He picked up her xu'ul again and headed toward the house.

She followed behind him. When they reached the eastern entrance of the compound, he set the baskets down outside the kitchen and the pottery sheds. Ahkan proceeded to unload the baskets, setting aside certain jars and pots, placing others in another smaller xu'ul. She took bunches of dried herbs and flowers and separated these, setting some aside to be used in the household and others to be taken the next day to the villagers at the far side of the city.

While she was busy with her task, her mother came out of the courtyard portico. "Where have you been, Ahkan? It seems to get later and later every day. I hardly ever see you anymore."

Ahkan looked up and smiled at her mother. A look of concern crossed the young woman's face. Her mother had aged in the last four years. Today she was looking exhausted and pale. "How are you feeling today, Na'?" Ahkan asked softly.

"I am fine," replied her mother. "Just one of my headaches," she said. "And cook has been in one of her moods, continuously on at me about the poor quality of the produce from the kitchen garden and from the fields. What does she expect in this dry weather? What does she expect me to do? I told her to go to the Temple with her complaints. Or better yet to the gods themselves." Her mother said with irritation.

Ahkan put her arm around her mother's thin shoulders. She could feel her mother's bones through the thin fabric of her summer dress. "Do not listen to that complaining old woman," Ahkan said with solicitude. "She would complain if everything in the world was going just right, just to have something to complain about." Ahkan guided her mother to the low wall outside the pottery shed and helped her to sit down. She then returned to the pots she had placed upon the ground and chose one of the smaller paayla. Ahkan turned to her mother. "Ko'lel sent this to you for your headaches. Come into the house and lie down in your room where it is cooler and dark. I will brew this in a warm drink. It will take the headache away and help you rest. But I am afraid I have nothing that will take away cook's irritation." The two women entered the house, one young and strong, the other aged and frail.

IV

December 10, 2011
12.19.18.17.3, 4 Akbal, 11 Mac
A basement ritual chamber somewhere in Mexico

The powerful man paced across the dark, musty room muttering to himself. He alternated between cultured Spanish and a strange, glottal language that was rhythmic in character, like a chant. He was clearly agitated, unsettled. He was alone in the basement room. Upon the altar in the center of the room was a large carved bowl containing thin scraps of wooden parchment, inscribed with hieroglyphs.

"The gods have set obstacles in our path. What more is it they ask of us? We have failed to please them. What can we do to appease them and regain their favor?"

He drew from within his scarlet robe a long wooden skewer that was incredibly sharp. Raising it above his head he intoned in that strange language a supplication to his gods, whoever they might be. He extended his tongue and drove the skewer through it. A great flood of bright, red blood poured over his chin and he lifted the sacred bowl to catch the flow. He stanched the stream with a pure white cloth that quickly turned to red.

The High Priest steadied himself on the edge of the altar, then taking up the burning candle at his right hand, lit the parchment now coated with blood. From a small pottery jar he added dried herbs and powders to the burning vessel and immediately an acrid grey smoke filled the room. He leaned forward, breathing in the pungent vapor. Slowly, he began to sway from side to side, then sank to his knees.

He was on what appeared to be a bombed out battlefield, alone. He tried to move and realized that he was no longer a man but had assumed the shape of a giant serpent with broad wings, made of feathers, upon his back. He had taken the form of the plumed serpent god, Ku'kul'kan, himself. He moved to the west, slithering across the desolate landscape. Suddenly, before him, rose a specter in the guise of a mighty green and gold bird, the Quetzal, symbol of the Maya people. In the mouth of the creature was a stone tablet embossed with the image of Ku'kul'kan. The bird dropped the tile upon the ground at his feet. The sun reflected off its polished surface, striking him directly in his eyes. He felt a moment of excruciating pain and crumpled to the floor.

CHAPTER EIGHT

I

576 CE
9.7.2.10.16

Mayan Myth

During the time of prosperity the Ah Kin
Placed a king, Ajaw K'inich, upon the throne.
A descendant of the gods,
The link between the gods and the people.
During the time of prosperity the sacrifice of the blood of the King
Was the tribute demanded by the gods.

And the gods were pleased with this blood sacrifice
And they blessed the Maya.
And the Maya prospered.

The years passed and the fortunes of the Maya declined.
The gods were dissatisfied with the tribute of the Maya people
And with Ajaw K'inich B'ox Kan, their King.
The gods had given their blood to create the Maya,
So the blood of the Maya was needed
To appease the gods and reverse their fortunes.

On the morning of the vernal equinox,
As the sun rose and cast its rays upon the high altar,
The King mounted the great pyramid, his queen at his side.
The King turned his face to the crowd below
Raised his arms to the rising sun.
A hush fell over the people.

The King took the sacred knife,[14]
Drew it across his palm.
Bright red blood fell, caught by the K'ubul Luuch.
The King motioned to the Queen, his wife,
And she stepped forward.
She knelt before him, her eyes on the King's face.

The Queen opened her mouth, her tongue extended.
The King raised the bloody dagger,
Pausing only a second, pierced the queen's tongue.
The Queen gave no outcry.
The High Priest mouthed the words of the ritual chant
That the sacrifice be acceptable to the gods.

And the people rejoiced.
And for a time the gods were appeased,
And the Maya prospered once more.

II

January 27, 2012
12.19.19.1.11, 13 Chuen, 19 Muan
The University: Archeology/Anthropology Department

Christmas comes and goes. Eduardo's phone calls come every day. He sounds better. He says he told the voices on the phone that he will stop asking questions, stop calling the Museo Mexicana de Arqueologia. After repeating this many times, he says the phone calls become less frequent and less threatening. Finally, they stop. Eduardo continues to complain about the museum's behavior. He still questions why someone doesn't want the existence of the Codex to become known.

I take some time away from visiting family and friends, and preparing for next semester, to take another look at the Codex. The front cover I have pretty well deciphered. Down the left hand side are the column of symbols and numbers that Calvin has deciphered. They indicated the Mayan date, 9.12.16.3.5, 11 Chicchan, 13 Xul. Translated to the modern Gregorian calendar it stands for June 10, 688 CE. Another column of

144

symbols and numbers on the right side of the cover, Calvin says, stands for, 10.5.17.2.5, 5 Oc, 13 Mac or August 28, 945 CE. Over 200 years separate the two dates. I wonder why? The first date occurred in the time of Chan Bahlum II's reign in Palenque. The second date occurred during the height of civilization in Chichen Itza. Odd.

The middle section contains two names with their accompanying titles. The first name is that of Chan Bahlum II, King of Baakal, son of Pakal. The second name, Chan Took Pak il Ahab Ch'e'en, is a name which meant small flint shield, son of the keeper of the cave. This individual is described as a priest scribe, Aj K'uhn. After some consideration, my assumption is that the manuscript was a copy of a document attributed to K'inich Chan Bahlum II. And that it had been copied by a scribe in Chichen Itza in 945 CE. No proof of this on the cover, but a workable hypothesis to start with.

The holidays pass quickly and by mid-January we are back at school doing it all over again. Back at the University I find a note from Brian waiting for me in my mailbox. It reads: "Some progress. Can we meet to review?'

"Great," I think. I e-mail him back with a time, late the next afternoon.

I also get a short e-mail from Daniel. "Have sent out queries to many colleagues re the existence of anything matching the Codex. Surprisingly, no positive responses. No response at all from either of the museums. Response from the Office of Antiquities was just a simple demand to know who I was and why I wanted to know. Very disappointing."

Carli is not back to school yet. She calls to say she will not be back for a week or two, as her mother is ill and needs her help at home. She sounds okay, her usual cheerful self. I hope that this will not interfere, too much, with her classes.

Brian arrives at my office half an hour early, carrying an untidy stack of papers. He comes in eagerly and begins talking before he is through the door. He bombards me with some long rambling, very technical, explanation. Little of this can I make heads or tails of; something about interfaces and compatibility. The gist of this seems to be he has found several programs used to translate hieroglyphics to a written language, some specific to the Mayan hieroglyphics. But, of course, the language it translates into is Mayan. The problem is, the Mayan language has had many permutations, over time. There are currently at least 32 different dialects spoken by descendants of the Maya. Not only that, but there were changes to the hieroglyphs, themselves, over time and between the different city-states, subtle differences in shape and placement of the symbols. These differences might change a word or phrase. Placement of the word within the phrase also changed the meaning of the word. And to complicate it, even further, the same symbol could have multiple meanings depending on the surrounding words, who was speaking, and the context in which it was found.

When Brian runs out of steam, I say, "But you managed it? You have the translation."

"W . . . well, not a complete translation. You s . . . see . . . ," and here he launches into another long technical diatribe.

I finally tap him on the arm to stop him. "I am practically computer illiterate and haven't the foggiest idea what you are talking about. I take it that it was very difficult, and I'm sure you're a genius to have managed it." I laugh and smile at him to reassure him that I am not making fun of him. "Sounds like it might be a good subject for your Master's thesis." His eyes light up, as if he hasn't thought of it already. "Let's save the technical stuff for that. What have you come up with?"

"Oh, oh, sure." he stammers and pulls out a sheaf of papers from among his pile and spreads them before me. I look down at them in anticipation. Each page contains a row of hieroglyphics, then a row containing Mayan words and a last row with the English translations. Brian points to each line in turn. ""This is the possible Mayan translation. Where there are p . . . parentheses there are two possibilities." He points again. "The l . . . last line is the closest English translation I can come up w . . . with. Imprecise still."

He shuffles to a later page in the pile, "There are some hieroglyphics not yet d . . . deciphered. Still working on those." He shuffles through the pile again. "This section," and he points to a page where there are few Mayan or English words, "is a b . . . bit of a mystery yet. But there's a diagram of some s . . . sort," and he points. "L . . . looks to be astrological, to me, but that's not my f . . . field."

I look closely at the drawing. "Yes, it does look astrological. We'll have to ask Dr. Brooks here at the University." I turn back to the first pages. "This is wonderful, Brian." He blushes, his face turning scarlet. "And what I said about your thesis I meant. You should think about it." I pause, still studying the pages. "Now I need to take time to review these."

"T . . . there's still a lot not fully translated," he says. "I'll k . . . keep working on it."

"But it's a great start," I gush. "A wonderful start." I look at him and smile. "I can't thank you enough for all your hard work."

"Oh, oh, t . . . that's okay," he stutters, blushing again. "I like p . . . puzzles."

"Can I copy these?" I ask, lifting the pages.

"Those are c . . . copies," he replies. "I made them for you." And he disappears out the door, before I can thank him again.

Carli returns to school at the end of January. She looks tired and pale, but tries to exude her usual cheerfulness and enthusiasm. She doesn't want to talk about her mother, just says she is still undergoing tests but is feeling a bit better. I can tell Carli is still very worried, but know that she will talk to me when she's ready. I see little of her over the next few weeks, as most of her time is taken up with catching up on her schoolwork and traveling home on the weekends.

Using Brian's pages of deciphered hieroglyphics, I begin making some sense of the manuscript. The first section is confusing and I leave it till later. The middle sections are more easily understood.

The second section seems to be a retelling of the Mayan creation myth. Nothing new here. A story is told in a variety of folk tales, legends and extant early Mayan writings. The gods create the universe, and everything in it, including man. The Mayan world is the center of that universe and the gods control their world and their lives.

The next section tells the history of the royal dynasty of Baakal, the Mayan name for Palenque. It includes the kings, Pakal, its founder, and his son K'nich Cham Bahlum II.

Just as I am about to leave the office for a departmental meeting, the phone rings. I think about not answering it, but I'd just have to return the call later. "Hello, Kate O'Hara," I say into the receiver. "Can I help you?"

"Senorita Professora O'Hara," says a voice I've come to know well. It is Eduardo and he sounds in a panic again.

"What's wrong, Eduardo? Are you alright?" I ask.

"The men, the voices, they are calling again," he says in a rush. "They accused me of going back on my word. They told me questions are being asked again. I tell them that it is not true. That I am not asking anyone, anything about the Codex and that I do not know who is. They called me a liar and say they will kill me, this time for sure." He ends in terror.

I feel a chill go through me. I know who has been asking questions. Daniel. Our interference has just made things worse. What can I tell Eduardo? The poor man is frantic. "Eduardo," I say. He doesn't answer. "Eduardo, are you there?"

"I don't know what to do," he whines. "What shall I do, Professora?"

How should I know, I think? But I can't tell him that. "Eduardo, call the police again. Tell them about the calls again. Tell the voice on the phone that you have contacted the police. Then keep telling them, the voices, that it is not you who is asking. That someone else knows about the manuscript and is asking the questions."

"The men will not believe me, Kate. And the policia did not believe me before. They will not believe me now."

"Then, tell them that the questions came from us. That the questions came from the University. Tell them that nothing they do to you will stop the questions." I am grasping at straws here, but it is all I can think of. Then, on the spur of the moment I blurt out, "And Eduardo, we'll be coming to Mexico to check with the authorities, with the museum, in person. Officials from the University will be coming to ask our questions in person." When he does not answer I ask, "Eduardo, did you hear me?"

"Si, Professora, I hear you. I do not think this is a good idea. I think it will be too dangerous for you." But he sounds as if it gives him some hope.

"Listen to me, Eduardo. Do what I say. Call the police. Give them my name and number. Tell them to contact me to confirm what you've told them. And Eduardo," I add as an afterthought. "Don't tell the voices our names. Tell them you don't know who it is from the University, only that it is someone important."

"Thank you, Kate. Thank you." he says with some measure of relief in his voice.

I hang up the phone, thoroughly shaken by the call. Now what do I do? I'm right in the middle of what is going on with Eduardo and I don't have any idea of what that might be. Now I'm in a panic. What am I going to do? Then I realize with a start, that it isn't just me I've gotten into the middle of the mess, but all of us, especially Daniel who had asked the questions. I have to tell them. I put in calls to each of them to set up an emergency meeting in my office, as soon as they can possibly get here.

Easier said than done. Each of us has a busy schedule and it isn't until the next morning that all of us meet.

I don't get a wink of sleep through the night. I am shaky and exhausted when I get to Professor Allen's office the next morning. I'd decided he needed to be informed about what is going on as well. I start out by telling them all what Eduardo told me the day before. They all look concerned, but I don't think any of them is convinced of the danger of the situation, but think this is just an extension of Eduardo's delusions. But they hadn't heard the panic in his voice. I take a deep breath, then tell them what I told Eduardo. There is complete silence and a look of incredulity on every one of their faces.

"You told him what?" screeches Adam.

"Wow," is Carli's only comment.

Brian nods his head. "G . . . good idea. A bit of misdirection."

"I don't think that was such a good idea," says Daniel. He looks sheepish. "I feel as if this is my fault. After all, I am the one who asked the questions. It was my idea."

The Professor looks at each of us astonished. "This is ridiculous, really. None of this is real, death threats from anonymous voices? The man is clearly unbalanced. He needs professional help, not endorsement of his delusions."

"I'm not so sure that I agree with you there, Professor," Daniel disagrees. "I know that it doesn't make sense, but neither does the fact that no one seems to be talking about the Codex. When has there ever been a possible find, of this magnitude, that hasn't gotten public interest as soon as it appears, whether an authentic find or not. I put feelers out there, with everyone I know, legitimate and fringe resources as well, and there is nothing. Somehow, someone has put a lid on any leaks. How they've done that I don't know. There must be some kind of significant power behind it, to keep it so quiet." All of us look at him expectantly. This change to a belief in Eduardo's story, on the part of the usually conservative and cautious Daniel, is daunting and, yes, a little frightening. "I'm not saying I fully believe in the conspiracy theory," Daniel continues. "I don't think we have enough information for that yet. What I am saying is that it is suspicious and because the threats are so serious, we need to consider them as real until proven otherwise."

I am surprised and, rather than thankful for his support of my opinion, his championship just frightens me further. I don't want him to agree with me. I want him to tell me I am being hysterical. I want him to tell me there is nothing to worry about. And here he is telling me to worry. "Daniel," I say plaintively, "what are we going to do?"

"I don't know," he says dejectedly, not at all what I want to hear.

"We're going to do just what you told Eduardo we were going to do. We're going to go on the offensive. We're going to go down there and find out what is going on?" says Carli decisively.

All the men look at her in horror. "I . . . I don't think that's such a good idea," Brian stammers.

"Ridiculous," scoffs the Professor with derision.

"I don't think that is a good way to go about it," says Adam thoughtfully. "I don't think there is anything to any of this really. I have to agree with the Professor. But if there is any truth to it, then confronting them isn't the way to go." And he looks at Daniel for support.

Daniel looks thoughtful but doesn't say anything. I am surprised, again. I've never known Daniel not to have an opinion or to take a back seat in any argument.

Calvin hasn't said anything so far. I'm not at all sure he is even listening. But he obviously is as he suddenly speaks up. "I have to agree with both Daniel and Carli," he says, quietly but firmly. He gets up from his chair and paces the room as he continues. "The more I study the artifact and research similar past findings, the more convinced I am that this one is real. Sure, in the past, when the Dresden and Paris Codices were first found, they were filed away on a shelf somewhere and not rediscovered for years, centuries. But this isn't the 18th or 19th century. This is the 21st century. What's more, with all the hype over the Doomsday Prophecies, lunatic fringe or not, someone, hell, everyone should've jumped all over this. That they haven't is suspicious in itself. That the only thing we've heard about it is not to ask questions and some threats, death threats if we do, to me says there's something more to it. What that is I don't know. But I think we should, we need to, find out." He slouches back into his chair, evidently finished with what he has to say.

The rest of us sit staring at him, at a loss for what to say. The silence goes on so long, it becomes uncomfortable. As I called the meeting and it doesn't appear that anyone else is going to take charge, I ask the question that hangs in the air. "So what are we going to do?" and I look at Daniel.

"I hate to say this, but since that is what you told Eduardo, someone will have to make a visit to Mexico. We need to see Eduardo, face to face, to see what his condition really is. And we need to talk to someone at the Museum to ascertain what they are doing to authenticate the manuscript." He stops considering, "The sooner the better, I suppose. The problem is I can't go right now." He pauses again, then adds, almost apologetically, "My dissertation defense is scheduled for two weeks. I can't realistically break away, until after that."

"Of course you can't." I really didn't expect him to go, but with his admission that he couldn't go, I find myself unrealistically disappointed. "I told Eduardo I was coming and I think I should be the one to go. I am in the best position to gauge his condition. After all, I'm the one who has been in contact with him in the last 6 months."

"I'd love to go with you," chimes in Carli. "But . . ." she continues guiltily, "with my mother ill, I can't really get away just now." She seems to be almost in tears.

I put my hand on her arm. "Don't worry," I say. "Of course you can't leave your mother right now. I can go by myself, no problem." I say this with more confidence and bravado than I feel.

"Don't be ridiculous," barks Daniel sharply. "You can't go down there by yourself. If any of this is true, any of it, then it is too dangerous for you to go by yourself. We'll just have to wait until I can go, or," he hesitates, "maybe I can take a few days . . ."

"Daniel, you can't take the time right now. No reason you should. I'm a big girl," I laugh, not feeling at all like one. "I intend to go later this week. Let's see." And I pull my day planner out. "Today is Wednesday. I have classes tomorrow. Could clear Friday, but don't think an official visit to the museum on the weekend will work. So say I fly out Saturday or Sunday. Yeah, that ought to do. I can get my TA to cover my classes in the beginning of next week." I am babbling, because to be honest, I am scared witless. Then I think, here I am making plans in front of my boss, about taking time off, without first asking him for permission. I look to Professor Allen and asked belatedly, "If that's okay with you, sir?"

The Professor has been quiet for so long, I think the rest of us have forgotten he is here. My question brings him back into the group. "I do not think any of this is a good idea," he says. "I really haven't any interest in this so called Codex."

I am shocked by this. The Professor, as a noted archeologist and scientist, should have been, if not excited, at least interested in what Eduardo has found. And as Eduardo's old friend, the Professor should have shown more concern about what is happening to his colleague. Why isn't he? He continues looking directly at me. "I do not condone your going to Mexico. Not because I think there is any danger," and here he looks at Daniel, "but because I do not feel you should interfere with the work of the Museo de Arqueologia. But, I will not tell you, you cannot go. Of course you can have the time off, but your trip must be unofficial. I cannot allow you to embroil the University in any of this. You cannot indicate to them, in any way, that you speak for the University. That just will not do."

I am shocked and disgusted. I have always thought the Professor a man of authority and strength, but he isn't showing any of that here. "Of course, Professor," I say coolly. Then I think, is his reaction because he is jealous of his friend? Is that the source of his unusual disinterest?

"You can't go alone," Daniel insists, totally ignoring the Professor. "It's just too dangerous. You'll just have to wait."

"I'll go with her," Adam says with a sheepish grin. "That is, if you'll have me?" He asks me.

"Thank you, Adam, but really I don't need anyone to go with me. I don't need a babysitter. Anyway, Eduardo will be there with me."

"No, really," replies Adam. "I'd like to go. I'm all caught up with my work here. No reason I can't miss a few days." And he smiles again, dimples and all.

"I think that's a good idea," says Carli.

"I think so too," adds Daniel. "I'll feel much better if you're not alone." There is something in his voice that I cannot identify, certainly not the usual mockery.

"Okay. Okay," I agree. "But," and here I become embarrassed. "I can't afford to foot the bill for both of us." I look uncomfortably at Adam.

"No problem. No problem at all," he laughs. "I have a little set aside. I think I can manage a ticket to Mexico City. No, really," he adds when he sees the doubtful look on my face. "It's not a problem." Then he adds to seal the deal, "Leaving Sunday will be better for me. I'll make the reservations, why don't I? You let Eduardo know when to expect us."

"I guess I'm outnumbered," I retort. "Thank you, Adam. I appreciate it. I didn't want to go on my own."

"Now that that is settled," says the Professor impatiently. "Can I have my office back? I have work to do, even if the rest of you don't." And he ushers us out of his office.

III

June 22, 942
10.5.13.15.8, 13 Lamat, 6 Yax
Chichen Itza, Central Plaza The Temple of Ku'kul'kan

Ahkan stood in the plaza, in front of the Temple of Ku'kul'kan, Chichen Itza's main temple. She stood near the front of the crowd amassed at the foot of the pyramid. The crowd was in a festive mood. It was the festival of the sun god, Ku'kul'kan, the plumed serpent. This holy day occurred at the summer solstice each year. The crowd was smaller and more subdued than usual. The drought continued into its tenth year and showed no sign of letting up. The fields were dry and the crops were more meager with each harvest. Though this was the feast in honor of the sun god, the prayers this day would be devoted to asking the sun not to shine. Further prayers would be offered to Chaac, the god of rain. The priests would pray that the needed water from the heavens be visited upon the earth. The deep cenotes of the city still held water, at least enough for the nobles and the priests. But the poor of the countryside were suffering and the animals were not multiplying. Rations were short, but the situation was not yet desperate.

The crowd was made up of men and women, young and old, nobles, free peasants, and slaves. They all wore their best garments. The nobles and merchants and their families stood at the front of the crowd. They wore garments of richly brocaded linens in festive colors. They were adorned with beautifully ornate jewelry and headwear.

As Ahkan watched, the procession entered the plaza from an opening at the base of the stone stairway. These steps ascended the western face of the Temple, leading to the platform and altar at its summit. First came the nobles of the Royal Court. Behind them came the Ah Kin, priests of the Order of the Chichen Itza Temple. They were dressed in the saffron robes of the fully ordained. Next came a contingent of the palace guard. They carried spears and lances festooned with brightly colored feathers and ribbons. They wore leather helmets upon their heads. In their wake processed the King himself, Ajaw K'inich B'ox Kan, resplendent in a glistening white cape edged with a Jaguar pelt, and upon his head rested a aj k'uh hun, the magnificent head of a spotted Jaguar. In his left hand he carried the rod of war. The queen, ix Ajaw, robed in the verdant green of the earth goddess, Chaac Chel, mounted the stairway at his side. There was a pause in the procession as the Royal guard and the King and Queen reached the platform at the top. The King took his place on the tunich tzam placed to the right side of the altar.

Then, the scarlet clad members of the Inner Circle of the Order entered the plaza and mounted the staircase. The Ah Kin Mai, Kaloome Ek Suutz, came next. He was robed in scarlet, as well, and upon his head he wore a headdress adorned with the green and gold feathers of a Quetzal, symbol of the Maya people.

Behind him, garbed in forest green, walked the three novitiates, who were to take their final oaths and be ordained into the priesthood today. Among them was Took Pak. He would be 21years of age in a few days and would today enter the priesthood as a fully ordained servant to the gods.

This was no celebration for Ahkan. Instead it was a day of sorrow, for on this day she would truly lose him forever. Once he made his final dedication, he would never leave the Temple and the company of priests again. She would never see him, except as she saw him today, on the steps of the Temple.

As the Ah Kin Mai and the Ah Kin of the Inner Circle attained the summit of the pyramid, they turned to face the crowd. The novices, Took Pak among them, remained on the step below, facing Kaloome Ek Suutz. The Ah Kin Mai raised his arms and addressed the people, "I dedicate this day to Ku'kul'kan, the sun god, and pray that he hide his face and spare the people." The other priests followed his lead, reciting the incantation to the heavens. The Ah Kin Mai continued, "And to Chaac, the bringer of rain, I ask that he send the rains that will save our crops and our people from starvation. Today, on this festival of the summer solstice, we ask that the gods accept our sacrifices and once more smile upon the Maya. The gods have asked much of us, but they are not yet pleased, for the rains do not come. We must increase our offerings to the gods."

There was a rumbling amongst the crowd and the good spirits of the people fell away. The crowd became restless. The Ah Kin Mai raised his arms again, to still the throng. He continued, in a loud voice, so to overcome the noise of the crowd.

"The young men, who will be dedicated this day, will sacrifice their blood to appease the gods." The novices mounted the final step to stand upon the high platform. The three turned to the right side of the altar and the King. They prostrated themselves before him. The Ajaw lifted the scepter of power and tapped each of them on the head in acceptance of their obeisance to him, as the symbolic representation of Ku'kul'kan, the Sun God. The novices stood. They returned to the center and faced the altar.

Kaloome Ek Suutz, standing before them, said to each of them in turn, "Do you dedicate yourself to the service of the gods and agree to act as intermediaries between the Maya people and the gods they worship? Will you offer up your blood as sacrifice[14] to those gods in hopes that the gods will find favor with that tribute and with the Maya people?" Each of the young men, in their turn, voiced their acceptance. They then, for the first time, turned to face the crowd.

Ahkan could not make out their faces or expressions from this distance. She could only imagine what Took Pak looked like from memory. The King looked upon the novitiates and, at his signal, the crowd gave a subdued cheer. Then the King motioned the first of the novices forward. The young man stepped to the side of the altar and knelt before the King. The priests intoned a long melodious prayer to the gods. The novice raised his head, extended his tongue, and with a sharp spine of the stingray, pierced his tongue. One of the priests stepped forward with the K'ubul Luuch and caught the blood that flowed.

Ahkan looked away, having no interest in the barbaric ritual, knowing that Took Pak's turn would come soon. She surveyed the crowd noting that many, like her, had their attention elsewhere. This was a trend that she had noted with increasing frequency. The people were not as absorbed in the religious rituals associated with the festivals as they once had been.

Ahkan felt a hand upon her shoulder and she started with alarm. "Did I startle you, hun p'iit?" came a voice that she knew well. She turned quickly to gaze into the smiling face of her brother, Ek Och. However, if she had not heard his voice first, she would never have been able to identify him. For standing before her was an old man. His bowed head was covered with an old woven hat and he was clothed in the tattered rags of a beggar.

"What are you doing here?" she whispered in alarm. "They have branded you an outlaw. If they find you here, they will kill you."

"But they will not find me," he said with a laugh. "Would you have known me, if I had not spoken?"

"This is too dangerous," she said, looking around to make sure no one was taking notice. She grabbed at his sleeve.

"They will take notice, if you continue to make such a fuss. I am here because I had business with my contacts here in Chichen Itza. But I cannot stay long. I dare not go near home, so I send my love to our mother through you," Ek Och said quietly. Then he looked up at the Temple. "So Took Pak will be ordained today? I wonder that such a smart one would do something so stupid." Ahkan looked at him sharply and would have made a remark, but he continued. "But to each his own. I am sure that what I do, he would consider just as stupid." Turning his attention back to her, he looked at her closely. "You have grown up, my little sister. I hear remarkable things about your healing powers. I hear you were even called to consult about the health of the King's son. Who would have thought it, not so long ago? I must be going, but I have things I must tell you. Meet me tomorrow morning at the old woman's hut." Ahkan nodded in response. But when she turned to say something more to him, he was gone.

There was a murmuring in the crowd and Ahkan's attention reverted to the Temple. The second novice had already performed his bloodletting sacrifice and soon it must be Took Pak's turn. Ahkan steeled herself for what was to happen next. A chill ran through her.

Took Pak stepped forward and stood before the King. He was numb and barely conscious of his surroundings. He was frightened, yes frightened. And he was exhausted. He and his fellow initiates had prepared themselves for this day for the last 48 hours: by fasting, by extreme physical activity working in the temple gardens, and by sleep deprivation. Took Pak was physically and emotionally exhausted, but he knew what he had to do and was determined to do so with honor. Took Pak looked up at the King, focusing his eyes on the Jaguar upon the Ajaw's headdress. The bright green and gold of the feathers that adorned it shimmered in the sun. He felt weak and was afraid that his knees would buckle under him. Someone, he assumed that it was Sajal Yax Ahk, the novice master, removed his robes. Took Pak loosened his loincloth and allowed it to slip to his feet. He stood naked, before the King and the crowd. But he was unaware of anything beyond what he was about to do.

He felt the stingray spine as it was placed in his right hand. Tool Pak felt physically ill. He took a deep breath and, trying not to think, raised the instrument and brought it down sharply, piercing his penis. The pain was excruciating, but Took Pak did not move or flinch. He made no sound. Again, he felt as if his knees would give way, but somehow he steadied himself. He could hear a rumbling in his ears that may have been the reaction of the crowd. He blocked this out, as he did the pain. All he was aware of was the blood, so much blood. It poured from his open wound in a bright stream of scarlet. Someone, another priest, stepped forward with the sacred bowl. The Luuch caught the warm, red sacrifice. Took Pak was becoming weaker by the minute. He swayed on his feet. Someone caught him and held him by the shoulders, while someone else applied a poultice, made from the sap of the gum tree, to staunch the bleeding.

Took Pak was half carried, half led back toward the altar. The sacred bowl containing Took Pak's blood was handed to the Ah Kin Mai. Small strips of parchment were placed within the bowl. On these were written exhortation to the gods. A lit taper was handed to Kaloome Ek Suutz and with it he lit the blood soaked papers. The parchment burned with a blue flame that sent the offering into the heavens, to the gods. A spiral of dark, gray smoke wafted its way upwards. This was Zikil Kan, the smoke serpent, god of the underworld.

The Ah Kin Mai raised his hands heavenward and chanted, "Oh gods of the heavens, and of the earth, of the rains, and of the sacred maize, please take this offering. Accept it as our homage to you and answer our prayers. Heap your blessings upon us." Took Pak came forward and, leaning against the altar for support, bent into the column of smoke. He inhaled deeply of the vapors that were laced with burning herbs. The world spun around him and his vision was distorted. The Temple and the crowd and the sunlight disappeared for him and he was transported to another realm.

For the spectators, the King, nobles, priests, and commoners, what occurred was very different from what Took Pak experienced, if no less miraculous. For as the smoke from the sacred parchment, carrying the incantations and sacrificial blood, drifted slowly toward the sky, a cloud appeared. A single cloud, in an otherwise cloudless sky, momentarily covered the sun. It obscured the sun's brilliant heat for the first time in many months. The spectators were amazed and took it as a sign that the sacrificial blood offering had been accepted and was pleasing to the gods. A cheer went up from the crowd. Took Pak did not hear the crowd or see the cloud. He was transported to another place.

He found himself on an empty plain, dry grass and bleached earth beneath his feet. The air was hot and dry and the wind, blowing from the east, swirled dust and debris around him. He was parched, his lips dry and cracked. He had difficulty seeing through the dust and the glare from an unforgiving sun beat down upon him. This world, all shades of red and orange and brown, no hint of green remained. And the sky was bright amber instead of a brilliant blue.

He heard in the distance the sound of thunder, but there was no indication of a storm. Then, out of the East came a figure, massive and frightening in its appearance. It was a huge bird, of brilliant green and gold, with outstretched wings and a head ten times the size of a man's head. It shrieked out a horrendous scream that made Took Pak's blood chill in his veins. The vicious bird bore down upon him, its sharp and hideous beak open with its cries. Took Pak was sure that it was about to run over him and trample him into the dust, but he was unable to move. The gigantic Quetzal kept coming. The monster came directly for him and would trample him he was sure. He closed his eyes, expecting the strike. Nothing happened. The bird blew right past him. It was as if it had run through him, as though he was not there.

Then he heard from the east the thundering once more. He was loath to see what loomed behind him now. But turn he must and so he did. What he saw terrified him even more. What came now was a gargantuan lizard, ten times the size of the Quetzal. The lizard, a putrid shade of green, was covered with foot thick scales and, behind, it dragged a tail 20 feet long and as thick and as massive as a tree trunk. Took Pak was horrified; his legs felt weak and could no longer hold him. He sank to his knees. The lizard trudged over the ground at a lumbering pace and the earth shook with each step. It came on relentlessly and, although Took Pak could divine from past experience that the monster would pass over him without touching him, he could not help but cover his head in trepidation. The beast came on. Took Pak could feel the air vibrate around him as it passed through him.

He heard a terrible shriek and the screaming of the giant bird. He lifted his head up in time to witness the battle. The Quetzal tore at the lizard with its razor sharp talons. However, the mighty bird was no match for the towering lizard. With one final swipe of its vicious tail, the lizard fell the bird and then finished it off by stomping it under his huge feet. The battle was over and the victor proceeded to devour his foe. Took Pak shook his head. He could not take his eyes from the wreckage of the magnificent bird.

Before Took Pak could recover from the shock, another figure loomed out of the east. This time it was a magnificent, black Jaguar. The cat ran with exceptional grace and speed toward him. The Jaguar had bright green eyes and long sharp fangs. It raced at Took Pak with the speed of lightning. Took Pak *was transfixed, immobile. Again he was spared, as the large cat passed through him without touching him. Took Pak turned to watch the Jaguar continue to the west. There to his horror, he watched as the cat caught up to the Lizard. It pounced upon the creature and, with an act of sheer malevolence, tore the slow moving though massive Lizard to pieces and devoured it. The blood and gore sickened Took Pak and he turned away.*

Took Pak was exhausted. He prayed that this was the end of the experience, but he had a feeling that it was not. He had no idea what to expect next. There was no thundering in the east. He hoped that no new beast would loom over the horizon. And then a wind, a hot, burning wind, came out of the East. The wind came at him, swirling the dust into his face and momentarily blinding him. Took Pak turned back to the East, not knowing what to expect, and fearing to find out. He saw, out of the dust cloud, a figure even more frightening than the lizard. For out of the distance came the heads of a mighty two-headed serpent, with eyes the color of the red setting sun. Its gaping maws opened and from them protruded long, forked tongues, which swished back and forth in front of it. Following the serpent's heads slithered the rest of its body, seemingly miles in length and as wide as the Temple stairway Took Pak hated snakes and this one paralyzed him. He could not move, as the snake slithered over him, but he could feel its progress.

The Jaguar, in the west, held its ground as the snake approached. As the battle began, the cat attacked with claw and teeth, but the snake repeatedly slithered out of its reach. At first, it appeared there would be no contest, as the Jaguar had strength and weaponry on its side. But the snake was cunning and it bided its time, keeping out of reach of its adversary's gaping jaws and sharp claws. The Jaguar lunged, the snake moved sideways, and the cat missed. Its charge carried it past the snake, and before it could turn to confront its opponent again, the snake climbed up its back and wound itself about the cat's neck, and tightened. The Jaguar thrashed and threw itself upon the ground, trying to dislodge the snake, but the snake squeezed tighter. This part of the battle took what seemed like an age to finish, but the outcome was not in dispute from that point on. Finally, the beautiful feline moved no more. The snake unwound itself from its victim, lifted its heads, and seemed to gaze at Took Pak. It flicked its tongues in his direction. Although Took Pak knew that the snake could not harm him, he flinched as the tongues approached him. The serpent then turned away and slithered off into the West. Took Pak was dizzy and sick with dread. What would come next? But nothing came. Slowly the swirling dust disappeared and Took Pak sank into oblivion.

Ahkan had not been able to watch. She had closed her eyes when Took Pak had taken the stingray spine and opened the wound. She had averted her head as Took Pak absorbed the spirals of the ritual smoke. Her heart sank and she feared for him when he collapsed upon the altar and was carried away.

The crowd around her was buzzing with excitement. She could hear them saying that this was a good omen. That Ku'kul'kan was pleased with Took Pak's sacrifice. That he was 'the special one' of the gods, for had the sun god not answered the prayers of the people and hidden his face when a sacrifice of this newly ordained priest had been burned in tribute. Surely Chaac would send rain to end the drought and the suffering of the people now. The crowd cheered even louder as the Ah Kin Mai helped Took Pak to his feet and draped the saffron robes of a priest around his shoulders. Took Pak was the one whom the gods smiled upon.

Ahkan returned home, hiding her face with her scarf to avoid letting anyone see her tears. In order to avoid interaction with the rest of the family, Ahkan retreated to the kitchen garden at the back of the house and took refuge under the branches of the gnarled old fig tree. But Ahkan found no solace here. She sat beneath the tree, knees drawn to her chest, her head buried in her crossed arms, and wept the tears she could let no one see. The sky darkened, but no rain came. As she fell asleep she heard the plaintive cry of the Quetzal, somewhere off to the west.

Early the next morning in the dormitory of the priests

Took Pak woke to find himself in a strange room. It was a small, barely furnished room with a single shuttered window. He was lying on a small cot covered by a mattress much softer than the one that he had slept on for the last four years. This was not a simple cot in the barracks he had shared with the other novices. Though not luxuriant, it was an improvement, and gave him some measure of privacy that he had not had before.

Took Pak felt ill. He felt weak and his head ached. He was thirsty and his throat was parched. When he tried to get out of bed, he found that he did not have the strength, not even to reach the ewer of water that sat on a small table at his bedside. He sank back into the mattress, closing his eyes. Slowly the memory of yesterday came back to him and, especially, the memory of the dream or whatever it was, that he had experienced. No, it was not a dream. It was a vision induced by the bloodletting ritual. It was a gift and a message from the gods. But what did it mean?

As he was pondering this phenomenon, there was a gentle knock at the door. He raised his head slightly and bade the individual at the door to enter. It was Chan Mach, the astronomer, who entered apologetically. "How are you my boy? Gave us a scare you did. Tell me what happened."

Took Pak shook his head in bewilderment. "I do not know what happened." He lay back on the cot, exhausted from that little bit of effort.

"Take your time. Relax and just think for a moment," said the old man with real concern in his voice. "Now tell me what it was that you experienced."

Took Pak closed his eyes, took a deep breath, and thought for a moment before he replied, a bit shakily. "I had a dream," he said at last, in barely a whisper. "I had a dream."

"Not a dream," said the old man, putting his hand on Took Pak's knee. "A vision!" he said with wonder in his voice. "And you so young. I am an old man and the only visions that I have had are those of the heavens at night. Never have the gods spoken to me as they have to you." There was a dreamy quality in his voice that indicated just how wonderful he thought this experience was. "Now, tell me exactly what it was you saw?"

Took Pak closed his eyes once more and with reluctance saw again the parched desert landscape of his vision. He proceeded to tell Chan Mach just what he had seen. The Quetzal trampled by the Lizard. The Lizard ravaged by the Jaguar. And the Jaguar swallowed by the Serpent. Chan Mach looked at him in horror as he finished, but did not make any reply.

"What does it mean?" asked Took Pak, alarmed by the look on his mentor's face. "What can it possibly mean?"

"We will have to study this very closely to determine what it means," said Chan Mach. Hurriedly getting to his feet and patting Took Pak on the shoulder, he said, "Don't you worry about that right now. You need to get your strength back. I will send a slave from the kitchens with some broth to nourish you. You get some sleep and I will see you again tomorrow." And he hurriedly left the room.

Took Pak settled back on his cot, wondering what it was that had shocked the old astronomer so. But he didn't have the energy to think about it right then. He quickly gave himself up to his exhaustion and slept.

The forest north of the city that same morning:

That same morning Ahkan left home for the forest before the sun had risen. She carried with her supplies for Ko'lel, foraged from household kitchens and gardens: maize and corn cakes, yams and beans and some scraps of dried venison, things that the old woman was unable to harvest from the forest herself.

Ahkan was weary, having slept little the night before. She trudged through the forest, trying not to think of the events of yesterday. Instead, she went over in her mind the tasks that she would have to accomplish today. There were dried herbs to be processed and stored. There was an unction to prepare for a weaver in the city and a tincture to deliver to a mother in an outlying village, for a child who had a fever. However, try as she might, flashes of the occurrences of yesterday kept invading her mind. She was also concerned with what her brother had been so eager to share with her, that he had bidden her to meet him at the old woman's hut this morning. With his name on the list of rebels and deserters, the palace guards and the city's defenders would have arrested him if he had been seen. If he had been arrested, he would have been killed. It was insanity for him to come to the city at all, and even worse to have stayed around for this length of time.

As Ahkan entered the clearing, she found it empty. The hide covering, over the door, was partially open and she could smell the odor of brewing herbs and wood smoke. As she crossed the clearing and neared the doorway, she was startled as a voice said from behind her, "Best you be more careful, little sister. I followed you for nearly a half mile and you never knew I was there. I could have accosted you at any time." And he laughed.

"I do not know why you are playing these silly games, Ek Och, when any of the King's soldiers would be glad to have you in their sights. I hear that there is quite a bounty on your head."

He laughed again, a merry laugh. "As you can see I am quite skilled at concealing myself. They do not have a chance of catching me." He took her burdens from her, pulled aside the leather covering from the doorway, and bowed to have her enter before him.

Once inside, she saw Ko'lel busily preparing a repast at the triangular fireplace in the far corner of the room. The old woman raised her head as the two entered the hut. "It is about time you got here, Ahkan, as your brother has been driving me insane with his constant pacing and impatience. You, Ek Och, come in and take this pot from the fire. Then sit down and have your breakfast. The two of you can talk while you eat." Ek Och did as he was told and placed the heavy pot from the fire onto the long wooden table in the center of the room. He sat and waited for the two women to join him, before he ladled some of the Sa', corn into a pottery bowl. The two women sat, but neither of them helped themselves to any of the porridge.

"Now what was it that was so important, that you needed to stay in this area where it is so dangerous for you?" said Ahkan in frustration.

"Is it not enough that I wanted to see my sister?" he said between mouthfuls of the rich, sweet concoction. "And, as I told you, I had other business in the city yesterday." He put down his spoon and looked at her intensely. "It is not about me that I wish to speak. It is about you. Even out in the deep jungle, I have heard of your exploits. It is not safe for you to bring the King's attention upon yourself. Then, to make your way to the palace and attend to his son was pure folly." Ahkan made to reply, but he brushed her words aside. "What do you think would have happened if your shaman ways had not benefited the boy? Do you think the King would have let you live for long, if the boy had died?" Ahkan started to speak again and, again he held her off. "And even without going to the palace and ministering to the royal child, your attentions to the peasant farmers and the slaves of the countryside have gotten the attention of the priests of the Temple. That does not bode well either, as the priests are very jealous of their standing in the hearts of the people. They will not long tolerate your interference in what they consider their prerogative." He stopped and picked up his spoon again.

Ahkan replied sharply, before he could stop her words again. "What I do for the people has nothing to do with the priests. And my care for the King's son is no different than my care for the farmer's son."

Ek Och looked at her in dismay. "If you think that, you are truly naïve." He said, shaking his head.

"I do what I do because I must. I have the knowledge and the skill that Ko'lel has given me. I must use it for the good of anyone who needs it. I cannot stop doing what I am doing, anymore than I might stop breathing. If there is an inherent danger, so be it." She looked at her brother with all seriousness. "And who are you to be lecturing me about the danger of my activities. I might ask you the same question. Why are you doing what you are doing, for you know that it is much more dangerous than what I do?"

He laughed. "You have made your point, little sister. It is true, what I am doing is dangerous. But there is a difference. I do not stay in one spot. I go from here to there. I rouse up the people and then I hide. You do what you do in the open, without a hiding place. But you are right about one thing," he added with another laugh, "I do what I do because I must." He paused once again, finished his porridge, put down his spoon, and stood. "I must be on my way before my presence here puts you both in more danger than you are already."

Ko'lel stood as well and, for the first time since they had sat down at the table, she spoke. "It is true that there is some danger in what Ahkan has accepted as her duty. I have lived with the vicissitudes of public opinion and of the King and the priests all my life. But I have chosen to hide myself here in the forest. Ahkan's increased danger lies in the fact that she lives in two worlds. She spends much of her time here in the forest with me, but she has her family and her ties to the city as well. This makes her much more visible to the Temple and the palace and increases her danger." She turned to Ek Och and said earnestly, "But I promise you, she will come to no hurt. I have seen that she will live to be an old woman, just like me. What will become of you?" she added with a tremor in her voice. "That is not so clear to me."

Ek Och nodded his head in acceptance. "What the gods will." And he gave both the old woman and his sister an embrace and left the hut. Ahkan and the wise woman did not say another word about him, neither of them wishing to express how fearful they were for him.

Later that same day: in the private chambers of the Ah Kin Mai:

Kaloome Ek Suutz was seated at the head of the wooden table with Sajal Ch'itz'aat, his secretary, seated on the bench to his right. The subordinate had an anxious look upon his face, and he wrung his hands as he talked. He said earnestly to the Ah Kin Mai, "Chan Mach has spoken with the boy this morning. What he relates is disturbing. The astronomer told me that Took Pak related what he calls a dream. Chan Mach is convinced that it was a true vision, a message from the gods. The old man says that what it tells us is not a good omen." Sajal Ch'itz'aat then proceeded to repeat the dream, as it was told to him by the old man.

The Ah Kin Mai was impassive, his face set and unreadable. He appeared to have none of the anxiety expressed by his second-in-command. "I am not concerned about what the vision may portend. One can read anything into the symbols and the omens of a dream induced by the bloodletting and privations that precede the ritual. I have had my share of visions, as have you. I do not think any of us have had visions of any great value or any that are true messages from the gods. Not since Chan Bahlum, the great prophet, so many katun in the past, have we had anyone who could foretell the future."

He paused and studied his hands for a moment, then continued. "What I am concerned about is not his visions, but that Took Pak, our newest of priests, seems to have a gift for other things. Chan Mach says that he has a great ability to read the stars and has, in the last few years, learned everything that the astronomer has to teach him. Cho Piitol, our chief scribe, though a jealous old man, has grudgingly admitted that Took Pak has a talent. That the young man excels at the writing and interpretation of the glyphs that he has been working so hard with over the last months. And you my friend," and he looked up at Sajal Ch'itz'aat across the table from him. "Have you not told me over and over, in the last few years, how his ability and understanding of the sacred calendars is beyond anything that you have ever seen, and beyond your own perhaps?"

"Yes, that is true," the undersecretary said. He wrung his hands even more vigorously. "Took Pak has talent in all these areas and he has superior intelligence as well."

Kaloome Ek Suutz nodded ruefully, but his face remained impassive. "He has one other trait that may be to our advantage," he said, and paused again, deep in thought.

"And what is that?" asked Sajal Ch'itz'aat, looking truly puzzled.

The Ah Kin Mai looked up at his companion and smiled for the first time, though it was an evil smile. "Why, it is the fact that he is unaware of his talents. He is naïve and that trait we can use against him. A man of guile would use the abilities that Took Pak has to gain power and importance. For is it not true, that within our order, knowledge is power?" And he paused again, contemplating this truth. "As long as we keep him ignorant of the value of what he knows, then we can retain the power and use him to that end."

Sajal Ch'itz'aat looked more perplexed. "Do you mean that we should keep him ignorant of all the mysteries of our order? Not allow him to learn any more of the movement of the stars, the use of the calendars, the writings of the sacred codices, or the prophecies of those that have gone before us?"

"No, that is not what I mean at all," the Ah Kin Mai replied with a grim laugh. "I plan to give him the opportunity to learn all that he can in all of those disciplines. To let him explore the mysteries. Who knows what he may be able to teach us. But the knowledge will be ours and the power will be ours. We must keep control. He must report to us, depend on us, and trust us, so that it will be possible. He is naïve, as I said. He is young and he is trusting. He does not know the ways of the world, the court, or of the Temple. He cares nothing for popular acclaim. We must keep him ignorant in that regard," the High Priest continued with another wicked laugh. "He has his mentors and he trusts in them now. You must keep those relationships strong. I am relying upon you."

"I will do as you say, but I am unsure as to what value this may have for us. And what of the others? What if he shares his knowledge with the other priests; with Chan Mach and Cho Piit? How can we keep them from stealing our power?" he asked with concern.

Kaloome Ek Suutz laughed again. "That is the beauty of this young man, in particular. Because of his superior intelligence and his obsession with his studies, he has few friends. He comes in contact with few of the younger priests and in no contact with others of the Inner Circle. I have seen to that. I have kept him so busy with his studies and with his tasks with the scribes, that he has had little time for interaction with others. And I will continue to keep it so. As for the astronomer and the scribe, they are dependent on me."

The High Priest paused and it seemed that he was finished with the audience. Sajal Ch'itz'aat began to rise, but before he could get to his feet, the Ah Kin Mai continued. "Keep me informed of how things progress. Continue to teach him the intricacies of the calendars as you know them. I feel he will be able to teach us something of their import. That information will serve us well in our dealings with the King. What we must guard against is Took Pak acquiring the ear of the King. No rumors of him must go in that direction. Never again must he take center stage in any ritual, as he did yesterday. The King had his eye on him and was impressed with what appeared to be his communion with the gods. I have downplayed what occurred and told the King that the boy swooned from blood loss, but had no vision. Make sure that no further information goes abroad." And with that, Kaloome Ek Suutz dismissed the other priest with a wave of his hand.

IV

January 22, 2012
12. 19. 19. 1. 6, 8 Kimi, 14 Muan
In a private home somewhere in Mexico

A man stood in the hallway of a well apportioned, but not ostentatious, apartment, talking on the phone. "Si, Monsiegnor." His voice was solicitous and anxious. "Si, Professor Gomez continues to make a nuisance of himself. He is always calling or visiting the Museo Mexicana de Arqueologia, berating them about the Codex."

The man paused to listen to what the person on the other end of the line was saying. He grimaced as if he had taken a blow. "Si, si, we are communicating with him often, warning him of what will happen if he does not desist. But the man is crazy, totally out of control."

He listened again. "Si, the Universidad has let him go. Given him a leave of absence."

There was another pause. "Si, we are having him followed, but he seldom goes anywhere except to the Museo. Most of the time he stays at home. No one is listening to him. Everyone knows he is loco."

After another few minutes he said, "Our informant at the American University gave me some disturbing news." He spoke hesitantly, as if afraid of the response he would get to what he was about to say. "It seems that the archeological team managed to take away reproductions and specimens of the Codex . . ."

He did not get to finish what he was saying. He held the receiver away from his ear as the other person screamed through the phone. When the torrent was over, he whined, "We did. We examined all of their boxes and bags, all the files and equipment thoroughly before it boarded the plane, both in Merida and Mexico City. Nothing was found."

He listened again. "Si, si, something was missed." Another pause, then, "Si, I will do that. I will contact our informant tomorrow and see what other information I can get. I could also make contact with our other acquaintances at the University." He stopped and held the phone away from his ear again. "No, no, of course, you have better affiliations and are better known and should talk to the contacts." He started to say good night, but the person on the other end of the line had already hung up.

Chapter Nine

I

424 CE
8.19. 8.6.4

Mayan Myth

A story is told in the villages and in the cities,
And all through the city-state.
The god twins, Hun Bstz and Hun Chuen,[15]
Journey to Xibalbal, the underworld,
There to ransom their father, Hachun,
Whom the gods of the underworld had stolen.

They travel far to the west
And vanish with the setting sun.
There they met Cisin and Xbalanque,
Gods of the underworld,
And said to them,
"Give us back our father, Hachun."

And Cisin and Xbalanque said,
"If you can defeat us in battle
We will give your father to you."
The twins, confident that they could not
Be defeated, agreed to the contest,
And took up their weapons.

Then the gods of Xibalbal said,
"And if you are vanquished, here you will remain

Never to return to the world."
And so they fought.
First Cisin and Xbalanque had the upper hand.
They battled on, first one side winning
And then the other.
Then Cisin raised up his mighty stone ax
And cleaved Hun Bstz's head from his body.
Hun Chuen, seeing his brother's fallen and bloodied body,
Was consumed by a terrible anger.

He took up his battle ax and shield
Ran at the gods of the underworld,
Slaying first Cisin and then Xbalanque.
Hun Chuen looked down upon his conquered foe
Then lifting up the head of his brother, Hun Bstz,
And with his father, returned to the world between.

And so the gods of Xibalbala were defeated
And came no more upon the earth.
So the story is told far and wide.

The gods came to the Ah Kin Mai in a dream.
They whispered in his ear,
"You must honor the twin gods, Hun Bstz and Hun Cheun.
The Maya shall recall their journey to Xibalbal
And their defeat of the gods of the underworld
Upon the playing field."

And so the Ah Kin Mai instructed
The Maya in the ballgame, Pitz,[16]
And the great ball courts were erected in the center of the city.
Here on high holy days the twin gods are honored,
And the head of the defeated is sacrificed
In their honor.

And the gods were pleased
And blessed the people.
And the Maya prospered.

169

II

February 20, 2012
12.19.19.2.15, 11 Men, 3 Kayab
Mexico City

Adam and I reach Mexico City late on Sunday night. Eduardo e-mails me that he will meet us at our hotel Monday morning for breakfast. He is here waiting for us when we come down at 7 AM. He is sitting in a booth at the back of the dining room, his back to the wall, watching everyone who enters the room. He has a look of acute anxiety on his face. He's scruffy and disheveled looking: ill-kempt, wrinkled shirt and pants, and a two day growth of beard. His eyes are red and swollen, as if he has not slept in days.

As we come into the room, he looks up at us and quickly searches the room as if checking to see if we've been followed. He nods slightly, evidently reassured, but does not smile or show any recognition. We sit down across the table from him.

"Buenos Dios, Eduardo. How are you?" I ask, truly shocked at his appearance. I reach across the table and put my hand on his arm. "Are you all right?"

He doesn't answer, just shakes his head and looks near to tears. Adam has said nothing so far. I can see him shaking his head, out of the corner of my eye. In pity or disgust, I can't tell. "Tell me about it," I continue, speaking quietly.

At that inopportune moment, the waitress comes over to take our orders. We order, then wait until she pours our coffee and leaves. Eduardo sips his coffee, takes a deep breath and begins to speak in a voice not much above a whisper. He is continually scanning the room nervously. He tells his story rapidly, not looking at either of us. He concentrates on the paper napkin in his hands, which he rhythmically shreds, as he talks. "I am not crazy," he declares. "I am not imagining all of this. They are following me, all the time. I can feel their eyes on me. And now, and now, they have left messages at my home, at my office. They know where I work, where I live, and where my family lives. They have begun calling me on the phone again, at home and at work. They are threatening again. But now, but now, they are threatening my family, my wife and my sons."

He pauses as the waitress brings our meals and refills our coffee cups. She asks if she can get us anything else, but we all shake our heads. We make a stab at eating, but clearly none of us is hungry. Adam catches my eye, briefly, and just shakes his head sadly, clearly believing the other man is just what he protests he is not, crazy.

Eduardo takes another sip of coffee, sighing deeply. "I told them that I had stopped asking questions, that it isn't me. I told them that it must be people from the American University, who are making inquiries. But I do not think they believe me. Still they call, but now they say nothing. They just hang up without speaking." He looks suddenly deflated, as if he has run out of steam. "And now they are watching me."

"Who are these people?" Adam asks calmly, with what appears to be real interest in what Eduardo has to say. But he looks over at me and shakes his head, again.

"I don't know," Eduardo says. "But . . . but it must be," he starts, shakily. "It must be the Order. The Order," he repeats, bewildered, as if he doesn't believe what he is saying himself.

"The what?" I say, not having the least idea what or who he is talking about.

"I thought that was a myth," Adam remarks.

Eduardo looks up at him, shakes his head, and says, "No myth. No, no myth. Just a secret."

"Wait a minute. What are you talking about? What order? What kind of order?" I say, totally confused, not knowing what either of them is talking about.

"The Order," says Adam, and for the first time I hear a hint of condescension in his voice, a note of superiority. "The Order is, supposedly, the modern equivalent of the ancient Mayan priesthood. When the Maya civilization fell or disappeared, the priests that were left slunk off and vanished into the jungle. Most reverted to the land, becoming farmers like their neighbors. Some, a few, converted to the new religion imported to the region from Spain, Christianity, or more exactly Catholicism."

Here Eduardo interrupts and takes up the story. "Still others hid in the forests and continued to practice their religion, continued to celebrate their rituals and perform their sacrifices. It still goes on today. Everyone knows of the itinerant shamans, who practice the ancient religion in the caves of the countryside." He pauses to take another sip of coffee, before he continues. "But a few, a very few, hid their true nature. They became rich and powerful men in the government and in commerce and even, some say, in the Church. These men make up the Order, 'El Sociedad,' a secret society that continues to believe in and practice the old ways of the Maya, but in secret." He finishes with more assurance than he has shown so far today, and looks at Adam, as if to ask the younger man to contradict him.

All of us are quiet for a time, attempting to eat a little of our mostly untouched and now cold breakfasts. Finally I say, "Myth or reality, why do you think they are threatening you? What is it that has made them angry? What is it about the Codex that is a threat to them?" I look at Eduardo earnestly. I don't know, yet, if I think him crazy or not, but am willing to give him the benefit of the doubt.

Eduardo waits, taking a bite of his fast congealing breakfast, taking the time to gather his thoughts, I suppose. "It's about the artifact, the Codex, that I found, yes. But I don't know why." And he shrugs with resignation.

Adam takes up the discussion again. "There has been nothing said about it at the Museum, as far as we know. Not a word in the journals or even by word of mouth in the archeological community. What makes you think that the Order, if it exists that is, will have heard of it?"

Eduardo looks up at him, obviously noting the doubt in the younger man's voice. "I started asking questions and becoming vocal about it. That is when the harassment started: the e-mails, the telephone calls and people following me. Following me all the time. The two events must, therefore, be connected." As he talks, he becomes agitated again, pulling his napkin to tiny pieces. He looks down, not willing to meet our eyes, afraid that we cannot possibly believe him. Half believing, I think, himself crazy. He stops talking. He seems exhausted, spent, defeated.

I reach over and put my hand over his, again. "I believe you," I say, not sure if it is true, but not ready to label him crazy either. He looks up and smiles weakly. "I don't know anything about this 'Order.' Never heard of it. Whether it exists or not, I don't see that there is anything we can do about it," I say. "But I'll tell you what we can do. What we came down here to do. It isn't much, but it might get some answers and, at least, it will take the limelight off of you, Eduardo. What I really don't understand are the actions of the Museum and the Office of Antiquities. Why the silence from them? Is it just that they don't want us to get any of the glory? Do they want to somehow steal it all for themselves? You'd think they would be shouting about a find like this, to all who will listen. Or do they know something that we don't? Have they determined that it's a fake, a hoax of some sort?" I say, confused by all of it.

Adam brightens a bit. "That's probably it. It probably is a fake and they are keeping it under wraps to avoid embarrassment. Or is it all about money?" he adds, when he sees my look of disagreement.

"Somehow, that doesn't make any sense to me. It doesn't make sense," I repeat. "There will be enough glory to go around, if this is for real. And why would anyone from the Museum threaten you, Eduardo, just for asking questions?"

"No," says Eduardo, 'if it is real, for some reason there is someone or something . . . . the Order perhaps," he looks up at Adam to see how he would respond to this. When he didn't, Eduardo resumes, "There is something that does not want this Codex to be made public."

"But why? The threats would indicate that the Codex is real. But the lack of publicity points to it being a fraud," I say.

There is a long moment of silence, as each of us thinks about this. Finally Eduardo breaks the silence. "Because, I think, there must be something in the Codex that they, whoever they are," he looks again from Adam to me, "there is something in the book that they do not want anyone to know."

Adam looks puzzled. He says at last, "What can something, written 1000 years ago, have in it to threaten someone today? If it has something to do with the Mayan creation myth and Mayan history, which is what some of our early decoding suggests, it doesn't make sense. No, that doesn't make any sense," he laughs. "One myth threatened by the possible existence of another myth, a secret society no less." He laughs again. "That's all I come back to, that it just doesn't make any sense. That it's all crazy."

"Maybe," I say, a little heated over his jeering remark. "Maybe that's all there is to it. That it doesn't make sense because they, the people who are threatening and following Eduardo, don't make any sense. That they are the ones who are crazy." Again there was a moment of silence.

"No," Eduardo says, "that may be true of the people who are harassing me, but it does not explain why I cannot get any information from the people at the museum. Or why there hasn't been any hint of the find in the archeological world. You are right." He said to Adam. "It just does not make any sense."

"There you go again." I said and laugh ruefully. "We always seem to get back to the fact that it just doesn't make sense."

"Well," says Adam, "what are we going to do next? How do we go about making it all make some kind of sense?"

"I don't know," says Eduardo, shaking his head sadly. "I am frightened," he whispers, not able to meet our eyes. "I am beginning to believe their threats."

"I don't blame you for being afraid," I say.

"I think you should lie low for a while," says Adam.

Eduardo looks up at us and gives us his first real smile of the day. "Mucho gracias," he says. "But that is what I have been doing and it does not appear to have helped."

No one says anything for a time. None of us has eaten much of our breakfast, but we signal the waitress to clear our plates. While she does so, we all seem to gather our own thoughts. When she is gone, Adam and I both begin speaking at once. We laugh and Adam gallantly waves his hand to let me go first.

I say, "While we are here, I think Adam and I should keep to our plan and make a visit to the museum. We plan to make some unofficial, official inquiries on behalf of the University."

Adam laughs. "What you mean," he says, "is we'll lie about what authority we have."

"Not lie," I bristle. "We are from the University and actually were part of the dig when the codex was found. If they assume that we are more important than we are, is that our fault? Anyway, how else are we going to get any information? We need information if we're ever going to make any sense out of this." I nod my head and am proud of myself for coming up with what sounds like a plausible explanation. Adam laughs again. Then, I say, more seriously, "You know the University does have a right to know what's going on, because the University co-sponsored the dig that gave them the Codex. I know we hated to give it to them, but we did, and they should share their information with us. At least keep us informed of what is happening to the artifact. It's only fair."

Eduardo nods vigorously in agreement, but Adam disagrees. "Actually, the artifact was not found at our authorized site and we didn't have permission to excavate where it was found."

"But Eduardo did find it, so it's only fair," I argue.

Adam continues, ignoring my complaint, "I think we should go through the proper channels. Have the University make the request formally and officially official." He looks pointedly at me.

I frown at him and shake my head. "But we're here now, on the spot. Since we're here, I plan to at least make an attempt at getting some answers." When Adam looks displeased, I hastily continue, "We'll go the official route too, when we get back. But I'm making a visit to the museum this afternoon. You can come with me or not. It's up to you." And I nod my head to emphasize my determination. "You can come or not, that's up to you," I repeat. I meet his gaze, challenging him.

"Oh, I'm coming along, if just to make sure you don't get yourself in any trouble and to keep me out of trouble with Carli."

"To keep me out of trouble," I mutter, but I am really very pleased that he is going to accompany me.

Adam turns to Eduardo. "Any suggestions as to whom we should see at the museum?"

Eduardo thinks for a moment. "I do think it might be a good idea for you to ask some questions on behalf of the University. Anyway, someone should. I think Senor Roberto Mateos, the Director of Acquisitions, is the person for you to see. It is he who would have received the Codex from the Merida Nationale Museo. He can't pretend he doesn't know what you are talking about." He pauses. "I think I should go with you. He is an old friend. Yes, I will go with you," he says, with determination.

I look at him and shake my head. "It's too dangerous."

Adam says, "I agree with Kate."

"I've worked with the Museo de Arqueologia for years," argues Eduardo. "I know Senor Mateos well, and I trust him. I have every right to go to the museum and speak with him. I will introduce you to him. I am going. They, the voices, will blame me for your being here, whether I go with you or not."

We could not dissuade him, so we made arrangements to meet at the museum in an hour's time. Adam and I return to our rooms to change into something more official looking. We both agree that if we are to be even semi-official, we need to look the part. Even though I believe, and Eduardo is sure, he is being harassed, it still, somehow, feels like a game. Things like this only happen in books, not in real life and not to ordinary people like us.

Just as I am about to leave my room, the phone rings. It is Father Domingo, the priest I met in Merida last summer. I had e-mailed him about our impending trip to Mexico City and the hotel where we planned to stay. He greets me warmly and we make plans to meet for dinner that evening.

Dressed officially: me in dressy navy slacks and white silk blouse, Adam in black pants and gray blazer, we meet Eduardo on the steps of the Museo de Arqueologia. It is an impressive building of lofty masonry and colonnades. We enter the building and go up to the 3rd floor. 'Director of Acquisitions' is stenciled on the door. We enter a small, but beautifully furnished, reception area, which is overseen by an equally, decorative secretary. Adam smiles at her winningly, and proceeds to introduce us all."

Buenas tardes. Mi nombre estas Adam," He smiles even more broadly, if that is possible. "Ella Professora O'Hara." He continues in his better than average Spanish. We are from the American University. And, of course, you know Professor Gomez. We are here to see Senor Mateos." He smiles his most gracious smile again. He is flirting outrageously with this very pretty young woman. She is, very obviously, responding. She barely looks at Eduardo and me, as she gushes back at Adam. "Do you have an appointment?" she asks sweetly, in excellent English.

"No," admits Adam, "we don't. We are on a rush trip here in Mexico City, on business with the Officia de Antiguedad. We cannot leave without stopping in to extend the compliments of the University to Senor Mateos, and also, to convey our thanks to him for his help over the years. Purely a courtesy call, but it would be highly impolite not to at least say hello." He lies very well, as if he's had lots of practice, so I let him do all the talking. Also, he has more influence with the impressionable secretary than I would.

I let him continue, "We didn't call to make an appointment because we didn't know if we'd have time. To make an appointment and then not be able to keep it would have been rude."

She seems ready to give him the usual response, that without an appointment she doubts Senor Mateos will be able to see us. Adam smiles again, and she smiles back. She is buying his song and dance completely. "I'll just go and see if the Director has a minute." She stands and walks to the inner door, opens it, and goes in, closing the door behind her.

"Way to go, Adam," I whisper, not entirely tongue in cheek. "It's always helpful to have charm on your side. You certainly managed that well."

The secretary comes out of the inner office, at that moment, smiling effusively and blushing slightly. "He is very, very busy," she says, "but he will be able to see you, just for a minute." She opens the door fully and stands aside to let us pass.

Senor Mateos is a tiny round, graying man in his sixties. He stands and comes around his desk, as we enter. He extends his hand and smiles a genuine smile. "Lovely to meet you, Senor Adam and Professora O'Hara." The secretary is obviously worth her salary. She had gotten our names and titles correct, first time out. "And Eduardo, so nice to see you again. How is the family?" he says pleasantly, shaking Eduardo's hand warmly. He continues without waiting for a response, "When was the last time we saw each other?" Eduardo shakes the Director's hand, but is left with his answer of, "Fine, thank you" unspoken as Senor Mateos blusters on. "The Museum fundraiser last spring, wasn't it?

When the Director takes a needed breath, Eduardo barges in with, "Yes, that was the last time we saw each other. But we spoke on the phone in October, about the artifact I found in the Yucatan last summer," he says aggressively.

"Oh, oh yes, of course. Of course," Senior Mateos replies, embarrassed. Clearly he does not remember the incident, until reminded, and is still a bit fuzzy about it. It obviously isn't of importance to him. The Director waves us to a group of chairs in the corner of the room. "Please be seated," he says.

I seat myself. Eduardo lags behind, still flustered by Senor Mateos' reaction. Adam takes over the meeting as he sits. "That's really what we wanted to see you about," he begins. "Just to get an update on what's going on with the artifact, you know. We haven't heard a word about the Museum's evaluation of the item, since it was transferred to you from the Nationale Museo de Merida. The University is eager to get your impression, of course, as you are obviously the experts. We have a vested interest, you might say, as we found it."

"Yes. Yes, I certainly understand." But he is clearly confused. "Let me think a moment." And he does.

Eduardo is exasperated and jumps in. "Don't you remember, Roberto? Last October? I called. I told you I had found an artifact that looked like a post-classical Maya codex. I told you the Museu Nationale de Merida told me they were sending it here to you. Don't you remember, amigo? You said you would look into it and let me know when it got here. But you never called. I called you, many times, but you never called me back. Don't you remember?"

Senor Mateos looks bemused. "I . . . I . . ." he stammers. "I seem to remember it now. Yes. Yes, I remember you called about then, but I never got any artifact from the Merida Museo. No, I am sure I did not." But he still looks like he doesn't remember any of it.

I watch the exchange. The Director's response is bemusing. Eduardo looks at his friend with horror. "You do not remember it any better than that?" he says accusingly.

"Things were very busy about then. I had a lot on my mind. Funding problems, you know? Always funding problems. But now, I seem to remember something about a find, yes. You called, yes." But Senor Mateos doesn't seem very clear on anything. "But nothing about any codex." He looks up at Eduardo, as if for assistance. He looks at Adam and me, as if we might give him the answer.

I'm stunned. Adam looks as if he has come to some kind of conclusion about Senor Mateos. The Director of Acquisitions rubs his head. "My memory is not what it used to be. So busy, so much going on. And I am not so young anymore." He is clearly confused, and upset by his confusion. I can see Adam nodding his head, out of the corner of my eye.

Eduardo touches the older man's hand. "Do you know what might have happened to the artifact if it arrived from Merida?" He says this with sympathy, as he, too, realizes that his friend is not the man he has known.

Well, yes, of course, I do. It would have come to the workroom downstairs, been unpacked, and then sent to the appropriate department. That is protocol, so that is what would have been done." But he doesn't sound so sure.

Adam turns to Senor Mateos and says gently, 'Do you think that your office can make some inquiries about the article?"

"Well, I think perhaps I can." He rubs his head again, not looking at all as if he can comply with this simple request. He looks from me to Eduardo.

Adam gets his attention again. "Perhaps we can ask your secretary to take on this little job for you? I know how busy you are."

"Yes, yes, very busy." He smiles up at Adam, looking relieved.

"Why don't we have her come in and ask her?" Adam says.

"Certainly," the Director agrees. He gets up, walks to the door, and asks his secretary to come in for a moment. He looks, at this point, as if he is again in control of the situation, as when he first greeted us. But all of us know that he isn't.

The secretary comes into the room. She smiles reassuringly at Senor Mateos. "What can I do for you, Director?" She holds his gaze and so his attention. He looks a bit bewildered, again, and seeks help from Adam.

Adam takes the initiative, again. "We have asked the Senor Director for some information, but know he is very busy and it is just a little thing. He suggests that you might be able to get the information for us." She looks at Senor Mateos, reassuringly. A pearl of an assistant, I think. She obviously knows her boss' problem and covers for him, does his job, in all probability. Unless she makes his salary, she is paid too little. She turns her attention to us. "What is it you want to know?"

Adam gives her a brief outline of the artifact and our interest in what had become of it. He leaves out any mention of exactly what the object might be.

She smiles again at him and shows no surprise at the request or any interest in any further information. "Of course," she says. "It may take a day or two, but I don't see any problem with getting the information you need. How long will you be staying in the city? Where can I reach you?"

Adam looks at me and I answer for us. "We will be here another day or so," I say. "It isn't definite yet. It depends on our other meetings." I know I am rambling on too much. I'm not an able storyteller, like Adam. I am uncomfortable in the lie. "We are staying at the Hilton Mexico City Reforma. Call us there. Thank you very much for your time," I add sincerely.

The secretary looks at me curiously. I know I have overdone it, for such a simple request, for an unimportant bit of information

We say goodbye to Senor Mateos. Eduardo shakes his hand and then gives him a prolonged hug. A final goodbye, I think.

Once outside the building Eduardo leads us to the park opposite the Museum. He turns to look in every direction, as if to see if he can spot any of his followers or anyone paying unusual attention to us. He seems not to see anything suspicious. "Poor Roberto," he says sadly. "He doesn't know what is going on, does he? He was such a brilliant man, truly brilliant.

And now . . ." He shakes his head; there are tears in his eyes. "How can something like this happen?"

"Yes," Adam says. "Looks like Alzheimer's. Wonder how long it's been going on? I wonder how long the secretary will be able to cover for him? But it may explain the missing Codex, or the lack of any progress on its evaluation."

"Yes, that may be true," Eduardo says thoughtfully. "It may have just been shelved, with no one taking any responsibility for it."

There is a pause. Then I comment on the obvious. "It may account for the lack of publicity, but it doesn't account for the threatening calls and the stalkers." Adam and Eduardo nod, but don't have anything to add.

There is a message at the front desk when we get back to the hotel from Senor Tierro, the Director of the Office of Antiquities in Merida. It says that he heard we were visiting Mexico City. He is as well. He invites us to a reception at the Oficina de Antiguedad here in the city the next evening. He hopes we can attend and he will send a car for us at 7 PM.

Eduardo refuses to go and Adam says he is meeting friends and can't possibly stand them up. I don't want to go either, but feel I can't refuse. I call the number Senor Tierro left, and leave a message accepting his invitation.

I meet Padre Domingo at a restaurant not far from the hotel. I arrive early and am already seated when he walks into the room. He is immediately greeted from all sides. Even the owner of the establishment comes to shake his hand. "A celebrity," I think, watching him. "Seems well loved and respected."

He approaches my table, smiling warmly and grasps my hand. "Professora O'Hara, how wonderful to see you." He sits across from me.

"Father Domingo, so good to see you, too. And please call me Kate," I reply.

"Only if you call me Father Alejandro," he says. "Tell me how have you been and how your research is going?"

"Things have been busy and hectic. Not much time for my personal research." We order our dinners, or rather he orders for both of us. He says he comes here often and knows the best things on the menu.

"What are you doing in Mexico City? Too early for Spring Break, I would think," he comments.

I don't know how much I should tell him. "My colleagues and I had some business at the Museo Mexicana de Arqueologia. Some loose ends left over from the summer dig."

"I hope you will get some time for some sightseeing. Ours is quite a beautiful city," he replies.

"I don't think I will this time. We have another meeting at the Museum, though I'm not sure yet when that will be. And I have an invitation to a reception at the Oficina de Antiguedad tomorrow evening." I tell him. A cloud seems to cross his face for a second, so quickly gone that I'm not sure I have seen it at all.

He changes the subject. "What will be your next area of research?"

I told him about the subject of my dissertation and we talk at length about the role of women through history. He is well versed in the subject. After my second glass of wine I am relaxed enough to bring up a subject I have been thinking about all day. "What do you know about something called the 'Order'?"

His expression turns suddenly grave. He takes a sip from his wine glass and then looks up at me. "Why the interest in this?"

"Just a casual comment someone made," I evade.

"I believe this person refers to a secret organization which is supposed to exist, both here in Mexico and elsewhere in the world. Sometimes, known only as the 'Order,' the term refers to El Sociedad. Some say it is pure myth, others insist that it exists and has existed for a millennium." He pauses to take another drink of wine. "El Sociedad is believed to be the remnants of the classical Maya priesthood. It is said that this secret organization still practices the ancient religion of the Maya, including polytheism and human sacrifice." A shiver runs through me. He continues speaking gravely, looking directly into my eyes. "It is an evil society. Do not speak of it to anyone else. Do not continue asking questions about it."

The tone of the evening has abruptly changed. We say goodnight soon after, promising to keep in touch. To my complete surprise, as we part, Padre Alejandro leans down and kisses me gently on the forehead, as if in benediction.

Senor Mateos' secretary calls us at the hotel the next morning. "I've found out at least part of what you want to know," she tells me in her precise, but heavily accented English. "I spoke with the Office of Evaluation. A friend of mine there looked into it for me. The piece seems to have been logged in on the 24th of September from the Museo Nationale de Merida. That is all my friend was able to find out, so far. She could not talk to the person who logged it in, because he does not work here any longer. It seems he quit, very unexpectedly, sometime in September."

"Oh," I say disappointed. "Is there any way of finding out where the artifact is now?"

She answers, "The notation in the log gives a room and a drawer or shelf number where each item is stored, but my friend did not have time to look for it."

"Do you think she would meet with us and take us to the location of the article? We would like to see for ourselves that it is safe." I feel awkward, putting it that way, and continued explaining. "Eduardo feels a bit proprietary about it, seeing as he is the one who found it." Again too much explanation, I sound funny even to myself.

Her answer is as gracious as ever, with no indication that she might find my demand out of the ordinary. "I'm sure she would be glad to do so, if she has the time. I will check with her and get back to you as soon as I can."

"Thank you so much," I reply and put down the phone.

It turns out that the secretary's friend can see us this afternoon, and so at 3 PM we are back at the museum. Eduardo is very nervous and jumps at every loud noise. He is sure that the watchers will notice two trips to the museum. "They were watching outside my house last night," he says. "I am sure of it. A big black car with no lights, two shadows in it, parked there across the street all night. It was not a car that belongs there." Adam and I look at him skeptically. "I thought about going out and knocking on the window, but what if they attacked me? There were two of them after all. Then I thought of calling the police, but what could I tell them? They would just laugh at me again. So, after all, I did nothing," he finishes dejectedly.

"Don't even think of confronting them," I say nervously. "They may be very dangerous men, if they're the ones behind the threats. You should call the police if it happens again."

"And tell them what?" Eduardo says. "They are tired of hearing from me and they do not believe me, anyway." Neither Adam nor I have an answer for that, but I think Eduardo is falling apart under the strain of the harassment.

We meet the secretary's friend, Mara, as arranged, in the Evaluation Department. She is a woman in her mid-twenties, short, heavyset, and with a dark complexion. Despite her weight, she moves with an energy and agility that leaves the rest of us hastening to keep up. She leads us down several flights of stairs, to the subbasement.

"This is the area where we store potentially perishable items. The vaults here are climate controlled for humidity and temperature. I take it the article you are interested in is of biodegradable material: cloth, or paper, or something like that?"

"Yes, it is," answers Adam cordially.

The woman stops outside a heavy metal door. On a small shelf, outside of it, is a ledger. "Each item contained in the vault is logged in and out in this book," Mara explains. "The description of the item, its museum ID number, the date it was entered, the date it was removed, and the date it was returned; are all recorded here. It also has the name of the person responsible for the action." I look over her shoulder at the ledger. All the information is entered in neat columns. Mara points to an entry and I read what is written. The entry for drawer 24E reads; September 24th, 2011—Codex-north central Yucatan—30 x 36 x 11.5 cms, hide wrapped parcel, not yet authenticated, Alejandro Juarez. There is nothing written in the column marked removed or returned. "So it is here," I breathe.

Mara enters a code into the key pad on the door, turns the handle, and we all enter. The lighting is dim and the room cool. It is about four feet wide and twenty feet long. The room is lined with numbered drawers on both sides, from the floor to the ceiling10 feet above. Mara leads us down the room, searching the numbers on the drawers as she passes them. Finally, she comes to a stop and points to a drawer on the left hand side of the room, about waist high. The drawer is marked 24E. "This is the one," she remarks and proceeds to open the drawer. Her, up till then, stoic demeanor is suddenly marred by a look of surprise, and then of anger. She spits out, "It's empty!"

We crowd around her, leaning over her shoulder to peer into the drawer. Sure enough it is empty. "It has been stolen," Eduardo moans.

"Or never put in," I say.

"This is impossible," Mara says loudly. "I'll have to get to the bottom of this." She appears for the first time to be put out at being involved with us, foreigners. She glares at us as if we are at fault.

"How could this have happened? I ask. "What about your security?"

The woman glares at me and snaps, "We have excellent security. Only those with proper authorization know the access codes and those are changed regularly. This isn't a high security vault, but not just anyone can get in." She is beginning to calm down. "No, it has to be a mistake of some kind. Someone has it out for evaluation and forgot to sign it out. Yes, that's it. Just an oversight, yes, that's it." She nods. Then another explanation seems to come to her. "Or it was just placed in the wrong drawer. That is easy enough to do." She slams drawer 24E shut, turns on her heels and heads back to the door, mumbling to herself. "I will get to the bottom of this. I'll check with everyone in the department, have every drawer checked. This is unconscionable. I'll find out who is responsible." She exits the vault and waits for us to follow. She continues muttering to herself, paying us no attention at all.

"You will keep us apprised of your investigation and notify us when the artifact is found?" asks Adam.

The woman starts, as she suddenly becomes aware again of our presence and the reason for it. "Yes, I will notify Senor Mateos' secretary and keep her abreast of developments," she says dismissively.

"Be sure you do," I say, with an edge to my voice.

Mara looks up at me with alarm, nods, and replies, "Of course I will." She hastily storms up the nearest stairway, leaving us to find our own way out. This we do with only minimal difficulty.

Once outside we make our way to the park again, and again hold a conference in lowered tones. I look at Eduardo. He is pale and shaken. "It is gone," are the first words he has spoken since the discovery of the empty drawer. "It is gone," he says again and he sinks onto a nearby bench."

"Yes," I say. "I wonder what it means? Is it just an error, a misplacement? But the fact that Alejandro, the person who received the Codex at the museum, resigned shortly after it was given to him, doesn't bode well for that being the case."

Adam nods and looks worried. Eduardo is paying no attention. He looks around furtively. "They are behind it," he says in a tight whisper. "They are behind it." Eduardo seems to be losing it, so shaken is he by the loss of the manuscript.

"Who's behind it?" says Adam looking at him closely. "We don't know who 'they' are."

Eduardo doesn't answer at once, again scanning the area. He seems to find nothing, but is obviously not relieved. "They took it," he says, as if making complete sense.

"But who are they?" I ask again in exasperation.

Eduardo shakes his head and looks defeated. "I don't know," he says. "I don't know who they are." He takes a deep breath and seems to come back to himself a little. He whispers to himself. "The Order. The Order." I strain to catch his words. "The Order." And he looks more frightened still, if that is possible. He stands up and walks away. Adam and I catch up with him. We make him promise to keep in touch, to keep a low profile, not to ask questions, and not make waves. Eduardo looks so depressed and frightened, we are sure he will keep that part of the promise, at least.

He walks away without looking back. Adam and I slowly walk back to the hotel.

The car sent by Senor Tierro, a sleek black limousine, arrives promptly at 7. The Oficina de Antiguedad is housed in an elegant, old building on the edge of the city. The large rotunda is crowded with beautifully dressed men and women. I feel underdressed in my simple, all purpose LBD, little black dress. I don't know anyone. I wish I hadn't come.

I am wandering around aimlessly, with an untouched glass of rather bad white wine in my hand, when a rich, melodious voice comes from behind me. "There you are, Professor O'Hara." He is smiling graciously, a handsome man, but all I can think of is Daniel's description of him, 'like a used car salesman.' "We have not yet met. I am Menos Tierro. I had the pleasure of meeting Dr. Allen and Senor Daniel Keith last summer." Here he looks around at the other guests nearby. "But where are your compatriots?"

"They had previous engagements and so were unable to come," I say.

"Too bad," he says, already having lost interest.

"What a beautiful room," I remark, just to have something to say.

"Let me show you about and introduce you to some of our guests." He takes my arm and guides me around the room, describing the works of art that grace the hall. He seems to know everyone and proceeds to introduce me to everyone we encounter. None of them seem the least bit interested in me, but all are flattered by his attention.

Senor Tierro asks the reason for my trip to Mexico. He seems unconvinced when I say it was just a pleasure trip. A little later, he remarks he has heard that my companions and I had visited the Museo Mexicana de Arqueologia the day before. I reply that, as we are all anthropologists, a visit to the Museum is to be expected. He smiles, but is not pleased by this answer. A short time later, he is called away to a discussion on the other side of the room, and I am mercifully left on my own. I don't like the man, too swarmy. I leave a few minutes later and take a cab back to the hotel. I'm bushed and fall into bed and asleep shortly after.

We fly back home the next morning.

III

February 16, 943 CE
10.5.14.10.5, 3 Chik'chan, 18 Sip
The Temple Library, Chichen Itza

It was late at night and yet Took Pak was seated at a small wooden table surrounded by many codices.[11] He had foregone his usual nightly stargazing as he had become mesmerized by what he was reading in these ancient manuscripts. His daytime hours were spent in copying more recent and less interesting works, often the rituals and incantations used in festival ceremonies or minor observations of seasonal variations in climate and astrology. After the other scribes had gone and he was alone in a small room in the basement of the Library, he would often pull the lesser known, more archaic tomes from the shelves. These works he would study, coming across information and mysteries that were new to him and actually unknown to most of the priests of the order. No one seemed to mind that he did this and no one ordinarily interrupted him in these late night sessions.

Tonight, however, Cho P'iit came to the doorway carrying a lantern. The old scribe peered into the room. "I see that you are still here, apprentice scribe. Rumor has it that you spend many nights in this chamber pouring over some odd manuscript or other. I take it you are not copying what has been assigned to you. What is it that attracts you so?" The old man asked as he entered the room.

Took Pak lifted his head in surprise as the head scribe entered the room. Never had he seen Cho P'iit here this late. "All of it interests me," he said. "But I do not do this when I should be doing what you ask of me. I do this late at night, when I will bother no one."

"So you work late at night and do not get the sleep that you require, even at your young age, and your work will suffer for it on the morrow. Your work is not so good that it can overcome a sleeping hand," the priest said snidely. He did not attempt to hide his dislike for his young apprentice. "And of what use could this study be to you? I think that you have aspirations beyond your station. Be that as it may," he continued, waving away Took Pak's attempt to reply, "I have another assignment for you, one that will take all of your insignificant talent to accomplish, even minimally. It is not my idea, I assure you. It comes from the Ah Kin Mai himself, I believe, by way of Sajal Ch'itz'aat, the High Priest's undersecretary, who seems to have some overinflated regard for your abilities. I told him that I would give you the assignment, against my better judgment. But, oh well, the worst result will only be the waste of good paper and ink."

Took Pak looked at the other man, knowing that Cho P'iit did not like him, but not knowing why. The truth was that Cho P'iit was jealous of Took Pak, for the older man saw in the young man intelligence and talent that he, himself, did not possess.

"What is this assignment?" asked Took Pak quietly, so as not to arouse Cho P'iit's contempt for him any further.

"It seems that the Ah Kin Mai wishes that a very ancient manuscript be copied. It is believed to be a codex produced in the time of Chan Bahlum II,[(4)] perhaps by his own hand. Be that as may be, it is very ancient. I have no idea why the Ah Kin Mai wants it transcribed now, after it has been ignored for so long. But this is what he wants and the task is to be given to you. Do not think that this will free you from your regular duties. It will not." Took Pak made to answer, but the older man forestalled him. "Follow me," he said tersely and left the room without another word or a backward glance.

He led Took Pak down a stairway and into a corridor that Took Pak had never been in before. At the end of the corridor, they came to an unremarkable door. Cho P'iit took the woven sash that he wore around his waist and from it selected a very old wooden key. This he inserted into a slot in the door and, with some manipulation, managed to unlock it. The door opened with significant effort. The old scribe entered, holding his lantern aloft, so as to illuminate a very small and narrow chamber. The room was lined with shelf after shelf of codices and smelled of dust and mold. From a shelf on the far wall, Cho P'iit took a large wooden box.

The box was heavy and it took a great deal of effort for the old man to get it down from the shelf and place it on the table in the center of the room. The box itself was unremarkable, but appeared to be old and was covered in dust. Using the wooden key he had used on the door, Cho Piit pried the lid from the box. From inside, he removed an object wrapped in fine leather made from deer hide. The leather was thin and worn with age, but was still soft and supple. He placed the bundle upon the table and, with great care, opened the wrappings. Took Pak leaned forward to see what lay within and what he saw took his breath away. Here was a beautifully bound manuscript. The cover was made from richly polished and ornately carved wood. The carvings depicted many intricate glyphs and astrological symbols. Took Pak gazed at them, fascinated, and reached out his hand to touch the wooden surface.

Cho P'iit pushed his hand away roughly and said, "Time for that later. These are the rules." He looked directly into Took Pak's face to get his complete attention. "No one else is to have access to this codex. It is not to leave this room. You are to speak of it to no one but Sajal Ch'itz'aat, the Ah Kin Mai or myself. And you are not to neglect your other tasks for this one. Do you understand?" He looked sternly at Took Pak, waiting for him to answer.

"I understand, and I will comply," Took Pak said. All he could think of was getting his hands on this beautiful manuscript and finding out what mysteries it might contain. The chief scribe slowly rewrapped the manuscript in its covering and replaced it in the box, which he left upon the table. He then turned toward the door. "It is late, time for you to get what little sleep you can before morning. You have a copy of the spring planting ritual to complete. This will have to wait until tomorrow night at the earliest," he said, with a nod of his head toward the box that lay on the table. He left the chamber and Took Pak followed without a word.

Took Pak could not sleep that night. All he could think of was that beautifully carved manuscript. What secrets could it possibly hold? And was it really the writing of Chan Bahlum II, said to be a long-ago king of the Maya from a far off city-state called Baakal. It was said that he was a great prophet and that he could foretell the future. Cha Mach, the astronomer, had told him that Chan Bahlum II had written down the paths of the planet and the ways of gods and the fortunes of the Maya people for many baktun into the future. Could this be what the manuscript held? If so, why had the Ah Kin Mai given the task to him?

The next day Took Pak went about his regular duties as if nothing out of the ordinary had happened the night before. Cho P'iit said nothing to him and gave no indication that anything had changed. Took Pak could not wait for the day to end. He found that copying the usual uninteresting manuscript he was working on to be more tedious than usual. Finally the day came to an end and all the others left. Took Pak did not even take time to go to the kitchens for a meal. Taking up a fresh taper, he made his way once more down to the small chamber in the sub-basement.

The door had been left unlocked and opened with the creak of disuse. On the table sat the box containing the codex. Took Pak opened the box and reverently took out the leather wrapped bundle. He sat at the table and opened it. He gazed down again upon the beautifully carved cover and ran his fingers over the glyphs and symbols. He recognized symbols for the sun and the moon and the sacred planet, Venus. He saw the symbols for Ku'kul'kan, the Sun god, Chaac, the god of the rain, K'u ix tz'it, the god of the maize, and Chaac Chel, the earth goddess. He saw the glyphs that proclaimed this as the work of Chan Bahlum II and the date on which it had been written, 9.12.13.8.6 (684 CE). Took Pak set aside the supplies he had brought with him, long sheets of parchment, corked vials of ink, and various quills. He needed first to examine the manuscript and this he did with wonder.

Took Pak ran his hand over the ornately carved wood that formed the cover piece of the manuscript. His fingers followed the carved symbols. He felt a warmth emanating from them. He could almost feel a pulsing sensation. He shook his head. "That cannot be," he thought, "This is a cold, inanimate object." But he could feel a power emanating from the article, as if the manuscript was releasing the spirits of the King who had written it centuries before.

Took Pak took a deep breath, and breathed in the musty smell of old parchment. He looked more closely at the hu'un and with trembling hands slowly opened the codex. Within the outer wooden covers, many sheets of very thin parchment were folded in accordion fashion. Each of these was covered with beautifully scripted hieroglyphs and pictographs. Took Pak gazed at the treasure before him, not taking in the meaning of the individual glyphs, but absorbing the majesty of the entirety. Somehow he felt connected to this work. Somehow he knew that he was meant to have the knowledge that it contained. Somehow he knew that this was why he was here, and that it would change his life.

From the dust that had collected upon the codex, he believed that he was the first person in a long time to have access to its secrets. He was honored and felt himself blessed. "But why," he thought, "had the Ah Kin Mai given this honor to me?"

With trepidation he went back to the first page and began to read, his fingers tracing the outline of each of the glyphs. That first page contained the Maya story of the creation of the world. It told of how the world was created and destroyed four times before this present creation. He knew the story well. It was the basis of the Mayan beliefs.

Over the next many months, Took Pak was fascinated by the revelations of the Chan Bahlum Codex. He spent long hours there in the chamber deep within the Temple Library, rarely leaving for food or sleep. He became thin and pale. He rarely went to the top of the Temple Observatory to watch the stars. Instead, he read of the stars and planets and their prophetic meanings as described in the codex. Chan Bahlum had been an intelligent man, as versed in the ways of the planets and stars and astronomy as Cha Mach was. He was as learned in the Mayan calendars as Sajal Yax Ahk, the master of novices, or any of the present day priests.

Halfway through the codex Took Pak came upon a section of the script that contained information that was entirely new to him. Here the writing was not just that of a King or an astronomer. Chan Bahlum was also a shaman, a seer, a prophet. Much of the rest of the codex was dedicated to prophecy. In its ancient pages Chan Bahlum had laid out the prophecies related to each of the kin, katun, bakun and each of the ages. Every day was given a prophetic meaning, every month, every year. Each kin (day) was prescribed an omen or forecast for good or for evil, and from these forecasts, prophecies designated the most auspicious days for the everyday occurrences in Mayan life. Chan Bahlum foretold when enemies from outside would attack, in what year the crops would be good and in which bad, and in what age the Maya would prosper and in which they would not.

Toward the end of the codex Took Pak came upon the most fascinating information of all. In this section, Chan Bahlum had described when and how the fifth, and last, creation of the world would end. To his great surprise, all of the many calendars of the Maya ended on that same day,

13.0.0.0.0, 4 Ahau, 3 Kankin and so the end of the fifth creation. Upon the last page of the codex was a depiction of how the world would end. The beautifully drawn illustration showed Chac Chel, the earth goddesses, pouring the waters of the earth, from clay ewers, upon the already sodden ground. The goddess flooded the world, drowning all that lived there; man, plant and animal. Took Pak stared at the illustrations in fascination and horror.

"And so our world, and the Maya, will come to an end," he whispered to himself. It was very late, the early hours of the morning, just before dawn. He should have long since been asleep, for he had to be back here to work in a few short hours. But Took Pak went back and reread the final passages of the codex. He returned to the calendars to determine just when the cataclysm was predicted to occur. After many tedious hours he came to the conclusion that the end would not come in his life time, or in the life time of anyone alive now. No, the prediction stated that the end would not occur for 3 batun (1200 years). Took Pak wondered who else among the priesthood knew of this prediction? Surely, the Ah Kin Mai, Koloome Ek Suutz, Chan Mach, and possibly Sajal Ch'itz'aat, would know of the prophecy. And yet none of them had made it common knowledge. Nowhere in the massive teachings of the priesthood could it be found. Why?

Took Pak heard the arrival of his fellow scribes in the corridors above his small cell and began to put the ancient codex back on the shelf. He left the Library to relieve himself and to get some bread and cacao for a meager breakfast and to provide a stimulant to help him get through the rest of the day without any sleep.

At the same time, the edge of the kitchen garden of the Ch'e'en household.

Ahkan sat in the small shed Nuxib Mak had built for her in the kitchen garden. He had built it almost a year ago, after Ko'lel had left this world for her final journey, to the underworld. She had been of a vast age and she had failed in the last months of her life. She told Ahkan that it was her time and that she was prepared for the journey and went willingly. Still Ahkan mourned her. The old woman of the forest was buried beneath the floor of her hut as was the custom.

Ko'lel had given Ahkan all her worldly belongings. These were few. She also gave her the tiny hut in the forest, as well. At first Ahkan had intended to move to the forest, to be where the people were used to going for treatment of their illnesses and wounds. But Ahkan's mother, Ak'a ch'iick, was doing poorly. Her health had been slowly deteriorating for many years, but in the last six months had showed a sharp decline. Ahkan did not feel that she could leave her mother alone with the servants, for the long days she spent caring for the Maya. Her aunt, NaabYutzil, was herself not well and spent most of her time cloistered in her apartments. Ahkan felt that her aunt's problems were due to the falling fortunes of the Ch'e'en family. Both of Ahkan's cousins, Janab ha and Kiichpak pas, were married and no longer lived in the family home. The girls seldom visited, consumed by their own households and young children.

This morning Ahkan was out in her shed before the sun rose. Yet early as it was, she already had three patients waiting. A local farmer had brought his head slave to have a festering wound treated. The heavy stone ax that the man had been using to clear the farmer's land had slipped and sliced into the man's leg. The wound, though swollen and red, was draining. Ahkan cleansed the wound with clean water and the juice of the aloe plant, and then applied a poultice of steeped corn silk and cacao. She bound the wound with the leaves of the bakalche' tree. She then instructed the man in the care of the wound and gave him a supply of the salve. She told him he needn't come back, unless the redness and swelling did not resolve. The man was young and healthy, so Ahkan was sure that he would heal without permanent damage.

She did not feel as hopeful about her next patient, a young boy of ten. He had fallen from a tree several weeks before. His family lived many miles from the city and was very poor, with many other children. The boy's grandmother, who had some experience caring for the minor illnesses and accidents of her family and the neighbors, had tended the break herself. However, the broken bone had gone through the skin and muscle of the boy's leg. It had become infected. The boy suffered from malnutrition as a result of failing crops and the family having too many mouths to feed. Too late, they brought the boy to Ahkan. The father carried him on his back for the long miles. They arrived, before the sun, having walked all night, and by that time the boy was delirious with fever. There was little that Ahkan could do. She bathed his burning body and cleaned the festering wound. She gave him a potion which she knew would not cure him, but would help to ease the torment he was experiencing. It might also hasten his death, but his death was inevitable no matter what she did. Better that he die sooner and suffer less. The father sat beside his son, holding the boy's hand and patiently waiting for what he now knew would come.

Ahkan spent the rest of the morning caring for a variety of minor illnesses. First, an old woman with a persistent cough, which Ahkan treated with a tincture made from the poppy. The cough would clear, as the rainy season came to an end, only to recur in the next cycle. But the tincture would make her feel good enough to return to her garden and cook fire. The old woman blessed her for her care and left with the healing brew. She left Ahkan with some medicinal herbs she had gathered on her way. Ahkan thanked her gratefully, as she would have had to gather them herself if the local folk did not provide them as payment for her services.

Ahkan looked at the bundle of oleander that she knew would be helpful for her mother's worsening headaches. Headaches that Ahkan knew would not be cured by any treatment that she knew. But the plants the old woman had given her would help to ease them and give her mother some much needed sleep during the long nights. Ahkan mused as she went out into the gardens to harvest the plants and herbs that grew there. Her father was aging as well, much of it caused by worry over her mother and the dwindling resources of the family. Ahkan knew that the time would come when she would be without both her parents; a time not so long in the future. Ahkan thought over all the losses she had sustained in the past few years; the death of Ko'lel, the wise woman and her mentor, her cousins who had married and so left for their husbands and children, her brother who was a renegade and fugitive, her mother, into illness, who could no longer mother her, and of course, most of all, Took Pak, who had abandoned her for the Temple. She had her patients and her calling, of course, and that sustained her. But she was lonely. She had to admit she was not happy, but she was somewhat content, or at least resigned.

In the chamber of the Ah Kin Mai that same day.

The Ah Kin Mai, Koloome Ek Suutz, and Sajal Ch'itz'aat stood before the small personal altar in the corner of the Ah Kin Mai's austere chamber. Each man faced the altar rather than his companion, as if communing with the gods, not each other.

"The boy came to me last night," said Sajal Ch'itz'aat in no more than a whisper, as if keeping a secret even from the gods. "He was greatly excited. He came to tell me of all the mysteries he had uncovered in that old codex of Chan Bahlum, as if he were the first to read the prophecies."

"It is good that he came to you before anyone else. It shows that he holds you in high regard and that you have his trust," replied the Ah Kin Mai, not turning to look at his subordinate, but keeping his gaze upon the small carved figures upon the altar. He paused for a moment and then added, "And what did you tell him?"

Sajal Ch'itz'aat hesitated for a moment and then said, tentatively, "I showed moderate interest. He rambled on at great length and with great enthusiasm. Once his initial outburst was over, I congratulated him on his excellent research. I assured him that those of us of the Inner Circle were aware of the writings and of the prophecies." The priest smiled to himself. "He looked crestfallen. I thought for a moment, he might cry." And he laughed unkindly. "What did he expect? Did he think that he was the first, in hundreds of years, to come across these momentous words?"

Koloome Ek Suutz ignored the other priest's remarks and, still not looking at him, asked again, "And what did you tell him?"

"I told him to keep this information to himself, to share it only with you or with me." The secretary looked a little confused and defensive. "I told him exactly what you told me to tell him."

The Ah Kin Mai finally turned to look at him. "Of course, of course you did," he placated the other man. There was a longer pause this time, as he turned back to the altar and studied the beautifully carved figure of the god of rain, Chaac. He took a deep breath, and finally continued. "How much do you think he understands of the implications of what we have allowed him to discover? Do you think he has any realization of the power that the information might give him?"

Although Sajal Ch'itz'aat realized that these questions were rhetorical, and that the Ah Kin Mai was really asking them of himself or of his gods, he could not keep himself from answering. "As you said before, your Excellency, he is but a boy and a naïve one at that. I do not think he has any wish for power."

"Not now, perhaps," the Ah Kin Mai mused. "But he is intelligent, very intelligent. Although he is now caught up in his fascination for the mysteries and the learning, there may come a time, in the future, when he will see beyond the mysticism and see the practicalities. We must watch him even closer; make a pretense of listening to his discoveries and assumptions, assure him that we have plans in place, and that the world is progressing as it should." Again he paused, marshaling his thoughts. This time Sajal Ch'itz'aat waited without speaking. "And the other thing that we must do," and the Ah Kin Mai turned and looked directly into Sajal Ch'itz'aat face. "And this is extremely important. We must keep him away from the King. He must have no chance of telling the Ajaw any of this, for you know that the King is a true believer, and he would take all of this, the mysticism, the prophecy, the warnings, to heart. This would give Took Pak more power than he could ever dream of." The Ah Kin Mai turned back to his contemplation of the altar and waved Sajal Ch'itz'aat away. The other man left the room without another word.

February 27, 943 CE
10.5.14.10.16, 1 K'ib, 9 Sots
The Temple gardens

Took Pak spent his midmorning break each day walking in the kitchen gardens of the Temple. He had spent the better part of the last year hidden away in the bowels of the Temple Library, pouring over his dusty manuscripts. At the end of this time, he found that he had lost weight and was paler than he had been the year before. He found that, at the end of the day, his eyes burned with the strain and his head ached. His muscles had grown weak and he found himself short of breath from simply climbing the stairs to the top of the Observatory. Feeling that his health was in jeopardy, he was convinced that he needed to do something to remedy the situation. And so, he returned to the midday work in the garden. Took Pak's body had grown firm and strong again in the last few months. His hands were calloused, his back straight, and his skin warmly bronzed.

Nuxib Mak, his father's old servant, tended the gardens at that time each day. Took Pak, as a further means of strengthening his weakened body, took to helping the old man with the digging and the removal of stones from the earth. The two men, the young priest and the old servant, spoke little. They were comfortable in each other's company and felt no need for idle conversation. Took Pak had not realized how much he missed the human interaction he had forsaken for his studies, until he had resumed even this meager contact. On the warm spring days, Nuxib Mak was engaged in the heavy tilling and turning of the soil in preparation for the spring planting.

Took Pak asked in a perfunctory manner, as he did each time they met, after his family. Nuxib Mak responded each time, in much the same manner, that little seemed to change over time. Today, however, when Took Pak asked, the gardener stopped what he was doing and leaning upon his spade, said quietly, "I have sad news." Took Pak braced himself for what he was about to hear. Nuxib Mak, seeing the young man's alarm, raised his hand in negation and hurried on. "No, no. Your parents and Ahkan are well. It is Ahkan's mother who is unwell. I fear she is dying."

"I am sorry for that," Took Pak said, but he visibly relaxed. "It must be very hard for Ahkan. Is there nothing that she can do for her Na?"

"This illness is beyond even Ahkan's considerable healing powers. Only the gods can intervene now. It is not a sudden illness. It has been coming on for years. I know that Ahkan is saddened, but she is resigned." Having finished what, for him, was a long speech, Nuxib Mak went back to his hoeing.

Took Pak did not go back to his work right away, but stood contemplating the truth that this news had brought him. In his mind, all those he had left behind in his childhood home remained unchanged. He remembered them as he had last seen them. And yet, the realization came, they would have aged in this time. He realized that both his sisters were married and had children of their own. They were no longer the young girls he remembered, but grown women. Both his parents were growing older. Did they suffer from the debilitation of old age? Had they been ill as Ahkan's mother had been? And what of his brothers? Chawak K'ab' was now running the family business. The business was failing, as all the other businesses of the city were, if the rumors that reached the Temple were true. And Ah Tz'on K'an was away with the weakened army in the northern reaches of the city-state. How were they faring? Took Pak felt ashamed of himself for not thinking of them more often. And Ahkan, sweet butterfly? She was a mature woman now, as well. He gradually brought his thoughts back from these useless regrets, and returned to the tilling.

After a moment, he said to Nuxib Mak, "Send my condolences to Ahkan. Tell her how sorry I am for her mother's illness. Tell her I will say a special prayer to the earth goddess, Chac Chel, to spare her Na further pain and make her journey to the next world an easy one." Nuxib Mak looked up in surprise, for it had been years, since Took Pak had sent any message to his family.

At the Ch'e'en home, the same day.

Ahkan knelt beside her mother's bed; bathing the dying woman's feverish forehead with cool water and wiping her mouth of the thick spittle that came with the incessant cough. Ak'a ch'iick had been unresponsive for much of the morning, but now she roused. She turned her eyes to the sweet face of her daughter kneeling next to her. "You must not be sad," she gasped. "I am so tired. I am ready for the journey and will not miss this world at all." She closed her eyes and Ahkan thought she had relapsed into sleep. But after a moment, she opened her eyes again and said weakly, "If only I knew that you would be alright. If only I knew that you would come to no harm."

Ahkan took her mother's skeletal hand in hers and soothed it gently. "Go peacefully, dear Na. You need not worry for me. The wise woman, Ko'lel, told me, long ago, that she saw for me a long life. She saw me an old woman, like herself, living in the forest and caring for the people long into the future."

Ak'a ch'iick breathing slowed and became easier. Her eyes closed. The grasp she had on Ahkan's hand relaxed and she was gone. Ahkan knelt there for a long time, thinking of the many things her mother had given her: her strength, her perseverance, her resolve, and the assurance that she was loved. Ahkan remembered all the times that they had shared, particularly in the last four years. She would miss her mother's company, but she would not want her mother to remain with the pain that she had suffered over the last few months. And so she let her go.

March 9, 943 CE
10.5.14.11.6, 11 Kimi, 19 Sots
The Temple Library

Took Pak had been spending every night into the early mornings pouring over the ancient manuscript, copying its intricate hieroglyphs and illustrations into a new, pristine codex. It was a labor of love. It was taking much longer than his usual work, because he spent as much time reading and digesting its contents as copying.

One night, as he prepared to put the manuscript away, tired and ready for his bed, he noticed a small slip of parchment protruding from the back of the h'un. He carefully removed it from between the ancient pages and gently unfolded it. It appeared to be a scrap of parchment, torn from another codex, perhaps. It was old and faded, but not as old as the Bahlum Codex. It was covered in hieroglyphs, penned by a skillful hand. Took Pak looked intently at what was written there.

'In the mouth of the serpent rests
The means of salvation.
When the two halves are of equal length,
Under the glorious sun find it, beneath the stone,
Where the serpent disappears.
Pass on what is written to the generations to come,
As I, a lowly Aj K'uhm, have done to yours.
So might the fortunes of the Maya be preserved.'

Took Pak sat studying the paper for a long time, but could come to no determination of its meaning. His head ached from the effort and he could no longer keep his eyes open. With reluctance he carefully placed the Bahlum manuscript back into the box and returned it to its shelf, but not before replacing the scrap of paper where he had found it.

IV

March 9, 2012
12. 19. 19. 3. 13, 3 Ben, 1 Cumku
The familiar room

The two men sat across from each other, as they often did. The man in authority sat behind the ornate desk. The subordinate sat in a straight backed chair facing the desk. This man sat forward, leaning earnestly toward his superior. He appeared to be in a panic, wringing his hands and talking rapidly in a whining voice. The man behind the desk was impassive, seeming to be unmoved by what the other man had to say.

"They were here," the man in the chair said, throwing his hands about in exclamation, "here in Mexico City, the Americans from the University.

They met with Dr. Eduardo Gomez. They all went to the Museum, looking for the Codex." He trailed off weakly, out of breath.

"I know," the man behind the desk said, unconcerned. He did not look up at the other man, but was absorbed with some papers on his desk.

"You know?" replied the subordinate. "But this is disastrous. They now know that the Codex is definitely missing."

His superior looked up and gave him a cold, pitying smile. "But they knew that already. It is of no importance that the Codex remains hidden any longer." The man across from him gasped in surprise and the man behind the desk gave an icy laugh. "The reason for taking the manuscript, in the first place, was so that I might review it before anyone else, to determine if it were the real thing and if it contained anything damaging to our cause. That I have done. The second reason, to prevent general knowledge of what the artifact might be and what it might contain, was to keep it from our enemies." He paused and again seemed to study the papers on his desk. "Even with the existence of the Codex known, I believe we have the authority and power, as a group, to keep its content out of the public knowledge for as long as need be. As regards our friends from the States, they have reproductions of the entire manuscript, according to the spy in their midst, and specimens to prove its authenticity, as well. Why should we panic over a bit of fuss they make at the Museo Mexicana de Arqueologia. It discredits them, not us."

The words of his superior did not seem to calm the other man. "What do you plan to do next, Monsignor?"

"I plan to continue to put obstacles in their way. The Codex will remain lost, for now. The Museo Mexicana de Arqueologia will put out the word that it is out being evaluated and that there was an error in documentation." He stopped and looked up menacingly at the other man. "The other matter is of greater importance and needs to be done immediately. You are to get in touch with our spy among the Americans. Get all the information you can about where these duplicates and specimens might be. Then you are to contact Carlos." He added snidely, "You remember our associate Carlos? You are to give him all the pertinent information and instruct him to find and retrieve all of it." An evil look came over his face. "Make sure you tell him, nothing less than success will be tolerated. No slip ups like last time."

"Si, Monsiegnor. This I will do."

CHAPTER TEN

I

880 CE
10.2.11.0.18

Mayan Myth

And to the Queen, a child was born,
At the winter solstice.
A boy child, the prayed for heir.
But the child was small, weak, and misshapen.
His skin was sallow, his eyes dull,
His right arm withered and his back bent.

The King refused to claim him,
The queen shrank from any contact with him.
A wet nurse was found for the queen refused to suckle him.
The Maya saw the child as an omen,
That the gods were displeased
And the Maya would not prosper.

The fortunes of the Maya went into decline,
The rains did not come
And the crops withered in the fields.
The priests demanded ever more tribute,
And more sacrifice
But nothing was sufficient to appease the gods.

The King fell into a deep despair.
He prayed and offered up blood sacrifice in atonement.
The queen retired to her chambers
Leaving the child in the care of strangers.
The Prince was unloved
And hidden away, out of sight.

The Ah Kin Mai lay the blame
For the misfortune of the Maya at the child's feet
And the Prince was reviled and shunned.
The Maya did not prosper and the people suffered.
They blamed the King and his heir,
And turned their faces from the throne.

The fortunes of the Maya changed.
The sun rose in the sky
And shone for days on end,
Scorching the earth
Burning the crops in the fields.
And there was no grain to harvest.

The rains did not fall.
The grains dried in the fields,
The fruit withered on the vine,
And the game and the fowl perished.
The Maya had little to eat,
And the old and the very young died.

What little they were able to harvest
From the fields and the gardens
Was demanded by the priests to appease the gods.
The Maya had nothing to feed their children.
The army did not have enough to feed their legends
And were too weak to protect the people.

There was no plunder to pay the tribute to the Temple.
And the Maya did not prosper.

II

March 7, 2012
12.19.19.3.11, 1 Chuen, 19 Kayab
The University

Our return to the university and work is anti-climatic. I really have little time to reflect on our trip, or to decide what to do next. My time is taken up with tasks I had put off for the five days spent away. Carli is still away, spending time with her mother, so I do not have my usual sounding board to talk over what had taken place in Mexico. Daniel is very busy, totally absorbed in preparations for his dissertation defense, so I do not see him at all in my first few days back. I'm not sure if I am ready to discuss the trip with him yet, anyway. I feel I need to come to some kind of understanding of it, in my own mind first, and I just don't have the time.

Eduardo begins calling again, every few days, but the calls are brief and give little new information. They are desultory. Eduardo sounds depressed and withdrawn. The contact is merely a formality. He calls because I had insisted that he keep me informed.

A week after our return, I feel I need to bring the others up to date about the disappearance of the Codex and get some input from them as to how we should proceed. I call Professor Allen's office, make an appointment for early the next morning, and then notify the others, requesting their attendance. Carli is still away, so I don't expect her to attend. All the others, Calvin, Brian, Adam, and Daniel, e-mail me that they intend to come.

Professor Allen is surprised and a bit bewildered to see all of us in his office the next morning. He takes it in stride, however, and greets us warmly, if absent-mindedly. He requests additional chairs, so that we can all sit, and settles us hospitably. Once the formalities of "How are you?" "How is the semester going?" are completed, I come to the reason for the meeting. I start by reminding everyone of Adam's and my recent trip to Mexico. Professor Allen seems surprised at first, as if it has slipped his mind, then suddenly remembers and asks after Eduardo.

"He is frazzled," I reply. "He looked as if he hadn't slept. He was unkempt and was constantly looking over his shoulder."

"Poor man," mutters the Professor, shaking his head sadly. "Poor man."

I continue, sure that the Professor took this description of his colleague as undeniable proof that the 'poor man' was unbalanced. "He was perfectly lucid," I interject, perhaps a bit too aggressively. "He is back to work and seems to have recovered from his injuries." I say.

"Good. Good," says the Professor, still shaking his head.

"But . . . ," I continue, "he is still receiving threats, death threats, as well as threats to his family." The Professor's brows rise quizzically and he frowns, obviously not believing a word of this. I plow on. "He is sure he is being followed. That someone is watching him, following him. But despite this, he went with us to the museum. He is still determined to find out what is going on with the Codex." I stop to both catch my breath and collect my thoughts.

The Professor breaks in to ask, "And what did you find out?" There is a note of impatience and frustration in his voice.

I am about to give an angry retort, as I find this lack of real concern for his friend disgusting. Adam, obviously picking up on my mood, takes over the narrative. He gives a complete, but concise, recital of our visit to the museum and our meeting with the Director of Acquisitions and his apparent disability. Adam then describes our trip to the underground vault, only to find the Codex missing. There is a general gasp of astonishment from Daniel and Brian. The Professor seems to wave off the pronouncement, as if it is of little consequence. Calvin makes no reaction at all, which is typical, I suppose.

"The C . . . codex is gone?" stammered Brian. "B . . . but how? Who? W . . . Why?"

I smile over at him. Just like him to get to the central questions immediately. "Exactly," I say. "All pertinent questions and put so succinctly," I praise him. This breaks the tension that the announcement had caused, as the others laugh quietly. It also gives me a chance to get my aggravation under control. "Exactly," I repeat. "How was it taken from a supposedly secure facility, like the museum, without anyone knowing?"

"Or," interjects Daniel, speaking for the first time, "had it ever been there in the first place? Did it ever leave Merida?"

"It must have," argues Adam. "It had been logged into the vault and assigned an ID number and a drawer. But the drawer was empty. Of course," he adds, as an afterthought, "the employee who signed it in quit suddenly in the interim and was unavailable for us to talk to." He pauses and then continues. "Senorita Mara, who showed us the vault, offered the explanation that the Codex had just been misfiled."

The Professor gets up while we're discussing this point and crosses to the window, where he is staring out at a fine snow that is falling on the courtyard below. "Of course, that is the obvious explanation. And, as you know, the simplest explanation is usually the correct one. All of this cloak and dagger intrigue is ridiculous," he says with finality.

"A check of the nearby drawers didn't turn up our Codex," comments Adam. "Senorita Mara assured us that she would personally supervise an intensive search of all the museum's collections. She seemed to take the Codex's disappearance as a personal affront.

"S . . . so we'll just, just have to wait?" asks Brian, clearly not liking the prospect.

"Looks like it," replies Adam, with a laugh and a hint of condescension that is his usual approach to anything Brian has to say.

"And the other questions?" queries Daniel. "The who and the why? I fail to think of any reasonable answer to either of those questions. Who would want an unauthenticated artifact and, more importantly, why?"

"Just what Adam, Eduardo, and I concluded. It just doesn't make any sense," I say with frustration.

"And if it doesn't make any sense?" says Daniel, again in his professorial voice.

"If it doesn't make sense with what we know, then we just don't have all the facts." I mimic him, with a rueful laugh, and smile over at him.

"But h . . . how do we go about getting more f . . . facts?" says Brian, looking from one to the other of us. We all look at each other with what feels like a collective shrug.

Adam finally breaks the silence. "Wait. I suppose the museum is on it. We just need to wait until they find the Codex, or don't find it. What else can we do?" And he actually does shrug his shoulders in resignation.

I, for one, am not willing to give up quite that easily and to my surprise neither is Daniel. "We are all going on about the missing Codex," he says, "and yes, the actual Codex is missing, but . . ." and here he looks directly at me, "the information from the Codex isn't missing. Is it?" Here he glances at Brian. "I understand you've made great headway at deciphering what the Codex contains."

"W . . . well yes, yes," Brian stammered. "I have it all de . . . deciphered. Don't know what it all means y . . . yet. But I have words for all the h . . . hieroglyphs."

"You do?" remarks Adam in surprise, clapping Brian on the back. "Great job," he adds, but there is something in his manner that makes me sure he doesn't really mean it. Jealousy, I suppose.

"And there are other sources of information that we have," Daniel goes on. He pauses for effect, then continues, "We have the pictures, detailed pictures of the artifact and the first examination of the Codex. These give us information about how and where it was hidden, its construction, and the character and placement of the glyphs. These clues should go far in allowing us to estimate a date for when it was written. And finally," he pauses again and looks at me. He has all of our riveted attention. "Finally," he says in a conspiratorial, half mocking tone, "we have pieces of the actual Codex, pieces of the parchment and the wrappings themselves. Don't we?" And again he looks directly at me.

"Of course we do," I almost shout in excitement. I had forgotten this in the general excitement of deciphering the manuscript and the disappearance of the Codex. How could I have forgotten our little act of smuggling and the contraband we had brought back with us from the Yucatan. "And we have soil and rock samples from the cave," I add. "We don't need the original Codex." I realize what I have just said and add guiltily. "I mean, we do need to find the Codex, but there is a world of information we can gain from these specimens, until we find it."

"So, that information is where?" asks Adam off handedly.

"With the files and boxes we brought back with us from the Yucatan, in the store room down in the basement, I suppose. That's where it should be. In the basement," I say. "We just need the key." I look over at the Professor, who is still standing at the window.

He pulls his eyes away from the scene outside that has held his attention for so long. He returns to where the rest of us sit. He takes a key ring from his pocket and extracts one of the keys from it. I reach out my hand to take the key, but the Professor folds it into the palm of his hand. He looks at me and says, "You know, I did not, and still do not, approve of our absconding with Mexican artifacts without the permission of the government. And I regret my complicity in it. Its legality is questionable at best." He pauses to impress us with the seriousness of the matter. "I should, even at this late date, notify the Mexican Office of Antiquities and return the materials to them." I gasp at the suggestion and begin to protest. "I won't however," the Professor continues, before I can respond. "It would be an embarrassment for the University and would certainly jeopardize our acquisition of permits for any digs in the future." He rolls the key in his hand, looks down at it with regret, and then hands it to me.

I take the key humbly. Any response to his objections is unnecessary and would be counterproductive at this point. I say with humility, "Thank you," and I leave it at that.

"Just do not make waves," the Professor admonishes, turning back to the window again, a gesture of dismissal. The rest of us rise and head for the door. "Don't make me regret this," he adds, as an afterthought, clearly unhappy with the situation.

Once out in the hallway with the door closed behind us, I put the key into the pocket of my jacket and turn to the others. I don't know what to say.

"Well, that certainly was uncomfortable," remarks Daniel with a frown.

I smile skeptically. I agree with Daniel, but have no intention of letting Professor Allen interfere with what I intend to do.

"So w . . . when do we, do we make a trip to the basement?" asks Brian.

"I'm afraid now isn't a good time for me," replies Daniel. "I have a class right now, for which I am already late."

I gasp and look at my watch. "So do I," I say. "We'll have to make it later today. I have class or appointments until after 5. What about the rest of you?"

"So do I," adds Daniel. "Let me know what you decide. Must go." And he takes off down the hallway toward his office.

"I have class this evening until at least 9," says Adam. "If you don't need my help, go when you can."

"I . . . I have classes tonight t . . . too," stutters Brian. "I'd like to . . . to come. But I can't miss class."

We reach the elevator while we talk and take it to my office on the third floor. The others follow me to my door.

"Have a class this evening. Can't get out of it," says Calvin, speaking for the first time since leaving Professor Allen's office. "And I'd really like to go with you. Would like to look through the files we brought back.

My original drawings of the Codex cover are with them. I want them for reference."

I am surprised at Calvin's expression of his wish to go with us and at his uncharacteristic burst of loquacity. "Well," I say with resignation, "we can put it off until tomorrow. The boxes wouldn't be going anywhere, I suppose. They've waited this long. How about 10 tomorrow morning?" I hate to wait, even a day longer, but I also don't want to make the trip down into an empty sub-basement, all by myself, either.

"That's fine with me," responds Calvin.

"Good, good for me t . . . too," adds Brian.

"I'll check my calendar," says Adam.

We reach my office. I deposit my briefcase on my chair, take the key from my pocket and lock it in my top desk drawer. I turn back to the other three, grouped in my office doorway, as I grab my lecture notes for class. "So until tomorrow. Ten AM. Here," I say, picking up my briefcase and heading to class. "Have a good day," I call over my shoulder.

I rush from class the next morning to find Adam, Calvin, and Brian waiting for me, outside my office. "Ready?" I say, as I retrieve the key to the storeroom from my desk drawer.

"S . . . sure," responds Brian. I can hear the excitement in his voice. It matches my own.

With a wide grin at him, I reply "Then let's get this show on the road." And I head down the hall to the elevator.

Calvin pulls himself away from the wall he has been leaning against languidly. "Sure, let's go. I have class at noon," he says, and follows us at a leisurely pace.

Adam smiles. "Onward and downward," he says with a laugh, clearly in better spirits than yesterday. We take the elevator to the sub-basement. Adam sings softly to himself, all the while, "Down, down, down, down, down."

"I . . . I never knew there was a s . . . sub-basement in this building," says Brian. "N . . . never been down here before."

The elevator doors slide open and we exit into a grey, ill lit, narrow corridor: grey walls, grey doors, and grey concrete floor. I look at the key in my hand. The number SB113 is engraved on its surface. "113," I say and begin down the corridor, checking the numbers on each of the doors.

"101 . . . 102 . . . 103 . . ." Adam recites as we pass each door. We come to the end of the hallway. The corridor continues to the left. As we turn the corner, we see Daniel standing outside a door a short way down the passage, waiting for us.

"Hi," I say as we approach him. I am surprised to see him and surprised that he knew which room it was.

"Good morning," he responds, good-naturedly. "About time you got here. It's kind of spooky down here, especially when you're all by yourself," he adds with a laugh.

The door behind Daniel reads SB 113. I insert the key into the lock. I have a feeling of acute anticipation and rising excitement. The key turns easily and the door swings open, noiselessly. I reach in and run my hand along the right side of the door, feeling for the light switch. I flick the switch up and a brilliant, overhead fluorescent light comes on, blinding me for an instant. I hear a gasp from behind me. As my vision clears I see why, and cry out in astonishment.

The room is a shambles. The four men crowd into the doorway at my cry, and survey the room silently, with equal astonishment. The small, windowless room is in total disarray. Emptied boxes and files are piled in the center of the floor. Papers and equipment are strewn around the room. All of the shelves that line the walls are empty. The five of us just stand in the doorway, unable to speak, unable to move, unable to believe what we see.

Daniel is the first to recover. "Oh, my God," he breathes. "What a mess."

"An understatement, to say the least, more like a catastrophe," I think.

"G . . . gone!" whispers Brian. "Do you think they t . . . took the ar . . . ar . . . things? Why, why?" He moans, clearly distraught. The rest of us stay silent. We don't have an answer. Brian continues shaking his head as if trying to clear it. "And, and how did they know the artifacts were h . . . here?" he adds, sounding bewildered.

"How indeed?" I think.

"Wait a minute," interjects Adam. "How do we know they found the artifacts or even if that was what they, whoever they are, were looking for?" I look at him as if he's crazy. I just know it has to be the artifacts that they were after. "Well, there is a lot of expensive equipment stored down here, as well," he continues defensively. "It is much more likely someone would know about the equipment than about what we brought back from Mexico. Well, isn't it?" He looks from one of us to the other for some hint of agreement. Getting no answer, he adds, "What's more, we don't even know when all this," he indicates the mess with a sweep of his hand, "happened."

"That is true . . . I suppose," Calvin says tentatively. "Before we jump to conclusions, let's look through this . . . stuff. See if the specimens are here or not."

Daniel seems to come to himself, looking thoughtful. "Sensible suggestion. Let's see if we can make some order out of this chaos and find out what is missing, shall we?" He enters the room and begins moving the empty boxes from the middle of the floor.

I sink down on an overturned crate against the wall next to the door. I feel deflated and defeated. My legs just won't support me any longer. I feel like crying, but am determined not to do so in front of the others. I feel like crying, and then I feel like screaming, and then I just get mad. "Damn 'them," I think.

Brian and Calvin begin picking up the empty files and scattered papers from the floor, placing them in neat piles on the empty shelves. Adam collects the pieces of equipment and puts them back into boxes. Daniel pats me on the shoulder, then pulls his cell phone from his pocket and calls the campus police.

The University cops arrive about a half hour later. By that time we have made some progress in bringing some order to the mess. The University police are unimpressed by the break in. They give the scene a desultory look and, then give us a hard time about disturbing the scene before their arrival. They are, otherwise, disinterested. They tell us to see if we can tell if anything is missing and to make a full written report in the next 48 hours. And they leave.

In the next two hours we go through every file, box, and piece of paper in the room. The files and the box containing the evidence from the Codex are nowhere to be found. No little zip-lock bags of dirt, stone, pieces of parchment, or shreds of cloth are here. None of the photos or notes we had taken when first opening the hidden bundle are here. I feel empty, flat. We are really at a dead end now. The Codex and all of the evidence are gone.

I return to my office defeated, dejected, all of the eagerness and anticipation of the morning gone. How can we possibly solve the mystery surrounding the Codex now? I feel, again, like crying. Then I laugh at myself. "Don't be ridiculous," I tell myself, "and don't give up so easily." True, we no longer have the means to authenticate the codex, in the absence of the original or pieces of it, but we still have the computer record in the photographs we had taken. We can still work at deciphering what it says and, perhaps, why someone is so intent on preventing us from doing just that. Certainly the theft is a disappointment, but it need not be a catastrophe or the end of our work.

Of course, I reason with myself, there is another and more ominous interpretation of the break-in. There are only 7 of us who knew of the existence of the articles and records from the Yucatan. And there are only 6 who knew that we intended to retrieve them from the storeroom that morning. "That means," I think, "that one of us is the thief. Since I am sure I am not the culprit, that means, one of the other five is the perpetrator or told someone else who instigated the break in.

But who? Which of them and why? Until I know the answer to that I can no longer trust or confide in any of them. This realization leaves me feeling isolated and alone. Then I think of Carli. Carli is completely above suspicion. She wasn't at the meeting in the Professor's office yesterday and, therefore, hadn't known of our plans regarding the evidence. Thank God for Carli. At least I still have one person I can trust. I just wish she'd get back to school soon."

I stay late, finish grading papers for the next morning's classes and make sure my lecture notes are in order for the following day. Tired and depressed, I know I won't feel like cooking when I get home, so I stop at a Chinese restaurant for take-out on the way. I park the car in the lot behind my apartment building, grab my bags and briefcase, and head for the door, groping for my keys in my purse as I walk. I open the security door, grab my mail from the mail box, and climb the stairs to my second-floor apartment. I am rifling through the mail, not paying attention, as I reach out to put the key in my apartment door. I stop, suddenly aware that the door is ajar. My immediate thought is that somehow I had forgotten to close the door after myself as I left this morning, but that's something I'd never done before. Locking my door, as I leave, is a habit, second nature. I do it automatically, without thinking.

I push the door open and enter. Then a second thought comes to me, someone has been inside. And then I think, they may still be here. I should, right now, run, but of course I don't. I reach up, instead, and flick on the light in the hallway. The hallway is empty. I stop and listen. Silence, I hear nothing.

I turn to the left and enter the living room, turning on the overhead light as I go. The room looks undisturbed, everything appears to be as I left it that morning. I drop my bags and briefcase on the couch and head for the dining room. I can see, by the light from the living room, that it too is empty and untouched. I tread softly, now, as I move from the carpeting to the hard wood floor. If there is someone still in the apartment, I don't want them to hear me. I then nearly laugh out loud, thinking, "What am I doing? If there is a burglar here, then I shouldn't be."

I listen again, still no sounds. I continue to the kitchen, throwing on the light as I enter the room. Again the room looks untouched and is empty. I begin to second-guess myself. Maybe I had forgotten to close and lock the front door when I left this morning. I quickly check the back door. It's closed, double locked, with the safety chain in place.

Emboldened, I proceeded more quickly. I reenter the hallway. The three remaining rooms are now on my left: the bedroom, the bathroom, and my study, each of them dark. I go into the bedroom. It is empty too and, at first I think, as undisturbed as the other rooms. But something is odd. I had made the bed that morning, but now the edge of the bedspread is turned up, as if someone has peaked under the bed. I look at the rest of the room, more closely, and find more evidence of an intruder. The drawer of my bedside table is ajar and, when I look inside, I can see that the odds and ends I keep here have been disturbed. I can't tell if anything has been taken, for I honestly don't know what I keep there. The top drawer of my bureau has also been disturbed, a pair of panty hose hang obscenely from its edge. Obviously, someone had rifled through my drawers. I shiver. I feel defiled.

Now that I know someone has been in my home, might still be in my home, I am frightened. I don't know what to do. Should I go back to the kitchen and get out through the back door? But unlocking the door will take time and make a lot of noise. Or should I make a run for the front door which is still open, but to do that I will have to pass the doors to the two rooms that are as yet unsearched. I listen, again, still not a sound. I, very quietly and very slowly, creep out into the hallway. The bathroom is dark. I reach my hand in, feel for the light, and switch it on. The room is empty, there isn't anywhere to hide. I catch a quick glimpse of my face in the mirror and see a look of terror on it.

I slip down the hallway to the last room. If my intruder is still here, this is where he has to be. I should get out, I tell myself. Run and get help. Call the police. But I don't. Instead, I slowly go through the door to my study. I actually cry out. The room is a shambles; every drawer open, papers strewn across the floor, boxes emptied and overturned. Where, in every other room, he had searched carefully and, yes, neatly, here he had vented his anger. This was obviously the last place he looked and his frustration, at not finding what he was looking for, shows. I know he didn't find what he was looking for, because what he was looking for wasn't here. I know, without a shadow of a doubt, that what he was looking for were the artifacts from the Codex. What this break-in and search of my apartment tells me is that whoever broke into the storeroom at the University, hadn't found the artifacts there, either. So where are they?

III

March 22, 944
10.5.15.12.7, 2 Manix, 15 Zec
The Temple of Ku'kul'kan

The 22nd of March, 10.5.15.12.7, 2 Manix, 15 Zec, the spring equinox, is one of two days every year when day and night are of equal length. On that day, at the Temple of K'u k'ul kan, Chichen Itza, a glorious spectacle occurs. On that day, as the sun passes its zenith, its shadow falls upon the Northern slope of the Temple wall. As the sun begins to descend, its shadow, in the form of what appears to be a magnificent serpent, slithers its way down the steps of the Temple. It reaches the bottom just as the sun is midway to the horizon, at approximately 3 o'clock in the afternoon.[17]

So, just before noon on 10.5.15.12.7, 2 Manic, 15 Zec Took Pak sat on the western side of the Temple. Here he would have the best vantage point from which to observe this phenomenon. Several weeks before he had fortuitously found a small scrap of parchment within the manuscript of Chan Bahlum. There was no indication of who had authored the note or who might have secreted it there. The glyphs upon the parchment made reference to something hidden 'where the serpent vanished' when the day and night was equal. "Where else could this be," thought Took Pak, "but

at the bottom of the northern staircase on the day of the Vernal Equinox?"
And so here he sat. He had told no one of his discovery.

Took Pak watched in fascination as the spectacle began. The sun was
hot and, as on almost every day of the last year, there was not a cloud
in the sky. The sun passed the halfway point. Took Pak gasped, as what
was clearly the head of the snake appeared at the top of the northern
steps. Slowly, excruciatingly so, the serpent slid down the Temple wall, as
if gliding over the oversized stones that formed the structure. Took Pak
was mesmerized. Although he had seen it many times before, he could
not tear his eyes away. The afternoon progressed and the sun moved lower
in the western sky. The serpent's head reached the bottom of the stairway,
its body stretched behind it, as long as the temple was high. Took Pak
moved from his vantage point and walked the few feet to the wall, so that
he could see the base of stairs. From that angle, he could see where the
serpent disappeared into the shadows at the corner of the stairway. The
spectacle was over. The serpent had vanished. The bottom of the stairs was
in complete shadow.

Took Pak walked to the foot of the stairs. The rest of the spectators
had dispersed. He felt along the bottom of the wall. He could just make
out a square tile, embedded in the earth there. He rubbed his hand across
the stone and could feel the faint indentation of some sort of carving. He
was familiar with all the many hieroglyphics and symbols and he discerned
that this was the symbol for Ku'kul'kan, the sun god. This was surely the
hiding place spoken of in the note. This was 'where the serpent vanished'
and what he was meant to find was here 'under the glorious sun' 'beneath
the stone.'

Took Pak realized he could not retrieve it now. There were still too
many people in the plaza and he would need something to pry up the
stone.

Sometime after midnight, he returned with a lit taper and a small
digging tool. The night was dark, receiving little illumination from the
scant quarter moon in the night sky. Took Pak made his way carefully
down the steps, feeling his way with his hand on the rough stone wall.
By the light of his small torch, Took Pak could barely make out where the
stone lay. Again relying upon his sense of touch, he found the corner of
the flat engraved tile. Took Pak wondered how long the stone had been in
its place. Kneeling on the ground, he placed the digging tool beneath the

stone. It came up easily with the gentle pressure of his stone implement. Took Pak lifted the stone from its resting place and found beneath it a parcel, wrapped in a leather hide. He lifted the object and carefully placed it in the satchel he brought for this purpose. He replaced the stone, quickly, tapping it into place, and brushing some dirt over it to hide where the area had been disturbed. Dousing his torch, he hurriedly made his way back to the Library in the dark.

He did not stop until he reached his small, subterranean chamber. Once there he opened the door, making as little noise as possible, though he doubted that there was anyone else in the Library this late at night. He removed the parcel from his satchel and placed it carefully on the table. It was late, and he really should be off to bed, but he could not resist knowing what it was that he had found. He slowly unfolded the moldering deer hide and found a very small, poorly bound h'un inside. The codex was in shoddy condition, having suffered damage from exposure to the elements. Took Pak ran his hands over the rough wooden cover. There did not appear to be any written glyphs or symbols upon the cover. He very carefully opened the cover and found, on the pages within, hastily written and poorly executed glyphs. Just a quick glance at them and he knew that it would take many hours to decipher them. Further investigation would have to wait until he had gotten some sleep. He closed the codex, rewrapped it in its shabby covering and placed it on a far shelf, behind a pile of old, dusty manuscripts, where no one else would look.

Took Pak spent most of the next day working on an unimportant volume of astrological observations. He copied summaries of the repetitive movements of the stars and planets. He was tired and could not keep his mind on this mundane task. His thoughts wandered repeatedly to the codex hidden in his chamber several floors below.

Cho P'iit prowled about the cavernous room full of benches filled with apprentice scribes toiling away with quills and ink. The chief scribe peered over their shoulders as they worked. In the years that Took Pak had worked for him, Cho P'iit's attitude toward the younger priest had not changed. The older man disliked him intensely. Cho P'iit recognized Took Pak's ability, but this recognition only intensified his dislike for the young man. Cho Piit knew that Took Pak's work would always be complete and expertly done. The master scribe generally left Took Pak alone, spending his spite on the other, less talented apprentices. However, he kept a vigilant eye on the apprentice he obviously saw as his competition and potential usurper of his position. Any indication of weakness or hesitation, any imperfections or errors on Took Pak's part were quickly admonished, but this happened seldom.

Cho P'iit noticed, today, Took Pak's lack of attention and his wandering thoughts. The old man was quick to address the issue, "Are you ill, Ahab Took Pak or do you find the work you have been assigned beneath you?" he said snidely, laying a hand on Took Pak's shoulder.

Cho P'iit's voice, coming out of the usual quiet of the workroom, startled Took Pak and brought him back sharply to his surroundings. He shook his head and came back from where his thoughts had taken him. He recovered quickly, having over the years developed a good defense against Cho P'iit's insidious attacks. "No, Master Scribe, I became so engrossed in the mysteries of the heavens that this marvelous book so expertly discusses, that I was transported. Thank you so much for recalling my attention to the task at hand, for the copying of this magnificent work is of extreme importance, I know." And with that outwardly obsequious response, Took Pak bent his head back to his work.

The other apprentices kept their heads down, showing no interest in the exchange. But they snickered to themselves and took pleasure in Cho P'iit's discomfort. As for Cho P'iit, although he suspected the insincerity and disrespect in Took Pak's response, he could find no legitimate reason to berate him further. "See that you keep your mind on the task at hand," he said. "Your job is to copy only, not to read what is written. The mysteries told in the codices are not for the likes of you." And the unhappy old man stomped away to the other side of the room.

Somehow, Took Pak got through the tedious day. After the others had packed up their quills and ink and gratefully left the Library workroom, Took Pak packed his own equipment without showing the impatience he felt. He made sure that Cho Piit and everyone else had left before making his way down the dark stairway to his dungeon-like chamber in the lower reaches of the Library.

Once he had firmly closed the door behind him, he went immediately to the far shelf where he had hidden the strange manuscript the night before. Pushing the other volumes out of the way, he carefully retrieved the hide-wrapped bundle and carried it to the table. He placed it there almost reverently.

He put his hands upon the book and, as he had when he first handled the Chan Bahlum manuscript, he felt as if it was alive. He felt as if it had a heart that was beating below the worn, battered cover. He felt a warmth and energy emanating from the small codex. He had an odd feeling, a premonition perhaps, that this tiny manuscript was of great import, that it would bring with it changes that would affect him and others. And yes, he felt that the world as he knew it was about to change as well.

He paused for a long moment, and pondered what he should do next. He knew if he continued, if he opened the book and delved into its mysteries, he would set into motion events he could not then stop. But he knew in his heart he could not do anything else. He could not, not continue. He knew that he did not have the willpower to push aside this gift, or burden. He could not put it back into the dark hiding place where he had found it any more than he could fly like the brilliant Quetzal.

So taking a deep breath, putting away his fears and premonitions, Took Pak opened the book. The pages inside, a few dozen at most, were covered with small untidy scratchings. Symbols, glyphs, and illustrations crowded the parchment sheets. They appeared to have been penned hastily by a shaky and inexpert hand. They were indiscreet, imperfect and, so, difficult to decipher. Took Pak leaned closer to the hu'un, smelling the old parchment. He began the painstaking task of decoding the ancient writing.

The frontispiece, just inside the cover, held fewer glyphs than the subsequent pages. As Took Pak deciphered the short line of glyphs, he was struck with a sense of dread. He felt a strange feeling at the nape of his neck, as if someone or something was breathing over his shoulder.

He rubbed his eyes, shook his head, not believing what it was that was written there. Surely, he was wrong. He had misconstrued what the passage said. He went back and he read each glyph, using his finger to follow along to ensure that he had not been wrong. But there it was, as he had read it at first.

'I, Chan Bahlum, High King of Bakaal, transcribed this work with
my own hand, trusting the information to no other.
You of the future, who find this codex, preserve it and use it well.
Pass it on with care to the generations to come so that the Maya may
triumph over the terrible will of the gods.'

Took Pak gasped, taking in a great lungful of air, realizing only then that he had been holding his breath for a long time. He felt weak and faint.

He heard a roaring in his head. His eyes blurred. He lost consciousness and fell from his chair onto the floor.

He was again in the place he had visited in his vision on the day of his ordination. He was standing alone in the hazy sunshine of a barren plain. He heard a roar and the flapping of great wings. He lifted up his head, knowing what he would see as he looked to the east. Racing toward him, again, was the giant Quetzal, its savagely sharp beak aimed directly at him. The magnificent bird flew toward him skimming gracefully over the sun baked earth. The bird came right at him, but Took Pak did not move. He knew what was happening, having been through it all before. The Quetzal reached him and flew right through him. Took Pak felt nothing but a puff of hot wind. The bird passed through him and continued unabated out the other side, moving off to the west.

Took Pak held his ground, bracing himself for what he knew would appear next. As expected, a thundering clamor began again to the east and out of the haze came the expected monster. A gargantuan, gray lizard appeared and followed the Quetzal into the west. The huge reptile fell upon the beautiful bird and trampled it under its gigantic feet.

Next came the majestic black Jaguar. It came streaking past Took Pak. The gracefully muscular cat fell upon the Lizard, tearing it viciously to pieces. Took Pak was appalled, as he had been the first time he had experienced the event, but he could not draw his eyes away from the carnage.

Finally, came the snake, a massive two-headed serpent. Both its swaying heads with forked tongues flicking from its gaping mouths. The vast serpent slithered over and through Took Pak, causing him to shutter in disgust. It advanced upon the Jaguar, coiled itself about the mighty beast, strangling the life from it.

And then the serpent disappeared. The barren plain was empty once more. Took Pak dropped to his knees and placed his head in his hands.

Suddenly, he found himself back in his chamber, lying upon the dank floor. His head ached. His mouth was dry, as if he had truly been stranded in the arid desert. Took Pak struggled slowly to his knees, and then to his feet, with the help of the wooden bench. He was spent, truly and completely exhausted. He sat down upon the bench and laid his aching head upon the still open book. He felt a pounding, but was unsure if it was his head that pounded or the codex that lay beneath it. He must have slept, for when he woke the taper in its sconce was sputtering and threatening to go out. He replaced the manuscript in its wrappings and put it back into its hiding place and, then made his weary way to bed.

IV

March 13, 2012
12. 19. 19. 3. 17, 7 Caban, 5 Kumku
In a cellar somewhere in Mexico

They were gathered, some ten or so members of El Sociedad, all robed in brown. They had been chosen particularly for a special ritual. None of them knew what to expect, except the man standing at the altar garbed in white. He raised his hands in supplication, intoning the words of the ancients.

"Our path is clear, but obstacles have been placed in our way. The gods are angry and demand tribute in the form of a blood sacrifice." He began to chant, swaying to the rhythm of the orosion, and the others in the room joined in.

Then the high priest silenced them with a motion and, lifting his face to the heavens, he raised his voice in supplication once more. His eyes were wild and unfocused, as if he were in a trance. "The blood of one who has failed us and the gods is demanded." He screamed out. "Bring him forward."

From the back of the room came two figures; one robed in brown sacking, the other dressed in a shabby brown suit. The robed figure was nearly carrying the other man, who stumbled his way unresisting toward the altar, obviously heavily drugged. The pair halted in front of the altar and again the chanting began. The many voices echoed off the walls of the chamber, soaring and entreating whatever gods they might believe in.

The supplication came to an abrupt end and the figure in white stepped out from behind the altar. He faced the drugged man and placed his hands upon his head as if in benediction and intoned, "Our brother, Carlos, may your sacrifice be pleasing to the gods." He turned the man to face the assembled congregants. Carlos's face was slack and his eyes glassy and unseeing. The High Priest placed a hand upon his shoulder and the man slumped to his knees.

Looking once more to heaven, the Ah Kin Mai took a knife from within his robes and slit the man's throat so swiftly that no one else in the room had a chance to protest. There was a general gasp of horror, but no one moved. The High Priest reached behind and removed the obsidian K'ubul Luuch and placed it to catch the scarlet stream. Most of the attendants hurried out of the room immediately; some retching and choking, others in panic and terror, still others in a daze of disbelief.

Chapter Eleven

I

961 CE
10.6.13.2.16

Mayan Myth

Ajaw K'inich B'ox Kan was King during prosperity.
He was beautiful and bronzed,
A shining reflection of the Sun and of the gods.
For many years the gods smiled upon him
And on the Maya people.
But the fortunes of the Maya changed.

The lack of rain was seen by the Maya
As abandonment by the gods.
The Maya lost faith in the Ah Kin,
Blamed them for the misfortune of the people.
The ceremonies and sacrifices of the Ah Kin
No longer appeased the gods.

The Maya gave what they could as tribute to the gods.
But the gods were not pleased
And the Maya did not prosper.

The army lacked sufficient food and weakened.
Where once they were ever victorious, they were no longer.
The warriors lost faith in their leaders.
Lost faith in the Ah Kin and the Temple.
Lost faith in Ajaw K'nich, their king.
They lost faith in the gods themselves.

Many warriors left
To join their foes,
Taking their families with them.
And the city was defenseless.
And the city was destroyed
By their enemies.

And the gods grew angry
And the Maya civilization declined.

II

March 14, 2012
12.19.19.3.18, 8 Etznab, 6 Cumku
The University

A few days after the break-in, the telephone calls start. At first they are just nuisance hang-up calls. You know the kind; the phone rings at any time of the day or night, and no one is there. Just silence. Not even heavy breathing. If it hadn't been for Eduardo's experience, I would just chalk them up to wrong numbers or crank calls. The ones that are the most annoying and frightening are the ones that come at 3 or 4 in the morning. The calls that wake you from your soundest sleep and immediately make you think of horrendous accidents or someone needing to be bailed out of jail. By the time you pick up the phone and your heart rate returns to normal, the empty phone line just makes you angry. I take to refusing to answer my phone, letting the answering machine pick it up, but this does nothing for my disturbed sleep or anger levels.

It's another week before Carli returns. She comes to my office on Monday morning. She looks pale and drawn. Her mother is undergoing chemotherapy and tolerating it poorly. Carli wanted to stay at home, but her mother insisted she return to school to finish her senior year.

I give her a big hug and ask after her parents, motion her to a chair and offer her a cup of tea. She tells me briefly about her mother and about how her father is bearing up. Not well. But she really doesn't want to talk about it and changes the subject, quickly, to ask about things on campus. I give her the lowdown, tell her the whole story of our trip to Mexico, the loss of the codex, the meeting in Professor Allen's office, and finally about the theft of the materials from the storeroom. I leave out the story of the break-in at my apartment and the late-night calls, for now, not wanting to worry her more while she has so much on her mind. I haven't told anyone yet.

She looks at me with a confused expression on her face that mystifies me. I think, at first, she has forgotten all about the articles we'd smuggled out of Mexico. Then, she suddenly breaks into laughter. I fear she has gone crazy or thinks I am joking, or something. "But they weren't in the store room," She announces, controlling her amusement. "They weren't stolen."

"Yes, they were," I argue. "We looked everywhere and they aren't there."

"They never were," says Carli, slowly, as if she is speaking to a child. "What I mean is they haven't been stolen. They aren't gone. They never were there."

"No," I insist, now thoroughly confused. "They were packed with all the things from the camp office and shipped back here. They were stored in the storeroom in the basement." I pause and look at her still smiling face. "What do you mean, they were never there? Of course they were. Where else would they be?"

"But they weren't packed with the other things from the office," Carli persists and she laughs again. "Don't you remember? I had the box containing the codex things: pictures, notes, and the rest. I had them, doing a final cataloguing."

"Yes," I say vaguely. "I remember you were working on them, but you took them back to the office. Didn't you?"

"No, I didn't," she tells me. "I meant to, yes. I took them back to the office, but by the time I got there the boxes were all packed and sealed. I didn't want to take the time and trouble to open one and then reseal it . . . So I took the box back to our tent. I told you that, then, and why. You were in bed already, but I thought you were still awake. I packed the box in my luggage and brought it back that way. Good thing they didn't look at my carry-on bags too closely at the airport. I was scared to death I'd end up in a Mexican jail for smuggling." And she laughs again.

I stare at her in astonishment, unable to say a word.

"I still have it," she continues, "locked in my file cabinet in my dorm." She looks very pleased with herself. "So the box wasn't stolen and it isn't lost," she says gaily. "Never thought to see you at a loss for words."

My spirits lift. I don't know when I have ever been so happy and relieved. I give her another big hug and tell her what a relief it is to know we still have the artifacts. We sit for a long time talking about the implications of the break-in and set our minds to what we need to do next. We know we need to get the specimens carbon dated. This will not constitute legitimate authentication, but it will tell us if the Codex is ancient, the real thing, and might shed some light on why someone wants it to disappear.

"But carbon dating is expensive," I moan. "How can we pay for it? And even if we scrape up the money, who can we get to do it? We can't go to the University to do the dating or to finance the testing. We can't admit to absconding with the artifacts and implying the University's complicity in it, even if inadvertently."

Carli is quiet for a moment and then she says tentatively, "My Dad could get it done. I'm sure of it." I start to protest, but she continues, "He's a CEO of a corporation. His company is a small one, but he has contacts. I'm sure he has contacts, somewhere, which can get it done." She smiles again, "No problem."

I'm not so sure. "But the cost," I argue. "We still don't have the money."

"Let's worry about that later," she says firmly. "Let's see what my Dad can do first, and go from there."

"You're wonderful," I say, meaning it, "always coming to the rescue."

"What's a sidekick for?" she laughs.

My spirits fall again, as I think about all that has happened in the last few days. "But we still have a problem," I say. "We still have a traitor in our midst. We have to keep this a secret. We can't tell anyone you have the artifacts or what we plan to do with them. We don't know who we can trust."

Carli's face falls. "I can't believe it of any of them. Why . . . why would any of them do such a thing? No, I just don't want to believe it. But you're right, of course, you are. Not a word to any of them. At least until we know the results of the tests." She stands, shrugs into her coat and picks up her purse. "Now I really have to go. I'll call my Dad tonight and let you know what he has to say."

She gives me a quick hug and hurries from the office, leaving me to marvel at the sudden change of circumstances. I think again of the break-in. One thing, even though the artifacts hadn't been there to steal, the attempt convinces me that the Codex is real, and that someone somewhere doesn't want it to surface. It tells me, too, that the threats to Eduardo are real. And finally it tells me that the disappearance of the Codex was no accident.

March 20, 2012
12.19.19.4.4, 1 Kan, 12 Cumku
Vernal Equinox 2012

Late in the day on March 20th I receive an e-mail from Brian with an attached video downloaded from YouTube. The short note reads, "Watch this, then refer to the Codex decoding." The video clip is titled *Vernal Equinox, Chichen Itza, Temple of K'u K'ul Kan.*[17] The video, obviously taken by a hand—held camera, is often jerky and out of focus. It shows a scattered crowd of people of various ages and genders. The congregation appears festive, like a holiday picnic. The people are sitting on blankets placed on the ground, or are milling about talking to their neighbors. There is an underlying current of anticipation. The day is clear and bright, with only an occasional high cumulus cloud to cast a shadow over the scene. In the background I can see the vast, towering pyramid that is the Temple of Ku'k'ul kann. Its steep stone steps lead upward into the afternoon sky. The sun, just past its zenith, begins its slow descent into the west. The crowd stands and, in unison, turns to face the northern face of the magnificent pyramid. As the sun drops below the pinnacle of the stone edifice, a shadow forms. I can hear over the audio static, a gasp of astonishment and awe erupts from those assembled. An echoing gasp comes from me as well. Of course, I have heard of the phenomenon, but never seen it. As the crowd and I watch, the shadow takes the form of a gigantic serpent. As the sun sets, the reptilian shape slithers down the Temple stairway. It moves slowly and with an unnatural grace, the reflection of the sun giving its back a shimmer, like shining scales. The event lasts only moments, but seems to go on much longer. The crowd is silent, mesmerized by the spectacle. Then suddenly, the mighty creature's head reaches the foot of the stairs and disappears, as if into the very earth. Its body follows seconds later. A cheer and clapping erupt from the spectators and the video ends abruptly.

I go to my file cabinet, unlock the middle drawer, and retrieve the file folder containing Brian's decoding of the Codex. I know what he refers to, without looking at the indicated page, but I turn to it nonetheless. Sure enough, the page tells how the writer of our Codex, the scribe, had found Chan Bahlum's hidden Codex. The directions had been couched in mythical terms that until now I have not understood, but now I do. The scribe recounted how the instructions led him to where the Cham Bahlum codex had been hidden. "It is hidden where the serpent disappears." Where the serpent disappears? Where else could it be, but there at the foot of the north stairway at the time of the vernal equinox at Chichen Itza?

April 1, 2012
12.19.19.4. 16, 13 Cib, 4 Wayeb

The semester from this point on is a busy one and leaves me little time to worry about the mystery of the Codex or about who was behind the break-ins and the phone calls. I don't get a break until Spring Break, which happens to fall on Easter week this year. I haven't planned anything for the time off. Can't afford a holiday after the trip to Mexico. So I plan some much needed at home time and some catching up, end of semester chores.

I come into school that Monday, when I figure the place will be empty and quiet. On my desk, under a pile of unfiled folders, I find the folder containing the work Brian has done decoding the Codex. I begin leafing through it and soon become totally immersed in its content. Brian has done a great job deciphering the hieroglyphs, but he left the interpretation up to me. I take out a pad of paper and go back to the very beginning. Over the next many hours, I work at taking the literal translation of each glyph and coming up with an interpretation that seems to make sense. On one side of the paper I write the word or words Brian says the particular symbol might mean. The problem with the Maya written language is that one symbol might have multiple meanings, depending upon its context and position with relationship to other symbols.

The cover we had deciphered, with Calvin's help, that first day. On the left side of the engraved Codex is a column of numbers and symbols representing a date on the Maya Long Count Calendar. Calvin verified that it stood for: 9.12.16.9.5, 1 Chincchan, 13 Ceh. He converts it to October 8, 688 CE Gregorian. Brian had written it out as: [3]

Baktun 9   x 144,000 = 1,296,000 days
Katun 12 x   7,200 =   86,400 days
Tun 16   x   360 =   5,760 days
Winal 9   x   20 =   180 days
K'in 5   x   1 =   5 days
Time since creation: 1,388,345 days = 3803 years

The numbers and symbols on the right side of the Codex cover Calvin had read as 10.5.15.17.17, 7 Caban, 15 Chen or June 30, 944 CE Gregorian.

Baktun 10 x 144,000 = 1,440,000 days
Katun 5   x 72,000 =   360,000 days
Tun 15   x   360 =   5,400 days
Winal 17 x   20 =   340 days
K'in 7   x   1 =   7 days
Time since Creation =   1,805,747 days = 4947 years

So far this is clear and straightforward, not open to interpretation. Two dates, two hundred fifty-six years and 4 months apart, occurring during the Classical and early Post-classical periods of Maya history. But why two dates? Usually a date on a manuscript indicates the date it was written. Was the later date the date the Codex was written and the first, earlier date, the history the Codex was written about? Possibly.

The middle of the cover contains multiple hieroglyphs. The uppermost is one that I am familiar with, from my research in the Merida Museum. The glyphs are those that are ascribed to Chan Bahlum II, the King of the Maya city state of Palenque from 684 CE to 702 CE. The glyph for this historic Maya king reads, literally, Jaguar Serpent. The second set of symbols, Brian has translated as three words: "Chan" meaning small, "Took" meaning stone or flint, and "Pakal" which could be the glyph for the word shield. The series of symbols are preceded by a symbol that indicates that this group of hieroglyphs refers to an individual and is, therefore, a proper name and indicates a second person. The last pictograph Brian has translated as Aj K'uhn, the word for a priestly scribe. So the cover of the Codex contains two dates and two names. Brian had scribbled at the bottom of his notes, "Is the Codex a copy of a manuscript that King Chan Bahlum II wrote on October 8, 688 and the priest/scribe, Chan Took Pakal copied on June 30, 944?" This seems logical to me and is a working theory, until proven otherwise.

So much for the easy part. On the second page, the glyph for Chan Bahlum II appears again, this time preceded by a symbol that stands for the personal pronoun 'I.' What follows seems to be an acknowledgement or introduction to the text. Here Brian has added a note: "What follows is an approximate translation only. What I have put in parentheses are alternate translations or spellings. Fascinating!"

'I, K'inich Kan Bahlum II (Chan Bahlum II),
Ajaw (high King) of Baakal (aka Palenque),
transcribed (penned) this Hun (book) with a hand of mine (my own hand),
trusting the knowledge (information) to no other man (person).
Men (warriors) at the end of this creation (of the future),
who find this Hun (book) preserve (protect)
it and use it well (with honor).
Give it as a gift (pass it on)
with care to the generations to come (in the future)
so that the Maya may triumph (vanquish)
over the terrible (there is no Maya word for evil) will of the gods.'

I sit for a long time in wonder. "My God," I think. "Is this, can this possibly, be for real? Can a document from the past with a message for us in the future come to light just when the Maya Prophecy is due to come to pass? Too much of a coincidence." For the first time since I saw the Codex lying in its stone hiding place in the Yucatan cave, I have doubts about its authenticity. This is too much to believe. It is just too, too much. It has to be a joke, some kind of elaborate and twisted hoax. Very funny, but what about the threats and the break-ins?

I've had enough. I can't think any more. I carefully gather all of Brian's translations and my notes, return them to their folder, and lock them in my file cabinet. And then I go home.

III

March 24, 944
10.5.15.12.9, 4 Muluc, 17 Zec
The next evening, the Temple Library

Took Pak did not go to his small underground chamber after working all day. He had slept little the night before and was still greatly disturbed by the vision he had endured. He did not feel he could face the secret codex tonight or the possibility of a repetition of the vision. So he made his way to the top of the Observatory and the company of his old mentor, Cha Mach, the temple astronomer. The old priest was the one person, within the Temple, that he felt he could still trust, and the one person he felt he could call a friend. So that was where he went in his confusion.

Cha Mach was there, sitting at the far side of the platform as usual, gazing up at the moon in the night sky. "Ah, young Master Took Pak, it has been a long time since you have come to join me in the contemplation of the heavens. Is it not?" the old man said, not turning to see the younger priest. There was no rancor in his voice at this abandonment, but Took Pak felt ashamed for having neglected his friend for so long. He blamed himself, even if Cha Mach did not.

"Yes, it has been a long time. I fear other things have taken my attention. I apologize that it has been so," said Took Pak with contrition.

"And what is it that has stolen your time and attention" asked the priest with real interest in what the answer might be.

Took Pak hesitated, wondering just how much he should tell the old man, wary of divulging anything about the secret manuscript just yet. Cha Mach noted his hesitation and, laying a hand upon his arm, said with concern.

"What is it that is troubling you, my son?"

Took Pak was touched by the show of concern and decided to share the immediate cause of his own distress. "I have had the vision again," he said quietly.

Cha Mach was surprised. Obviously this was not what he had expected. "The vision?" he repeated.

"Yes" nodded Took Pak. "The one I had after my ordination. The one about . . . ."

But Cha Mach stopped him from elaborating. "Have you been practicing the bloodletting ritual alone, without supervision?" he said in alarm.

Took Pak heard panic in the priest's response, but felt he must have misread what was actually just overconcern. "No" he replied. "No, no bloodletting, except what we all participate in on the high holy days. And no visions come to me on those occasions." Took Pak thought for a moment. How was he to explain how the vision had come without divulging the part that the hidden codex had played? "I was overtired, had slept little and eaten less. I was working alone in my Library chamber, long into the night. I fell into a faint and found myself once again within my vision." He paused and then continued, tentatively. "I am worried about what it might mean," he said slowly. He looked over at the other man and caught a flicker of . . . what? Fear? Was that what he saw in the pale eyes of the old priest? But the look was gone before he could identify it.

Cha Mach looked away from Took Pak's intense and inquiring gaze. Then taking a deep breath said, "Tell me again about the vision; be explicit. Tell me exactly what it is you see in your vision." He waited patiently while Took Pak composed himself and gathered his thoughts.

Then Took Pak gave him a very detailed and exact account of the vision, ending plaintively with, "What does it mean?"

Cha Mach thought a moment and then said slowly, "Now I remember. Last time you recounted it I did not really take in the particulars. I was so surprised and, yes, a little jealous that a vision had come to one so young and so newly ordained into the Temple." He made a motion with his hands as if pushing away an errant and pesky thought. He then continued, just as thoughtfully. "I think we must look at the vision symbolically. He looked quizzically over at Took Pak who nodded but said nothing. "What does the Quetzal represent to you?" he prompted the young priest.

The Quetzal is the sacred bird of the Maya." Took Pak replied. He paused and then continued, "And I suppose it represents the Maya people in my vision."

"Yes, I think you are right. It represents all of us: you, and me, and all the Maya people," the old astronomer agreed. "And what of the great reptile, the Lizard? What do you think it represents?"

"It could mean several things, but the glyph of the lizard is most often associated with K'u ix tz'it, the god of the maize," said Took Pak.

"Again I agree. This is made clearer if we remember that this is your vision, so your association is most surely the right one." Cha Mach paused and looked up at the heavens and said as if to himself, "Now what came next? Oh yes, the Jaguar. What might its meaning be?" He spoke again to Took Pak, this time with a smile. He was obviously enjoying himself, in his element solving puzzles.

Took Pak was enjoying the exercise as well and had relaxed. "Again there may be many interpretations. Two in particular come to mind. The first, the Jaguar represents the King of the Maya and the royal power of the city state."

"Yes, that is true. And the second?" questioned the priest, sounding like the teacher that he was.

Took Pak responded eagerly. "The god Ku'kul'kan is often depicted as the black Jaguar."

Cha Mach nodded and asked, "And the last apparition, that of the two-headed serpent?"

Here Took Pak appeared puzzled. "The Serpent represents many gods, Ku'k'ul kan himself is, at times, depicted so. Ah Uincir Dz'acab, the god of healing, might also be seen as a snake of some sort, and the two headed serpent may mean, Xibalha, the god of the underworld, as well."

"I agree, the answer here is most nebulous, but I think I have an interpretation that will fit. But we will come to that later," Cha Mach said with a hint of a laugh, clearly enjoying keeping Took Pak in the dark a little longer. "Let us first look at the other symbolism within the apparitions. What is it that occurs in your vision?" He looked expectantly at the younger priest.

Took Pak took a deep breath and then ventured, "Each successive monster kills the preceding creature." Cha Mach nodded and Took Pak continued. "The Lizard kills the bird. The Jaguar kills the reptile and is in turn killed by the serpent."

"Yes," said the priest. "Now substitute the symbol for the image."

Took Pak thought for a moment and smiled. "Well, the symbol of the Maya people is killed by the god of the maize, or, perhaps, more explicitly by the lack of its sustenance." He felt triumphant and was energized by the look of approval on the face of his mentor. He continued, excitedly. "Then the maize is destroyed by the sun in the guise of the Jaguar. This is an allusion to the drought, no doubt." He paused thoughtfully. "Or, alternately, if one sees the Jaguar as the King, one might interpret this as the depletion of maize and other products by the heavy taxation and tribute required by the throne."

Here Cha Mach looked disapproving. "That is a stretch, I think. Look at the larger symbolism of the environment in which you found yourself in the vision. You are in a desert, in an arid and barren countryside. In that context, do you not think that the allusion to drought and the Sun God's destruction of the maize, a more likely one?"

"Yes, I see, that is a much clearer interpretation." Took Pak's pride was a bit deflated with Cha Mach's criticism.

"And the last appearance?" asked the astronomer.

Here Took Pak hesitated, knowing the answer, but unsure if he should reveal his knowledge of things he should not know.

"The interpretation of the symbol of the Jaguar may be broader." Cha Mach answered for him. "The Jaguar, symbol of the sun, the Sun god and the power of the throne, may be interpreted here as the whole: the earth, the heavens, the universe. And the serpent, as you said previously, may represent many of the gods. So as it, the serpent, destroys the Jaguar, so the gods destroy the world. Is this not a representation of the end of the current creation prophesied by Chan Bahlum II, himself?" At Took Pak's shocked expression, Cha Mach chuckled and said, "I know you have read the Chan Bahlum Codex and understand it. Nothing goes on in our little community that is not soon universally known." And he laughed again.

But Took Pak was not amused. A cold chill of foreboding ran through him and he was silent.

Cha Mach did not notice, he was deep in contemplation, and thought to himself. "This was a very impressive vision for such a young man and its repetition lifts it almost to the level of prophecy. Does he have the gift of prophecy?" But this was not really a question, and Cha Mach lost all his merriment as he thought it.

Several days later in the chambers of the Ah Kin Mai

Kaloome Ek Suutz and Sajal Ch'itz'aat were again alone in the room. "Cha Mach came to me with some disturbing information," Sajal Ch'itz'aat said.

"He has the ear of the young Ch'e'ne, does he not?" Kaloome Ek Suutz asked.

"Yes," the secretary responded. "The boy came to him several nights ago, on the night of the new moon." He paused and the high priest waited impatiently, tapping a ceiba switch against the palm of his left hand. The secretary finally continued, timidly, noting his superior's impatience. "Cha Mach said that Took Pak came to him with a disturbing story. He told the old man that he had a repetition of the vision he had on the day of his ordination. The vision came unbidden, without the aid of herbs or bloodletting." Sajal Ch'itz'aat paused again, expecting a response from the High Priest, but got none. He laughed, a halfhearted laugh, and said, "The old man is getting addled. He thinks that the vision is a prophecy. He thinks the boy has the gift, and that the repetition of the vision is an omen foretelling continued hard times for the Maya, for the dynasty, and for the priesthood itself." He stole a sidelong glance at the other man, but Kaloome Ek Suutz's face was impassive and he kept his attention on the thin switch in his hand. Getting no response, the other priest continued. "Cha Mach connects the boy's vision with the unrest and uprising of the legions." And he laughed again, becoming increasingly unnerved. He did not say anything more.

After an extended pause, the Ah Kin Mai finally asked, "What was the boy's interpretation of his vision?"

Sajal Ch'itz'aat was surprised at this question. He had expected Kaloome Ek Suutz to denounce the astronomer's theory as ridiculous and the repetition of the vision by a novice priest to be of little consequence. Instead, Kaloome Ek Suutz seemed to be giving credence to the young priest's opinion of what he thought he saw. "Cha Mach did not say, except that Took Pak had come to him to find out what it might mean. It seems that he was frightened and concerned about the experience." Sajal Ch'itz'aat concluded.

"And did the boy describe any other visions?" the Ah Kin Mai asked.

"Chan Mach said the boy denies any other visions. Just the one, the same one he had at his ordination," answered Sajal Ch'itz'aat.

"Tell me again, what Cha Mach told you of the vision itself," said Kaloome Ek Suutz, and Sajal Ch'itz'aat proceeded to describe the vision as Cha Mach had related it to him.

Kaloome Ek Suutz made no comment in response. He just continued to tap his palm with the rod. Sajal Ch'itz'aat became more and more uneasy, not knowing if this was a dismissal or if he should say something more. He did not know what to do and so did nothing.

Finally, the Ah Kin Mai stopped his tapping and said, "So we have a prophet in our midst. Very unfortunate."

The secretary was shaken at this response. "Did the Ah Kin Mai take any of this seriously?" he thought. But he had the foresight not to ask it aloud.

Kaloome Ek Suutz commented thoughtfully, "We must keep an even closer eye on the young priest." Finally turning his attention to his subordinate, he continued, "The time may be coming, soon, when we will have to do something about the would-be prophet." His voice held such a sinister note that it frightened the other man. "Make sure, Sajal Ch'itz'aat, that he talks to no one but Cha Mach or yourself, and that the old man brings any new information to you and only to you."

"Of course," Sajal Ch'itz'aat said, now thoroughly frightened. The Ah Kin Mai waved him away and he hurried from the room gratefully.

IV

April 1, 2012
12. 19. 19. 4. 16, 13 Ceb, 4 Wayeb
An office in Merida

Señor Tierro sat behind his desk in a large, well furnished, but obviously, bureaucratic office. He was talking on the telephone. His voice was pleasant, but authoritative, rather than friendly, as if speaking to a high ranking subordinate.

"The request has come from the Museo Mexicana de Arqueologia in Mexico City." He paused here to listen to the individual on the other end of the line. "Yes, I know that it may upset our relationship with our friends at the American University. We have had a good collaborate affiliation with them for many years. In fact, Professor Allen has been a friend of mine for nearly 20 years." There was another pause.

"No, I do not foresee that this will be a permanent action, but I can see the Museum's point. Having outside archaeologists, especially students, at a dig site so close to the site where this mysterious Codex was found, would be a hindrance and might cause difficulties, especially as they were the ones to find it."

He listened for a short time, then continued, "Yes, please inform the University, officially, that its permits for the dig at Seros Pezo have been revoked for this year. This year only. Say that the decision came from Oficina de Antiguedad here in Merida. Make it clear, however, that the request came from the Museum. Reassure them that they may resubmit a request for next year and that we hope to work with them again in the future."

He hung up the phone with a faint smile on his face.

CHAPTER TWELVE

I

992 CE
10.8.4.11.8

Mayan Myth

And the Maya did not prosper.
The people were saddened
And then they were frightened
And then they were angry.
They grumbled amongst themselves saying,
"Our tribute and our sacrifices were not sufficient."

And then they said to the King,
"We have nothing more to give in tribute,
To appease the gods.
We cannot feed our children or ourselves."
And they blamed the King
Who was the incarnation of the gods.

And they blamed the priests
Who could not read
The will of the gods,
Whose prayers no longer reached the ears of the gods.
And they blamed the gods
Who had forsaken them.

So the farmers and the soldiers,
The hunters and the merchants,

Came no more to the city.
They had no crops or crafts to sell.
No venison or plunder. and no tribute to give.

And so, they moved away
To find fertile land and water.
They followed the herds
And the flocks of fowl.

They deserted the city.
And they did not look back.

II

April 24, 2012
12.19.19.5.19, 10 Cauac, 2 Uo
The University

The telephone calls continue to come, disturbing my sleep every few nights. I don't ever sleep through the night, for even when the phone doesn't ring, I sleep fitfully, anticipating the calls. In the middle of April the calls change in character. Now instead of a creepy silence on the other end of the phone when I pick it up, a disembodied, heavily accented, male voice speaks. "Stop what you are doing or you will be sorry." That's all, but I believe him. I don't tell anyone. I'm not sure why. Everyone is so busy and what can they do about it anyway? And the police? There haven't been any definite threats and I don't have any idea who it might be. The police won't take it seriously, I'm sure.

Dr. Allen calls us all into his office early in May. We all assume it is to start planning for this summer's dig. We haven't heard anything, so far, and it is getting a bit late. But that isn't what the Professor has on his mind, at all. Once we are all seated around his desk, he begins somberly, "I received word four weeks ago, from the Mexican Office of Antiquities, that they are not renewing our permit for an archeological excavation in the Yucatan this year." A gasp goes up in the group and then we are silent with astonishment. The Professor continues gravely, looking intently

236

down at his hands, not meeting any of our inquiring eyes. "I objected, contested their decision, but to no avail. I had the University make a formal complaint and pulled all the strings that I could, but they will not change their ruling."

"But w . . . why?," stammers Brian. "You've been g . . . going to the s . . . site for y . . . years." His agitation makes his stuttering so much worse that he is practically unintelligible.

I don't say anything. I don't ask why the Office of Antiquities refused Dr. Allen's permit. I have the sinking feeling I know why and, by Daniel's silence, I am sure he does too. The Professor's reluctance to look at us, which I at first attribute to his disappointment and embarrassment, I realize is anger instead. Anger at us, or rather at me, I'm sure. Or am I just being paranoid? His next words make it quite clear.

"This has put the University in a precarious position. It may impact all future relations with the Mexican Office of Antiquities and our work in the Yucatan in general." There is a hard edge to his voice, a barely concealed rage. He looks up here and stares directly at me with a steely gaze. "They did not give any explanation beyond that it is not convenient for us to be there. The Museo Mexicana de Arqueologia inMexico City is beginning its excavation of the cave site and will be using our camp for their headquarters. They made no mention of . . ." Here he pauses and looks around the group, as if including all of us in the complicity. This makes me feel even guiltier. He continues gravely, "No mention of your absconding with artifacts or of Eduardo's erratic and intrusive behavior." Though I am sure these are the underlying reasons for their decision. "You will not continue with your interference into the Museum's investigation of the artifact or involve the University, or myself, in any of this," he pronounces with finality. He looks back at his hands, a gesture I take to indicate that this is the end of the discussion.

Carli looks as if she is about to say something, but I put my hand on her knee and shake my head silently. I get to my feet, gesturing for the others to do the same, and say without feeling, "Thank you for your time, Dr. Allen." However, I am not about to accede to his request, or rather his command. Neither am I going to apologize for anything we have done. I'm not sorry and I have no intention of stopping my investigation of the Codex. There is no point in arguing, for neither of us is about to change our position.

Without another word I leave the room and the others follow in my wake. I think they all understand the implications of what Professor Allen has said and are still in too much of a state of shock to respond. We are all silent until we reach the elevator, when Daniel says, "We need to talk, but not here, not now. Anyone who can, meet me at the Coffee Shop in an hour." He continues down the hall, toward his office, without another word or a backward glance, leaving the rest of us staring at his receding back, open mouthed.

It is less than an hour later when we all, except Calvin, meet in the back booth at the Coffee Shop, a local hangout just off campus. Calvin sent word, through Brian, that he has an appointment he cannot change and his part in researching the Codex was finished anyway. The rest of us sit, with cups of tea or coffee in front of us, not speaking. I look around at this group of people, whom I had gotten to know over the last year, and realized I really don't know them well at all. What I do know is that we all look, to varying degrees, guilty and disturbed. I speak first, unable to stand the silence any longer. "Well, that was surprising."

"Y . . . yes," Brian adds. "D . . .didn't see that coming."

"You don't really think it is our fault? You don't really think we are the reason the Office of Antiquities denied the permit, do you?" Carli asks, a note of real anxiety in her voice.

Daniel replies, his voice holding more distress than I've ever heard in it before. "It really isn't such a surprise, is it? I must say, I saw something of the sort coming."

"You did?" says Carli in surprise. "Why?"

"I have a confession to make," he says.

I look at him, shocked. "My God," I think, "what does he have to confess? What has he done?"

"There is something I haven't told you." He looks directly at me. I'm not sure I want him to tell me, whatever it is. "I have been receiving threats, telephone threats, over the last month or so."

Carli gasps. Brian's eyes grow wide. I let out a sigh of relief. Daniel looks at me oddly, having noted my reaction obviously. "I have too," I admit hastily.

"You have?" Daniel says, lowering his voice in rebuke, but there is a hint of his usual amusement in his demeanor.

"Well, yes. But I didn't say anything to anyone. Everyone was so busy with the end of term and all. I mean there wasn't anything anyone could do about it. It was just a voice on the telephone. Not a real threat, just some vague bit about stopping what I am doing, or else. I didn't want to worry everyone over nothing. I mean . . ." I've been rushing on so rapidly, that I have to pause to take a breath.

Daniel jumps into the void. "Just so, my conclusion as well." And he actually smiles for the first time. "But it brings up a concern and is the reason why I am not surprised by the Professor's announcement today. These individuals, whoever is behind the calls, seem to have a lot of information about us: our positions at the University, our home phone numbers, and our involvement with the Codex and Eduardo." He stops here to see how the rest of us are responding to this conclusion.

Brian looks even more surprised, blown away really. Carli frowns, a frightened expression on her usually smiling face. I'm not surprised at all, of course. I've thought of all of this already and share Carli's fear.

"And the fact that they have this information and are concerned enough with what we might learn, what the Codex has to tell, to try to deter us," Daniel continues, "worries me. Add to that the power and connections they must have to influence the Office of Antiquities and the museums, worries me even more." He pauses and takes a sip of his coffee. The rest of us wait. Finally, he continues seriously. "So what, knowing what we do, do we do now? Do we do what Dr. Allen told us to do? Do we stop what we are doing as the phone calls have been telling us?" He looks over at me and smiles, obviously noting the look of obstinacy on my face. "I know, Kate, giving in is totally out of character for you. But I think we should consider it. This whole thing, whatever it is about, might just be too dangerous to pursue." I start to comment, but he stops me with a motion of his hand and continues. "Something is going on here that is sinister and we haven't a clue what it is. Until we know why the Codex is valuable or dangerous, I think we should stay out of it." He put down his cup, looks at us, and waits for us to respond.

All of us are quiet, thinking. Then I take a deep breath and jump in. "I think you're right, there is something important about the Codex, something I think, beyond the intrinsic value of an authentic Maya Codex. I think perhaps Brian found a hint of what that might be.

"M . . . me?" Brian says, his voice raising several octaves in his surprise.

"Your translation of the Codex," I tell him. "In particular, the acknowledgement on the first page." And I tell them all about Chan

Bahlum's invocation to the reader, to us in the future, the reason for his writing the manuscript.

"But what does that mean?" asks Carli, leaning toward me intently.

"I'm not sure," I begin.

Here Brian takes over with enthusiasm, his stammering almost gone with his excitement. "What I thought it meant when I first read it is g . . . going to sound crazy, but maybe no crazier than people threatening you. Bahlum II was called a prophet as well as a king. As a prophet he foretold events far into the future. The most well-known prophecy of the Maya, especially now, is what is being called their D . . . Doomsday Prophecy. There are two indicators that people point . . . point to as foretelling disaster. First, that all Mayan Calendars end on the same day, December 21, 2012. This has led many to say that this means the world will come to an end on that day. Second, the last extant page of the Dresden Codex shows a picture of C . . . Chac Chel, the earth goddess, pouring water from a ewer upon the already sodden earth. There is a notation that this depicts the end of the fifth creation of the w . . . world."

"But that's crazy," protests Carli. "Do you believe it?"

"W . . . well n . . . no, of course n . . . not," he says, clearly concerned that Carli thinks he is crazy and so he's having more difficulty getting his words out. "B . . . but Bahlum's words made me think he was referring to the, the p . . . prophecy. Maybe what he is s . . . saying is that there is a way to p . . . prevent the prophecy from . . . from coming t . . . true. Maybe that's w . . . what the Codex has to s . . . say." He looks over at Carli, appealing to her to understand him. He continues apologetically. "N . . . not that I . . . I believe it. But th . . . there are crazy people out there who do. M . . . maybe that's who's threatening you." He turns to me for confirmation. "D . . . did you read the last part yet?" he asks me.

"No," I admit. "I haven't gotten past the first section, the creation myth."

"The last few pages," he explains, "are v . . . very confusing. Something about the winter s . . . solstice and a serpent that is attacking the world and a shield of some sort. I couldn't m . . . make any sense of it, but Bahlum seemed . . . seemed to be giving instructions of some kind. What if . . . if h . . . he was giving instructions, of just how to prevent D . . . Doomsday?" He stops here, seeming to have run out of steam.

We just look at him. It certainly is crazy, but then the whole thing is crazy. Hasn't that been what we have been saying from the start, that it just does not make sense?

Adam speaks for the first time. "I don't buy any of it," he says more vehemently than is needed. "It's ridiculous. I don't pretend to know what's going on, but I agree with Daniel. It's all too dangerous and we need to back off. Leave it alone."

Daniel nods, but whether in agreement or just recognizing Adam's concern, I don't know. His reply, in a calm unemotional manner, is in sharp contrast to Adam's outburst. "As I said, there may be danger involved in continuing our investigation, but I really can't see why at this juncture. I'm curious enough to want answers, but I don't know if I am foolhardy enough and brave enough," here he smiles over at me. Is he implying that I am brave or foolhardy, or both? He continues, "I think I am leaning toward caution at this point." When I start to protest he adds, "But this is a democracy. Whatever the group decides, I will go along with. I am not going to let any of you leap into danger without providing backup." And here he looks at me again, intently.

I smile. What I think he was telling me is, he knows I won't give up no matter what he says. And, despite his better judgment, if that is what I choose to do, he is with me. I am touched and gratified, but this also puts the responsibility on me if anything goes terribly wrong.

Before I could answer, Brian speaks up. "I'm hooked, I'm a . . . afraid. I want to k . . . know what it is the C . . . codex or what Chan Bahlum is telling us. Silly as it is, I think the Doomsday f . . . fanatics may . . . may have something." He laughs apologetically and looks at Carli for validation.

I smile at him and pat his hand. "You all know where I stand," I say, glancing Daniel's way. "I promise not to do anything stupid." Daniel laughs. "Well, not too stupid, anyway. But I'm not going to give up on the Codex. I have a feeling that we were meant to find the Codex. Eduardo said it, when he was still in the hospital, and I have to agree with him. From the beginning, I got a feeling from the artifact, as if it is alive, as if it is speaking to me. I know that sounds ridiculous, but that's how I feel."

Adam looks at me as if I am insane, shaking his head in disbelief. Daniel says nothing. Carli nods and rejoins, "I felt the attraction too. I felt, when I touched it, a warmth, an essence." She has a bewildered, confused look. Then she laughs and adds, "It does sound silly, very new age and all.

Anyway, I'm with Kate. I want to know more about the Codex, and what's more, I want to know why someone doesn't want us to know."

"I'm . . . I'm with you too," chimes in Brian. He avoids looking over at Carli this time.

"I don't believe you guys," admonishes Adam. "Are you all out of your minds?"

"All right," says Daniel with resignation. "It looks like the ayes have it. But there have to be rules, safeguards. No one is to do anything without letting the rest of us know. We need to consider all the ramifications before forging ahead."

"No more secrets, right," I say with a smirk and then wish I hadn't, for Daniel isn't the only one who has kept secrets. Carli and I still have, at least, one secret we haven't shared with any of the others. I look quizzically at her and she nods in ascent. "Then I guess Carli and I need to come clean."

"What have you not told us?" inquires Daniel, with a grin.

"What did you find out?" Adam says at the same time, but his tone is accusatory."

I start guiltily. "The box of artifacts we brought back from the Yucatan is not lost or stolen. It never was in the storeroom."

"What?" all four men cry out and everyone at the surrounding tables stare at us.

"Yes," Carli takes over. "You see, I had the box all the time. I brought it back in my luggage and had it in my dorm room when the break-in took place." She looks sheepishly around the table at the men.

"Where is it now?" Adam demands.

Carli and I tell them the entire story; from why she had the box in her luggage to our request for her father's assistance. We conclude with the details of the testing we are having done and by whom. Daniel's only response is to ask why we kept it a secret. Rather than telling him the truth, that we didn't trust any of them, I tell him it just seemed like a good idea at the time. He nods. I think he knows what I'm not saying.

Adam seems to have a brief flare of anger on his face that is gone so quickly I'm not sure it is there at all. He probably guesses why we kept the information a secret and I don't blame him for being angry. He smiles then and asks, offhandedly, "When do you expect the results?"

Carli answers, "Soon, I think. In the next few weeks."

"I think," Daniel says quietly, "under the circumstances, we have already taken our next step. Now we just wait for the results and go from there."

There is an uneasy silence, all of us immersed in our own thoughts. I change the conversation to relieve the tension. "Since we won't be going to the Yucatan this summer, what are your plans?"

"I . . . I think I'll take a summer c . . . course or two," offers Brian. He sounds disappointed. "I was really looking forward to the d . . . dig."

"I'll probably do the same," adds Adam, "unless something better comes up."

"I'm relieved that the dig is off," Carli confesses sadly. "I couldn't have gone anyway. Not that it was at all a sure thing that Professor Allen would have included me in the course. I haven't officially been accepted into the graduate program yet. Come to think of it, now I may not be if Dr. Allen rescinds his recommendation."

"I'm sure he will still recommend you," Daniel tells her. "But why were you not planning to go to Mexico, if I may ask?"

"My mother is ill," she whispers. "I need to be home with her this summer."

"I'm so sorry," Daniel consoles. "If there is anything I can do, please let me know." He, then, glances at his watch and remarks, "I have a class. Sorry to break this up. The next few weeks will be busy for all of us, but do try to keep in touch."

We leave together and head reluctantly back to work.

A week later I get an excited call from Eduardo. "They found it," he says so loudly I have to hold the receiver away from my ear.

"What?" I ask. "Who found what? What did they find?" But, by this time I have gotten my bearings and know what and who he means.

"They, the Museum, found the Codex. I got a call this morning. They called the secretary in Senior Mateo's office who called to tell me."

"What explanation did they give for the Codex being missing?" I ask.

"The secretary, the lovely senorita, said that the manuscript was returned from an outside authenticator. It was not missing at all, just a problem with paperwork. It was not properly documented, an unfortunate mistake," Eduardo concludes. He seems to be satisfied with this explanation. I'm not sure I am, but I don't disallow his enthusiasm by contradicting him.

"That's great, Eduardo. Keep me informed," I request and I ring off. Interesting, I think. Was it just a mistake? If not, why has the Codex suddenly turned up now? "No," I tell myself, "you're just seeing conspiracy in a perfectly commonplace bureaucratic error. But what about the threats?"

May 15, 2012
12.19.19.5.10, 1 Co, 13 Pop
The University

Carli finishes her senior year and graduates Summa Cum Laude. Daniel successfully defends his dissertation and receives his PhD at graduation, as well. We celebrate both in very different ways: Carli's with loud music, pizza, beer and much laughter; Daniel's quietly with wine, a few friends, quiet conversation, and a deep sigh of relief that it's done. Carli leaves for home, right after, to spend some time with her mother who has not been well enough to make the trip. Daniel leaves for a short period of R and R, but will be back in a week. Brian, Calvin, and Adam are around, but I don't hear from them in the first weeks of the summer.

I think all of us are at a loss as to what to do over the summer. I know I am.

III

March 28, 944
10.5.15.12.11, 6 Chuwen, 19 Sek
In the basement of the Temple Library

Over the next few days, Took Pak painstakingly decoded the secret manuscript. It began, simply enough, with the recounting of the much told myth of creation. It recounted how the world had been created and destroyed four times and the fifth and current creation had begun some 10 Baktun (4000 years) ago. It told the story, known by every Mayan child, of how the gods created the heavens and earth and the Maya. There was no new information here and Took Pak was able to decipher the text quickly.

The next segment of the manuscript turned to the heavens. It began with an explanation of the movements of the heavenly bodies: how the sun traverses the sky from east to west every day; how Uh, the moon, makes a similar but less regular journey across the firmament, while shedding and retrieving her gossamer robes every twenty-eight days; how Venus, at times the Evening Star and at others the Morning Star, makes a completely erratic circuit across the heavens. The manuscript spoke of the tree of life, Yax Cheel Cab, which bridges the heavens and the underworld and is the sky portal where the Milky Way crosses Hunab Ku, the center of the universe. All of this Took Pak was familiar with from his sessions with Cha Mach atop the Observatory and from his own observations.

The codex turned then to prophecy. Chan Bahlum II, in his secret manuscript, told of a rare convergence of the celestial bodies. This was an event that, though cyclical like all the movements of the stars and planets and of all life, was so infrequent that it had not occurred in the memories of any living man or creature. In fact, it had last occurred more than 10 batun ago, at the end of the fourth creation and beginning of the fifth.

The manuscript recorded how it would not occur again in his lifetime or in the lifetime of anyone living at the present time. It would not, in fact, occur again in the lifetimes of many generations. The next occurrence of this phenomenon would occur 3 baktun in the future. The exact day, according to Chan Bahlum's prophecy, would be 13.0.0.0.0, 4 Ahua, 3 Kankin.

"Why does that sound so familiar?" thought Took Pak to himself. He gasped when the importance of the date became clear to him. He thought, "That is the day on which all the Mayan calendars end. It is also the day the other Chan Bahlum Codex predicted the fifth and final creation of the world would come to an end. The day on which the gods would destroy the Earth, and so, all of creation would cease upon that day."

Took Pak shook his head and put the manuscript aside for the time being. He needed to ponder this new and alarming revelation. The end of the world would come because of the alignment of the heavens. How fitting. Did not the stars order what occurred here on Earth? The sun divided the day from the night. The moon controlled the tides. The position of the planets forecasts the proper scheduling of earthly events: the planting and harvesting, the conception and birthing, the death of the old and infirm, the outcome of battle. Why not the creation and destruction of the universe itself? There was a symmetry to this, as there was to all of life.

That night

Took Pak slept fitfully and near morning fell into a dream, a vision, like the other visions. He suddenly found himself in the barren place standing alone, as before. This time, however, he felt no fear, for he knew what was about to happen. Unlike the first two occurrences of the vision, this time he felt himself prepared, armed against what was to come. The vision or dream progressed, as it had before. First came the Quetzal, then the Lizard, then the Jaguar. The dream did not deviate in any way from its predecessors. Took Pak stood impassively, unmoved by what took place around him.

And then a great wind stirred and a cloud passed over the sun. Out of the East came the great two-headed serpent, twisting and writhing more furiously then in either of the previous visions. Took Pak felt a moment of near panic, but he held his ground and the feeling quickly vanished. He realized that something different was happening this time, but he also knew that somehow he had the answer. The snake continued to advance menacingly, slinging its two mighty heads from side to side. The great forked tongues lashed out at Took Pak where he stood firm and resolute. Suddenly, in his hand appeared a shield, a flat stone tile, square shaped and the color of sand. Embossed upon its surface was a glyph, the emblem of the Sun God flanked by two outward facing Jaguars. Took Pak felt a power he had never felt before course through his arm from the stone shield. The energy reached his heart and he felt strong and invincible. He felt able to face and defeat anything that might come, including the mighty, two-headed serpent that now faced him, even, he thought, all the gods of heaven.

He held the shield before him. The snake continued to advance and would have slithered through him, as it had before, when a miraculous thing happened. The serpent reached the place where Took Pak stood; its flicking tongues touched the upheld shield. It drew back its heads, as if to strike, but instead the snake recoiled. Took Pak felt the energy of the shield flare outward. There was a mighty blast of lightning and a crack of thunder and, suddenly, the serpent dissolved in a flash of smoke and ashes.

Took Pak felt an impact which threw him to the ground. He looked up, the snake was gone and the black Jaguar was safe behind him. He realized that the world was safe, as well.

Took Pak woke with a start and found himself lying on his cot in his sparse quarters. He rose, confused, and yet invigorated by this new vision. What did it mean? He slept no more that night.

Several days later in the subterranean chamber of the Library

Took Pak turned to the fourth section of the manuscript, only after he fully understood what preceded it. When he finally decoded this segment, he was astonished and elated, for what Chan Bahlum wrote here was beyond anything Took Pak could have expected. Chan Bahlum II wrote that the end of the world would be a direct result of the position of the planets at the time of the convergence. He included an illustration of the placement of the heavenly bodies on 13.0.0.0.0, 4 Ahau, 3 Kankin.[18]

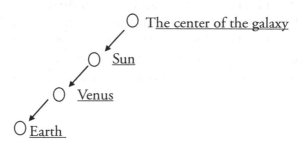

At the exact moment the sun reached its zenith, the center of the sacred tree of life, the planet Venus, the sun and Earth would be in perfect alignment. The energy from the three celestial objects would reach the Earth's Center and the four would be connected. The power that connects them, wrote Chan Bahlum, would destroy them all, all of existence.

Took Pak came to the last few pages of the manuscript. He continued reading with trepidation. Chan Bahlum continued writing about a theory: if the flow of energy could be broken, then the destruction of the world could be averted. Took Pak pushed the book aside. He was fascinated with this concept. It seemed logical, but he also felt disquieted by the theory, for it took the will and power of the gods out of the equation and, therefore, was heresy. He felt a chill of foreboding. And what of his latest vision? What did it mean in the context of Chan Bahlum's prophecy? And, more importantly, what was his role in all of this? This was heresy and his knowledge of it might put him in mortal peril, might seal his fate.

He pulled the manuscript back across the table. There was but one final page left undiciphered. He must know the end of it. What he read was cryptic and astonishing. Chan Bahlum wrote,

'In the mouth of the serpent rests the means
of salvation beneath the glorious sun.
He who finds it shall place the image upon
sacred ground at the center of the earth.
At the moment the heavens align,
so shall he save the world from destruction.'

Took Pak gasped and said out loud. "The manuscript gives to men of the future, a means to avert the end of this era, to interfere with the will of the gods, and to save creation from destruction." He then recalled his latest vision. In it he stood in the way of destruction, but how could that be, for he would not be alive in that far distant future? What did his vision mean? He did not know, but he was sure it pointed to what he was meant to do. But what that might be, he did not know. This would take much thought, and that is what he did over the next few weeks

IV

April 28, 2012
12.19.19.6.3, 1 Akbal, 6 Uo
A private home somewhere in Mexico

The man picked up the phone from the hall table and dialed a number that he knew by heart. The number rang three times and then a voice answered.

"I am sorry to be calling so late, but I have information I think you would wish to know," the man stammered, evidently expecting an angry response, but there was silence on the other end of the phone.

So he continued tentatively. "I received a call from our informer in America." He paused again, but still got no response. "Our spy reports that the specimens from the Yucatan Codex have been sent to be carbon dated. He says he just found this out."

Another pause, while the individual on the other end said something in reply. The man grimaced and recoiled at whatever had been said. "No, he says he does not know where they have been sent, just that it was outside the University."

He listened for a few minutes then replied, his voice quavering and his hand that held the phone shaking so badly he almost dropped it, "I will try to get that information." He winced as the voice must have answered loudly.

He said, then, almost in a whisper, "I will do so." But the line was dead.

Chapter Thirteen

I

1012 CE
10.9.5.7.15

Mayan Myth
The cities were abandoned
And the Temples were empty.
The sun shone down relentlessly,
And the stones turned to powder.
The winds came out of the east
And with a mighty blow, blew away the dust.

The rains came in torrents
And wore away the stone,
Washing away what the Maya had built.
And the mighty monuments
Reverted to the earth and rock,
From which they had been made.

Time passed and the trees grew
Thick and lush.
The forest encroached upon the city,
Extending their roots toward the silent temples,
Toppling the structures
And dismantling the shrines.

They spread their canopy
Over what remained,
Hiding all from view.

And the city was no more,
Except in the memory of the people
And in legend.

The Maya empire was no more.
And the gods were pleased.

II

May 28, 2012
12.19.19.7.13, 5 Ben, 16 Zip
The University

I plan to take a few days off to relax, but I find that all I can think about is the Codex. In the end, I take the files containing Brian's translation to a quiet and empty corner of the library. This is my special place and I come here often for some solitude. It is in a far section, behind the stacks containing little used volumes covering ancient, long dead languages. Here is an overstuffed chair, a small low table on which I prop my feet, and a window that overlooks the back of the greenhouses and gardens of the biology department.

I settle in and gaze out at the colorful bed of tulips and greening carpet of grass and plants. I relax for the first time since the semester began, or perhaps since I had returned from Mexico. I think about all that has happened in that period of time, and how much in my life has changed. Last year at this time, I was a dedicated, rather isolated academic. I was totally involved in my own research and self interests. My acquaintances were my colleagues at the University and my interactions were confined to those individuals and my students. In the past year I have gotten to know a new group of people. True, they are still colleagues from the University, but they have also become friends. I have gotten to know them, in this short time, better than I have known anyone in a long time.

Besides expanding my social environment, my interests and involvement in the world has changed as well. I'm no longer entirely concerned with my own research and myself. I am now involved, I feel, in something outside myself, something bigger and more important than I am. Maybe I'm deluding myself. Maybe the Codex is a fake and all that has happened in the last year, just one big hoax. But I don't think so. I hope not.

I pull myself out of this reverie and open the file on my lap. I decide to read through the translation from beginning to end first. I haven't done this yet, instead of reading bits and pieces in no particular order. I reread the cover page and the first page of what appears to be the introduction to the rest of the text; Chan Bahlum's explanation of how and why the manuscript has been written. Fantastic. I feel as if this long ago, long dead King is speaking directly to me.

The next section is a recital of a traditional Maya creation myth. It tells the story of how the gods created the world and humans from the corn of the fields and their own blood. Nothing new here, but I am entranced by the fact that this retelling of the story comes in the words of one who believed it to be the truth about the beginning of the universe.

The next section contains many numbers and dates, along with the Mayan symbols that denote the sun, moon, Venus, Mars, and other heavenly bodies. A note here from Brian says that these are, according to Calvin, astrological observations. A memo from Calvin is attached that gives an interpretation of the mathematics involved and a rough estimation of their correlation to what would have appeared in the night sky in the 8th century in Palenque. I glance at this, but it's beyond me.

The subsequent section looks much the same to me, but Brian's interpretation is quite different. His note scribbled in the margin says, "See astrological convergence predicted by modern astronomers to occur sometime around 12-21-12." I read something about this while researching the Doomsday prophecies, but make a mental note to go back and look at it again.

The translation here contains more numbers and dates and astrological signs. What makes it clear for me, however, is a diagram, showing the alignment of the center of our Milky Way galaxy, Venus, the Sun, and the Earth.[18] The Codex predicts that this will occur on 13.0.0.0.0, 4 Ahau, 3 Kankin, or December 21, 2012 Gregorian. The Codex gives one further prediction here, but I'm a step ahead and already relating the date to the Doomsday prophecy. I read on. Brian's translation says,

"When the sun (Sun god, Ku'kul'kan) reaches the top of the sky (zenith),
and the center of the sacred tree of life (the galactic center),
Venus (the morning star), the sun and the earth (middle world) align.

The will (energy) of the celestial objects (stars, planets)
will reach the center of the Earth.
And so, the power of the gods will connect with the heavens.
And the will of the gods will destroy the world (universe)
and all of existence.
And the fifth creation will come to an end."

So here is the Maya Doomsday Prophecy. Okay. Thinking about it, I realize this is just a more detailed account of the end of the current creation as intimated in the Dresden Codex. Why had Chan Bahlum felt this so important, that he must include it in a manuscript he had written by his own hand? And why did someone want it to stay hidden?

The next few pages of the manuscript give a partial explanation. Brian's translation continues,

'In the mouth of the serpent rests the means of salvation,
beneath the glorious sun.
He who finds the stone (shield) must place the face (image)
of Ku'kul'kan (sun) upon sacred ground(holy place)
at the center of the earth (world) at the moment the heavens align,
To deny the will of the gods,
so shall he save the world from destruction."

Here there is another note from Brian. I can almost feel his excitement from the erratic look of his script. He has written, "Does this mean what I think? Is he saying the end of the world can be prevented if we can find this stone or shield or whatever? Wow!"

Wow is right. I sit back, contemplating what I've just read. Again I wonder if this is just a gigantic hoax, or is the Codex an authentic, ancient artifact? The authentication of the Codex is of paramount importance and I don't know how I am going to survive, until we get the report back.

June 7, 2012
12.19.19.8.3, 2 Aknal, 6 Zotz
The University

I spend most days in my office working on lectures and syllabi for the fall and on my lit search for my dissertation proposal. Adam stops in, from time to time, just to see what is up and if there has been any word about the Codex results. Brian is back on campus, taking several classes. He stops in occasionally to say "Hi." I tell him I've been studying his translation of the Codex at length and am still trying to figure out what I think about it. He admits he is in the same place, just waiting for the authentication results. I don't think either of us is ready to talk about the implications, if it proves to be real.

Daniel is still away. He's spending time with his family in Boston and will be back in the next few days. Carli is home with her mom. We talk on the phone every few days. She sounds tired and depressed. I wish there were more I could do for her.

On June 7th I receive a newspaper clipping from Eduardo. It is a small article. It reads:

"The Museo Mexicana de Arqueologia today announced: an artifact, found in the Yucatan last summer, and purported to be of ancient origin, has been declared a hoax. The Museo firmly denies its authenticity. No further details are available."

Eduardo didn't include any other information or comment. There is a short note asking if I am well and expressing disappointment over the cancellation of the dig for this summer. Okay, I think, so the museum made public that, according to their experts, the Codex is a fake. Big deal. After their little stunt with the misplaced Codex, I don't believe anything they have to say.

Several days later I got an excited call from Carli. "Assemble the troops," she says.

"You got the results," I shout into the receiver. "What do they say?"

"Calm down," she laughs. "I haven't opened them."

"You haven't opened them? How can you have such restraint? I couldn't have resisted."

"I know you couldn't," she teases. "But I feel this is something we have to do together. I'll be on campus next Tuesday. See if everyone can gather at the Coffee Shop some time that morning. Okay?"

"Okay, but I don't know if I can survive that long. See you then." And I hang up the phone, not knowing how I can possibly wait that long.

June 12, 2012
12.19.19.8.8, 7 Lamat, 11 Zolz
The University

I get to the Coffee Shop a few minutes before 10 AM. The four guys are there already, sitting in the back booth where we had met before. I grab an iced latte and join them. Daniel looks tanned and more relaxed than I have ever seen him. He is telling the younger men about the sailing he and his brothers had done off the Cape. Obviously, the source of his tan and probably of the relaxed air, as well.

Carli arrives several minutes later, smiling widely, slightly out of breath, her short, blonde hair tousled and her cheeks flushed. "Sorry I'm late," she gasps. "But it was such a beautiful day, I came the back roads rather than the Interstate. It took a lot longer than I expected, but it was glorious." She laughs and runs her fingers through her hair in an attempt to tame it. "Had the top down on the Bug. Must look a fright." That explained the flushed face and windblown hair. Despite the high color, she looks worn out and thinner than just a few weeks ago.

"How is your mother doing?" Daniel asks sympathetically.

"About the same. Some days better than others. Tired and nauseated most of the time." Carli looks away, evidently not wanting to say any more. I can see the tears starting in her eyes. She smiles weakly and changes the subject. "What are you all up to?"

Brian asks her what she wants to drink and goes to the counter for an iced tea. Daniel and Adam regale us all with amusing stories of their recent trips. When Brian gets back, Carli thanks him and turns to me with a smirk on her face. "I'm surprised you're sitting here so quietly and so well-behaved. I expected you to jump at me with a demand to see the results, as soon as I came through the door." She laughs, bends down to pull an 8 x 12 manila envelope from her backpack, and waves it in the air over her head. I grab for it, but miss and she snickers. It is good to see her old spirits surface. "I won't tease you anymore," she concedes and hands me the envelope, giggling. We are all laughing by this time. It feels good. But I think we are all overdoing the frivolity in an effort to take Carli's mind off her worries at home.

I take the envelope from her fingers and gaze at it in anticipation. The return address in the upper left hand corner reads, 'IBG Laboratories'. I know that this is the subsidiary of a well-known, multinational corporation which specializes in biogenetics. Carli's father obviously has friends in very important circles.

"Well, are you just going to sit there looking at it?" hisses Calvin. "Open it already." Is that a hint of excitement I hear in his voice?

"W . . . we've waited long enough," adds Brian, still laughing.

"All right, already," I say smiling. "Hold your pants on." I slip my finger under the end flap and proceed to open the envelope with exaggerated ceremony. I pull out about a dozen sheets of paper. The cover sheet is an invoice detailing the articles we had sent to the lab. These included: small scraps of the outer leather covering and inner cloth wrap, a splinter from the cover of the manuscript, several tiny pieces of the parchment, some with writing on them, a small sample of the soil of the cave where the book was found, and, finally, two small stones from inside the container chiseled into the cave wall.

I give a quick look through the rest of the documents. Each of the remaining pages gives details of these articles. Each page looks similar in format. First, a detailed physical description of the article. Then, a description of the examination and testing that the article was subjected to with the results. Finally the conclusions of the examiners. I have the urge to go right to the final page and the final conclusion. But this feels like cheating, like flipping to the last page of a mystery. I resist the urge and go back to the beginning.

The first report is for the outer wrapper of the Codex. I begin reading, but Daniel interrupts to ask that I read it out loud, which I do. The report for this item begins:

> "2.54 cm by 2.54 cm by 0.3048 cm section of russet material.
> The specimen is supple and somewhat oily in appearance
> and texture."

The next section describes the specific tests and techniques employed, as well as the technical, very scientific results. I begin to read this for the others, but stop mid-way.

"This is totally beyond me," I complain. Calvin begins to explain what I have just read, but I stop him. "I'll let you study this later, Calvin. I don't think any explanation is going to help me. If it's alright with the rest of you, I'll skip the details and get right to the conclusions." I look around the table. Everyone, but Calvin, nods with what I take as relief. I continue to read from the bottom of the page;

> "Conclusion: This specimen is a section of organic material, specifically a preserved animal hide. DNA testing identifies it as Odocoileus virginianus, white-tailed deer, indigenous to the continental United States, Canada, Mexico, and as far south as South America. Carbon dating[19] indicates that the specimen has a calibrated value of 1050+/-30 BP. Techniques and chemicals used in the preservation of the specimen are consistent with this dating and with the reported area of the find."

I stop reading and look up at Calvin. "What does this mean? Does it mean what I think?"

He takes the sheet of paper from me and studies it intently. "I did some reading up on carbon dating," he explains. Then, pointing at the page, continues. "This value is the actual dating. 1050+/-30 BP means 1050 years with a standard deviation of 30 years before the present. Traditionally, BP indicates the number of radiocarbon years before 1950, because of the increased atmospheric quantities of C_{14}^+, radioactive carbon isotopes, due to the industrial revolution, fossil fuel usage and atomic bomb testing. Calibrated means that these variables are accounted for and the date represents an approximate date before today." He looks up to see if we were following.

"I think I understand that," I say. "So 1050+/-30 BP means," here I take out a pen and begin to do the math.

"Somewhere between 1020 to 1080 years ago, or between 932 and 992 CE," Carli squeals. "That means it's real, really real." She jumps to her feet in excitement.

"W . . . w . . . wow!" says Brian in astonishment, an understatement.

"Oh, my God," is all I can say, unable to take it in fully. Daniel takes the paper from Calvin's hand and studies it closely, as if he too is having difficulty taking it in.

"But just how accurate is carbon dating?" asks Adam contentiously. "I mean, one hears of mistakes and hoaxes, verified by carbon dating, only to be found out later."

Calvin is prepared for this as well, countering with, "Carbon dating is actually quite accurate where it can be calibrated. These dates fall well within that range. Carbon dating is based on the half-life of C_{14}, about 5,730 years." Seeing the confused look on Carli's face, he adds, "A half-life is the amount of time it takes half the carbon ions to be released from organic material. Dates longer than 50,000 years aren't as accurate. For the most accurate work, variations in atmospheric amounts of Carbon must be compensated for by means of calibration scales." He looks at us again to see if we are following. For the first time I realize just how smart he is and what a good teacher. "I'd say this date is accurate and what we have here is an authentic Maya artifact."

Daniel hands the paper back to me. "Much to my surprise, I have to agree. I did not expect these results." I can't tell if he is disappointed or just astonished, but he doesn't seem to share my excitement.

"I knew it. I just knew it," sings Carli. She clearly shares my response.

"W . . . wow," exclaims Brian again.

Adam gives Calvin a sour look. He looks as if he is about to dispute his pronouncement, but Daniel breaks in to forestall any argument. "Let's look at the rest of the results before we start celebrating. The piece of leather may date from the 10th century, but that does not necessarily mean that the Codex dates from the same time period."

I haven't thought of this, and from the gasps around the table and the looks on their faces, neither have any of the others. But, of course, Daniel is right. I pick up the other pages and, with a feeling of trepidation, begin to read the next page, skipping directly to the conclusions at the bottom. This is the report on the white fabric, the inner wrapping of the Codex. It concludes that the fabric is made of woven, bleached cotton fibers. Carbon dating is almost identical to that of the leather wrap and consistent with a date in the mid-tenth century. Good, but the flaw in using this as authentication of the Codex is the same as for the animal skin wrapper. The fabric might have been made in approximately 950 CE, but the Codex itself could still date from a much later time.

"Okay, no help there," I say, reaching for the next page. "But the Codex, itself, is next." Again I feel a rise of excitement. The description of the item states:

> "a 4.5 cm by 0.25 cm splinter reported to have come from the cover of a book found in the Yucatan Peninsula on June 22, 2010.

The specimen is a segment of wood from the fig tree, Ficus yoponensis, native to central and south Am. Carbon dating indicates that the specimen has a calibrated value of 1043+/-30 BP".

Carli gives a short whoop as I read this. "Home run," she yells and the people at the next table turn to stare at us.

I turn to the next page. This page contains the results of the examination of the small sections from the pages of the Codex. The laboratory scientists had determined that the scraps were parchment made, again, from the wood of the fig tree. Carbon dating gave a result of 1056+/-24 BP. I look over at Calvin questioningly.

"That's 956 CE with a standard deviation of 24 years which puts it sometime between 932 and 982 CE. Puts our target date right in the middle. Conclusive enough for you?" he says to Adam, with a note of superiority. "I'd say that makes the Codex authentic, the real deal."

"Oh, my God," I breathe. "Oh, my God."

Carli has a wide smile and an air of loosely suppressed exhilaration. Suddenly her smile slips from her face and a look of concern replaces it. "Eduardo should be here. He should have been the one to open that envelope. He's the one who has had faith in the Codex from the beginning. It is his find and he should get the credit. I have a feeling that won't happen."

I've been thinking the same thing. Carl's pronouncement takes some of the celebration out of the atmosphere. "I'll call him this evening and give him all the details. He'll be pleased, but I don't think he'll be at all surprised."

"The dating of the parchment is conclusive, I agree," Daniel interjects, "but there is more to the report. Before we break out the champagne, let's see that all the articles we sent for analysis fit the criteria. If one of them does not, it throws all of the results into doubt." Ever the Doubting Thomas. "Continue reading please, Kate."

I pull the report to me again and shuffle through the stack of papers. I read out loud to the others. The gist of the remainder of the report is that all of the specimens and samples are consistent with the techniques and practices available in the 10th century and in the area where the artifact was found. This included the ink as well as the fabric and parchment. The report also identified the soil and stone as consistent with the western Yucatan. I put aside the pages and look up at last.

"G . . . good, good," Brian stammers, smiling with satisfaction. He'd been convinced of this outcome before the report.

Daniel nods, "So the carbon dating of all the organic articles found in the cave is consistent with each other and indicate a date sometime between 930 and 982 CE. Furthermore, the chemical analysis of all the articles submitted for evaluation is consistent with the area in which they were found. Lastly, the craftsmanship and techniques used in their production are consistent with the time period we are looking at and with the culture of the Maya of the period." He ticks off each of the points on his fingers as he makes them. "What is of equal importance," he continues, in his most professorial manner, "is that nothing in that report contradicts the conclusion that this is an authentic Codex produced in the late classic or early post-classical period of the Maya civilization. There are still many unanswered questions, but I am convinced."

I show them the article Eduardo had sent. "I doubt the Museum will change their conclusion," I reflect, disgruntled.

"To Hell with them. We know these results are accurate. I guarantee it," Carli says staunchly.

"So is it time to break out the champagne?" Calvin interjects, and he laughs.

She then adds more seriously, "What do we do next?"

"I'm afraid what we do is wait," Daniel says, looking directly into my eyes and holding my gaze intently. "We wait for the Museum to report further findings about the Codex or for the archeological community to take up the issue. Now that they have announced their findings, that shouldn't be too long."

"But w . . . why don't we announce our findings?" asks Brian.

"For two very good reasons," Adam breaks in. "First, we aren't supposed to have these items in the first place. We took them without permission, you will remember." His tone is highly condescending. "Since we do not, officially, have them, their source is, therefore, suspect. Their authentication will not justify the authentication of the Codex itself. What is more, the Office of Antiquities might have something to say in the matter. And that will not be a good thing for any of our careers." All of us look crestfallen, except Adam, whose expression is one of disdain.

Daniel takes over here. "I'm afraid I must agree with Adam's assessment. I assume the second point he was about to make is that we cannot announce these results because someone is threatening us, to prevent us from doing just that." He looks at each of us in turn, as if to make sure we are taking him seriously. "It is just too dangerous."

Our celebratory mood has completely evaporated. "I hate to cave in," I say with resignation, "but I guess I have to agree with you." I tell Daniel. "But what do you suggest we do now? Besides wait, that is."

"We c . . . continue to look . . . look at the Codex, to see if we can f . . . find any explanations for the threats," Brian comments somberly.

"I'll look into the astrological calculations and the 2012 predictions. The threats might come from the Doomsday fanatics," asserts Calvin.

"Excellent idea," comments Daniel. "I intend to look more closely at the history of Chichen Itza during the relevant time period. Kate, might I suggest you use your creative talents and come up with a meaning for the instructions the Codex seems to be giving us." He is laughing at me again, but I nod in compliance.

"I'll do some more research into Chan Bahlum II," Carli offers. "He fascinates me."

"Seems like we have a plan," Adam sneers. He looks at his watch and adds, "Hate to break this up, but I have to go." He pats my shoulder. "Keep in touch." He turns to Carli, gives her a quick kiss on the top off her head. "Take care of yourself." And he leaves without a word to the others.

Carli says, reluctantly, that she too has to leave and the rest of us follow her out. "Call me to let me know you get home safely," I say, giving her a big hug. "I hate to see you go," I add. Both of us are close to tears.

Daniel and Brian each give her a hug and tell her to call if she needs anything. We watch her drive away. What started as such an exciting day has certainly turned oddly depressing.

"Lunch tomorrow?" Daniel asks. I am surprised, but agree immediately.

Sure, why not? The day feels a tiny bit better, all of a sudden.

III

June 21, 944
10.5.15.16.18, 2 Etznab, 6 Yax
Chichen Itza

Took Pak read and reread the secret Codex, re-deciphering each hieroglyph, each symbol. He tried to determine if his initial analysis was correct, or if there might be an alternative interpretation. He paid particular attention to the final passage. Three months passed and, on the day of the summer solstice, while strolling in the Temple gardens, Took Pak watched the sun moving across the sky. It reached its zenith and began its slow descent. He was reminded of the spring equinox, when the Sun's shadow had formed the image of the serpent. He remembered how the serpent's head had slithered down the north Temple wall and had disappeared at the bottom of the stairway.

"In the mouth of the serpent rests the means of salvation." Chan Bahlum had written on the last page of his manuscript. Took Pak closed his eyes and pictured, again the moment the serpent's shadow had reached the foot of the stairway with extended mouth agape. What had he found at the place where the snake disappeared? He had found the secret manuscript, but he had also found the flat stone with the symbol of the sun god upon its surface.

Chan Bahlum had written, "He should place the image upon sacred ground at the moment the heavens align, so shall he save the world from destruction."

Chan Bahlum's words echoed in his mind. Then he recalled his vision. The emblem engraved upon the shield, placed miraculously in his hands, had been that of the sun, the emblem of Ku'kul'kan, the Plumed Serpent god. Through its intercession he had stopped the advance of destruction in the guise of the serpent. Could it mean that this tile, found at the bottom of the Temple stairs, was the salvation of the world? Took Pak shook his head. How could it be and what should he do with the knowledge that he alone had?

He sat under the ceiba tree in the Temple gardens and thought. Chan Bahlum had written a secret Codex. He must have left the secret of its location with someone, a priest or priests, within the Baakal Temple. Had they carried it here when Baakal was abandoned? Had they hidden it where it would not be found until it was needed. Then years later, a scribe within the Temple Library had added a small note to the known Chan Bahlum Codex, pointing to the existence and location of the secret codex. He left that message there for someone in the future to find and so ensure that the book was found when it was needed. By luck, or was it fate, Took Pak had found the message in Chan Bahlum's manuscript. It had fallen into his hands through some twist of fate. So what was it that fate intended him to do with it?

Took Pak thought laboriously, "I must do what Chan Bahlum and the nameless scribe had done. I must protect the information from those who would destroy it and preserve it for those who would need it in the future. I must hide the stone tablet to keep it from destruction. But how can I do that?" This he did not know.

He thought again. "I have two choices. I can return the manuscript to its hiding place and depend upon fate to protect it and ensure that it is found when it is needed. Hoping that those who find it are not those who wish to destroy it. Or," he continued thinking to himself, "I can hide both the manuscript and the tablet elsewhere. But how then will it be found?" He thought longer and it came to him that there was a middle path. "I can do both," he thought. "I can preserve the information in another hu'un, hide that elsewhere, and return Chan Bahlum's secret manuscript to its original hiding place. I will leave directions to that hiding place. But the tile? I must hide it elsewhere for it is too important to leave to the fates. I will include in my writing where I have hidden this stone shield." Took Pak thought through his plan again and found himself satisfied with his solution.

On the night of the next full moon, with the aid of this heavenly body's light, Took Pak made his way again to the north Temple wall. All in the Temple slept. He crossed to the base of the stairway. His fingers found the stone tablet where he had left it. He lifted it out and replaced it with a common courtyard tile. The original tile he placed under the folds of his robes and stole back to his bedroom. He hid the stone within his mattress under the shucks of corn that cushioned his nightly sleep.

Took Pak lay on top of the mattress, staring up at the ceiling. He could not sleep, but lay awake pondering the meaning of all that had happened, trying to decide what he was meant to do next. Finally, in the wee hours of the morning, he slept.

IV

June 2, 2012
12.19.19.7.18, 10 Etznab, 1 Zotz
The familiar office

The two men sat across from each other as they did so often. The man behind the desk was impassive and actually looked serene. The other man, in contrast, looked about to jump out of his skin, trembling visibly and sweating profusely, in obvious terror of his superior.

"The American academics have proven to be more persistent than expected," the man behind the desk intoned. "They have shown such tenacity that one must almost admire them. Worthy adversaries." He paused here and looked thoughtful. "Or perhaps it is merely their stupidity. They do not know the full import of the situation. They do not know just how out of their depth they are."

He sat, contemplating his hands, folded upon the desk, for several minutes. When he spoke again, it was with a tone of resignation. "We have done all we can to make it clear to them, but they still fail to desist."

The man in the chair facing the desk shrank down in his seat and trembled even more, if that was possible. He seemed to expect the blame for the failure to fall on him. He did not say a word.

His superior continued. "The public announcement of the finding of the Codex was inevitable. We are still in control of that situation. We can deny access to everyone but those we know will agree with our point of view."

The man behind the desk looked up for the first time at his associate. When he spoke again, the tenor of his voice had changed. It had become menacing, almost sinister. "Let us move now to the report I have here." He tapped the pile of papers on his desk. "This, I understand, is the report of the carbon dating our American friends had done on the specimens they stole. Nothing really surprising here, though I am surprised they got the results back so quickly. The evaluation is as I expected it would be, for, of course, we have known all along that the Codex is authentic." He smiled snidely. "I do not, however, have any idea what they will do with the results. Unless they are very foolhardy, I do not expect that they will make them public."

The other man could see the suppressed anger in his superior's face and hoped that it would not be directed at him. "What we need to do now is to get the word out in the professional community that the Codex is a fake. We have enough experts in our back pocket to do the job nicely."

The man behind the desk went back to his papers in dismissal. His subordinate slunk out of the room, glad that lightning had not struck him.

CHAPTER FOURTEEN

I

1056 CE
10.11.9.12

Mayan Myth

In the forests and the villages,
In the valleys and on the hillsides,
In hidden caves and small warab'alja,
The remnants of the ancient priesthood remained.
Here in secret they kept the beliefs,
The rites, and the rituals of the Maya alive.

Here they kept the Maya gods alive.
And so the circle was complete.
For here a new order of shaman was created
To carry on what Halach Uinic began so long ago.
Here they passed along the knowledge
To the next generation of wise men.

Here in the secret places,
They told the stories of the glorious Maya.
Shared knowledge of the stars and the heavens,
Of the seasons and the days,
That had been given to them by their forefathers,
From the beginning of creation.

Here they prayed the prayers,
Performed the rites and rituals
As the gods ordained.
Here they paid tribute
As the gods were due.
Here the soul of the Maya was preserved.

And the gods were pleased.
And the Maya endured.

II

June 25, 2012
12.19.19.9.1, 7 Imix, 4 Zec
The University

I call Eduardo the next day to tell him the carbon dating results. He is pleased his belief in the Codex's authenticity is confirmed, but he is not surprised. He had known it all along. He is much more interested in complaining to me about the latest altercation he had with the Museo Mexicana de Arqueologia. They continue to deny him access to the Codex, giving him one excuse after another.

"All I want," he whines, "is to see it. To see for myself that it exists, that it is real. But they keep giving me excuses. What do you say? The run around?"

I don't have an answer for him, so I change the subject. "What about the phone calls?" I ask. "Are you still getting them?" I haven't told him of the calls Daniel and I have been receiving for fear of increasing his fears.

"No, no more calls since the Codex was found. They do not seem to be following me anymore, either," he answers, but he is clearly not interested in this and cannot be distracted from his complaints. "I am sure it is the work of the Order," he continues, not waiting for me to comment. "The legends tell the story. The grandmothers and the old men have told it through the generations. I remember mi abuela telling me the story, like your grandmother told of the boogeyman. Si?" I could hear a smile in his voice. At least the memories have calmed him.

267

"The big bad wolf my grandmother used, to scare me into good behavior," I laugh.

"Si, the big bad wolf," and he laughs as well. "Mi abuela warned me if I did not go to mass 'El Sociedad' would come to get me." And here he laughs ruefully. "Mi abuela told of how when the great ciudad, cities, of the Maya were abandoned and the people no longer came to the Temple, the priests deserted the holy places. She told of how many of these sacredote fled into the forests and there they hid from their enemies. And there they continued to minister to the people and to make their homage to the old gods, with their rituals and their sacrifices, and their black magic. Some others of these sacredote moved to the cities of their enemies in the west, and there they hid, and there they wove themselves into the fabric of the new society. In time they grew in wealth and in power, but they still remained hidden. And so these two parts of the same whole kept the knowledge and the culture of the Maya alive. In time they formed the Order, 'El Sociedad,' hidden in secret, hidden underground. 'El Sociedad' watches from the shadows and sees all that goes on. It knows when even the smallest child is malo, bad. And so if I did not do as I was told,

'El Sociedad' would come to get me and spirit me away." And again he laughs.

"But that is a story told to little children to keep them in line," I argue.

"Si," Eduardo agrees. "But as with any legend, the story is based upon a truth. The shamans still exist in the forests and the caves of the countryside. There they continue to practice the rituals and the magic of the past. There they continue to minister to the people, using the old ways, praying to the old gods, taking tribute from the people and making sacrifice to the gods in the old ways. That is truth. This we know to be so."

"Yes," I agree reluctantly, "the village shamans still exist, but that is a long way from implying the existence of a huge, very powerful underground successor to the ancient priesthood."

"'El Sociedad' exists," he says with finality. "That I know."

I realize that I'm not going to change his mind and he, I'm sure, knows he hasn't changed mine. I change the subject instead. I ask that he continue to keep me informed of any further announcements from the Museo Mexicana de Arqueologia and that I will let him know any new ideas we come up with regarding the translation. On that note we say good night.

Several days later I get a rather frantic message on my home answering machine from Eduardo. "Look at the e-mail of the latest malicious announcement from the Museum and tell me there is not a conspiracy." And he hangs up.

I immediately go to my email and open an article Eduardo has forwarded to me. The article is from *El Heraldo de Mexico* (*The Mexico Herald*), a daily English language newspaper published in Mexico City. The headline reads, "Museo Mexicana de Arqueologia announces the recently discovered Yucatan Codex a fake." The article is dated today, June 27, 2012. The article continues, "The Museum officials suspect the fraudulent forgery of ancient Mayan artifacts." I feel my indignation rising as I read on. "Senor Mateos, Director of Acquisitions, spokesman for the Museum, announced yesterday, that regretfully a recent find which appeared to be an ancient Maya manuscript proved to be a modern facsimile, as determined by independent experts. When asked if this forgery was an intended hoax, his only comment was that he could not see how any perpetrator could expect to deceive an authority such as the Museo Mexicana de Arqueologia." The article goes on with vague hints that link the Codex to the rising hysteria over the fast approaching Doomsday prophecy deadline.

I push myself away from my desk and pick up the phone, meaning to call Carli with this infuriating news. I think better of it. Her life is difficult enough at the moment, without dumping my anger on her. My announcement of the news to her can wait until I calm down. But I need to vent to someone. I think of calling Eduardo, but think better of this, anticipating a cosmic explosion if the two of us try to discuss the issue. A cooler mind is needed here and I naturally think of Daniel. So I call him.

He answers on the second ring. When I identify myself, he responded sweetly, "Kate, how lovely to hear from you." I'm sure he says this facetiously when he heard the edge to my voice. I can almost see the smirk through the phone.

I tell him about the article in the Heraldo de Mexico, giving him the particulars with frequent expletives and editorial comments, repeating frequently my opinion of Senor Mateos' mental status. "We know he is suffering from early Alzheimer's. They could tell him to say anything to the press and he'd do it. I think they are trying to point the finger at us. Their latest threats have not been death threats. They just say we'll be sorry. I'll be very sorry if I get arrested for forgery."

"Calm down," he says when he can get a word in. His voice is serious now, all hint of humor gone. "E-mail the article to me," he requests. This I do while he murmurs, "Interesting," over and over. Then, "Go get yourself a cup of tea, while I read through this." His unruffled, soothing voice calms me somewhat, and I docilely do as I am told, setting the receiver down on my desk.

Five minutes later, a cup of herbal tea in my hand, I return to pick it up again. "So?" I say into the phone defiantly.

"We know," he begins tentatively, "that the Codex is authentic from the carbon dating and analysis of its composition. So why the difference in our conclusions and those of the museum?"

"Isn't that obvious?" I say argumentatively. "The Museum is lying."

"That is one possible explanation," Daniel remarks slowly. "But it isn't the only explanation. The other explanation is very odd, I admit, but no stranger than that the Museum would lie about it. The other explanation is that the Codex that the Museum has evaluated is not the one we found, but a forgery that has been substituted for the original. Why that should be so I have no more of an explanation than for why we are receiving threats to prevent our talking about the find in the first place. Either explanation for the Museum's announcement makes no more sense than any of this has from the beginning." He finishes with finality and I don't have anything to add. His logic has taken the edge off my anger.

"I hadn't thought of that alternate explanation," I say, contrite. "Whichever answer is the right one, what are we going to do about it?"

"Nothing, absolutely nothing," he says decisively.

"Nothing!" I yell into the phone. "We can't do nothing. The results they announced are a lie. We know the truth. What we found is a fantastic find. It is an authentic Maya Codex that has the potential of changing how we understand the entire civilization."

"I won't go quite that far," he laughs, "but I agree it is a significant find. However, the same arguments against our publicizing our results have not changed." I don't reply and he continues. "We cannot announce our findings because we are not supposed to have the samples and someone is threatening us to not do just that." I don't have a rebuttal, so say nothing. Daniel continues, "We need to think about this, think it through. We can't do anything hasty. Perhaps we should think about getting some outside independent experts of our own." When I don't answer, he adds, "Think about it. We'll talk soon." And he says good night.

August 1, 2012
12.19.19.11.9, 3 Mulac, 12 Yaxkin
The University

I am surprised when several days later I get another call from Eduardo. "You received the article?" he asks. "What was your response?" He sounds very calm and in control of his emotions. I tell him how angry I was, at first. I then go on to tell him, in detail, my conversation with Daniel and his conclusions. To my astonishment he agrees completely with Daniel and says he too has decided it would be unwise for us to say anything about our contrary findings yet. He agrees it is much too dangerous.

He also has no objections to our seeking some outside verification. He pauses for a time. I assume he is thinking of whom these experts might be. His response, however, takes me completely by surprise. "I suggest that we talk to Enrice` Sanchez. He is one of the leading proponents of the 2012 Maya prophecy. He has a local radio talk show and a blog dealing with its implications."

"Consult with a fanatic? Go to the fringe element for confirmation of our ideas regarding the Codex?" I bellow. "Are you crazy?" Then I wish I hadn't put it that way. But I hear him chuckle over the line. I add hastily, "What makes you think they aren't the ones who are threatening us?"

"If your assumptions about the meaning of the Codex are correct, those individuals who believe that December 21, 2012 may be the end of the world would want its authenticity broadcast far and wide, as proof of their assertions." He sounds so logical and so much like his old self, I have to give his suggestion consideration. He continues, "I know Enrice` socially and I find him an intelligent and levelheaded person, despite what we might think of his rather bizarre ideas. I begin to think not quite as bizarre as I once thought."

"Do you think you can consult him and have him agree not to publicize what you tell him? I mean, after all, he makes his living making news." I really don't think Eduardo can guarantee this individual will keep the information off the record.

"I don't know that I will try." When he hears my sharp intake of breath, he adds, "I will make him promise to keep our names out of it, of course, but I think that he might be the only way we can get the existence and authenticity of the Codex to the public, without putting ourselves in jeopardy."

"Do we want the information out there?" I ask.

"Don't we?" he rejoins. "What else are we to do with the information it contains?" I have no answer for this. "If the Codex is giving us information about how to prevent the end of the world, as you seem to think is its message, don't you think the rest of the world has a right to know?"

"But the whole idea is fantastic, pure science fiction. I mean, the writer of the Codex might have believed what he was saying, but it's not real. I mean, do you really think the world is coming to an end on December 21st? Now?"

"At this point, I do not believe." I sigh with relief too soon, for he continues, "nor do I disbelieve. I do not know. But what if there is one small possibility that the ancient Maya were correct? What if there is one chance in a million, in a trillion, that the world is scheduled to come to an end in four short months, and we have, by some freak of fate, been given the means to prevent it, isn't it our duty to try to do so?"

Put that way, what can I say? "Yes," I reply weakly, not at all convinced. "But it's preposterous!"

"Preposterous or not, I think that those who believe it to be a surety are our allies rather that our enemies. They have no reason to want the Codex and its information discredited. Nor, if you think about it, do the fanatics have any way of knowing of its existence. Until the recent announcements, that is."

"No, they don't," I think, "and neither does anyone else outside the museums and the Office of Antiquities."

"That brings me to the real reason for my call," Eduardo says. "I want you to come to Mexico again, soon. I know it is a lot to ask of you, but there is someone I wish you to speak with and we can talk to Enrice` then too. It will be better for the information we give to Enrice` to come from us both, particularly, with the rumors of my behavior at the Museum going about." When I start to say something in response, he interrupts me with, "I am not going to tell you who I want you to speak to until you get here, but believe me it is important and may help us solve the mystery."

He'd say no more despite my entreaties. I tell him I will think about it and hang up with a promise to let him know in a few days. I don't tell him I have already decided to make another trip to Mexico, this time to Chichen Itza to see in person the great Temple of Ku'kul'kan where the Bahlum Codex had been hidden. I need to think through Eduardo's suggestion of speaking to this radio personality and am a bit put out with him for refusing to tell me who this mystery person is he wants me to speak to. And I have to discuss all these new ideas with Daniel and Carli. What is more, I really don't want to make the trip alone. Although I deny it, even to myself, the persistent telephone calls and the enigmatic threats that they make have me scared.

Carli, when I speak with her that evening, thinks Eduardo's idea of the publicity provided through a talk show host is awesome. Which I assume she means is a good thing. She is a bit less enthusiastic about my going to Mexico, either to meet with Eduardo and his friend, or to visit Chichen Itza, where this all began. I allay her fears, as much as I can, but since I share them I don't think I make such a good job of it. I do assure her, however, that I will not go by myself. I'm not sure that is entirely honest, however.

Daniel and I meet for coffee the next day. I quickly fill him in on my conversation with Eduardo. To my surprise, his response to Eduardo's suggestion is much the same as Carli's, though in very different words. He sits for a moment thinking, then says, "Really a very good idea. Wouldn't have thought of it myself, of course, but it fits the need. We want the information regarding the Codex made public, but dare not do it ourselves. So we take a hint from the government, leak it. And who better, and most likely to do so, than those who have been publicizing the Doomsday farce in the first place?"

"If you think it is such a farce," I say irritably, "why play into it? Don't you think Eduardo's feeling, that there might be an outside chance the Maya may be right, has any merit?"

"No, I don't," he says with conviction, "but I do want the thing publicized without it coming from us, to remove the pressure and the threats."

"Oh," I say, disappointed. I then tell him of Eduardo's request that I come to Mexico and my wish to see Chichen Itza again.

He is adamantly against my doing any such thing and says so very clearly, but ends with, "But I suppose it is a waste of my time trying to talk you out of it? So I guess, I will just have to accompany you."

I am overjoyed when he suggests this, but try hard to contain my enthusiasm. "Aren't you busy? I mean, it would be great to have company, if you'd like to come along."

"I really don't have much going on right now. I think I can clear my calendar for a week or so." He pauses and looks me in the eyes and says, "I do not want you to go on your own. It is not safe."

"Okay," is all I say, but I'm delighted and realize this is what I wanted all along.

Several days later, Brian and Adam show up at my office, having heard of the planned trip, probably from Carli. Brian is all enthusiastic, telling me over and over, exactly what to look for at Chichen Itza. He reminds me, again and again, what the Codex said about where the Bahlum Codex was found.

Adam is much less enthusiastic, actually implying it will be a waste of time. Then, just as he heads out the door, he says nonchalantly, that he isn't taking any classes this summer session and might like another trip to Mexico. When I don't respond to this off handed suggestion, he says, "Do you think Daniel would mind if I tagged along?" As if I have no say in the matter. "Let me know your plans," he says over his shoulder and leaves before I can respond.

III

June 22, 944
10.5.15.16.17, 1 Kaban, 5 Yax
Chichen Itza

The next day Took Pak left the workroom early and made his way to the southern side of the city. He went to the woodworker's compound where he found his friend, Ah Cho' B'aat. The craftsman had taught him to make the wooden parchment and the fan folded manuscripts when he first started his apprenticeship. Took Pak saw the woodsman routinely, at the Temple Library, when the artisan brought new books for the scribes to copy into. However, this was the first time Took Pak had returned to Ah Cho' B'aat's place of work since he had spent those weeks with him. Ah Cho' B'aat was surprised when Took Pak entered the compound and greeted him warmly.

"Master Scribe, it is good to see you. How might I be of service to you, for I take it, this is not just social visit?"

"No, it is not just a social visit, though I am glad to see you as well," said Took Pak, trying to keep the urgency he felt out of his voice. "I require a favor of you, my friend."

The woodsman looked closely at the young priest. "Anything that is in my power to do, I will do for you," he said.

"I require a hu'un, a new codex, for my own use. But I have nothing with which to pay you," Took Pak said apologetically.

The bookmaker smiled broadly. "That is certainly within my power and something I will do for you gladly." He turned toward his work bench. "Pay me with prayers and incantations," he said over his shoulder. "I have an ache in my bones, as I grow older, which makes my work difficult." He withdrew a small book with polished wooden cover[11] from a pile upon his work table. It was finely made, the suede cover a rich and warm brown, soft and supple to the touch.

Took Pak smiled back at the wood worker. "I will pray for you, certainly, and offer up incantations for your relief, but I think I have an idea that will work better then my prayers, that will work only when the gods are willing."

"What other advice can you give me?" Ah Cho' B'aat asked.

"I know of a healer, a wise woman, who lives on the other side of the city. Her potions and salves may work better than my prayers," Took Pak replied and gave his friend directions to his family's home and Ahkan. "Tell her it was I who referred you to her, with my compliments and good wishes."

"That I will do and if her potions work, I will bless you," and he laughed.

The next day, after he had finished his day's work, Took Pak repaired to his basement chamber, taking the empty hu'un with him. He began the arduous task of preparing the codex by drawing a number of red lines, using a straight edge. First he drew lines across the parchment sheets, then added lines to form columns. These intersecting lines formed a grid of squares that would contain the hieroglyphics and symbols that told his message. The task took most of the night. When he was done he wrapped the beautiful book in clean linen wrappings and placed it in an old wooden box. He hid the box behind some dusty volumes on the other side of the chamber from where he had hidden the secret Codex of Chan Bahlum. He then went back to his room and slept, pleased with his progress.

In the kitchen gardens of the Ch'e'en compound that same day:

Ahkan had not moved from her childhood home after the death of her mother. She had planned to move to the forest hut, but kept delaying the move. She felt comfortable and content here. She told herself that she stayed because it kept her closer to her father, who was aging rapidly. But in reality, he needed her little.

She told herself as well that the kitchen garden, so close to the central city, was more convenient to her clients. But actually, her clients were so scattered throughout the city-state, that they traveled great distances to reach her anyway. Also, she spent much of her time traveling from one corner of the city? to another visiting people in need.

The full truth was that here, in what had always been her home, she felt closer to the memory of her mother. She was not yet ready to give this up. Here too, she felt, was where her brother would look for her on his infrequent visits to the city. But, of course, Ek Chuk'in Och knew of the hut in the forest and could find her there as well as here.

The most pressing reason for remaining here, though she did not admit it even to herself, was that here she felt closest to Took Pak. She seldom heard word of him, but here she was close to her memories of her childhood with him and, therefore she felt, to him. From time to time, Nuxib Mak brought some news of Took Pak. She knew that the two men met in the Temple garden and exchanged brief conversations. Nuxib Mak's terse reports told her little, but it kept Took Pak alive and vivid in her mind.

One bright moment, in an otherwise uneventful late summer day, was the unexpected arrival of Ah Cho' B'aat, the woodsman, at her garden shed. "The priest, Took Pak Ch'e'en, sent me to you with his good wishes. He told me that your herbs and potions could do more for me than his prayers and incantations." He laughed.

Ahkan smiled and took a liking to the man immediately. "If he told you that, then he has grown in wisdom since I last saw him," she replied.

Ah Cho' B'aat, much more loquacious than Nuxib Mak, was able to give her a clear picture of Took Pak's health, state of mind, and something of his daily life. The man's words brought Took Pak home to her in a way he had not been for a long time.

The treatment of Ah Cho' B'aat's minor ailment was a work of little time. It could have been accomplished in one visit; however, the woodsman began coming every few weeks, ostensibly to replenish the herbs and potions she had prescribed for him. But in reality, he came because they enjoyed each other's company. He told her of his family, his wife and children, and the humorous drawbacks of being a husband and father. She, in her turn, told him of the joys and sadness of caring for the people of the community. They spoke of common interests, their love of the forest and the land. Ah Cho' B'aat loved the trees and the vines of the forest. He told her how he used them to form his carefully crafted books. Ahkan told him of her love of the forest plants and berries that she used in her salves and potions. She described their various medicinal properties and uses.

They became fast friends; something that Ahkan had not had since Took Pak had left her. She cherished this friendship for its own sake and for the link it gave her to Took Pak.

Back in the basement of the temple library

Next Took Pak began the detailed work of inscribing the glyphs and symbols that would preserve his message for far future generations. He first made an outline in his mind of what it was he wanted to say. Only then did he take up his quill and ink. The quill he used was the one made from the Quetzal feather that Ahkan had given him so long ago. As he picked it up and began to use it, he thought of her.

Took Pak began his task with much apprehension, surprised that he had the audacity to follow in Chan Bahlum's footsteps and write a Codex of his own. On the soft brown suede, he wrote Chan Bahlum's name and the date the prophet King had written his secret codex. Took Pac then wrote his own name and that he was a scribe at the Temple in Chichen Itza, and finally the date on which his codex was written.

Took Pak next reproduced the information

Took Pak ended the document with details of what it was he had done and was going to do with the tile and this codex. He told whomever in the future might find his manuscript where the original Chan Bahlum manuscript could be found. He included where he planned to hide the stone tile and what was to be done with it and why.

Took Pak wrapped the hu'un in linen wrappings and placed it in the box and once more hid it where it would not be found. He must now make his other arrangements.

IV

July 6, 2012
12.19.19.9.12, 5 Eb, 16 Zec
The familiar office

The man was not sitting behind his desk, but pacing in front of it, in some agitation. He was holding a phone to his ear and screaming into it. "What do you mean they are coming to Mexico? Why? What is their purpose?" He stopped to listen but cut off the answer with more questions.

"What do you mean they are coming to meet that fool Eduardo Gomez? I thought you had him intimidated enough to keep him in control?" He frowned at whatever the person on the other end of the line had to say.

"What is this about them meeting with some radio personality? Who is this Sanchez?" He began pacing even faster, covering the entire width of the large room in seconds.

"Si. Si, I have heard of him. A crackpot, a fanatic. Makes his celebrity by stirring up the masses, fueling the hysteria." He was quiet for a few minutes, deep in thought. "This is not good. Sanchez is not one that we will be able to control. Look into him. Find out all you can about him."

He listened again, then ranted at his caller. "Set up watchers. We need to know everything the Americans do while in Mexico, everyone they meet, every conversation they have. Can you manage to do that much without messing it up?"

There was another pause. As he listened, his face reddened and his mood darkened even further. He stopped his pacing abruptly and screamed into the phone. "They are going where? To Chichen Itza? Why didn't you tell me this at once? This changes everything. It can mean only one thing, they have decoded the Codex. They are ahead of us. They are ahead of me."

He was silent again for a longer period of time. Then his visage relaxed and he seemed to grow calmer. An evil smile creased his face. "This changes everything," he repeated. "We need a further, final deterrent. We must show them that our threats should be taken seriously." He stopped to listen again. "No. I ask nothing of you this time. I need to know that it will be done and done right. I will do it myself." And he slammed down the phone.

CHAPTER FIFTEEN

I

1376 CE
11.7.14.3.10

Mayan Myth

The shaman foretold the coming
Of a strange new god.[20]
He would come out of the East.
The god would come on an island that floated
Over the water from a land far away.
And his name would be K'nich Kay Lak'in

The wise men told of the god with skin the color of the moon
And eyes the color of the sky.
His hair like the silk of ripened maize.
He would come with fearsome warriors
Clothed in breast plates as hard as flint
Borne upon the backs of mighty beasts.

The god would demand tribute
In the form of golden stone,
Said to come from the distant mountains.
But the people would have none.
And the god would be angry
And the people would suffer.

II

August 8, 2012
12.19.19.11.5, 12 Chichan, 8 Yaxkin
Mexico City

Eduardo picks us up at Benito Juárez International Airport one week later. He looks very different from how he looked when I had last seen him. He is neatly dressed, his face shaven, his hair cut and combed. He smiles at us as he loads our luggage in the back of a well-worn, scratched and dented jeep. He drops us at the Mexico City Hilton 10 minutes later and asks if we'd like to have a night cap before heading to our rooms. I decline. It's been a long trip and I'm beat. All I want is a hot shower and a soft bed, and I say so. Adam agrees that bed sounds like the better idea. Daniel begs off as well. Eduardo seems disappointed, but he bids us good night in good humor, reminding us, "We have an appointment with Enrice` Sanchez at ten tomorrow morning, after his early morning talk show. I will pick you up at 8 for breakfast. Si?"

After a hearty breakfast at a local café, we head for Chapultepec Park at the end of Paseo de la Reforma. Eduardo explains that it is the largest expanse of open ground and century old forest within the urban center.

"Why meet here?" Adam asks, "Why not at his studio or at our hotel?"

"Because it will be very difficult to eavesdrop on our conversation here in the open," Eduardo says with a touch of irritation, obviously catching the hint of derision in the younger man's voice.

I make myself comfortable on the grassy ground, reveling in the warm sun and the breeze that sweeps across the commons. Adam saunters off toward the trees. The other two men stand nearby, surveying the area: Daniel nonchalantly, Eduardo intently. We are all quiet and in the silence, two grey squirrels come bravely near, foraging the area for whatever they can find. I am totally engrossed in their antics, as they fight over a half empty Snickers wrapper, when I am startled by a voice I do not know.

"Buenos Dios, Eduardo, mi amigo," entones a rich, melodious voice. I turn to see a short, balding man wearing thick, black rimmed glasses. The voice doesn't, in any way, match the person. Eduardo smiles broadly and greets him warmly, in rapid Spanish which I can't follow. The man then turns to us and reverting to heavily accented English says, "And you must be our visitors from the States. Enrice' Sanchez."

He reaches out and shakes Daniel's hand as Eduardo introduces him, "Dr. Daniel Keith from the University of Western New York." Then turning to me, "And his colleague, Professor Kate O'Hara."

The small man with the large voice takes my hand, as I get clumsily to my feet, squeezing it rather than shaking it and says, smoothly, "A pleasure to meet you, I am sure, Senorita Professora." Adam returns to the group and is introduced in his turn.

"An interesting setting for a meeting," Enrice says jokingly to Eduardo. "I take it you don't want what you have to tell me, or ask me, to be overheard. Such cloak and dagger, mi amigo. Or is it that you do not want to be seen with a disreputable individual, such as myself?" And here he gives a full, hearty laugh.

"Some of each, I think," replies Eduardo with a smile. He turns serious. "I have a great revelation for you, and yes, it is a secret. We come to you because of your interest in a certain event . . . the prophecy," he gives his friend a searching look. Enrice' looks confused but interested.

Before Eduardo can continue, Daniel breaks in. "Before we continue this discussion, I feel we need some assurances."

"You are not about to tell me that you are going to share with me some great secret, but that I can tell no one about it? Why then come to me at all?" he says with some irritation.

"Not at all," Daniel responds, smiling. "The information we are about to give you, we want you to publicize." At the other man's look of surprise, he laughs. "That is why we have come to you. The information you can share with your radio listeners, we want you to. What we ask you to keep secret is where you got the information." He pauses, waiting for this to sink in. "It will become clear when you hear the whole story, why we must ask you this. Do I have your assurance, your promise, which you will tell no one, absolutely no one, our names." And he waits for a response.

"You have my word," Sanchez replies solemnly, without another question.

"All right then," Daniel says. "This may take some time. Shall we make ourselves comfortable?" and he seats himself gracefully on the ground. Quite out of character I think, but he appears as much at ease as he would in the rocking chair in his office. The rest of us seat ourselves next to him.

All except Adam, who remains standing, probably not wanting to soil his pristine white slacks.

"The story starts with Eduardo." Daniel gestures to him to begin.

Eduardo starts the story with his return to the dig site last summer. He tells of his hike to the ancient mound and his sighting of the enormous Quetzal and his fall. He tells Enrice` of the predicament he found himself in, the broken ankle, and his despair of being found in time. He is a good storyteller and has all of us mesmerized by his tale, even those of us who know the story very well. He pauses here, before continuing to the denouement. When he continues, his voice has taken on a dreamy quality. He tells of the finding of the hiding place carved into the cave wall, of his opening the worn wrappings, and the discovery of what lay within. He describes the Codex and his conviction of what it is.

Enrice`, attentive at first, is now staring at him open-mouthed. He has been silent throughout the narrative. He now exclaims in wonder, "¡Dios Mio. The artifact. The announcement from the Museo. But they say it is a forgery, a hoax!"

"Si, that is what they say." Eduardo cannot keep the anger from his voice. "I think Daniel should continue the story from here, as I remember nothing further until many days later."

Daniel takes up the tale. His style is much different: factual and unembellished. He tells of our arrival in Mexico and Professor Allen's message. He then goes on to describe the search and the recovery of Eduardo. He explains how, from Eduardo's note, we find the Codex. He then describes for Enrice` our return to the cave the next day and our recovery of the hidden manuscript. Daniel continues with a description of how we documented and recorded our examination of the Codex, ending with the samples we had taken. "That is, obviously, one of the reasons we want our names kept out of it. We didn't ask permission of the office of Antiquities to take the specimens out of the country. Not entirely legal," he admits.

"I see your point," Enrice` nods. "But it does complicate authentication of the Codex."

"Let us finish our story," Daniel requests. "Kate, you can probably tell this part of the story better than I." And they all look at me expectantly.

So I take over the telling. I tell Enrice` of our return to the University and Brian's translation of the Maya hieroglyphs. I tell him about the threats Eduardo began receiving, the break-ins, both at the University and at my apartment, and of the threats Daniel and I are getting. He just nods in understanding. I then give him a much abbreviated synopsis of the first few sections of the manuscript and the dates found on the cover.

"Chan Balham II!" he says in astonishment. "Do you think it is real? Even if it is just a copy, what a find." He pauses here and thinks for a moment. "But why did the Museo dismiss it out of hand?"

"I'll get to our conclusions regarding that, in a bit," I say. I continue my story with how we sent the samples off for evaluation and the results of the analysis.

"¡Dios Mio." is his only response.

I rifle through my hand bag and come out with a rather large file folder. "I have copies of the translation and the analysis you can have to study later." He reaches for it, but I do not relinquish it immediately. "Let me finish the story first." He looks at the file longingly. I go on to tell him about the rest of the Codex: of the astrological symbols and diagrams, of Calvin's interpretation of their meaning with regard to the coming convergence, and the repetition of the date, 13.0.0.0.0, 4 Ahau, 3Kankin, December 21, 2012.

"The Maya Prophecy," he gasps in wonder.

I come finally to the end of the story. I tell him of the final section of the Codex and, taking one sheet of paper from the file, read Chan Bahlum's own words.

"In the mouth of the serpent rests the means of
salvation, beneath the glorious sun. He who finds it
shall place the image upon sacred ground at the
center of the earth. At the moment the heavens
align, so shall he save the world from destruction."

"What does it mean?" he asks in confusion.

"We aren't sure, but we think, I think," I amend, "Chan Bahlum is telling us we can prevent the end of the world. How we are to go about doing that, I don't have any idea. Something about a shield placed over the center of the Earth to prevent the completion of the line formed by the cosmic alignment. Farfetched, I know, but as Eduardo pointed out to me, even if you have only a one in a million chance of preventing the destruction of the universe, you have to go for it." I smile over at Eduardo.

He laughs. "Not quite how I put it, but the sentiment is right."

Enrice` looks at all of us. "Fascinating. I do not ascribe to the belief that the end of the Maya calendars, the Maya Prophecy, means that the world will, literally, come to an end. I am of the more moderate fanatical group," here he laughs. "My belief, and what I believe the Maya predicted, is that the next cycle will begin with the 13th Baktun, bringing a new order, great changes in the world. The Maya were great believers in cycles.[21] They saw everything in the form of cycles, everything repeating itself. The sun rises in the east and sets in the west everyday and it will continue to do so until the end of time. The seasons follow one another, summer, fall, winter, spring, in the same order and at the same point in the heavenly cycle, and so are predictable. They believed that the world has been created five times, each lasting 5,125 years, the length of the Long Count Calendar. Each previous creation ended with some kind of catastrophe. The fifth creation will end on 12-21-12. But, though the fragment of the Dresden Codex that still exists implies that there will be catastrophic flooding, it does not say that the world will be destroyed. This new information may lead me to change my opinion." He is quiet for a time, looking pensive. Then he seems to pull himself back to the present and asks, "What is it, specifically, that you want me to do?"

Daniel takes over again here. "We want you to publicize this information. I would suggest that you begin by saying you have heard rumors about a message from the past. Then gradually add pieces of information attributing it to reliable sources." He stops here, noting the amused expression on Enrice`'s face. "Well, that is really your area of expertise. You'll know how best to go about it without revealing where your information came from."

"Si, I think I can handle that part of it," the talk show host says in good humor. "Tell me though, what is the outcome you wish?"

"We want people to start asking questions. Questions that we cannot ask ourselves," I interject. "We want to be able to find out what it is exactly that Chan Bahlum is telling us. What is it we have to do and why someone wants to stop us. From what I know of your group, your interests are the same. Will you help us?"

Enrice` responds without hesitating. "Si, I will help you, and with pleasure." I hand him the file and he takes it with a smile of appreciation. He clutches it to his chest as if it is the most precious thing in the world, and maybe it is.

Enrice` nods to all of us in goodbye, turns and walks off to the car park, north of the commons. The four of us turn in the opposite direction, to where Eduardo had parked the jeep. As we walk, Eduardo grabs my arm and pulls me away from the others.

"Do you think you might get away from Adam and Daniel tomorrow night?" he says quietly.

"Why?" I ask in turn, glancing at him out of the corner of my eye.

"There is someone I wish you to meet," he answers.

"Who is that, Eduardo? Why all the secrecy?"

"I will tell you tomorrow." He smiles and then adds, as if a new thought has just come to him. "Maria asked that I invite you to dinner while you are here. She wishes very much to see you again. That is a good excuse, no? And it will not be a lie, for we will go to my home for dinner first."

"That's fine with me, Eduardo. I can use some time away from those two," I nod toward the others. "And I do want to see Maria. I am dying to know who this mysterious person is." By this time we've caught up with the others and so fall silent.

Eduardo picks me up at the hotel at six. Daniel, Adam and I had spent the day exploring the city. Daniel intends spending the evening with some friends, fellow archeologists he had met over the years. Adam says he thinks he can find some way to amuse himself. We plan to meet for breakfast the next morning.

I have a delightful dinner with Maria and Eduardo. Maria is an excellent cook and the conversation is relaxed and pleasant. Not once is the issue of the Codex or the threats broached. We speak of art, music and philosophy, and, of course, about their two boys, who are spending the summer in France as exchange students. At a little after ten, Eduardo says it is about time he gets me back to the hotel. He tells his wife not to wait up, as he will probably have a night cap with Daniel and Adam, if they are still awake. I wonder why the deception. Where are we going, that he doesn't want his wife to know.

Once back in the car, I demand, "Just where is it we're going and who is it we're going to see?" Eduardo drives through the dark and quiet suburban streets heading in the opposite direction from the hotel, northwest if my sense of direction is accurate.

"We are going out into the countryside, to a small village that I know. Perhaps an hour's drive or so. We are going there to see a shaman," he adds sheepishly.

"A shaman," I exclaim. This isn't at all what I expected. "One of your underground El Sociedad?"

"Underground, yes, in that none of the village shamans are officially condoned by the government, but not a member of the Order I do not think."

"And why are we going to see a shaman?" I am about to tease him about going to have our fortunes read, but seeing the serious expression on his face, think better of it.

"We are going to hear a story, a legend," he replies.

When he does not continue, I ask, "What kind of legend? Something connected to the Codex?"

"It is best that you hear it from her." He is obviously going to continue the mystery.

"She?" I query. "I thought most shaman were men."

"There are a great number of woman who are healers, medicine women," he explains. "Though some are wise women, seers, as well. The woman we are going to see is one such, Ko'lel ix K'aax, a wise woman of the forest."

We are silent for the rest of the trip. I know Eduardo is not about to tell me anything further and ruin the surprise. I doze a little; the last few days have been tiring.

I wake with a start, as Eduardo parks the jeep in front of a brightly lit building. I look around and see we are in the central square of a small village. There appears to be a dozen or so other buildings surrounding the square: houses, businesses, and the church at the end of the street. All of these other buildings are dark. From the lit building comes the noise of people talking and of music. I realize this must be the village tavern and, at this late hour, the only establishment still open.

Eduardo gets out of the jeep, saying as he does, "Stay in the car. I'll be right back." He walks toward the bar and as he reaches the foot of the steps, a figure comes out of the shadows to meet him. They speak for a moment, the other man gestures toward the other end of the village, out beyond the church. Eduardo nods his head in agreement with whatever the man has said and the two of them come over to the jeep.

"This is Carlo," Eduardo introduces the man, but doesn't give him my name. "He will show us the way."

I nod in greeting and get out of the car. Carlo goes back to the shadows at the side of the tavern and returns with two lanterns, one of which he hands to Eduardo. We walk toward the church and then around to its far side. To my mild alarm, we enter the graveyard. The cemetery is very old and poorly tended, with the weathered headstones chipped and awry. Grass and weeds grow, uncut, between the graves. The night is overcast and the lanterns only add to the eerie aspect of the scene by casting furtive shadows about us. Once out of the grave-yard we enter an ever thickening copse of trees with only a narrow path open enough to allow us through. The two men walk in front of me. They have no difficulty making their way over the uneven ground, while I stumble and trip over every fallen branch and tree root on the path.

We walk for about 15 minutes. The terrain becomes steeper and the forest deeper around us. Eduardo and Carlo come to a halt in front of me. I see the path has come to an end and directly ahead is the side of a hill. Where are we to go from here, I wonder? Through the side of the hill, or under it? I'm not far wrong, for just then a opening appears and flickering light pours out from a leather draped doorway. A cave, I realize. A figure, much shorter that either Eduardo or Carlo, holds open the door's covering and motions us in.

In the center of the room we enter is a fire pit with a badly smoking fire. This provides the only illumination for the small chamber. The cave smells of burning vegetation, pungent herbs, thick smoke, and the awful stench of old blood, like a not very clean butcher shop. As my vision grows accustomed to the dim light, I can make out a bundled figure, seated tailor fashion, on the far side of the fire. The Shaman. She is wrapped in a once brightly colored serape, much faded now to a uniform grey. Her head, bent with her chin resting on her chest, is feathered with a thin thatch of fine white hair. Her hands are tiny, shrunken and gnarled. They move incessantly, kneading a worn leather pouch. She does not look up as we enter.

Carlo hands a sack to Eduardo I haven't noticed him carrying. He leaves the cave, pulling the door covering closed behind him. The attendant, who had let us into the cave, motions for us to sit on the floor before the fire, and we do. No one says a word. The attendant takes a small container from somewhere in the darken corner of the room. He kneels beside the Shaman and throws a powder onto the fire. The fire blazes up with bright green flames and an acrid smell fills the room.

Finally, the old woman speaks in a strange dialect. Eduardo answers her haltingly, obviously not well accustomed to the language. The Shaman speaks again, this time Eduardo hesitates and the attendant speaks as translator. I realize, on hearing him speak, that he is a young boy, barely into his teens. He says, to my surprise in English, "The holy one asks why you have come?"

Eduardo responds, "We have come to hear the tale of the Priest and the Wise Woman."

The Shaman says nothing for some minutes. She rocks back and forth slowly, humming softly to herself or perhaps communing with her spirits. Finally, she speaks again, looking directly at Eduardo. The boy translates into English. "I see that you are connected to the story and to the Ah Kin, the priest. You know more than I, perhaps?" Her gaze turns to me. "And the catedratica" the attendant pauses, unsure of the translation, then adds, "the professora, she sees, but does not understand. The leyenda may open her eyes. I will tell the story as it was told to me by mi abuela and she by hers, and so through the generations."

The old woman stops here, nods at the attendant, who throws something else upon the fire. This time the flames shoot up brilliant blue and the aroma is sickly sweet. She begins to rock slowly again, in time with her rhythmic recitation. The boy translates in unison with the old woman's words, as if he knows the story as well as she.

"Many Baktun in the past, when the Maya people were still strong and the Temple still held power, there lived a nina chica, a young girl in a city far to the east. She was wise and a clarividenta, seer. She learned the shaman ways and was a great healer to the people. It is said she was called once to the palace of the King to minister to his son. And so she gained much renown. She was given the title Ko'lel ix K'aax, wise woman of the forest. And so she has been known through the intervening years. There was also an Aj k'uhm, a priestly scribe known as Piedra Escudo, whom she loved."

Here Eduardo whispers in my ear, "Piedra Escudo, stone shield." I gasp in surprise. Our whispered conversation does not disrupt the Shaman's singsong recital. She continues without pause and the boy translates.

"The priest was a wise and learned man. He knew the movement of the stars and the planets, and how they guided the fortunes of the people.

He knew the history and the legends of the Maya. He had the skill of the written language and knew the written history of the people. The great Ajaw Bahlum came to Piedra Escudo in a dream and told him of a time in the future, when the gods would become angry with humankind. They would align the stars to set in motion the end of the world. And the mighty King whispered in the priest's ear the secret of how the men of the future might outwit the gods. He gave to Piedra Escudo a holy shield that would protect mankind from the wrath of the gods and prevent the destruction of the earth. Bahlum told him he must pass this information on through the generations.

And so, Piedra Escudo wrote of Bahlum's prophecy and his instructions in a sacred book. He gave the book and the holy shield to the Wise Woman and told her to hide them where they would be found when they were needed. So Ko'lel ix K'aax hid the book in a cave far to the north. The shield she hid on sacred ground near the center of the earth. The gods were angry with Piedra Escudo, and demanded he be sacrificed upon the high altar to appease their anger. And this was done.

The wise woman mourned his death. She lived for many, many more years in her hut in the forest. There she ministered to the people and told them of the future. When she was a very, very old woman, she finally left this world, but her waay, spirit, still haunts the warab'alja, forest shrine, near her woodland home. It is said that when the end of this creation is near she will return in the form of the Maya sacred bird, the Quetzal, to guide the way."

I hear Eduardo's deep intake of breath and remember his insistence that a large Quetzal had led him to the Codex. The old woman leans toward us and asks a question. The attendant translates, "She asks if you wish to have your fortunes read?" I hesitate, but Eduardo nods. The Shaman speaks to me, pointing at the brightly colored bracelets I wear on my arm. The boy interprets, "What have you to give to placate the spirits?" The bracelets are inexpensive tourist trinkets I bought in the city. I part with them easily, slipping them off my wrist and handing them to the old woman. She takes them eagerly and places them on her own skeletal arm with, what appears to be, a nearly toothless grin.

At a signal from the Shaman, her attendant throws another powder upon the fire. This time the flames turn bright scarlet and the air fills with a sweet flowery perfume. The Shaman takes the small pouch, petaca, she holds in her hands and with gnarled fingers slowly opens its drawstring.

Intoning some unintelligible incantation, she shakes its contents onto the faded woven fabric on the ground in front of her. An array of objects land on the mat: small pieces of jade in greens and blues, tiny bits of blackest obsidian, smooth river pebbles, and an assortment of seeds and corn kernels. The Ko'lel ix K'aax bends forward, gazing at the objects intently for a few moments. Tapping one or another of them, she changes their position, infinitesimally. Satisfied with what she sees, she looks back at me and speaks in halting, heavily accented English. "You conexio`n wise women of leyenda." She reverts to her own tongue and the boy repeats in English, "She says you are related to the wise woman of the legend and have come to fulfill the prophecy. You must find the shield that is hidden and use it to protect the world."

The old woman pauses and is staring again at the objects on the mat. She looks up at me once more, looks directly into my eyes. She reaches across the smoldering fire, and grabs my arm with her claw-like fingers. Speaking with an urgency, she entreats me. "She says you must be careful, for there is a serpent in your midst who will try to divert you from your course." She lets go of my arm and seems to wilt with the effort of her revelation.

When she raises her head after a moment, her face has cleared. She gathers up the objects from before her and replaces them in her suede pouch. She turns to Eduardo. "What have you brought for the spirits?" the boy translates. Eduardo hands him the sack Carlo had given him when we entered the cave. The attendant opens it and takes out a white cock, whose feet and beak are bound and who appears sedated. The boy takes the cock to the back of the chamber and there he swiftly slits the rooster's neck. Its blood he catches in a small ceramic bowl. The bowl he brings back to the fireside and hands it to the Shaman. She receives the bowl into her hands and intones a prayer over it. As she completes the incantation, she sprinkles the blood upon the flames, producing a sickly sweet odor. The wise woman shakes the items from her pouch once again. She studies their configuration fixedly, for a long moment. Her face pales and I can see a shiver go through her. She pushes the mat roughly away, scattering the objects, and makes a frantic hand gesture at the boy. She says something to him in strident tones, which he does not translate. He turns back to the rear of the cave and brings forward the carcass of the cock, which he throws hastily and with obvious disgust into the fire. "Malo. Muy Malo," the old woman repeats to herself, beginning to rock rhythmically once again. She refuses to look at us, as the attendant hurries us from the cave. Eduardo tries to protest, but the boy forces us away from the doorway, repeating again and again, "The Ko'lel ix K'aax is ill. Go. Go."

We leave without further debate. I think Eduardo is as disturbed as I am by the sudden turn of events. But he doesn't say a word as we walk back to the village. We make the return trip to Mexico City almost entirely in silence, each of us immersed in our own thoughts. It is after 2 AM when Eduardo drops me at the hotel. I drag myself to my room, exhausted from a long, emotionally packed day.

The red light on the phone is blinking. There is a message from Daniel. "Enrice` Sanchez called. He said we should tune in to his talk show tomorrow morning, 7 to 9 AM. He thinks we might be interested. I made arrangements with the Hotel staff for a radio in the lounge off the lobby. Meet you for breakfast at 6, if you are up to it."

I set the alarm for 5:30 and fall into bed without bothering to shower. Three hours sleep is not going to do it.

At 10 minutes to 7 I make my way groggily to the diningroom. I had decided to forgo breakfast in favor of an extra ½ hour of sleep and a hot shower. Daniel and Adam are both there. I slide into a chair and order a cup of coffee. "How was your evening?" Daniel asks. "You got back rather late."

"I had a wonderful visit with Maria," I reply. I'm not ready to share the other experience of the night before, just yet. "What did you guys find to amuse yourselves?"

"We split up," Adam says. "Each of us hooked up with friends. I went out to dinner and then to a club. Didn't get back here much before you did, I suppose."

"I didn't know you had friends here in Mexico City," I comment. "Daniel, did you meet with your colleagues from the University here?"

"Yes," he answers. "I met with Michael Emery and Constantia Lopez. You've heard of them, I'm sure. We ran into Senor Tierro from the Office of Antiquities in Merida. He asked about the Codex, said he was here to get a look at it. He seemed very interested."

I was a little alarmed. "What did you tell him?"

"Nothing really. Just repeated what we had already told him last summer. I don't think he has any idea of the specimens we took with us, if that is what you're concerned about."

"No, I don't suppose he can." But I don't like anyone asking questions and showing an interest.

It is time for the radio program, so we make our way to the lounge. The Hotel staff has set up a small radio for us and the desk clerk is tuning it to the program as we enter. After a short piece of introductory music, we hear Enrice`'s voice wishing all his listeners good morning. My Spanish is limited, so I will have to rely on Daniel and Adam for translation. Their command of the language is better than mine. Enrice` opens the program, saying he has new developments to announce regarding the 2012 Doomsday Prophecy. He recounts the Maya Prophecy and its origin. He pauses for effect, then adds, "Rumors around town have linked the newly found artifact, a Codex found in the Yucatan, to the prophecies of Chan Bahlum II and the Maya Doomsday Prophecy. The Museo Mexicana de Arqueologia denies its authenticity, but I have it on good authority that it appears to be the real thing, or an ancient copy of a manuscript. What do you think? Give me a call." Here he breaks for a commercial and the three of us look at each other in resignation.

Adam breaks the silence. "Well, that lets the cat out of the bag. No keeping it quiet after this. I'm just afraid Enrice`'s 'good authority' is going to lead right back to us."

"Not necessarily," Daniel says, but he has a worried look on his face that belies this assurance.

Enrice` comes back on. "The phones are ringing off the hooks here at the studio. Let's take a few and see what you think." He takes twenty or so calls in the next hour. The comments seem to vary from outright disbelief to enthusiastic agreement. From what I can make out the ayes seem to have it. Enrice` signs off at 9 o'clock, assuring his listeners that he will take up the discussion again the next day. He urges them to be sure to tell their friends to tune in as well.

Adam is right, this sure does let the cat out of the bag. Publicity is what we wanted and publicity is what we are about to get, big time.

The three of us have plans to leave for a visit to Chichen Itza tomorrow morning. I decide to spend the day at the various museums and cultural centers. Daniel tells us he has some research he wants to pursue and will spend the day at the University library. Adam says he made arrangements for a round of golf with his friends. We make arrangements to meet for dinner later that evening. Eduardo is to join us in a farewell dinner.

On the spur of the moment, I decide to call Padre Alejandro, to see if he is free. He is and is delighted to hear I am in town. We spend the day wandering around the city, thoroughly enjoying each other's company. We talk about the history of the city and he shows me all his favorite sights. He is proud of his city and its history. He shows me the ruins, the remnants of the ancient Aztecs who founded the city. I think it odd, but rather endearing, that he is more interested in the pagan origins and monuments, than those of his Catholic religion. But as he reminds me they, and not the Spanish conquistadores, are his ancestors. We don't speak of the Codex or El Sociedad. I push any misgivings of this morning's radio show out of my mind for the time being.

The four of us, Eduardo, Daniel, Adam, and I, have a wonderful dinner at a local bistro of Eduardo's choosing. Then we go back to the hotel for a nightcap. While Adam and Daniel are getting our drinks at the bar, Eduardo leans over and whispers to me, "What do you make of the Shaman's fortune? Who could be the snake in our camp that she spoke of? And," here a look of terror shows on his face, the old panic returning, "why did she refuse to tell me my fortune? Is it a premonition, an ill omen?"

"I don't give much credence to anything she had to say," I reply, trying to calm him. But this isn't entirely true. The legend fits too well with the message of the Codex, and I've suspected for a long time there is a spy close to us. But I don't believe in fortune tellers. Then why do I believe in the prophecy of the Codex? I am sure, now, that I do.

"I feel evil in the air," continues Eduardo. "You must be careful. The Shaman told you it is your destiny to solve the mystery and find the shield. She did not tell me of my destiny though, did she?" He sounds despondent and, yes, somehow resigned. I begin to say something reassuring, but we are interrupted as Daniel and Adam return to the table.

We finally say goodnight near midnight, promising Eduardo we'll let him know what we find in Chichen Itza. He in turn says he will keep us informed of events here in Mexico City and at the museum. I hug him warmly and he holds on tightly for longer than usual. I think he actually has tears in his eyes as we part.

0

III

July 7, 944
10.5.15.17.14, 5 Ix, 2 Zac
In the Temple gardens:

Several days later Took Pak walked again in the Temple gardens at midday, so as to meet Nuxib Mak. He had a request to make of the old servant. As soon as Nuxib Mak saw him enter the garden, the old man made his way toward Took Pak, not hurrying, but obviously anxious to speak with him. Took Pak looked at his old friend's face and forgot his own concern over what he was going to ask of him. "What is it, friend?" he asked, fearing the worst.

"All in your family are well," Nuxib Mak told him hurriedly, realizing that the young priest had mistaken his anxiety. "It is not of them that I have concern. My fear is in regard to you, yourself."

"What is it that could possibly worry you so about me?" Took Pak said, though he knew what it might be.

"I was in the Temple courtyard yesterday, over by the north wall, trimming the bushes that grow there. Two men came strolling through the gardens. They did not see me where I was working, or saw me but paid me no more attention than they would a slave. Whichever it was, they walked and spoke unguardedly, as if I were not there." The gardener paused and looked at Took Pak to see if he had the young man's attention. Took Pak was listening with courtesy, rather than real interest. Nuxib Mak continued, "And so I heard what I was not meant to hear. The two priests were Kaloome Ek Suutz, the Ah Kin Mai, and Sajal Ch'itz'aat, the secretary.

This got Took Pak's attention. He looked at the other man in surprise. "Sajal Ch'itz'aat and Koloome Ek Suutz?"

"Yes, and they were speaking of you," said the gardener solemnly.

"Of me?" Took Pak asked, but he was not surprised at this; rather he felt a chill and a premonition of what was to come.

"They were speaking of you, yes," the old man continued. "Sajal Ch'itz'aat said that Cho P'iit is getting more and more suspicious of what you are doing. The chief scribe has evidently been watching you. Sajal Ch'itz'aat said that the scribe told him that you were staying late every night in your basement chamber. That though, previously, you spent this time reading every old Codex you could find, now you were writing a Codex of your own. Sajal Ch'itz'aat said that the chief scribe asked you what you were writing and that you told him you were transcribing your astrological observations. Cho P'iit said that he picked up the manuscript and that it appeared to be what you said." Here Nuxib Mak paused again and looked at Took Pak seriously. "But Cho P'iit does not believe you. Of course, he does not like you either."

The gardener paused again. Took Pak said nothing. Then Nuxib Mak continued, "Kaloome Ek Suutz seemed to be fascinated by what Sajal Ch'itz'aat had to say. Then the High Priest said that this information did not bode well." Here the old man recounted exactly what Kaloome Ek Suutz had said, "The high Priest said, 'I believe the boy is lying as well. I do not think he is writing about the stars, but what is it that he is writing? What has he found in the ancient manuscripts? I think it is time we spoke with our young prophet and then we may need to rid ourselves of him.'"

Nuxib Mak continued to relate what he had heard. "The Ah Kin Mai said that your destruction may serve them in two ways. He said that it would rid them of an annoyance, before you became a real danger. Then he said something about using your sacrifice to appease the gods and to quell the rebellion among the people. I do not like the sound of it," said Nuxib Mak. "They see you as a hindrance and mean to get rid of you, Took Pak." The old servant was near to tears; fear evident on his weathered face. He looked at Took Pak and what he saw on the boy's face surprised him. The young priest showed no fear, but rather a look of relief. In truth, that is what Took Pak felt.

"I am not surprised," he said. "I knew this time was coming, but it is here sooner than I expected. It just means that what I have to ask of you must be done quickly."

Nuxib Mak looked at him baffled, "If you knew that you were being watched and were in danger, why then did you not protect yourself?" he asked with confusion.

"We do what we must," Took Pak said thoughtfully. "I did what I had to do. I will continue to do what I must, with what has been placed in my hands. "Nuxib Mak made as if to protest, but Took Pak stilled him and continued. "What I need of you should put you in no danger."

"Anything I can do for you, I will," responded the old gardener.

"I want you to set up a meeting between Ahkan and myself," said Took Pak.

P. A. Faber

The gardener was totally taken by surprise with this request. Took Pak seldom spoke Ahkan's name or asked about her, much less asked to see her. "If she will come," Took Pak added.

"Of course she will come," Nuxib Mak said. "But it is against the rules of the Order. Will it be safe for you?" his friend said.

"Nothing is safe for me now," said Took Pak mournfully. "If she comes to the wall near the ceiba tree, at the far side of the Temple gardens, late at night when all in the Temple are asleep, it should be safe enough. Just tell her I must see her for there is something I must ask her to do for me."

"When, young master?" Nuxib Mak asked resignedly.

"As soon as possible. After what you overheard, we have no time to waste." Took Pak replied, and then continued. "There is one more thing you must do for me." He looked into the other man's eyes and said, seriously. "This is something you must do in the future. You will know when the time is right." And Took Pak told Nuxib Mak what else it was that he must do.

Several nights later

The small sliver of moon shone in a clear sky and lit the Temple gardens, but only dimly. Took Pak knew the route well and made his way without difficulty. He moved quickly, but silently, through the shadows, carrying a woven basket over his arm.

As he reached the ceiba tree, he heard a small voice from the shadows say, "Is that you, Took Pak?" The voice continued before he could respond. "I have been waiting. I came early, afraid if I waited any longer, I would wake and find it was only a dream."

Took Pak, on hearing her voice, was transported back in time to the last time he had seen her and heard her voice. It was the same sweet voice he heard in his heart so often. "I am here and it is not a dream, hun p'iit," he said softly. "This is a time I thought would never come."

"I have missed you," Ahkan whispered.

"And I you," Took Pak answered.

Ahkan came to him and put her hand upon his arm, unsure if she should touch him or if this would offend him. He took her hand in his and led her to the base of the tree. He put his basket upon the ground and sat, pulling her down beside him. He looked lovingly at her beautiful, familiar face. She had aged surely, for she was mature now, no longer the little girl he had known so well. She was beautiful still: her warm brown eyes, smooth bronze skin, and silky long ebony hair. He breathed in the still familiar smell of her, lavender and Yucca. He drank in the sight of her, not realizing, until this moment, how much he had longed for the sight and smell of her. He was so overcome, he could not speak.

So Ahkan spoke for him. "Nuxib Mak told me of the conversation he overheard the other day. What does it mean?" her voice tremulous and frightened. Still he did not speak, not wanting to cause her the pain his story would give her. "Why are they so fearful of you? What is it that you know that is a danger to them, and so to you?" she whispered, afraid of the answer.

Finally Took Pak spoke, "I will tell you all of it, but it is a long story." And Took Pak told her all: of his first audience with the Ah Kin Mai, of the sessions with the astrologer under the stars, of the manuscripts that he had read, of the visions or dreams or whatever they were, and finally, of the hidden codex he had found and what it revealed.

Anker marveled at all that Took Pak said. She also saw why Kaloome Ek Suutz was determined to rid himself of the young priest. And she was terrified by what she realized would be the inevitable outcome. "It is heresy against all that this stands for," she breathed and swept her hand toward the Temple.

"Yes, it is heresy," said Took Pak "but it is what the prophet Chan Bahlum has written. I believe it has been given to me, so I might pass on this information to the future."

"Why not just return the Codex and the tile to where you found them. Leave clues for men of the future to find. Say no more about what you have found," Ahkan pleaded, "and save yourself."

"I cannot do that," said Took Pak hopelessly.

"Why can you not?" she cried.

"Because they were given to me for a reason. In my vision I am holding the shield that saves the world. I am meant to do this. I feel if I do not intervene the world will end as the Mayan myth foretells." After a short pause and a deep breath, Took Pak continued. "I may be arrogant, but I believe it is my fate."

Ahkan saw that she could not dissuade him. She dropped her eyes to her hands folded in her lap. Tears fell upon them, unchecked. After a moment she continued changing the subject. "Nuxib Mak said that you had some things you wished me to do it for you. What is it that I can do?" she said. And he told her.

Took Pak pulled the basket he had brought toward them and gently, almost reverently, removed the bundle tightly wrapped in cured deer hide from inside. He placed it in his lap, his hands holding onto it as if he feared to let it go. He looked from the object to Ahkan's solemn face that he could see only faintly in the moonlight.

"This is my Codex. The original Chan Bahlum manuscript I have returned to where I found it, at the foot of the Temple stairway. But not before I copied the pertinent material here." And he touched the top of the bundle. "In this, my manuscript, I tell how the Chan Bahlum codex came to me. I recount what had been written there about the end of the world. Finally, I have written how those in the future might prevent it." He smiled up at her, hoping that she would comply when he asked her for the help that he needed to complete his plan. "This is where your part begins. I need a way to hide this, far from here, some place where it will be safe; so that sometime in the far distant future it will be found, when it is needed." Ahkan began to ask a question, but he stopped her. "I need you to get this to your brother, Ek Och"

"My brother?" Ahkan said in surprise.

"Yes, your brother. I know he is part of the rebellion. He knows the outlying villages and roams them freely. I know of a place outside a small village, where there are many small caves and cenotes. It is there I wish him to take this Codex and hide it. Tell him to hide it in the cave we found when we were boys, so many years ago . . . He will remember. Tell him to chisel a space into the rock and there place the manuscript."

"He will do this for you. I am sure," she said. Then, Ahkan asked the question she had been waiting to ask. "But how will the people of the future find it? How will they even know that it exists?"

"That task I have given to Nubix Mak, with your help. Nubix Mak, when he feels the time is right, is to start a story . . . a myth. A myth about a heretic priest and the beautiful wise woman of the forest. It will be the story of how they set in motion the means to foil the gods and their part in preventing the end of the world." He smiled at her and she smiled back.

"It will make a good story to hand down to the Mayan children to come," she said softly

Took Pak reached into the basket once more. "And now the most important and, perhaps, the most dangerous thing I must ask of you," he said regretfully. He lifted out of the basket the stone tile with the glyph of the sun god etched upon it. He laid it on top of the bundle that contained his codex. "This is the shield that I saw symbolically in my vision," he said. "It must be placed in the precise place at the exact moment as foretold by Chan Bahlum." He ran his hands over the carved surface of the stone.

Ahkan looked at the tile in awe. "What is it you want me to do with it?" she asked.

Took Pak replaced the stone and the Codex into the basket and handed it to her. He told her where the tile must be on that fateful day in the future and asked her advice. And she told where it should be hidden. She knew what it was she must do with the precious artifact.

They sat quietly, not speaking, just being in each other's company. They watched the faint shimmer of the stars overhead. Finally Took Pak broke the silence. "There is one more thing that I must ask you to do for me." His voice was grim, so grim that it frightened her, but she knew he would not ask if he did not feel that it was of great importance. "There will come a time when Kaloome Ek Suutz will demand information from me. When I refuse to tell what he wants to know, he will use whatever means he must to get that information." Ahkan gasped at the realization that this was true and what it would inevitably mean. "I need your services as a Ko'lel ix K'aax." He laughed ruefully "I require some potion or herb that will help me to resist telling him any of this and especially of your and Nubix Mak's role in it." She would have interrupted, but he held up his hand and continued. "Your brother is already a fugitive and can take care of himself. But you and Nubix Mak cannot go into exile, so I ask for a way to protect you and the tile from discovery." He paused, looking at her intently. "Can you do this for me?"

Ahkan nodded, weeping again soundlessly. She reached up and touched his face gently and then emboldened, when he did not pull away, kissed him tenderly on the lips. "I will send what you need with Nubix Mak." She rose and left without another word, knowing full well that this would be the last time they would ever be together.

Took Pak watched her leave and knew he had broken her heart once again. He walked back through the Temple garden, as if he had been unable to sleep and was out for a stroll. No one was about to see him and he returned to his room and his bed undetected.

IV

August 10, 2012
12.19.19.11.7, 1 Manik, 10 Yaxkin
Mexico City

Eduardo left the hotel a few minutes before midnight. He was saddened at parting from his friends and uneasy regarding the events of the last two days. He felt the heavy weight of the Shaman's words, and her silence even more.

He turned right out of the Hotel entrance and, then, right again into an alley way. This would take him to the side street where he had parked his car. The alley was exceptionally dark as he left the lights of the street behind him. He entered the shadows cast by the buildings on either side. He heard a noise from the main street, the sound of an engine starting. It reminded him of the shrill cry of the Quetzal, from the clearing on the mound a year ago. A shiver ran through him. Another premonition?

The car, without lights, silently entered the alley behind him. The car advanced slowly in his direction. It gained momentum. Eduardo became aware of something in the alley with him. He looked back and realized the car was there. He increased his pace, glancing frequently over his shoulder.

The car kept pace with him, then began to accelerate. Eduardo started to run. The car came on faster. He knew there was no way he could outrun the car. He looked ahead. The end of the alley was fifty yards or more ahead of him. Too far. The buildings on either side were too close, no way for him to get out of the vehicle's path. He looked in desperation for a doorway, any alcove that might protect him, but he found none.

The car sped toward him and he knew he was about to die. His last thoughts were of his wife, of the look upon the face of the old wise woman in the cave, and of the long ago priest who defied the heavens and paid the ultimate price. He wondered what he had done to anger the gods ?

Chapter Sixteen

I

1548 CE
11.16.9.3.14

Mayan Myth

And the time came when what
The shaman foretold came to pass
And out of the East came the great god,
The people brought to the god, K'nich Kay Lak'in,
Maize and squash, fruits and berries,
Fish and game and fowl.

These the god K'nich Kay Lak'in rejected
Saying, "Bring to me the stone the color of the sun."
Then the people brought fine linen
And intricately decorated pottery,
Beautiful jewelry of polished stone, jade,
And brightly colored beads.

These offerings they placed before the god.
But the god rejected all that they gave.
K'nich Kay Lak'in grew angry, demanding other treasure.
But the people had no more to give
And so the god commanded his warriors
To turn against the people.

And this they did.
Slaying the people where they stood

II

August 14, 2012
12.19.19.11.11, 5 Chuen, 14 Yaxkin
The University

Our trip to Chichen Itza is postponed due to Eduardo's death. On our last night in Mexico City, I am awakened at 3 in the morning by furious knocking at my hotel room door. I open the door, cautiously, to find two grim faced police officers on the threshold. They are polite, but insistent that I get dressed immediately and accompany them downstairs to the hotel lobby. They refuse to tell me why, just that their superior wishes to speak with me, and to hurry. All I can think is the Office of Antiquities is having me arrested for stealing pieces of a national treasure.

When we get to the lobby, Daniel and Adam are already there: Daniel looking stoic, Adam white faced with anxiety. A good-looking, dark haired, middle aged gentleman greets us and introduces himself as Capitan Nicalos Diego of the Metropolitano Policia. He ushers us into the entirely empty lobby and asks us to have a seat. His manner is grave, his voice conciliatory, which frightens me more than the curt insistence of the police officers earlier.

"I have some disturbing news for you, I am afraid," he begins. I feel a sudden feeling of overwhelming despair. I know what he is about to say, before he says it. Eduardo, I think, and see again the face of the Shaman as she stared at the ? stones cast for Eduardo's fortune. "Your friend, Eduardo Gomez, has met with an unfortunate accident. He is dead," the police Capitan concludes.

"How? When?" Daniel pants as if he has just been hit hard in the stomach.

Adam gave out a strangled, "What?"

Daniel reaches over and takes my hand, then wraps his arm around my shoulder. I can feel myself trembling. I am lightheaded and, if I had not been sitting, I would have fallen to my knees. I can feel Daniel's heart beating rapidly and hear his breath coming in quick inhalations, an indication of the emotional turmoil he is undergoing as well. I am shaking all over, but the tears have not come. They will, but not yet.

The Capitan allows us a moment to absorb the news, then continues, "I believe you were friends. I am sorry for your loss." He pauses a moment in respect. "He was hit by a car in the alley next to this hotel at approximately midnight." I gasp in shock. The policeman continues. "We believe he was leaving the hotel on his way to where he had parked his car. We found the car parked on the street several blocks away." He pauses again. When none of us make any comment, he continues, taking a small notebook out of his pocket. "Since you were the last to see him . . ." He doesn't add 'alive', but I do, in my head. "I'm afraid I must ask you some questions." And he does. How did we know Eduardo? How long? What was our relationship? Why had he been here at the hotel? Why had we come to Mexico City? Did Eduardo have any enemies that we knew of?

I tell him everything: about the Codex, about the death threats, the meeting with Enrice' and his radio program that morning. Daniel grips my arm in an unsuccessful effort to stop the flow of my testimony, but I can't stop. I even tell Capitan Diego of our visit to the Shaman and her odd response to Eduardo's fortune. This, of course, is news to Daniel and Adam. I shake off any question they have, at least for the time being.

Capitan Diego listens attentively, taking copious notes, but does not seem overly impressed by my story. When I finish, he closes his notebook with finality, and tells us, "We do not think there is any foul play involved, just a most unfortunate accident." I start to protest, but the tightening of Daniel's grip on my arm stops me. The policeman continues, "But as the driver did not stop, nor report the incident, it is still to be considered as a crime, a hit and run. We will be continuing our investigation. If I have any further questions, where can I reach you?"

Daniel answered for us. "We had plans to visit Chichen Itza, leaving later this morning. Under the circumstances I believe we will be postponing that trip. If the hotel can accommodate us, I think we will remain here, at least for a few more days. See what we might do to help the family. Stay for the funeral."

"The family," I gasp, suddenly thinking of Maria. "Have you notified his wife yet?" I ask.

"I will be going there directly," Capitan Diego replies.

A chill goes through me. Eduardo is dead and Maria doesn't even know yet. She is at home, sleeping or sitting up waiting for him to return, worrying because he is so late. Waiting, not knowing he isn't coming home. "Tell her . . . tell her," I stammer, "I will be here if she needs someone." I think of the other evening, their beautiful welcoming home, their loving relationship, their pride and pleasure in each other. Gone. I put my head in my hands and weep for the loss, for the waste of a good man. And I think to myself, "This was no accident. This was murder, the execution of the threats that had been plaguing Eduardo for so long. This was murder and I'll be damned if I will let them get away with it."

The funeral takes place three days later. It is a nightmare. Sudden, unexpected deaths always are, I guess. Maria, pale and dazed, clung to her sons for support throughout. She has a large family, as did Eduardo, and her sons so she does not need my support. Daniel, Adam, and I leave for home the next day.

October 15, 2012
12.19.19.14.13, 2 Ben, 16 Yax
The University

Carli is devastated by the news of Eduardo's death when I call her from Mexico City. She's sorry she cannot make it to the funeral. She is so distraught that I do not tell her of my suspicions about Eduardo's death and of my visit to the Shaman. I don't want to worry her further and really those are things I'd rather tell her in person, not on the phone.

Professor Allen does not come to the funeral, which I find very odd. I thought he and Eduardo had been good friends for such a long time that he would have made the effort.

We get back to the University just in time to complete our preparations for the fall semester. I'm afraid my heart isn't in it. I go through the motions: getting lectures ready, meeting with new students, arranging for guest lectures, and breaking in this year's crop of new teaching assistants.

Carli isn't coming back this semester. She's postponing her first year of grad school because of her mother's continuing illness. She has a position as a teacher's aide for her local Head Start. The hours are only half days which works well for her right now.

I do not see Professor Allen at all in August or September. He doesn't return to school until mid-October. There is a rumor going around that he was ill, but there's no confirmation. He appears his usual self on his return, but spends little time on campus and none of us see much of him.

I hear rumors and vague references, in the department and from students, about the talk show host in Mexico City making news over claims regarding the Maya Doomsday Prophecy. Gradually, the media picks up the story and news-casters and talk show personalities in the U.S. join the frenzy. All this publicity is fueling the hysteria that is building as 12-21-12 approaches. Its magnitude is far beyond anything I expected. Opinion seems to fall equally on both sides. The Museo Mexicana de Arqueologia in Mexico City is being bombarded with demands, from both sides, that they give further information about the artifact and release a copy of the manuscript to the media. So far the Museum has done neither. If Eduardo had intended to produce a storm, he would have been well pleased.

School is in full swing and I'm caught up in the day to day routine. I realize, once back, that I had, essentially, wasted the whole summer. I had planned some really intensive research time for my dissertation and further work on chapters one and two. None of this had I even thought about, much less worked on. I am behind schedule, feel guilty, but don't have the energy to do anything about it.

What I do, late at night when I can't sleep, is go over and over the story of the Wise Woman and the Priest the Shaman had told us. I think of it and compare it to the Codex. Had there really been a Mayan Priest and had he been the priestly scribe who wrote the hidden Codex? Had he given his life to send this message through the ages? And what exactly is the message? What are we, what am I, if the Shaman woman is right, to do with the information? And most pressing of all, has Eduardo died, like the ancient Priest, for this undertaking? I spend long sleepless nights contemplating these questions.

Finally, I can't stand it any longer. I need to do something, anything, if I am ever to get another night's sleep. I call a meeting of the team. Daniel and I have seen each other frequently, since our return from Mexico. We, of course, see one another in department meetings and committees. We have also gotten into the habit of having lunch together, once or twice a week. We either brown bag it and sit outside or in the faculty lounge, or we go off campus, usually to the Coffee Shop. I haven't seen Calvin or Brian, but Daniel spoke to them about Eduardo's death. They were shocked and saddened, but hadn't really known him well. Adam seems to have disappeared. I know he returned to campus, but neither Daniel nor I have seen him. He isn't in any of our courses.

Carli arrives into town to meet with us at my apartment on Saturday afternoon. I feel we need to meet somewhere we can talk uninterrupted and where we will not be overheard. Adam comes, arriving last. He seems to have gotten over the shock and distress he'd exhibited at the funeral and appears his old self, smiling and joking.

I jump right in after our brief hellos. I start with the reason I called them together. "I want to go to Chichen Itza as we planned in August." None of them seem at all surprised.

Daniel, as always, takes the path of logic. "What is it that you expect to find there?" he asks.

"I don't know," I admit, pathetically. "But I feel I need to see where the Codex was written. See if I can find the original Bahlum manuscript where our Codex says it was hidden," I explain in desperation.

"Do you really think," Adam interrupts sarcastically, "that the manuscript could still be there, after all these centuries?"

I ignore him. "I need to see if I can find out what this shield or tile can be and, if possible, find where it is hidden?"

"Do you really believe these things are real?" Daniel's disbelief is as evident as Adam's, but his comments are kind and without mockery.

I look at all their faces, some questioning, others disdainful, and for the first time tell them the whole story of Eduardo's and my visit to the Wise Woman in the cave. I tell them the legend of the long ago wise woman as the Shaman told it to us. I tell them of the fortune the old woman cast for me. And then I tell them the fortune she cast for Eduardo and her refusal to tell it to us. I describe her look of shock and revulsion that I still see in my dreams. I don't think my story changes any of their minds about the import and truth of the Codex. Daniel is kindly skeptical, Adam more aggressively so. Calvin mildly interested, but non-committal. Brian, my one ally from the beginning, remains a believer. Carli supports me as usual, though I don't think she believes it wholeheartedly. And then I say, "I believe what the Shaman told me. I believe what Eduardo believed. Eduardo believed that fate had led him to find the Codex for a reason and the Shaman confirmed that. The Shaman told me I am to find the shield and . . ."

"And what?" said Daniel gently, and they all waited expectantly for an answer.

"And . . . I don't know what," I answer, tearfully. "I don't know what. All I know is that I have to do something. It's crazy, I know. But what if the end of the world is near? What if the Maya were right? What if the shield, or tile, or whatever, can prevent it from happening? What if the Wise Woman was right and I am meant to find it? What if Eduardo was right in his belief?" I looked around at their incredulous faces and make one more effort to convince them. "I have to do this for Eduardo." And

I see, though I haven't changed any minds, they at least understand this reason and will support my intentions.

"Okay," Daniel says with resignation. "When do you plan to go?"

"As soon as possible. As soon as I can make arrangements for my classes," I tell him.

"I can't get away right now," he says with concern.

"I don't expect you can. I'm perfectly able to go by myself," I reply.

"But I don't want you to," he responds, talking only to me, as if we are all alone in the room.

"I might be able to get away for a short time," cuts in Adam, languidly.

Daniel gives him a venomous look and begins to object, when Carli speaks up quietly. "I'd like to go with you."

I look at her in surprise. "Are you sure? Can you leave your mom?"

"Yes, I can. She's doing much better, right now. She's off the chemo for now. I think she might welcome my being away for a little. She accuses me of hovering, smothering her." And she laughs self-consciously.

"Well, that settles it then. Carli and I will go, with Adam as protection." I can tell Daniel isn't happy with the arrangement, but he makes no further protest.

October 20, 2012
12.19.19.14.18, 7 Etznab, 1 Zac
Chichen Itza

It takes us nearly a week to make all the arrangements. By the time we reach Merida in the Yucatan, I am exhausted and in a panic because I don't have any idea what I am doing here. I haven't thought beyond getting here. Now what? We decide to spend the night in Merida and rent a car in the morning for the trip to Chichen Itza.

Adam insists we go out for a night on the town and calls us old ladies when we refuse. He laughs and goes out on his own, saying he is sure he can find other company.

Carli and I spend a relaxing evening at the hotel, take a swim in the pool, have a pedicure at the spa, a leisurely dinner in the hotel diningroom, and make an early night of it. I tell Carli, in more detail, about my visit to the Wise Woman. Through the telling, a clear idea of what it is I am meant

to do comes to me. And for the first time, I am able to articulate a plan. The problem is I don't have any idea how I am going to go about it.

This morning as we are checking out of the hotel, we receive a telephone call from the Office of Antiquities. The call is from Senor Tierro's, the director, office. His secretary asks if we might come in to see the director while we are in Merida. We tell her we are planning to leave for Chichen Itza this morning. She asks us to hold for a moment, then comes back on the phone. "The director has some time at ten, if you can delay your departure until then. He would really appreciate your thoughtfulness." We agree. What else can we do? On hearing that the director of the Office of Antiquities wishes to see us, my first thought is that our past indiscretions are about to catch up with us. However, the polite, gracious manner of the request dispels this fear. But if not to arrest us, why does he want to see us?

Senor Tierro meets us in the anteroom to his office. He is a debonair grey haired gentleman: tall, muscular, well manicured. He greets us warmly, shaking hands with each of us, and calling us by name. He is obviously well informed. We are led to a small sitting room across the hall. He must see the looks of confusion on our faces and laughs gently. "I am sure you are surprised by my request that you come to see me," he says once we are seated. "I was informed of your request for professional access to the site at Chichen Itza." He smiles again, probably noticing the fleeting expression of irritation on my face despite my attempt to hide it. Daniel had insisted that we arrange for a curator of the site to meet us and give us special access. So much for our visit remaining undercover.

My attention comes back to the present. Senor Tierro is still talking. He's apologizing profusely about the misunderstanding of this past summer. "I am most sorry I was compelled to revoke Professor Allen's license for the archeological dig in the Yucatan. The Museo Mexicana de Arqueologia has mucho power. How do you say it? Clout?" He smiles deferentially. "On your visit, if there is anything I might do to assist you, please allow me to do so." When none of us respond he continues, "I have been following all the to-do made by that fana`tico on the radio. I do not know what to make of it all. What do you think?"

"Ridiculous," Adam says, his smile is as ingratiating as Senor Tierro's. "Just a bid for publicity. That guy, Sanchez's fifteen minutes of fame."

"And your opinion, Professora O'Hara?" he looks questioningly at me.

I don't know what to say. He sounds sincere, but I don't know that I trust him. He is, after all, the government. "It's all fantastic," I agree finally.

"What is it you are researching at Chichen Itza?" he asks, still looking at me.

"My dissertation is about the role of Maya women in the post-classical period," I respond truthfully. "In the last few years, I've not had the time, while in the Yucatan, for a protracted visit to Chichen Itza. I am completing my preliminary research and wish to make sure I haven't missed anything here."

"I see," he replies and appears to accept this explanation. Our audience seems to be at an end. "Again, if there is anything I might do to assist you, do not hesitate to ask." He escorts us back to the hallway and says goodbye with a broad smile.

"What was that all about?" asks Carli, as we leave the building.

"He was just covering his ass," comments Adam. "Wants to stay on the good side of the academic community in the States. Kicking out a well respected archeologist isn't the way to make friends and encourage international cooperation." I'm not sure it's that simple; after all, Professor Allen isn't such a big fish in the archeological world.

Our trip to Chichen Itza is uneventful. Adam insists on driving. He's a good driver, so I don't object. We've made reservations at the Hacienda Chichen in the small village of Piste` about a ten minute walk from the ancient city. We check in at about 1 o'clock and make plans to meet in the lobby in 30 minutes. I change into jeans, long sleeved shirt, and heavy hiking boots; pack a bottle of water, my camera, phone, and my notebook in a backpack, and am ready to go. I feel excited. I feel sure there has to be something to find here.

We make the short walk from the hotel to the archeological site along a well-manicured pathway through the jungle. The day is already steamy and it is predicted that the temperature will be well into the nineties. We pass through a turnstile, entry fee 166 pesos, about $14 U.S. To the right of the entrance is the visitors' center, where we are to meet our guide at 2 o'clock.

The visitors' center contains exhibits; photos of the excavation of the site, and artifacts found here. A man approaches us as we enter. He is short, heavyset, and grey haired. He appears to be in his late sixties, his skin wrinkled and coarsened by exposure to the sun. "Buenos Dios," he says in a gravelly voice, extending his hand. "My name is Jorge, Professor Jorge Casteo, retired. I now enjoy the position of guide into the history of Chichen Itza. Much more enjoyable than spending my time in a classroom all day. I have been asked to give you the VIP treatment. Anything you wish to see and any questions you may have, it will be my pleasure to provide." He smiles, warmly. I like him immediately.

"Buenos Dios, Senor Casteo," I say, shaking his hand. "Our primary interest is in the Pyramid of K'ul kul'kan, though, of course, we want to see it all."

"Call me Jorge, please. Of course, El Castillo, the Spanish name for the pyramid, is the best known structure at the site. And it is magnificent, but there are many other magnificent things to see. You know that it is no longer possible to climb the Pyramid steps, a great shame for the view from the top is breath-taking. But the numbers of tourists climbing the stairs were contributing to their deterioration. Let's start there." And he leads us from the building. He gives us a running commentary about the features and history of the site as we walk.

In front of us stands the Ossiary, a smaller pyramid than the Pyramid of Ku'k'ul'kan and thought to be the burial site of the high priests of Chichen Itza, Jorge tells us. He then directs us east, past the end of the ball court. As we round the corner, the grand pyramid comes into view across a wide expanse of lawn. It takes my breath away, so much more beautiful and awe inspiring than in any photograph. It rises from the flat ground 75 feet (22.9 m) into the clear blue sky and is 181 feet (55.3 meters) across. Each of the Pyramid's four sides has staircases with 91 steps. When added together and including the temple platform on top as the final 'step,' there is a total of 365 steps, one for each day of the Haab' (the Maya sacred calendar and our year).

We walk across the grass to the foot of the northern stairway. This is the location of the equinox spectacles each spring and autumn. At the base of the massive steps, formed by huge limestone blocks, are two sculptured heads of Ku'kul'kan, the plumed serpent. El Castillo served as a temple to the god Ku'kul'kan. This was the place where the priest scribe had recorded he found the hidden Bahlum manuscript and where he had replaced it. Jorge tells us that the Pyramid had undergone reconstruction in the 1920's and the north side of the structure was excavated by the Mexican government in the 1930's. He assures us that no documents or any artifact resembling the tile or the Codex had been found. I am disappointed, but not at all surprised.

As I kneel at the foot of the giant Pyramid, the sun is momentarily covered by a passing cloud. A shadow falls over me and with it a chill. In the air, above the Temple atop the structure, I see a massive bird. Its wide swept wings reflect bright glints of emerald and gold. I hear a high pitch cry from the creature. I turn to see what the others make of the sight, but they do not appear to be aware of the apparition. I draw my gaze back to the Pyramid's summit, but the bird is gone. Had it been real? Or has the atmosphere of the place induced a hallucination? Whatever the reason, the shadow and the chill are gone.

Our next stop is the Ball Court. Jorge tells us it is the largest ball court in ancient Mesoamerica. "It measures 166 by 68 meters (545 × 223 ft). The walls are 12 meters (39 ft) high. In the center, high up on each of the long walls, are rings carved with intertwining serpents. Archeologists believe that the ball games, Pitz, played here were a ritualistic re-enactment of the myth of the twin gods' Hun Bstz and Hun Chuen, and their battle with the gods of the underworld. It is thought that the game was brutal and often ended with sacrificial beheadings." A shiver runs through me again.

The western wall holds a faded mural depicting the game itself. Players are shown with heavily padded elbows, knees and shins and large ornate helmets on their heads. They are knocking about a rubber ball, using feet, arms and heads, much like our modern game of soccer.

Built into the east wall are the Temples of the Jaguar. The Upper Temple overlooks the ball court. It has an entrance, guarded by two large columns carved in the familiar feathered serpent motif.

It is nearing mid-afternoon. We stand near the eastern wall. The sun, descending in the west, illuminates the eastern wall behind the figures of the god Ku'kul'kan carved on the pillars. On the face of a stone, placed between the columns, is embossed a Mayan glyph, the symbol of the sun god himself. This seems significant to me, but I can't quite make a connection.

We move on to the Caracol, what was supposed to be the Maya observatory. It looks like just that and I can imagine the ancient astronomers watching the stars from its heights, so long ago. The entire archeological site gives me the feeling of what it must have been like to live here in the time of the Wise Woman and the Priest, when the Codex was written.

The day has become excruciatingly hot and I am exhausted. We walk back through the restored city. Though our visit has yielded nothing concrete, it has given me an even closer connection to these ghosts from the past. We say goodbye to Jorge at the visitors' center and make the short walk back to the hotel.

That evening we have a surprise visit from Enrice` Sanchez. He says he had heard of our presence in Chichen Itza from one of the frequent callers to his radio talk show. He wants to know why we are here and what new information we might have gained. I give him a brief synopsis of our trip, including our audience with Senor Tierro of the Office of Antiquities.

"I am not surprised by Senor Tierro's interest. He has called me several times over the last few months," Seeing the astonished look on my face, Enrice` adds quickly, with a laugh, "Oh, not to my talk show. Private calls to me. He wanted to know what I knew and thought. He seems very informed and as interested as my most ardent listeners about the Maya prophecies. I think he might be a secret believer."

"He's an archeologist by profession and an expert in Mexican and Mayan antiquities, after all," Carli muses. "His interest in and knowledge of Maya mythology is understandable, don't you think?"

"I agree," said Adam with dismissal. "Nothing unusual there."

"I suppose not," I agree, but I'm not at all sure of that. "I'm not sure I trust the Senor of the Office of Antiquities."

Enrice` changes the subject. "My real reason for coming to meet you is to find out what you plan to do on the great day?" When we do not answer, he adds, "I have a suggestion." He tells us his plan for an international extravaganza. A worldwide telecast on 12-21-12, at the exact moment the prophecy is to occur. What he needed from us was the exact place.

"I don't know that," I tell him honestly.

His whole body slumps and a look of extreme disappointment crosses his face momentarily. He rebounds quickly and says, "But you will. You are still investigating?"

I laugh ruefully, "I wish I had as much faith in our ability to do that as you do. And I'm not entirely in agreement with your plan for a televised spectacle either."

"I don't think any of us can prevent it," he answers. "The whole 2012 phenomenon is going to come to a climax on that day no matter what we do. We might as well orchestrate it in order to keep some control."

I am not convinced and tell him so. "Do not make up your mind quite yet. Keep an open mind," he suggests and gives me a knowing wink.

Adam comes suddenly to life and sputters, "That isn't a good idea at all. I'm against it. Unprofessional. Unethical. Just wrong. I'm sure Professor Allen will be against it. And the University, too. Not good, not good for our careers, either." He finishes red faced. I'm surprised by his vehemence and put off by it. My response is too thin; maybe I should think it over some more and postpone any final decision.

Before we leave for home the next morning I get a call from Senor Tierro. He says, 'I am calling to see that your visit to Chichen Itza has gone well. Have you seen all that you wanted to see? Was your reception courteous?" I assure him that our visit has been wonderful and sing the praises of Jorge. He then says, "Please call upon me again, if there is anything I might do for you, or if you come again to my country."

I think he wants to know what we have discovered, but I do not tell him anything further about our visit. I thank him again and say goodbye. Curiouser and curiouser, I think.

III

July 13, 944
10.5.16.8.18, 7 Etznab, 1 Uo
The Temple of K'ul kul'kan, Chichen Itza

They came for him several days later in, the middle of the night while he was sleeping. There were two of them, Temple servants or slaves that he had seen on occasion outside the Ah Kin Mai's chamber. "The Ah Kin Mai wishes to see you," the taller of the two guards said gruffly.

"What?" Took Pak mumbled groggily, shaking his head and rubbing his eyes, not fully awake. Neither guard said anything further but pulled him roughly from his bed. Took Pak got shakily to his feet and pulled his coarse robe over his head. "What does the Ah Kin Mai want of me?" he asked, knowing that these men did not know, or if they did, would not tell him. The guards unceremoniously led him from the room.

They led him, not to the Ah Kin Mai's quarters, but into the Temple itself. They hurried him down the Temple stairway, deep into the Temple proper. They took him to the small underground chamber Sajal Yax Ahk

313

had taken him, many years ago before his induction into the novitiate. The room was lit only by candlelight and was empty. The guards pushed Took Pak into the room and left, slamming the door behind them. Took Pak surveyed the room. It contained only the low stone altar, unadorned except for two small candles. A crudely carved tunich tzam (stone throne) stood before it. The air in the room was damp and chill. It smelled of faint reminders of the herbs and incense that had been burned here in the past.

Took Pak stood in the center of the room still half asleep. He had known this time would come and, now that it was here, felt an unnatural calmness, rather than the fear he had expected to feel. The fear had been in the anticipation. He knew what he had to do. He must get through this ordeal without breaking and await the final chapter. His hand reached beneath his robe to where the small packet Ahkan had sent him was secured. With this reassurance he knew he could make it through whatever was to come.

Took Pak waited. He did not know how long, nor did he care. He spent the time recalling the beautiful face of Ahkan, as he had seen her in the moonlight those few nights before. Finally, there was the sound of footsteps in the corridor outside the room. The door burst open and Kaloome Ek Suutz swept into the room in a swirl of scarlet robes. His sycophant, Sajal Ch'itz'aat, followed closely on his heels. The Ah Kin Mai took his place before the bare altar. Sajal Ch'itz'aat stayed behind, out of Took Pak's line of sight.

Kaloome Ek Suutz stood there a moment, smiling at Took Pak, tapping his open left palm with a slender ceiba switch. "Well, Took Pak il Ch'e'en," he said in what sounded almost like a purr. "It seems we have some questions to ask you." And his smile turned malevolent. "Sorry to wake you and disturb your sleep, but I hear that you are used to late hours. Being unable to sleep myself, I felt I must get some resolution to my concerns in order to ease my mind." And he smiled again. "It seems that you have been busy in your basement cell. Cho p'iit tells me you have been spending every night, late into the night, in your chamber under the Temple Library. What is it that you have been doing, I wonder?" When Took Pak did not answer, he continued, still smiling. "Cho p'iit says you have been spending your nights reading all the old manuscripts you could find from every part of the Library: volumes on astronomy, myth and the history of the earth and our people. And lately, he tells us, the works and prophecies of the great K'nich Chan Bahlum. Were you able to decipher these ancient writings? To understand them?" He paused again, as if waiting for an answer.

Took Pak made no response. He stared back at the Ah Kin Mai. This seemed to anger Kaloome Ek Suutz. He lashed out with the ceiba switch, striking Took Pak across the face with it. His smile turned dark and malicious. The switch had cut a long gash across Took Pak's cheek and the young priest could feel a trickle of his warm blood slide down his face. The cut burned and he had to exert all his will power to resist putting his hand up to wipe it away.

"Kneel before your Ah Kin Mai," said Sajal Ch'itz'aat from behind. Took Pak felt strong hands upon his shoulders, forcing him to his knees. He knelt on the cold hard floor before the Ah Kin Mai. Kaloome Ek Suutz hit him again where he knelt. Then, as suddenly as his anger had come, it seemed to pass. The Ah Kin Mai's voice came softly, almost cooing. "Cho P'iit tells us that of late you have taken to writing, as well as reading. What might it be that you know, that is so important, that you must put ink to parchment to record it?" When Took Pak did not reply, Kaloome Ek Suutz continued in a sickly sweet tone. "Cho P'iit tells us that what you showed him appeared to be astrological notations. But he thinks there is more to your labors than mere astrological observations, and so do I."

Took Pak raised his head to look into the hard black eyes of the Ah Kin Mai. He looked back at the other man with no hint of fear, for he had none. The course was set, nothing that he said or did not say would alter the eventual outcome. "He told you correctly. I am transcribing my astrological observations," he answered coolly. "Cha Mach taught me that careful recording of what occurs in the sky each night allows us to predict what will occur in the future."

Kaloome Ek Suutz's face became livid with returning anger. "Do not lie to me boy." And he hit Took Pak repeatedly across the shoulders and back. Took Pak caught his breath, but was able to suppress the groan that rose to his lips. The Ah Kin Mai struck him repeatedly about the face, but Took Pak said nothing further. Kaloome Ek Suutz stepped back, seeming to regain some of his composure. "You will tell me what I wish to know or we will beat it out of you," he snarled.

Kaloome Ek Suutz seated himself in the stone seat before the altar. He realized that he was getting no results. The Ah Kin Mai signaled to Sajal Ch'itz'aat, who went to the door, opened it, and called in the two Temple guards. They lumbered into the room and, at a nod from the high priest, stepped to where Took Pak knelt. Took Pak felt the menace that emanated from the Ah Kin Mai, but felt no similar emotion from the guards. Their faces were impassive and they seemed to bear no malice toward him.

At another nod from Kaloome Ek Suutz, the guard on his right raised his arm. He brought the heavy wooden club he carried down, with great force, upon Took Pak's back. Took Pak gasped but otherwise made no sound. He did not cry out. He was determined not to show any sign of weakness to the wretched man who lorded over him.

The Ah Kin Mai asked him again. "What is it you have found? What is it you are writing?" Took Pak said nothing. Kaloome Ek Suutz nodded again and the guard brought the rod down again, and again, and again.

Took Pak finally fell, from the force of the blows. He landed on his side and lay unmoving on the hard stone floor. He did not know how much more he could take. He reached under his robe to where the pouch containing Ahkan's potion was secured. Surreptitiously and with great effort, so that the other men in the room would not be aware of what he was doing, he removed the tiny tablet of compressed powder from the pouch. He raised his hand, ever so slowly, and slipped the object into his mouth. The powder was terribly bitter and it was all that he could do to keep himself from gagging. The effect was almost instantaneous. He felt a lightness and a dulling of the pain in his back and shoulders. A calmness came over him.

He heard, as if from a great distance, "Get him back to his knees," the Ah Kin Mai hissed. The two guards pulled Took Pak roughly to his knees, but the young priest was beyond caring. "Tell me," Kaloome Ek Suutz screamed. "We have searched your room and the Temple Library chambers, and have found nothing. We have searched the gardens where you spend so much of your time, and found nothing." He continued to scream. Then, he seemed to come to his senses and more calmly whispered, "But you will tell us." He motion to the guards again and they resumed the assault, but Took Pak felt nothing.

Took Pak heard a roaring in his ears and the room faded. He was in a lush, green forest glade. The air was sweet with the fragrance of lavender and Yucca, the fragrance of Ahkan. And then he saw her enter into the clearing. She was dressed in a saffron dress, gossamer like. Her hair fell free and blew in the gentle breeze. A sweet smile was upon her face. Her eyes were bright and smiling too. She appeared to him as she had at 15, when she was first coming into her womanhood. She glided, not walked, toward him.

She smiled coyly up into his face. She reached up, taking his face into her hands, still smiling. She kissed him on his lips as she never had in life. Then she whispered, "We will meet again someday, I promise." She let go, stepped back and, before he could respond or reach for her, she stepped away. Her image began to glow, becoming misty. Slowly she turned into a beautiful bright yellow butterfly, which spread its wings, and flew away. Took Pak watched helplessly.

He was left in the forest alone and bereft. "Goodbye, my little butterfly." Unexpectedly he felt no sadness or feeling of loss but rather experienced a feeling of completeness. A feeling that things were as they were meant to be, that all, somehow, would be well. He was sure that they would truly meet again, in some distant place or time, when the stars and the planets were right.

Took Pak woke lying upon the hard cot in his chambers. His body ached. His head throbbed, whether from the beating or the drug, he did not know. He realized, with regret that he was still alive, and that the ordeal was not over. He lapsed into a dreamless sleep.

Sometime the next day

Cha Mach came to him. He did not know when. He had no sense of time. The old astronomer came to him in the guise of a friend, cajoling him, "TellKaloome Ek Suutz what he wants to know and he will forgive you your stubbornness." But Took Pak no longer trusted his old mentor and told him nothing. Cha Mach went away disappointed.

Took Pak was brought food and drink at intervals, tempting morsels of venison and bitter cacao. He refused it all, taking only sips of water to quench his thirst. Hours passed. Several days passed. Finally the two guards appeared again at his bedside. They announced that his presence was required in the Ah Kin Mai's chambers. Took Pak could not stand and so they drew him up, each supporting him on either side. They half dragged, half carried him to the Temple annex.

As the three of them entered the Ah Kin Mai's chambers, Took Pak realized it was filled, almost overflowing, with what appeared to be all of the priests of the Temple. Every station and status was represented, designated by the color of their robes: the brown robes of the Temple school boys, the green of the novitiates, the saffron of the ordained, and the scarlet of the Inner Circle. In this company Took Pak was determined not to show any sign of weakness. Summoning all the strength he could muster, he pushed away the support of the two guards and stood up straight under his own power.

At the end of the room stood Kaloome Ek Suutz, while behind him were gathered the Inner Circle, all of them robed in their full regalia, the staffs of their offices in their right hands.

Took Pak stood in the center of the room alone.

Kaloome Ek Suutz raised his hand, gaining the attention of all in the room. The room was completely silent. Then the Ah Kin Mai, without any preamble, intoned, "Took Pak il Ch'e'en, priest of the Temple of Ku'kul'kan, you are accused of the crime of heresy against the Order and all the gods of the Maya, You are, here, brought to judgment." He turned to the red robed priests of the Inner Circle and continued to them. "You have heard the charges. You have seen the evidence. You have listened to the witnesses. How say you?" He looked back at Took Pak, where he stood alone, and asked again, "How say you all? Guilty?" And the twelve priests of the Inner Circle, to a man, raised their staffs and, in unison, pounded them upon the floor.

Kaloome Ek Suutz smiled evilly down at Took Pak and pronounced his sentence, which Took Pak knew before he spoke, "You will, to appease the gods for your sacrilege, be sacrificed upon the high altar atop this great Temple. May the gods accept the sacrifice of your blood and heap blessings upon the Maya people."

Took Pak said nothing. What was there to say? He merely smiled at the Ah

Kin Mai, nodded his head to the assembled company, turned on his heel and, without the Ah Kin Mai's leave, walked from the room, his head held high.

IV

October 21, 2012
12.19.19.14.19, 8 Cauac, 2 Sac
Chichen Itza

A man, dressed in khaki pants, a brightly colored shirt lose over his trousers, and a straw hat, prowled about the ruins. If it were not for the large aviator sunglasses, he would have looked like any other Mexican tourist.

He was following a small group of Americans and their local guide as they toured the site. He hung back but was sure that he would not be recognized even if they saw him. He knew them though. He knew each of them very well by now.

They stopped at the base of the Temple of K'ul kul'kan's north stairway. He knew what they were looking for, but he had been there before them and knew they would find nothing. There was nothing to find.

When they moved to the Ball Court, he became more interested. They walked to the center of the field, the guide talking constantly and pointing out the area's highlights.

The redhaired woman seemed drawn to the two tall columns carved in the form of the Feathered Serpent god. She stood between the two pillars and stared at the ground beneath her feet. He saw a look of intense concentration on her face and then she looked perplexed, as if trying to remember something she had forgotten. She shook her head and the group moved on.

He advanced slowly until he stood in the exact spot where she had stood. He looked at the ground, as she had done. He then looked at the pillars on either side, and back at the ground. Instead of a confused expression to mirror hers, a look of enlightenment spread over his face, and then one of triumph. He knew. He knew where the 'sacred ground at the center of the earth' was, and she did not.

CHAPTER SEVENTEEN

I

1562 CE
11.17.2.17.18

Mayan Myth

The pale gods came from the east,
As the legends foretold.
They came for gold and for jewels.
But treasure they did not find
Here in the land that was
Once the land of the Maya.

What they found were the empty cities,
Once the thriving Maya civilization.
They found massive temples
Overgrown with the lush vegetation of the rain forest.
The conquerors took the land
And enslaved the Maya people.

All that remained of the once proud
And powerful Maya people.

II

November 23, 2012
12.19.19.16.12, 2 Eb, 15 Ceh
The University

I return to the chaos of a semester in progress: to lectures not fully prepared, student papers uncorrected, final exams to update, and faculty committees with resolutions I knew nothing about. This leaves me with little time or energy to spend on the fast approaching 12-21-12. What little time I have, I seem to spend pondering the prophecy but making no headway in solving its remaining mysteries. I meet with Daniel, Brian, and Calvin shortly after my return from Mexico. Adam is there, but Carli can't come.

I fill them in on the highlights of the trip: the surprising summons to the Office of Antiquities and Senor Tierro's interest and offer of help, our visit to Chichen Itza and failure to find anything related to the Codex, and finally the appearance of Enrice` at our hotel. I tell them his idea regarding the momentous day. To my surprise, Daniel is thoughtful over this suggestion, rather than immediately against the plan. Brian and Calvin are immediately enthusiastic about it.

Calvin looks at us with an expression of excitement, totally out of character for him. "It's going to be a circus, was bound to be even without the discovery of the Codex. Add that, and there's no way out of it. We might as well take center ring, to continue the metaphor. Use the media involvement to our advantage." He looks at me. "That is, if we know what it is we are supposed to do."

"Of c . . . course we do," Brian says with confidence. "We are to t . . . take the shield, the tile, and place it at the point where it . . . it will prevent the completion of the alignment. R . . . right?" My stomach drops. Of course, that is what the Codex tells us we are to do. It sounds simple, but we are no closer to knowing how than we had been a year ago.

Calvin voices the obvious reality of it. "Problem with that, we don't have the tile and we don't have any idea where the Codex means us to put it. Where is the center of the world? The Maya world? Bahlum's world? Or Chichen Itza's world?" I look at Daniel, but he says nothing. I have no answers to these questions either. "I have been working at the where, and I have come up with some ideas," Calvin adds, to my complete surprise. He smiles smugly and says, "Nothing definite yet, but I'm making progress. I'll let you know in time." Nothing we say would make him give any further details. He changes the subject. "What about the tile?" he asks me.

I've been afraid they were going to ask me about that. "I don't know," I say, hesitantly. "I thought I had some idea while I was in Chichen Itza. Just a feeling, I guess, but it didn't stay with me. I think there was something in the Codex that matched something I saw at the site, but I just can't place it. I need to go back to the translation and see if I can find it." I drift off uncomfortably. They all look at me with disappointment.

Finally Daniel speaks. "I don't know that I put any more credence to the whole Doomsday phenomenon than I ever did, but someone evidently does. Eduardo's death is evidence of that. Which means we are all in danger. Especially you, Kate." His expression is grave. "So, as we determined previously, the more publicity surrounding the event the better. The more fanfare and hoopla, the safer we are. So I'm in favor of Enrice`'s plans."

"Hoopla?" I laugh. "Okay, so the consensus of the group is that we go along with Enrice`'s extravaganza. In the meantime Calvin continues to work out where the center of the world is. And Brian and I," here I look expectantly at Brian, he nods, "will work out from the Codex where the tile might be." Problem is I don't have any idea where to start.

"In the meantime," Daniel concludes seriously, "all of us need to be careful. All of us need to report any strange or unusual occurrences: strange phone calls or emails, communications or threats, anyone following us, any break-ins or disruptions. Anything at all out of the ordinary, we need to tell each other." Rather chilling, I think, especially coming from unshakable Daniel.

The middle of the night phone calls start again the next night. No one on the other end of the line, no threats, just hang-ups without a sound. I report them to Daniel, who says he has received one as well. When we approach Adam, he admits, after an embarrassed pause, that he too has received a call but thinks it was just a wrong number. The annoying calls persist, several a night.

None include threats. Nothing more sinister occurs.

I keep thinking, over the next few weeks, that there is something I am not remembering. A piece of the puzzle that I was given in Chichen Itza, but that I'm not putting together.

I don't get around to any real work on the Codex until the Thanksgiving holiday break. On Friday, Brian comes to my apartment, bringing with him all his original notes and photos of the Codex. We spread them out on the dining-room table. The sheer amount of information was daunting. Where to begin? We sort through the piles of paper, trying to make some order of it all.

"Let's go back to the original photos," I suggest. Starting at the beginning always seems like a good idea if you don't know where to start. "There is something in Chichen Itza that resonated with me. Something seemed familiar, but I don't know what. It's right here, you know, like a name that you know you know but just can't remember."

"On the t . . . tip of your . . . your tongue," Brian offers. "When that happens to me I go . . . go through the alphabet, until I get it. Why don't you walk through your visit to Chichen Itza. Maybe s . . . something will come."

I do that, telling him about each part of the site we'd visited, each monument we'd seen, and my impressions of each. The recitation brings the whole trip vividly back to me. Brian is enthralled. He asks questions that clarify what it was I had seen and put all the locations into the context of the Codex. When I am done, he takes me back to the Temple of Ku'kul'kan. He hunts through the many papers on the table and brings out the passage in which the priest scribe explained where the Codex of Chan Bahlum had been hidden. 'In the mouth of the serpent rests the means of salvation' it read.

"Yes," I say, "that refers to the sculptures of the Plumed Serpent at the foot of the northern staircase. That's clear."

"The next line reads, 'He who finds the stone must place the face of Ku'kul'kan, the sun god, upon sacred ground,'" said Brian. "Th . . . that refers to the tile or shield he writes of later. I am sure this is a description of the tile. It has an image of the sun god on it."

"Okay," I say. "So we'll know it when we find it, if we ever find it." My feeling of discouragement is coming through.

Brian pulls a sheet of paper from the bottom of the pile. 'This is from the last page of our Codex." He hands the page to me.

What is written there, I only vaguely remember. It reads, "It shall be placed where the pillars of K'ul kul'kan point the way'. I stare at the line. I repeat it slowly, to myself, then again out loud. Something buzzes in my head. I can feel the heat of the day and see the sun as it made its circuit across the sky. I am standing, once again, in the great ball court of Chichen Itza, watching the sun set in the west. As it descends, the two giant stelae that flank the doorway into the Temple of the Jaguar are highlighted. On each of the columns I can see the carved image of the Plumed Serpent, each facing toward the ground between them. "That's it," I scream, startling Brian from his perusal of the passage.

"W . . . w . . . what's it?" he stammers, looking at me as if I have gone suddenly crazy.

I rush out of the room, returning in a moment with a pile of photographs. They are the ones I had taken in Chichen Itza. I paw through them until I come to the one I had taken in the ball court at the eastern wall and the doorway into the Jaguar Temple. "Here! Here!" I say excitedly, and point to the two pillars and the images of Ku'kul'kan facing down at the ground between them. "That's it," I repeat. "That's the center of the earth. That's where we need to place the shield." I catch my breath and calm down. I look at Brian with triumph. He is grinning at me. My feeling of elation is shortlived. "Now all we have to do is find the tile."

Brian thought for a moment, then begins looking through the mass of paper on the table again. It takes him some time, but he finally comes up with a sheet of paper and hands it to me. "This is from the last page of the Codex, too," he explains. "Here the priest tells what he did w . . . with the tile and the Codex. He says he gave the Codex to the wise woman to be hidden in a cave far from the city. That's where we found it."

I point at the paper. "But all he says of the tile is that she was to place it nearby, where it would be close when it was needed." I sigh in frustration. "That doesn't tell us anything, except that it must be somewhere in Chichen Itza." Another dead end. "I'm not s . . . so sure. There must be more to it. Let me go back to the hieroglyphs, to . . . to see if I missed something."

We spend the rest of the afternoon combing through the copies of the last pages of the Codex and Brian's translations. No matter what variations of the translation of the hieroglyphs we use, we don't come up with any clearer location for the tile. We finally give up for the day, too exhausted to make any sense of it. We both promise to continue working on our own and say good night.

December 14, 2012
12.19.19.17.13, 10 Ben, 16 Mac

I make no progress at all, no matter how many times I go over the material from the Codex. In mid-December, Carli comes for a visit. She looks tired and pale. Her mother is undergoing another round of chemo and is not tolerating it well. Carli's father has insisted that his daughter take a few days off while he cares for his wife. So she comes to spend a few days with me. She tells me about her concerns about her mother, but then says she'd rather not talk about it anymore. I tell her about Brian's and my discovery regarding the ball court at Chichen Itza and our lack of a clue as to where the tile might be. She offers to try her luck at it and I leave her with the mounds of paper on the diningroom table when I head off for campus.

When I get back that evening, I find her right where I left her, among the papers. She has reordered them so that each section of the Codex has its own pile containing photographs, copies of the hieroglyphs, and the translations. "Have you found anything?" I ask, setting a cup of coffee down beside her.

"Well, sort of, I guess. I mean, the only mention in the Codex of where the tile was hidden is on the last page, where it says it is to be hidden nearby. I thought at first must mean it was placed back where the priest had found it, at the base of the northern staircase. But, if that were the case, you'd think he would have been more explicit, as he was about the Bahlum manuscript."

"And if so, it was lost over time, just as the Bahlum manuscript has been," I agree in disappointment.

"But then, I thought of another explanation. I thought of Poe's *The Purloined Letter,*" she muses.

"*The Purloined Letter,*" I say in surprise, not knowing at all what she's talking about.

"Yes, *The Purloined Letter*. Do you remember the story? The clue, the lost letter, was found in plain view in the desk among all the other letters. The moral: if you want to hide something, sometimes the best place is in the most obvious place. If you apply this to the tile . . ." She waits for an answer from me, but I don't have one, so she continues with a twinkle in her eye. "The Codex says the Wise Woman was to hide the tile nearby where it would be needed in the future. So where do you suppose that might be? Where would the most obvious place be? Think like a woman. If a man was to hide something, he would most likely hide it in a secret place far away, so it would be safe. Like the Priest told the Wise Woman to hide the Codex in a cave far away. A woman, on the other hand, would be more likely to hide something nearby, so it would be right there when it is needed. So she could put her hand on it in time, even if she was running a bit late."

I look at her, still in the dark.

"Where is the obvious place to hide the tile?" she taunts. "Hidden, but exactly where it will be needed."

I look at the papers on the table and then at the pile of pictures. The one of the doorway to the Temple of the Jaguar lay on top. "Oh," I exclaim. "There." And I point to the spot of ground between the stone pillars. The spot is flat and covered with hard packed dirt. "There. Do you think it's there, right where it will need to be on the 21st? Do you think it could be that simple?"

"Yes, I do," she laughs. "Of course, we can't be entirely sure until we look, but I can't think of any other answer to the puzzle."

"And how do you suppose we're going to go about checking?" I ask. She doesn't have an answer for that. I think for a moment, then say pensively, "We may need to call on our 'friend' at the Office of Antiquities for a favor. In the meantime, let's keep this discovery to ourselves, shall we?" I am elated. Finally all the pieces are in place.

Enrice' calls periodically to report on how the plans for the 21st are going. "My radio followers have grown in such numbers, I don't think there is anyone in my broadcast area who isn't listening. And every one of them has an opinion and is willing to express it on the air." By mid-December he reports he has obtained promises of help from: the Mayor of Merida, the Director of Mexico's Instituto Nacional de Antropología e Historia, the directors of the two museum, the Arch-Bishop of the Catholic Church of Mexico and, of course, Senor Tierro of the Office of Antiquities. Quite an auspicious collection of allies, as he calls them.

The semester ends: finals taken, papers graded, and grades submitted on the 14th. Only one week, seven days until the ill-fated day. I make my arrangements and leave for Mexico the next day. Daniel, Adam, and Brian go with me. Carli can't get away.

December 15, 2012
12.19.19.17.14, 11 Ix, 17 Mac
Chichen Itza

We split up once we get to Mexico. Adam and Brian stay in Mexico City. Adam is to connect with Enrice` to work on the last minute arrangements. Brian meets with the director of the Museo Mexicana de Arqueologia. Daniel and I fly to Merida. Daniel has an appointment with Senor Tierro at the Office of Antiquities. I rent a car and drive to Chichen Itza. I have not told any of them Carli's theory about where we might find the tile. My idea is that the fewer who know, the less likely the information will get out.

My task is to determine if the tile is where we think it might be. That, I am sure, will be tricky. Digging in a national historic site is frowned upon, not to mention illegal. I need help and there is only one person I can think of who might fit the bill, Jorge. The problem is he works for the Instituto Nacional de Antropología e Historia, the conservator of the site, and it is his job to protect the site. Somehow, though, I feel he will be willing to help, if I explain it to him. It is a risk, but it is the only solution I have.

I walk to the ruins and ask at the visitors' center for Jorge. He is out with a tour I am told, but should be back in an hour. I leave a message for him and walk over to the ball court. The pillars mean so much more to me now. I look up at the twin images of Ku'kul'kan and note the patch of earth at their bases. I know now what I will find there. It calls to me.

Jorge meets me at the visitors' center an hour later. He's pleased to see me and asks how he might help me. This isn't the place to tell him what I want. I ask if he would like to have dinner with me that evening. He agrees with a laugh, saying he will have to get permission from his wife. We make arrangements to meet at the hotel at 8 o'clock.

Jorge arrives exactly on time, greets me warmly, then says, "I take it this is not a social engagement." When he sees the look of surprise on my face, he adds, "From your demeanor I deduce that this is more a matter of business, for your research, perhaps."

"You're right it isn't just for the company, although your company is most welcome. It's not related to my personal research, either. I'm going to tell you a story and then I'm going to ask a favor of you. A big favor." I tell him the whole story, starting with the discovery of the hidden Codex and ending with the prophecy of the Shaman. We have dinner while I talk, but I don't think either of us notice what we are eating. Jorge asks occasional questions to clarify our findings, but he shows no real surprise at what I tell him.

In fact, as I start to recite the legend of the Wise Woman and the Priest, he takes over and tells it to me. "My abuela told me that story when I was just a pequino nino, little boy. A long time ago," he laughs.

I go on to tell him of the threats and finally of Eduardo's death. I ask him if he has ever heard of El Sociodad? He grows pale at the mention of the order. "Si, of them I have heard. Mucho malo. They are said to be the ghosts of the ancient Ah Kin. The old ones practiced human sacrifice and it is rumored they still do. I do not believe in ghosts, but I do believe in El Sociodad." He shivers, a response we used to say was the result of someone walking across our grave. "I can see that they would be interested in the Codex you found, but not why they would kill to prevent its disclosure."

I then say, "I believe what the Shaman told me. I felt a connection to the Codex from the moment we found it. I believe, as Eduardo did, that it was his fate to find the manuscript, and it is mine to find the shield. To find the shield and to use it." I study his face for any sign of skepticism, but find none. Taking a deep breath, I tell him the end of the story. I tell him, trusting him with the secret of the hiding place of the tile and how I intend to proceed.

"And your request of me?" he asks, but knows already what it is.

"I need to know, before the 21st, if I am right, that the tile lies beneath the Temple of the Jaguar's doorway. If I am wrong, I will need to keep looking."

"And you wish me to help you to do so, to dig in a national historic site? To break the law? Why do you think you can trust me? That I will do such a thing and not turn you over to the authorities?" he asks quietly.

"You're the only one I could think of. I felt I could trust you from the moment I met you. I feel you are an old soul, a kindred spirit. Was I wrong?" I ask tentatively.

"I will help you," he answers simply. He then lays out a plan for how we are to go about it. I had thought we should make the attempt late at night, under the cover of darkness. He says, "This would not be a good idea. People sneaking around in the dark would be easily detected. It isn't as if it does not happen often enough. No, we will go in the early morning, when the maintenance and gardening crews do their work. Not only can we see what we are doing, but we will blend right in, as if we belong. The only problem is that we cannot do it until Lunes, Monday, morning, as tomorrow, Domingo, the workers do not work."

So Monday it must be, though I would rather do it as soon as possible, in case I am wrong. Time is running short.

As arranged I meet Jorge a few minutes before five on the morning of December 17th, just outside the visitors' entrance. He is wearing grey overalls, a bright red bandana, and the traditional straw hat. He unlocks a nearby utility shed and gives me a bundle and tells me to change. When I am similarly attired, he hands me a burlap sack. It is heavy and clanks.

"Carrying that will help to disguise your build and gait," he says. "Now, let us go."

We head into the ruins and over to the ball court. I glance nervously around, but do not see any other person. We skirt the eastern wall, walking in the shadows, until we come to the center and the entrance to the Lower Temple of the Jaguar. The doorway is flanked by the two columns bearing the images of the Plumed Serpent god. The whole area is deep in shadow.

I kneel on the ground between the two pillars. The same feeling of awe comes over me. A feeling of a presence, like I had felt from the Codex, overtakes me. I place my hands on the spot in the center of the doorway, and I know what we are seeking is here. I have the urge to dig it up hurriedly, but know we have to leave the area as we find it, so it looks untouched.

Jorge joins me and pushes a long metal dowel into the center of the area. He inserts it about 6 inches and hits something solid. He repeats the process, 3 inches out from the center, in every direction. It meets a solid object at the same depth in each direction. He then moves the dowel out another two inches; this time the metal enters to its full length without hitting an impediment. By repeating this process, Jorge marks out a square approximately 30 cm on a side. We cut along these lines, incising the square to a depth of two inches. This piece of sod we lift out and place to the side. Next, we dig out the soil from the hole, until we expose a flat stone at the bottom. I sweep the last of the dirt carefully from the object.

What is revealed is a completely smooth black tile. Taking a soft cloth from my bag I wipe the stone clean. It shines, reflecting the early morning sunshine from its ebony surface. I signal to Jorge, and we reach into the hole and carefully remove the tile from its hiding place. The surface is pristine, unmarked by any image of the sun god. My spirits sink. Then I tenderly turn it over, exposing the other side. On it is engraved the image of K'nich K'in, the sun god, as the Codex had described. This is the shield, found where it is meant to be. Found where it is to be used in four short days.

Jorge and I kneel there in awe. We have not said a word. There are no words to express how I feel. No words are needed. I feel the majesty of the moment and I think Jorge feels it as well.

It is getting late. We need to be out of there by 8 AM when visiting hours start. We fill the hole with the loose soil we had removed and tamp it down to make it level. Then carefully and reverently, we place the stone on top as we found it with the reflective surface facing up. We cover the tile with the square of sod and dust the area with dirt to hide that the ground has been disturbed.

I rise to my feet and reluctantly leave the tile hidden as it has been for more than 10 centuries.

I call Carli as soon as I get back to the hotel. She sounds worn out and depressed. My recounting of my morning's adventure brightens her spirits somewhat. "It was you," I tell her. "You came up with the answer. If not for you, I never would have found the shield. If the world is saved, the credit goes to you. As Eduardo once told me, the spirits will bless you for your labors." I believe this benediction to be true.

"Give the credit to Poe," she laughs. "Wish I could be there," she adds wistfully.

"I wish you could too," I reply. I tell her to give her mother my love and say goodbye.

Daniel and Brian show up at the hotel later that day. Each has varying reports of success. Brian reports that the Director of the Museo Mexicana de Arqueologia wants nothing at all to do with the nonsense, as he described it, revolving around the so called Maya Prophecy. On the other hand, the Archbishop contacted him before he left Mexico City. He had been adamant that, though the Church hierarchy put no credence to the Maya Prophecy, the archbishop himself would like to be present at the occasion to bless the event and dispel the heterodoxy of the past.

Daniel's meeting at the Office of Antiquities had gone very well, to Daniel's surprise. Senor Tierro was as gracious and welcoming as he had been the last time he met with us. He was overly enthusiastic about the plans for the extravaganza on the 21ˢᵗ. According to Daniel, he said, "All the civic leaders and local merchants are behind it as well. They all feel it is a real coup for tourism in the area. The eyes of the world will be upon Chichen Itza and the State of Yucatan." Daniel did not think Senor Tierro has any belief in the truth of the prophecy. In fact, Daniel says he feels an underlying insincerity in everything the Director said. The museum Director at the Merida Nationale Museo, where he stopped on his way to Chichen Itza, is enthusiastic about the publicity surrounding the event as well. He told Daniel that the museum wants to be a part of it and anything he can do, just ask.

Adam calls that evening and speaks to Daniel. Adam tells him that things are going swimmingly. Everything is in place. All the major American TV networks are coming. There will be worldwide coverage. Daniel says Adam sounded in high spirits and seems to be in the thick of the preparations. We expect Adam to arrive on Wednesday with Enrice` and his crew.

"With every weirdo and doomsday f . . . fanatic in the universe," Brian mutters under his breath.

III

August 13, 944
10.5.16.1.11, 3 Chuen, 19 Ceh
The Temple of K'ul kul'kan, Chichen Itza

And so the time came. The anniversary of his 23rd year passed without any observance. Ahkan alone noted the anniversary and celebrated it by herself with thoughts of Took Pak. She burned herbs and incense to honor him on the day of his birth. She kept to herself on that day, as if in mourning for a death that had not yet occurred.

The next day she rose early, before the sun had risen and before anyone else in the house had stirred. She washed herself in the cool water of the courtyard well and covered her body with a fragrant lotion made of the lavender that Took Pak loved so much. She dressed in her best finery, a dress of bright gold cloth richly embroidered with flowers and butterflies.

Around her waist she knotted the thread with the red shell she had worn since puberty. She dressed as if she were on her way to her wedding.

Ahkan left the house shortly after daybreak, slipping out the front doorway into the plaza before anyone else in the household had risen. She intended to get to the plaza early so as to get a place in the front row.

She stood alone there for hours, as the sun rose slowly in the east over the center of the great pyramid. The grand plaza gradually filled in around her with a crowd of noisy festively attired people. Somehow they seemed to sense something in her stillness, an unsettling aura, so that they kept their distance, leaving her alone, even in the crowd.

As the sun reached its zenith, there was a movement to the right of the plaza at the southern base of the massive pyramid. The crowd stirred and focused its attention there. Eventually a procession entered the plaza from that direction. Twenty or so young boys of the Temple school came first. Each looked frightened and kept their eyes focused on their feet as they marched solemnly in. Next the novitiates and the young priests marched in. Behind them came the older priests of the Order, carrying the staffs of their office. They numbered thirty or more. Their faces were grave. Next came the priests of the Inner Circle dressed in robes of red, deep red, the color of blood. Ornate aj k'uh hun were upon their heads, decorated with brightly colored beads and feathers. Then came the Ah Kin Mai himself, dressed in the brilliant white robes that he wore only on high holy days. Last of the dignitaries was the King and his consort. He was robed in dazzling gold, symbolizing his earthly incarnation of K'nich K'in, the sun god. The Queen was resplendent in a gown of sky blue. Each of the royal pair was laden with jewelry of jade and obsidian.

As the procession reached the foot of the pyramid, drums began to pound and horns to blow. Ahkan, whose attention had wavered as the profusion of priests filed in, lifted her head and once more focused on the far entrance to the plaza. Just then, Took Pak came into view. He was dressed in a loin cloth and a robe of brilliant, pristine white. He stood erect and carried his head high, but Ahkan's knowing eyes saw that he seemed unaware of the crowd, his fellow priests, or to anything that was going on around him. Ahkan knew that he was under the influence of the drugs she had smuggled to him. She was thankful for this.

Last in line, in somber contrast to the richly colored entourage that had come before, the executioner and his four assistants entered wearing robes of black. Black robes symbolic of the gods of the underworld.

The procession continued its slow ascent of the Temple stairs as the drums and the horns played rhythmically. The procession mounted the steps as the sun moved slowly to its zenith. At the top of the pyramid the Ah Kin Mai took his place in front of the altar, the red clad Inner Circle to his right and left. He turned to face the crowd. Finally the King and Queen mounted the temple platform and took their seats to the right of the altar.

The four black robed executioners stopped short of the summit and stood on the last step of the stairway, directly in front of the Ah Kin Mai. Took Pak took his place between them. He stood for a moment, his head raised and, in a sudden moment of clarity, gazed into the Ah Kin Mai's eyes, and smiled defiantly. Koloome Ek Suutz jerked in surprise, accurately reading the look of triumph in the young priest's gaze. The Ah Kin Mai looked away, refusing to give in to Took Pak's challenge.

At a nod from the high priest, the four executioners forced Took Pak to kneel at Koloome Ek Suutz's feet. Took Pak complied. The High Priest did not look at him again, but focused his attention upon the crowd. The Ah Kin Mai raised his arms into the air, his palms facing upwards to the sky and the sun. He intoned an orosion extorting the gods to find favor with the day's sacrifice. He asked that they find Took Pak worthy of their favor, so that the sun would shine when needed and hide its face when not. He asked Chak, the god of rain, to send the needed water to nourish the fields and the crops. He called on the maize god to provide for the Maya. The other priests and the crowd responded, adding their pleas to those of the Ah Kin Mai.

Koloome Ek Suutz moved to the right, away from the altar. The four men in black came forward. They touched Took Pak on his shoulder and raised him to his feet. Took Pak did not fight the intervention but complied almost eagerly. He turned to face the crowd, his head still held high, his eyes unseeing.

Ahkan wished that he would look at her. That he could see her face one last time. But she realized, even if he were not in a haze induced by the drugs, he could not see her from that height and distance. She felt that he knew she was there. She poured her energy out to him, hoping to give her strength to him.

The executioners took hold of Took Pak's arms and lifted him into the air. He did not resist. They mounted the last step to the Temple summit, approached the altar, raised Took Pak to shoulder height, laid him upon the altar.

The Ah Kin Mai stepped forward and took his place to the left of the altar. In his left hand he held the ceremonial knife of ebony obsidian with a handle carved of bone. The blade was razor sharp. The sun glinted off the knife's smooth surface. The assembled company of priests intoned the mournful prayers of supplication and sacrifice. The entreaty was lifted on the wind to the heavens as if in one voice. The High Priest raised his hand and every sound ceased: the drums and horns fell silent, the supplicants' voices were stilled, and the crowd hushed. The entire plaza, the entire world, waited in anticipation.

The High Priest lifted the knife into the air. He raised his head and eyes to the heavens, and looked across the young priest's recumbent form to the far side of the altar, to where the King sat. Ajaw K'inich B'ox Kan made an almost imperceptible nod and a lift of his dynastic staff and focused his eyes intently upon the altar.

Koloome Ek Suutz, the great Ah Kin Mai, was the center of everyone's attention. He looked again toward the heavens, to the gods who resided there, and intoned a final prayer. "We entreat you to accept this sacrifice in the name of the Maya people in atonement for our offenses. We ask that it assure your continued blessings upon us."

Took Pak did not move. The crowd held its breath, Ahkan along with it. She felt as if her heart had stopped as well. The Ah Kin Mai raised the knife high above his head. Took Pak looked up at that moment, a look of triumph and challenge upon his face. Koloome Ek Suutz knew that he had been outwitted by this brilliant young man, but he did not know how.

The High Priest paused for a moment, the knife still raised above his head. Then, with a sigh of resignation and a look at Took Pak of surrender, he brought the knife down with all his might.

The knife sliced through Took Pak's chest. His body jumped with the force of the blow, but he made no sound. A gasp and a moan came from the crowd. Koloome Ek Suutz reached down into Took Pak's open chest. With his right hand he grasped the still beating heart and lifted it up for the crowd to see. The High Priest took the knife and severed the major vessels that connected the heart to the body. Took Pak's body made one last lurch and was still. The priest raised the still quivering heart high over his head and drank in the bright red K'ubul K'ik'dripping from the organ.

As the heart grew still, the blood dripped down the priest's chin, soaking the front of his white robes. The blood slowed and finally stopped.

The crowd roared and cheered, excited by the savagery of the spectacle. The four executioners claimed the body and carried it from the altar. Took Pak's body would be placed upon a funeral pyre and burned. The smoke from the pyre would carry his sacrifice to the gods.

Ahkan watched the execution as witness and as friend. She kept her head up, eyes wide open and fixed unblinking upon the scene. Ahkan turned away from the scene. It was over for her. She made her way through the crowd, head still held high and eyes still dry. The crowd moved out of her way, allowing her to pass, chilled by the angry look upon her face. She returned home, speaking and looking at no one. She went to the far kitchen garden, avoiding contact with anyone from the household. She went to sit under the fig tree at the edge of the garden. She sat with her knees bent and her head bowed on her folded arms. She was hidden by the low lying branches of the sacred tree. And she gave herself up to her grief. She shed all the tears that she had not shed for the last twelve years. Shed tears for the love that was never meant to be.

IV

December 17, 2012
12.19.19.17.16
A hotel room in Chichen Itza

"They are all here in Mexico. She is here in Chichen Itza and the other will join her soon. All the pieces are in place, all but the last one." He was speaking into the telephone.

"Did our informant make contact? Did he have any information regarding the missing object?" He listened again and his face grew stormy at the reply

"We must have the object or know its whereabouts, now." His voice raised on the last word. "I have our agents in place here. See that things are under control from your end." There was a protracted pause while the person on the other end of the line spoke.

"Yes, yes," he replied irritably, seemingly uninterested in the other's conversation. "I will be here for the duration." A pause.

"No one will think it odd. I have every right to be here. In fact, it is my duty. I expect you here on Thursday. Buenas noches."

He hung up the phone. There was an odd smile on his face, one that showed satisfaction, but held an evil glint that spelled misfortune for someone.

CHAPTER EIGHTEEN

I

1562 CE
11.17.2.17.18

Mayan Myth

The men from across the sea
Brought their own beliefs and customs.
They brought with them a new religion and a new God.
And Priests of their own to honor their God.
They imposed upon the Maya their own rites and rituals.
They called themselves Franciscans, followers of Christ.

The Maya relinquished the old gods
And the old ways reluctantly.
A Franciscan priest, Diego de Landa,[12] came to the region.
He walked the land and preached in the villages.
He came armed with his beliefs and religion.
The Maya added Christ to their other gods.

The Church had no tolerance for the old ways.
They saw them as witchcraft.
They condemned the evil before it could entice the people
Back to their old heathen ways.
The Inquisition debased the Maya people
With physical abuse, torture, and death.

And the gods were angry
And the Maya suffered.

II

December 18, 2012
12.19.19.17.17, 1 Caban, 0 Kankin
Tuesday: Chichen Itza

The small village outside the archeological ruins, suddenly overnight, swells to 100 times its original occupancy. Foreign correspondents, archeologists, film and television crews, Doomsday fanatics and ordinary tourists begin arriving in droves on Tuesday, December 18th. It is a good thing we reserved our rooms for the week, as accommodations are at a premium. Every available space is booked and I'm sure latecomers will be camping out in every field, barn, and hayloft in the region by Friday.

I spend the day wandering around the ruins while it is still relatively empty. I explore those structures we did not have time to visit in October. The Caracol, believed to be an astrological observatory, is of particular interest. I can imagine the ancient priests stargazing from the top of the monument. I spend the warmest part of the day in the cool glade that houses the Cenote Sangura, the holy well. I feel the spirits of the place, the ghosts of the sacrificed and the gentle spirits of the supplicants.

I think about the Wise Woman and the Priest and wonder what their lives had been like. I feel close to them here in this sacred place, feel their spirits most of all. And I feel Eduardo's spirit, his the latest sacrifice for the Maya Prophecy. Hopefully his will be the last.

By the time I get back to the hotel it is late afternoon. It is swelteringly hot and clouds have gathered. I stop in the gift shop to pick up the day's newspaper, then make my way up to my room. I find the door open a crack and expect to find the maid changing the sheets and towels. I call "Hola" as I enter. No one answers. I call again. Still no answer. I peek into the bathroom. Empty.

A chill runs through me. Someone has been in my room. I look around. The brochures and papers on the desk are askew. One of the bedside table drawers is open part way, the phone book from inside lying on top. The clothes in my closet have been moved. Nothing seems to have been taken. Luckily, all of my valuables, extra cash, credit cards, and passport, I had locked in the room safe. When I open it, I find them all still there, untouched.

I feel frightened, then I feel violated, and then I get mad, spitting mad. I pick up the phone thinking to report it to the front desk. I think better of it and dial Daniel's room instead. He shows up at my door in less than five minutes.

"Are you alright?" he asks troubled. He looks around the room. "Nothing missing, I assume." There is concern in his voice, but no surprise. Seeing my puzzled look, he adds. "My room looks the same. A very sloppy burglar in a big hurry. He seems to have known what he was looking for. I wonder what that might be?"

"If he didn't find what he was looking for in my room or in yours, I wonder if he broke into Brian's room as well?" I pick up the phone and dial again.

Daniel leaves the room, calling over his shoulder, "Tell him I'm on my way up."

They arrive back in ten minutes. "Your r . . . room l . . . looks better than . . . than m . . . mine." Brian is stuttering so badly he can barely get the words out. "M . . . my r . . . room is t . . . trashed."

"I think Brian's room was searched last and by that time our burglar was angry or frustrated, or both." Daniel explains. "Brian's clothes were thrown all over the room. Papers shredded and the bed torn apart."

I turn to Brian in alarm, "You didn't bring any papers with data from the Codex, did you?"

I see a hurt look on Brian's face. "W . . . we agreed we wouldn't bring any. I . . . I didn't. Except on my iphone. And that . . . and that I had with me. I didn't bring anything in w . . . writing," he declares defensively.

I apologize profusely, then turn to Daniel. "What is it they are looking for?"

"I would assume they are looking for any information to tell them what it is we plan to do," he answers.

"Do you think they know about the tile and that we are looking for it?" I ask shakily. "If they do, where could they have gotten that information?"

"I know you think someone is leaking what we know to 'the enemy'." He laughs, trying to take some of the fear out of the situation. "There is a less sinister explanation to all that has gone on." When I look doubtful, he continues. "We are not the only intelligent individuals with access to the Codex. The independent authenticators and museum officials at both museums all had the opportunity to see the manuscript. Do you think we are the only ones to translate it? There are many with more expertise in

Maya hieroglyphs here in Mexico than we have. Add to that the media frenzy and the fanatic fringe . . . After all, it's been a year since Eduardo found the Codex. Plenty of time for someone else to come to the same conclusions we have." He pauses, here, to see if he is getting through to me. He is, I suppose, at least a little. "And finally," he says earnestly, "I trust the six of us. Don't you?" He looks sincerely into my eyes, with his brilliant green ones, and waits for my answer.

I'm not sure I trust them all, but I trust Daniel, don't I? I had feared a leak since the break-ins at the University last spring. But yes, I do trust them all, don't I? And then I remember the warning of the Shaman Woman, "Beware the serpent in your midst."

Daniel must see the indecision on my face and changes the subject. "In the meantime, should we report this to the authorities, hotel management, police, or not?"

I shudder. I just can't face all the red tape and questioning. "Oh, I really don't want to do that. After all, nothing was stolen and no one was hurt. I don't think the police will be much interested, or have the time for an investigation with all this going on."

Both Brian and Daniel nod in agreement. "B . . . but we need to be careful," Brian says anxiously.

"Exactly," Daniel takes up the theme. "None of us goes anywhere alone." They both look directly at me.

"Safety in . . . in numbers," Brian quips with a smile.

"Quite right. We check our rooms with the doors open until we are sure no one is lurking inside. And don't let any strangers in," Daniel concludes, glancing seriously at both of us, in turn. "It's late, I'm tired, and I'm off to bed." He gives my shoulder a squeeze, tells me to lock and deadbolt my door, and he and Brian leave.

I get little sleep that night. I keep turning over in my head the pertinent questions. Who had broken into our rooms? What were they looking for? And most important of all, what are they about to do next?

December 19, 2012
12.19.19.17.18, 2 Etznab, 1 Kankin
Wednesday

I sleep late the next morning and wake to the sound of rain pounding on the windows. It is a torrential rain, common to the tropics, but unusual this time of year. I think about pulling the covers over my head and going back to sleep. The day is a wash, anyway. Can't go to the ruins in this weather. Just when I decide to tuck myself back in the phone rings. It's Daniel calling to see if I am ready for lunch. Lunch? Surely it can't be that late.

I tell him to give me a half hour. I shower and dress. I'm just about done, when there is a knock at my door. I open it to find a very angry Daniel standing on the other side, with Brian beside him looking sheepish. "I could have been anyone," he bellows. "You opened the door without checking to see who it was, didn't you?"

"Well, yes," I stammer guiltily. "But I knew it was you."

"Right," he growls.

As we get off the elevator a wave of sound assails us. The lobby is packed: lines of people waiting to check in at the front desk, groups hauling luggage toward the elevators, others standing at the edges of the room talking excitedly. We push our way through the crowd and into the diningroom.

I pick at my salad, my attention focused on the conversations taking place around me. Everyone seems to be talking about the coming event. Some speak with a note of panic. Others joke about the end of the world. Still others are only interested in the celebrities and the media that are expected to converge here in the next few days. Whatever their take on what is coming, everyone is in a state of high excitement. The feeling of being where it is happening is in the air.

As we move across the lobby, on the way from the diningroom, a gaggle of what I assume is the media, descend upon us.

"Dr. Keith" "Professor O'Hara" Voices shout over the general clatter. "What are you doing here?" "Where did you find the manuscript?" "Do you believe in the prophecy?" "Do you think the world is coming to an end?"

They crowd us into a corner. Brian looks terrified. Daniel is livid. Just when I think I am going to be trampled to death, the hotel manager pushes his way through the throng with a security guard at his heels. "That is enough. You will leave our guests alone," he shouts. Turning to us, he says quietly, "Perdonar? I am so sorry, Senorita, especially after your unfortunate experience yesterday." He leads us toward the elevator, while the security guard forces the reporters out of the lobby.

I'm confused. What does he mean, after my experience of yesterday? Does he know about the break-in? Had Daniel or Brian reported it, after all? A glance at the two men tells me they are as confused as I am. I catch the manager's arm. "What do you mean by my unfortunate experience of yesterday?" I ask.

He looks confused in his turn. "I heard that you had been accosted last evening," he falters. "A purse snatcher, I was told."

"I wasn't accosted," I refute. "Where did you get this information?"

"I . . . I just assumed it was you, Senorita." He sputters. "Ilo siento. But I was told a woman, a pequeno, American woman with rojo, red hair. I naturally assumed it was you. Again I apologize."

"When did this happen?" Daniel asks in alarm. "Where?"

"Last evening," the manager replies, becoming alarmed himself. "At about 7 o'clock, at twilight. On the path from the ruins."

"What exactly happened," Daniel says, getting himself under control.

"I was told," the manager replies, disclaiming firsthand knowledge, "a man jumped out at the woman, from the forest. He grabbed her and knocked her to the ground. She screamed and others came running. The police believe he was trying to steal her purse." He sees the shock on our faces and adds in conclusion, "She was unhurt, fortunately." He makes his apologies once again, for what I'm not sure, and goes back to the lobby.

The three of us stand for a moment in stunned silence. "Oh, my God!" is my explosive response when I finally get my wits back.

"Oh, my God is right," Daniel exclaims. "They thought it was you. Too much of a coincidence otherwise. Does this prove to you just how dangerous this all is?" He grabs me by the shoulders and gives me a shake.

He looks at me paternally, a role not totally out of character. I have an almost irresistible urge to laugh. He brings his face close to mine. I think, at first, he's about to kiss me. Instead he grips me even tighter and shakes me roughly. "No walking to the ruins or the village on your own. Understand?" I nod meekly. He is the closest I have ever seen him to being out of control. "After what happened to Eduardo, do you need any further warning?"

"No, sir," I whisper. And then, "Daniel, you're hurting me."

He let go of me, reddening, embarrassed. "Sorry. But you do realize how serious this is? I should really send you home, right now."

I bristle. Who does he think he is? "You and who else?" I fume.

He laughs and the tension clears. "I forget just how feisty you are. Okay, I don't expect you'll go home, but you will be careful, won't you?"

"I will if you will," I retort and he laughs again.

I spend the rest of the afternoon in my room. I call Carli and give her an abbreviated update. Enough to keep her posted, but not enough to scare her. I then take a long, luxurious bubble bath and a short nap. When I wake I decide I cannot face the hordes downstairs or another run-in with the press. I ring Daniel's room and suggest, "Room service, my room, twenty minutes." He jumps at the proposal, says he'll grab Brian and they would be down.

They arrive in under the allotted time. When they knock, I check the peep hole to see Brian waving at me from the other side. "Who's there?" I sing out. "What's the secret pass word?" Then I open the door. They enter laughing, Daniel carrying an ice bucket with a chilling bottle of wine. "Are we going to have a party? I ask merrily. I suddenly feel lighthearted. I don't know why, except these are my friends and we will look out for each other.

Dinner is wonderful, more for the company than for the food. We are just finishing the meal and I am contemplating dessert, when there is a knock at the door. We look at each other, astonished. Who can be knocking at our door this late in the evening? Daniel gets up and goes to look through the spy hole.

"Calvin," he exclaims and opens the door.

"Thought you weren't coming," says Brian.

"Couldn't let you guys have all the fun," he says languidly, as he slouches into the room. "Carli called and told me you were having some difficulties. She twisted my arm and I promised to come rescue you."

Noting his backpack and the suitcase he is dragging behind him, I ask, "Haven't you checked in yet or aren't you planning on staying?"

'There isn't a room in the inn," he quips. "Thought I could bunk with one of you," he says looking from Daniel to Brian.

"My room has twins. You're w . . . welcome," Brian offers.

Calvin drops his bags at the door and collapses on the bed. "Now fill me in on all the gory details." I laugh and Daniel tells him everything that's happened since yesterday. I am about to tell them my discovery of the tile and how Carli had been the one to figure out the clues. But before I can do so, the phone rings.

"Hi there, Kate," says a familiar voice.

I put my hand over the receiver and tell the others, "It's Adam." Going back to the phone I ask, "How are things going there?"

"Great. Great. The whole crew will be coming your way tomorrow. Everything is set to go." Adam sounds excited and rattles on and on about the plans for the extravaganza. I can't get a word in. He, at last, slows, pauses a moment and finally asks, "What about you?" But he doesn't wait for my answer. "Have you found the tile yet?"

A thought comes to me. I don't want to give the information over the phone. I trust these guys, but the secret is still safer the fewer who know about it. Best leave it between Jorge and me, until the last minute. "No, nothing definite there yet."

"No headway?" he says, sounding disappointed. "Better get a move on, we're running out of time. "See you tomorrow," and he hangs up.

The sparkle had gone out of the evening. I say goodnight to the other three without telling them the secret.

III

August 17, 944
10.5.16.1.15, 7 Men, 3 Mac
Several days later; the Ch'e'en compound

Ahkan had two more things to do for Took Pak. The last things she would ever do for him. She would keep the promise she had made to him. She must take the package containing the manuscript and give it to her brother, Ek Och, along with Took Pak's instructions of where to hide it. Then she must take the other treasure he had entrusted to her and hide it as he had requested.

She made her way to the shed in the garden. She was drawn and pale, her eyes and her hair dull. The last spark of the happy girl of years ago was gone. She looked like an old woman, world weary and bent with care and sorrow. Ahkan went to the west corner of the shed and lifted the brick she had placed there weeks ago. She dug the thin layer of soil from the hole and carefully lifted out the package Took Pak had given her. The package was still wrapped in its many protective coverings. She placed it in a small xu'ul and placed a layer of herbs over it. She added a small bundle of clothes, corn cakes, dried fruits and nuts to the basket, enough to feed herself for a few days. She left without saying goodbye to anyone.

At the edge of the garden she passed Nubix Mak. She smiled at him and he gave her a nod, but neither of them spoke. They did not need to say anything, all words had been said. He knew where she was going and why.

Ahkan made her way along the edge of the milpa where the corn was growing in the fields, all of it dry and short for this time of year. She waded across the stream, but the stream held only a trickle of water. She entered the forest. It had retreated over the years of drought. Ahkan made her way to the hut that had once belonged to Ko'lel, the old woman of the forest. The hut had been empty for several years, since the old woman had made her last journey, her journey to the underworld.

Ahkan had sent word to her brother, through rebel contacts, to meet her here on this day and she was sure he would be there. As she got to the hut, she saw smoke coming from the outside oven and saw her brother standing in the doorway. He too looked weary and seemed to have aged beyond his years. He took the xu'ul from her and led her into the hovel. It had not changed since the last time they had met here, but Ahkan felt the absence of Ko'lel, who should be stirring a heavy cauldron over the indoor fire. Instead, the grate was cold and the room empty.

Ahkan sat wearily at the bare table and Ek Och caressed her hair gently. "I was in the plaza on the day of the ritual," he told her. "I too bore witness to the sacrifice Took Pak made for his beliefs." He told her that the rebellion, though still active, was doing poorly. "We have lost many, some to capture and death, more to loss of spirit and the need to return home to tend their fields and feed their families. A small uprising took place the day after Took Pak's . . ." and here his voice caught in his throat, "but it was weak and easily curtailed by the generals and the King's men." He fell silent.

They ate a dinner of quail Ek Och had bagged on his way from the city. They finished the meal with the dried fruits and nuts Ahkan had brought with her and herb tea brewed on a small fire set in the hut's triangular fireplace. Then, as the long summer day was drawing to a close, they sat on the bench outside the hut sipping their herb tea. They finally got to the reason they were there.

"Your request that I meet you here, I assume, has not been prompted entirely by a feeling of sisterly regard." He laughed quietly. Ahkan did not respond at first but stared down at her hands folded in her lap. Ek Och continued, "Not that I am not always happy to see you, but this is not a safe time for either of us. This meeting puts both of us in greater danger."

She looked up at her brother and smiled sadly. "Much as I do love to see you and enjoy your company, you are right. I do have an ulterior motive." She paused, wondering where to begin. "I come at Took Pak's request."

"At Took Pak's request?" he repeated in confusion.

"Yes." She replied. "I met with him several weeks ago and he told me a fantastic story. A story that explains what has happened to him and why his life was forfeited." Tears filled her eyes and slid down her cheeks. She ignored them and proceeded to tell him Took Pak's story from the beginning: what he had found and how, what it had told him, and what he believed it meant. Finally, she told her brother what it was Took Pak wanted him to do. Ek Och gazed at her in astonishment.

Ahkan gently drew the package from her basket, carefully removed the wrappings, and showed the manuscript to Ek Och. "Took Pak said that you would know the place where it is to be hidden. He said to tell you to remember your first hunting foray, when his Father, our Uncle, took the two of you north following a herd of white-tail deer. He said there was a small cave."

Ek Och broke in, finishing the story for her. "It was no cave. More like a small crevice in the rock face. We ran into a jaguar and Uncle had us hide there while he drew it away toward the rest of the hunting party. I do not think I had ever been that frightened before, or since. Took Pak did not seem frightened at all. He just kept putting his head outside the cave to get a look at what was happening. Then his Father came back to get us and told us they had killed the mighty cat." He laughed at the memory. "Took Pak insisted on seeing it and then sat and cried over its beautiful broken body. He never went hunting with us again." He shook his head and his eyes were bright with unshed tears.

"That is the place," Ahkan said, her eyes wet with tears as well. "Took Pak told me to tell you to chisel a space out of the rock inside the cave, air tight and made so as to keep out the damp. If Chan Bahlum's predictions are correct, it will have to be there a long, long time." She replaced the bundle in the basket and again covered it with the plants.

They stayed the night in the old woman's hut and parted at dawn the next day. They went their separate ways, Ek Och north to the remote area where he would secret the manuscript, Ahkan back to the city and the last task she had to do for Took Pak.

IV

December 19, 2012
12.10.19.17.18, 2 Eyznab, 1 Kankin
An estate north of Chichen Itza

Four men stood in the early evening shadow of a large Banyan tree in front of a palatial hacienda. One man, the oldest of the four?, was garbed in a well-tailored suit and carried himself with an air of confidence and authority. The other three men appeared to be common local laborers, dressed in faded jeans, white loose fitting shirts, and bright colored bandanas. They were short, broad shouldered and very muscular. None of them gave off the bearing of a peasant. Each was assertive and controlled, with a hint of violence just under the surface.

The man in the suit glared suddenly at the other three as they finished giving him a report that had not pleased him. "So, you could not find what we are looking for in any of their rooms? And then you attacked the wrong woman and stole her purse?" He stopped talking and walked over to the tree and broke a small branch absentmindedly from it. He walked back, tapping his palm with it. The action seemed to calm him. "You could not open the safe, you say. That is an oversight that must be remedied." He stared intently at the oldest of the three.

"Juan is not a safe cracker," the man said, nodding toward the youngest. "But I can get it done."

"See that you do." The man in the suit paced in front of them, continually tapping the twig against his palm. "If that proves to be fruitless, then the assumption that they are carrying it on their persons is a valid one. This time make sure you assault the right person. Some overt intimidation would not be amiss, but do not call attention to yourselves. The contingent of policia is excessive and I do not want you to end up in jail. I will have need of you later."

"Vale, I hear you, jefe," said the spokesman of the three.

"Keep me informed," the man said as he strode toward the house.

CHAPTER NINETEEN

I

July 12, 1562
11.17.2.17.18, 10 Etznab, 16 Cumku

Mayan Myth
Father Landa found the Maya codices,[12]
Writings that contained all the knowledge of the Maya,
To be the work of the Devil.
And so, he burned them all, along with
Many Mayan images and idols
In a ceremony called *auto-da-fé*.

The Maya mourned the loss of their sacred writings
For with them was lost
The wisdom and the knowledge
Of the once magnificent civilization of the Maya.
But the Maya shamans, hiding in the forests,
Kept the old rituals alive.

And the people
Wove the old beliefs and the new beliefs
Into a new religion.
And in this way the myths
And the history
Of the Maya survived.

II

December 20, 2012
12.19.19.17.19, 3 Cauac, 2 Kankin
Thursday: Chichen Itza

The next morning the rain stops, but the sky is overcast and the air hot and muggy, a desultory day all around. My elation and good feelings of the night before are gone, replaced by anxiety and, yes, dread. I don't want to face the prying media or the crowds, but I also don't want to spend another day in my room. I call Daniel and suggest we all make a trip to the ruins to see how the preparations are going. After a half-hearted argument, he agrees but insists on driving the car around to the visitors' center, rather than walking the short distance and exposing ourselves to unwanted attention.

I don large sunglasses and a wide-brimmed, floppy hat to cover the easily recognizable red hair and am ready to face the masses. Daniel pulls the car around and Brian, Calvin, and I meet him at the front entrance to the hotel. "What do you say to breakfast at a small café I know of, just south of here?" he asks as we climb in. "It is a bit out of the way and shouldn't be as crowded as the establishments here in the village."

"S . . . sounds super," stutters Brian. "I'm starving."

"Fine by me," interjects Calvin. I nod, wondering how it is Daniel knows the area so well?

The café, when we get there 15 minutes later, is really a dingy bar, the local watering hole. The wooden exterior is unpainted and the steps in disrepair. However, as we enter the shabby dining room, the aroma of fresh baked bread assails us. There are several farm workers seated in the corner of the room eating avidly, but saying little. As we seat ourselves at a table near the door, a rotund grey haired woman comes out from the back.

"Buenos Dios," she says with a scowl that belies her greeting. "Que` usted desean?"

Daniel orders for all of us in his fluent Spanish. When she has poured us coffee and left for the kitchen again, Calvin asks, looking down at his cup intently and stirring it deliberately, "Did you happen to notice we were followed from the village?"

349

"What," I yelp, and the workers at the other table look up at us in surprise.

"Yes," says Daniel coolly. "A car caught up with us shortly after we left the village. Turned off onto this side road when we did. Didn't see them pull into the parking area though."

"P . . . probably just reporters," said Brian.

"I doubt that," says Calvin. "If so, they would have been in here by now asking their stupid questions."

"The car probably wasn't following us at all," I say hopefully.

"Seems another coincidence, and I don't like coincidences. We'll need to be extra careful when we leave," Daniel concludes. Our meals come then and we drop the subject. The food is wonderful, but some of the pleasure in it is eclipsed by worry.

When we are done eating, Daniel throws the car keys to Brian. "Bring the car right to the stairs and pick us up there." I start to object and assure him I certainly walk across the parking lot safely in the company of three men. But he waves away my protest. We pay the waitress, thanking her profusely, but don't get so much as a hint of a smile. As we get to the porch, I hear a commotion coming from where our car is parked. I look across the lot and see another car, a much battered and dusty sedan, parked next to ours. Three very large Hispanic men are confronting Brian. They are grabbing at him and seem to be trying to force him into their car. He's putting up a valiant fight. I scream, and Daniel and Calvin sprint across the lot, shouting aggressively.

The farmers come out of the café at the noise and stand on the porch watching, thoroughly entertained. The three strangers look up at the two men running at them, then at the crowd on the porch, and let go of Brian. They are obviously not willing to fight, if the numbers aren't in their favor. They jump into their vehicle and peel out of the lot.

I run over to join the men. I am shaking with anger, rather than fright. Daniel is winded. Brian is a bit disheveled and uneasy. Calvin is grinning broadly. "Pack of cowardly bullies," he remarks. Daniel takes out a notebook and scribbles what I assume is the license number and a description of the car.

"W . . . what w . . . was that all . . . all about?" says Brian still shaky, as we get into our car.

"Haven't a clue," says Calvin, which sums it up quite nicely.

When we are just about back to the village Daniel breaks the silence. "I think we should go back to the hotel."

"No," I exclaim defiantly. "I will not spend another day cooped up in a hotel room. I plan to go to the site, whether you go with me or not."

He gives me a sidelong glance, shakes his head and shrugs, obviously realizing he isn't going to talk me out of it. He drives to the parking area next to the visitors' center and turns to me. "You will wait here." It is an order that brooks no argument. "You three, wait here while I alert security and get us an escort." I start to say I think this is unnecessary, but he is already out of the car and walking away.

Calvin laughs from the back seat. He seems to find all of this amusing. I don't know what Daniel told them, but security guards come back with him, two of them. They are pleasant and don't seem to mind acting as babysitters. Maybe this assignment is better than herding the massive crowds that I am sure fill the archeological preserve today. We make our way to the Ball Court with our escort. The area is cordoned off and we are about to be denied entrance, when I feel a hand on my shoulder.

"Buenos Dios, Profesora O'Hara," comes a sonorous and vaguely familiar voice. I turn to see the smug, smiling face of Senor Tierro. He speaks briefly to the security man at the barricade, and we are immediately allowed in. "I stopped at your hotel to pay my respects this morning when I arrived, but I did not find you there," he continues, smoothly, taking my elbow and guiding me across the expanse of open field.

"No," I answer sweetly, "we went out for breakfast at a quaint little café outside of the village."

"Ah, just so," he replies, totally uninterested. He is watching the preparations going on near the Lower Temple of the Jaguar. A frown crosses his face for an instant, as if he is displeased by the turmoil going on there. The look passes so quickly, I'm not sure it has been there. He turns back to me. "Are you prepared for tomorrow? Is everything arranged as it should be?" he asks in a purely conversational tone, but I can see that the answer to this inquiry is of interest to him.

"Oh yes," I say nonchalantly. "Everything is in place." He smiles again, this time not so broadly.

By this time, we reach the Temple entryway in the east wall of the Ball Court and the two huge stone pillars. The carved figures of the Serpent god look more sinister to me today and I shiver. The scene is much different from the last time I'd seen it. The doorway is now flanked by massive lights and thick coils of electric cables. Folding chairs have been erected on the western side of the field and the area right in front has been cordoned off. I shiver again, disgusted by the farce being made of what should be, or might be, a momentous event.

Senor Tierro leaves me standing there and approaches a group of men who seem to be supervising the work. I can see Enrice` among them and then the familiar figure of Adam. He is standing in the middle of the turmoil, seemingly calling directions enthusiastically to the workers. None of them seem to pay him any attention.

Senor Tierro moves on to a group of what I assume are the media. He appears to be answering their questions, giving them an interview. I think of how people respond differently to the limelight. Daniel, Brian and I shrink from the attention. Adam and Senor Tierro seem overly eager for their fifteen minutes of fame.

I turn to Daniel and the others. "I've had enough of this," I say in disgust and turn to walk back to the car park. As we reach the gate near the visitors' center, I see Jorge standing next to the building. He looks as sad and disturbed as I feel. I smile and nod to him. He nods back, but we do not speak.

When we get back to the hotel, the news media is still congregated out front and the lobby is full to overflowing. I tell Daniel I really don't want to return to my room for the rest of the day. He goes to ask the hotel manager if there is somewhere we can sit outside, but have some privacy. The young man smiles graciously and says, "We have closed the pool area. Because of the sheer number of guests it is a safety issue. You might like to sit out there." He shows us to the secluded, and now empty, patio at the rear of the hotel. Here, fortified with cold drinks, we spend the afternoon, basking in the sunshine and the quiet. Daniel reads the day away, some best-selling novel, a thriller I think. Brian is working on Sudoku puzzles. And Calvin and I just luxuriate in the sun. I actually think I fall asleep.

I am walking in the hot sun. I feel weak and very thirsty. I am carrying something very heavy on my back. I know I have to get somewhere. I have to get there very soon. My burden keeps getting heavier and heavier, and I am getting more tired and weaker with every step. I can see an old woman ahead of me, smiling and beckoning me on. Beside her is a young man wearing a forest green cape and a tall headdress in the form of a bird. I try to reach them. I know that is where I need to go, but the load on my back is too heavy. I cannot take another step. I fall to my knees. I cannot get up. Then I feel something behind me. Two pairs of hands lift me up, and another pair takes the burden from my back. In this way the four of us advance slowly to where the two other figures are waiting.

I hear a loud shriek and open my eyes with a start. Have I been dreaming? I hear the cry again and see, spiraling in the air above my head, a large green and gold bird.

"What's the matter?" says Calvin, with some alarm.

I look over at him to question him about the bird, but he's looking at me, not at the sky. I must have cried out. When I look back up, the Quetzal is gone. Neither of the other men seems to have seen or heard anything. "Nothing, nothing," I mumble. "Just a dream."

"Did you have a nice nap?" teases Daniel.

"Not really," I answer, still between the dream and wakefulness. "I had a dream." I tell them what I dreamt and how I felt.

"What do you think it means?" asks Brian seriously.

I have an idea, but before I can answer, Adam comes out onto the patio, a bottle of beer in his hand. "Had a hell of a time finding you," he accuses. "The desk manager seemed to think I was part of the press and wasn't going to reveal your whereabouts. Had to show him my University ID before he'd let me in on the secret." He plops down in one of the deck chairs.

"Saw you out at the Ball Court," drawls Calvin. "Quite the Hollywood big wig, aren't you?"

'Just lending a hand," Adam retorts acidly. "What have you all been up to?"

Brian tells him haltingly of our encounter with the three thugs that morning. Adam seems unconcerned, except to say he is sorry he missed all the action. He then turns to me and asks mater-of-factly, "What's the plan for tomorrow Enrice` wants to have some kind of timeline this evening, so he can block out the program."

They all look at me expectantly. I know what it is they want to ask, but are too polite or embarrassed to do so. I know what they are thinking. I have failed to find the shield. The whole thing is going to fall apart, that we are all going to be a laughing stock without that piece of the puzzle. They have a right to know, and at this point what does it matter? Everyone will know tomorrow. Then I remembered the dream. It's a message telling me I can't do this on my own. I need to trust my friends.

I tell them the whole story, beginning with Carli's working out of the cryptic clue and her reference to Poe. They look a bit skeptical, but their expressions change to amazement when I tell them of Jorge's and my early morning excursion a few days before. I tell them of our finding the tile just where Carli and Poe said it would be. Daniel nods his head, as if he should have figured it out as well. Brian is ecstatic. Calvin claps me on the back in congratulation. Only Adam seems a bit put out, perhaps that I hadn't told them sooner.

"Where is it n . . . now?" asks Brian.

"It's somewhere safe," I answer. "And it will be available when it's needed."

Brian looks around the empty patio, as if someone might be listening. "Right, best . . . best not to say anything here."

I think again of my dream, and then of the Shaman's warning, and leave it at that.

We talk over the schedule for the next morning. Daniel says he will call me in my room at 7 AM and we'll drive over to the site and park where we did today. He'll notify the security guards to keep an eye out for us. We would be in place long before the zero hour, 11:11 AM. Adam says he is meeting Enrice` for dinner and will give him the schedule.

"Adam," I say grabbing his sleeve as he is about to leave, "remember don't tell anyone that I've found the tile." I look at the others to include them in the admonition.

"Of course not," he says sincerely. And he bends down and kisses me on the forehead

The rest of us sneak out the back gate and walk to a nearby restaurant, braving the crowds, but not encountering any members of the third estate. We get back to the hotel at about 10 PM. I am tired and ready for bed. We meet Adam at the elevators. He seems in high spirits and, perhaps, slightly inebriated. Brian and Calvin announce they are going to the bar for a nightcap. Daniel and Adam walk me to my room. Daniel gallantly takes my room keycard and opens my door for me. As the door opens, someone large barrels out of the room, knocking me to the floor. The intruder runs down the corridor, Adam on his heels. They vanish into the stairwell at the end of the hall.

Daniel helps me to my feet and places a protective arm around my shoulders. He asks me if I'm alright and helps me into the room. Chaos greets us. The room is torn apart: bed stripped, dresser and cupboards emptied, my clothes thrown around the floor. In the bottom of the closet, the room safe is wide open; money, credit cards, and passport lying beside it. I look at the mess, sit down on the bed and start to cry. Daniel sits down beside me and cradles me in his arms.

Adam comes back into the room, out of breath and puffing loudly. "Lost him on the stairs. He went up and could've gotten out at any floor." Seeing the empty safe, he asks, "Was anything stolen?"

"No," I say between sobs. "Everything that was in the safe is there on the floor."

"Good. Good. You're not hurt, are you? Are you going to call the police?" he asks, his breath finally under control.

"No," decides Daniel. "I think it best not to make too much of this," indicating the mess in the room.

"Yeah, right," is Adam's answer, as he leaves. "See you in the AM."

Daniel helps me pick up the room and remake the bed. "Would you like me to stay here tonight?" he asks. "I can sleep in the chair."

I think it might be nice and then picture Daniel curled up uncomfortably in the chair and laugh. I wipe my eyes and blow my nose. "I'll be fine. But thank you for the offer. They won't be back. They know now the tile isn't here." I'm sorry I turned down his suggestion as soon as I do, but can't think of any way to gracefully change my mind.

"Do you think that's what they were after?" he asks.

"What else?" I reply.

I followed him to the door. He looks back at me, a serious expression on his face. "Lock and deadbolt the door when I leave. Don't let anyone, anyone, in until I call you and let you know the coast is clear. Call me if you need anything." He bends, kisses me on the forehead, and leaves. What is all this kissing on the forehead anyway?

Before I fall asleep, the phone rings and it's Carli. "Just want to wish you well for tomorrow. Oh, how I wish I was there. You know, I tried to get a flight down today but couldn't get a reservation. My mother was pushing me to come. We saw the doctor yesterday and the latest CT shows no sign of the cancer right now. A clean bill of health and no more chemo, for a while anyway. You know I'm there with you in spirit, don't you? Take care." And she wishes me goodnight.

III

September 4, 944
10.5.16.2.13, 12 Ben, 1 Kankin
Chichen Itza

At the next new moon, when the many stars shining in the lofty heavens gave little light to illuminate the night, Ahkan and Nubix Mach met in the shed at the end of the kitchen garden. Ahkan once more lifted the brick from the northeast corner of the shed and dug to reveal the second artifact Took Pak had given her, the carved tile. This she wrapped in a fine linen cloth and secreted it in the folds of her skirt.

Ahkan and the old gardener walked silently through the darkness toward the center of the city. They passed no one and were not observed by anyone. They skirted the Temple of Ku'kul'kan to the west and continued toward the southwest edge of the city. Here was the ceremonial Ball Court, a large rectangular, open field with high slopping sides. It was here that the ritual ball games were played. The games often culminated in the sacrifice of the captain of the losing team.

The court was empty and dark. Ahkan felt a chill run through her. Nubix Mach must have been feeling the same disquiet, as he said, "The waay are abroad tonight surely. I can feel their presence."

"I do not know that I believe in the sprites that are said to haunt our dreams, but I can feel the spirits of all who have lost their lives here, over the many katun." Ahkan whispered.

"Whatever or whoever is here, I do not like it. Let us get on with what we have come to do; so that we can get out before whatever it is gets us," exhorted Nubix Mach, his voice gruff with the emotion.

They entered the Ball Court and made their way toward its center. On the eastern wall in the very center of the court stood two tall stelae on which was carved the image of the Feathered Serpent god, Ku'kul'kan, himself. There was a circle etched in the smooth flat stones of the wall. Within the circle was carved the image of the sun god.

Ahkan knelt down upon the ground between the two pillars and Nubix Mach knelt next to her. She removed the linen wrapped tile from her skirt. At that moment there was a loud harsh shriek. Ahkan gave a gasp of surprise and fright, and dropped the bundle to the ground.

Nubix Mach yelled out a startled, "What!"

Ahkan felt something pass by her head.

"What was that?" Nubix Mach said again, but this time he spoke in a strangled whisper.

"Something flew past me," Ahkan said. "A bird of some sort. Perhaps an owl." There was an unearthly shriek, sounding far to the west. "No, not an owl," she said, as if to herself rather than to the old man. "That is the sound of the Quetzal."

"Not in the middle of the night," replied Nubix Mach. "It is the waay, for sure. Hurry, let us get this done before they come back to get us." He took a small stone digging tool from his mecapal and began to dig in the soil between the columns. He did not dig deeply, just a foot or so. He then turned to Ahkan. She reverently removed the linen wrappings and gently placed the ancient tile in the depression he had made. She swept the dirt back over it to cover the tile completely. Nubix Mach smoothed out the soil and packed it down firmly, then swept some loose dirt over the area so that no one could tell that it had been disturbed. "I do not see how it can stay hidden for all the generations you say it must," he said skeptically and rose hastily to his feet.

Ahkan rose as well, as she replied, "Took Pak said that the stars and the planets would protect it, and that they would reveal it when it was needed. I trust in his visions," she said quietly, brushing the dirt from her hands on to the edge of her skirt.

They returned home to the Ch'e'en compound without saying another word. Nor did they speak of what they had done this night, ever again.

December 21, 944
10.5.16.8.1, 3 Imix, 4 Pop
Chichen Itza

Not many months later Ahkan returned to the hut in the forest. She made it her home. She seldom went into the city, for she no longer had ties to the household. The forest provided her with what she needed. There she harvested her plants and her herbs to mix her salves and potions. What else she might want Nubix Mach brought to her. She journeyed to the surrounding countryside and small villages to minister to the sick scattered over the countryside.

As she grew older the people came to her for healing. She lived out the rest of her days there in the hut, in the forest that she loved. Her life was a long one, living alone there. She had become Ko'lel ix K'aax, the old wise woman of the forest.

Years later a story began to be told in the many small villages that dotted the lands of the Maya. The city of Chichen Itza had been abandoned long before. The farmers had returned to farming the land for the provision of their families only, not to sustain the Temple. And the priests had disappeared into the forests or to other, still flourishing, cities farther north and west.

The story of a hero of the Maya people began to be told: the tale of a priest of the once mighty Temple and a Wise Woman, whom he loved and who loved him. It told of how, together, they saved the world, or would save the world, from destruction. It told of a magic shield they had found at the center of universe; that they had hidden the clue to its hiding place in a cave far to the north.

The story, it was said, was first told by a lowly gardener to his grandchildren who repeated it to their children, and they to theirs. And so it is told even today.

IV

December 20, 2012
12.19.19.17.19, 2 Cauac, 2 Kankin
An estate outside Chichen Itza

The two men sat facing each other. The room in which they sat was a large brightly lit sitting room filled with overstuffed couches and chairs. There was a palpable excitement in the room, like a strong electric current was running through it. The two men sat for a long time in silence, each wrapped in his own thoughts.

The smaller man, more timid and anxious than his companion, thought to himself, "And what will come next? What new insanity will possess him when the Prophecy does not become truth, when the world does not disappear? And what will become of me?"

The man's, in the well-tailored suit, thoughts were much different. He thought, "By this time tomorrow the new order will be in place and I will be at the pinnacle. It is my destiny."

He then spoke out loud, either to his companion or to himself. "I know the secrets. All the pieces of the puzzle are in place. I know where the shield is hidden. No one can stand in my way now."

Suddenly becoming aware of the other man's presence, he turned to his companion and addressed him directly. "It makes no difference that she found the stone before me. She made the mistake of leaving it where it was found. I will destroy it before the hour, and she will not stop me."

The other man said nothing and soon the first continued. "The plan is in motion? The informant knows his part? For which, I must say, he has been well paid. The other arrangements have been made; each player knows his part?"

The other man nodded reluctantly, for he had not been the author of these other arrangements. He was sure, however, if they were not successful, it was he who would be blamed.

CHAPTER TWENTY

I

December 21, 944
10.5.16.8.1, 3 Imix, 4 Pop

Mayan Myth

In the Ninth Baktun of the Fifth Creation,
In the great city-state of Baakal,
Ajaw K'inich Chan Bahlum II, sat upon the throne.
A great king, son of the mighty Ajaw K'inich Pakal,
He was a seer and a prophet
One who could read the stars and foretell the days.

He foretold the fortunes of the Maya
Far into the future.
Chan Bahlum foretold the end of creation,
When the will of the gods would destroy the world.
For the Fifth time the world would come to an end,
This time by water.

He foretold the exact day, the exact hour.
13.0.0.0.0, 4 Ahau, 3 Kankin,
As the sun reaches its zenith

Chan Bahlum looked to the stars
And in the Heavens he saw the answer,
And so devised the means to thwart the will of the gods.
This he wrote within a secret Codex
Which he hid, for future generations
To discover when the time was right.

Many Baktun passed,
The Maya people were still strong
And the Temple still held sway.
In a city far to the North
Lived a nina chinca, a young girl.
She was wise, a Shaman, and a seer.

She learned the shaman ways
And was a great healer to the people.
She was called Ko'lel ix K'aax,
Wise woman of the forest.
And so she has been known
Through the intervening ages.

Then too lived an Aj k'uhm,
A priestly scribe,
His name, Piedra Escudo,
Meant stone shield.
The wise woman loved him
And he loved her.

The priest was a wise and learned man.
He knew the movements of the stars
And of the planets.
How they guided the fortunes of the people.
He knew the history
And the legends of the Maya.

One night, the great Ajaw Bahlum
Came to Piedra Escudo in a dream.
The King told him of a time in the far future
When the gods, angry with humankind,
Would align the stars
To set in motion the end of creation.

And the mighty king whispered
In the priest's ear the secret,

361

How men might outwit the gods.
He gave to Piedra Escudo a holy shield
To protect mankind from the wrath of the gods.
And a book to instruct them in its use.

These he must pass on
Through the generations.
Piedra Escudo gave
The holy shield and sacred book
To the Wise Woman,
Ko'lel ix K'aax.

She hid the sacred book
In a cave far to the north,
The shield she placed in sacred ground
At the center of the earth.
And so they remain
To be found when they are needed.

The gods were angry.,
And so they demanded
Piedra Escudo's sacrifice
Upon the high altar,
To appease their anger,
And this was done.

Ko'lel ix K'aax mourned his death,
Living many, many years in the forest.
There she ministered to the people
And told them of the future.
When she left this world
Her waay remained.

Her spirit haunts the warab'alja still.
And the legend says,
When the end of this creation is near,
Ko'lel ix K'aax will return
As the sacred Quetzal,
To guide the way.

II

December 21, 2012
13.0.0.0.0, 4 Ahau, 3 Kankin
Friday, Doomsday

The Hotel

6:30 AM

I am awakened by the ringing of the phone at 6:30. It is Adam. "Daniel told me to call you," he says cheerfully. "We'll be waiting in the car out front at 7. Get a move on." He hangs up before I can ask him why the change in plans.

I shower and dress quickly. I'd slept well, though I hadn't expected to. But I'm still a bit groggy. I dress for the cameras: tailored khaki pants, bright green sleeveless blouse, and beige jacket. As an afterthought, I grab my floppy hat and sunglasses.

7:06 AM

At a few minutes after 7, I am out the front door of the hotel and can see Adam sitting behind the wheel of a bright, red Mazda. I walk over to the car and get in. "Where's Daniel?" I ask, somewhat uneasy.

"He was called to the police station. Probably something about the break-in last night," Adam says easily. "He said he'd meet us at the ruins."

"That doesn't make sense," I argue. "We didn't report it to the police." I pull my cell phone out of my bag and begin to dial Daniel's cell. Before I can complete the call, Adam reaches over, snatches the phone from my hand, and throws it onto the back seat.

"Don't bother him," he says with a short laugh. "Maybe it was the security people he said he was meeting." Adam puts the car into gear and begins to pull away from the curb.

I remember the last thing Daniel had said to me the night before, "Don't let anyone, anyone in until I call you and let you know the coast is clear."

"Something isn't right here," I say out loud. As I reach to open the car door, Adam slams the brakes on, bringing the car to an abrupt stop.

He reaches over and pulls my hand away from the door handle. Before I can protest, he takes a set of handcuffs from somewhere, and clasps one around my wrist and the other around the shoulder strap of my seat belt. "What are you doing?" I scream at him.

"Making sure you take a little ride with me. Nice day for it, don't you think?" He laughs, still smiling goodnaturedly

7:11 AM

My cell phone rings. Both Adam and I turn to look at it in the back seat. I can't reach it and Adam ignores it. It rings until it goes to voice mail.

Adam pulls out of the hotel drive and turns the car north, in the opposite direction from Chichen Itza.

"Adam, why?" is all I can say. I am so shocked by what is happening, by his betrayal. I know he's trying to prevent me from getting to the Ball Court. What I don't know is how far he will go to prevent it. "Why?" I ask again with a feeling of terrible betrayal.

"For the money, of course. People are paying a lot of money to make sure you don't make an appearance at the Ball Court this morning. All I have to do is take you for a little ride, keep you occupied, say until noon or so." He glances over at me and must see the look of disgust on my face. His expression becomes contrite. "It's for your own protection. Don't want anything to happen to you. Not like what happened to Eduardo," he says with a pleading note in his voice.

"You didn't have anything to do with that," I say in horror.

"No. No, nothing at all. I was with you and Daniel when it happened. Remember?"

"But you agreed to work for the people who did that to him, who killed him?" I say accusatively.

"Not the same people. They assure me they had nothing to do with that. It was an accident." He doesn't sound at all convinced of what he is saying.

7:25 AM

I'm quiet for a long time. Adam doesn't say anything either. My displeasure and disappointment in someone I trusted and thought a friend is a real presence in the car. Finally I say, as a command, not a plea, "Turn around Adam. It's not too late. I have to get to the Ball Court by 11. It's important." He says nothing. He won't even look at me. "It's not too late," now I am pleading.

"It's all a bunch of nonsense. Doomsday. Armageddon. The end of the world. All nonsense," he says angrily. "And you thinking you're going to save the world with the help of a message from the past. Shit. You're a scientist. You don't really believe that drivel, do you?" he sneers.

"I don't disbelieve it," I whisper. I am quiet again, trying to think of a way to convince him to go back.

7:40 AM

"The others know what to do," I say, breaking the silence. "It doesn't matter if I'm not there."

"The others have been taken care of, too," there's a bitter edge to his voice.

"What do you mean 'they've been taken care of?'" I say, with alarm. "What have you done to them?"

He laughs. "Don't get in a panic. They've just been detained by the police. My employer has a lot of friends in high places. The police wish to speak with them about a small matter of the theft of the national treasures of Mexico." He glances at his watch. "Right about now, I'd say, they are cooling their heels in a tiny cell in the village jail. I'm sure everything will be cleared up by this afternoon, with no bad feelings."

I look at my watch as well. Only three and a half hours left. It's been a half hour since we left the hotel. "Where are we going?" I ask. "How much further?"

"Not far. Not far" is his reply.

I slump back in my seat, at a loss of what to do.

8:10 AM

We pull off the main highway onto a rutted dirt road. The scenery looks vaguely familiar, flat open country with dry, mown cornfields on either side of the road. Then a group of tents and wooden buildings comes into view. It is the site of the dig from last year. "How apropos," I say. "Back to where it all began." At least I know where I am, forty-five minutes and about 30 miles northwest of where I am supposed to be.

8:15 AM

Adam pulls the car up in front of the camp office, parks, and turns off the motor. "Now what?" I ask, not sure I want to know the answer.

"We wait," he replies. He gets out, walks around the front of the car and opens my door. He unlocks the handcuff from around the seat belt and then the one from my wrist. He points the way to the office. We enter. It's unchanged from a year and a half ago, except it's empty of equipment and boxes.

"There's water and soda in the fridge," he says. "I won't cuff you if you behave. I'll be right outside."

I don't say a word. He leaves and I hear him turn the key in the door. I'm locked in. I look around in desperation. Some kind of weapon is what I need, but I don't have much to choose from: a chair, a desk, a lamp. I could call him in on some pretext and hit him over the head with the chair. No, the lamp is lighter. I pick up the lamp, walk to the door, and stand beside it. "Adam," I call, trying to make my voice firm, but not angry. "Adam, I have to go to the bathroom." No answer. Has he left, when he said he wouldn't or is he sitting in the car listening to the radio and ignoring me. "Adam," I scream, now angry. Still no answer.

I look at my watch again. 8:20 AM. Only two hours, 51 minutes to go.

IV

Back at the Hotel

7:00 AM

Daniel pulls the nondescript, grey sedan into the hotel drive at just 7 AM. He parks a distance from the front door, behind a large delivery van. He pulls out his cell phone and calls Kate's hotel room. No answer. "Probably in the shower," he thinks. He watches as two burly farm laborers empty the truck of fresh produce and local poultry. They go about their job leisurely, conversing in rapid Spanish all the time. They are complaining about the tourista and the traffic.

7:05 AM

Daniel dials Kate's room again. Still no answer. "Damn that woman," he said out loud. "Where has she got to?" The van has been emptied by this time and the two delivery men climb into the cab.

Daniel begins to open the car door when he sees a woman coming out of the hotel, floppy hat, big sunglasses, over-sized moral (native bag) on her shoulder. "Kate," he growled. She didn't hear him. She turns in the opposite direction and walks away from where he is parked. Just then the van pulls out and he could see a bright red sports car that has been parked in front of it. Kate heads right to the car, opens the car door and greets the driver as she steps in. "Damn her," he curses again. "What does she think she's doing?"

The two in the sports car are talking. They look to be arguing. Daniel sees the driver reach over and take something from Kate's hands and throw it into the back seat. When the man turns to profile, Daniel realized it is Adam. "What the hell?" he mutters. The two in the car seem to be fighting, or is Adam just helping Kate with her seat belt?

7:11 AM

Daniel picks up his cell phone again and dials Kate's mobile number. It rings and rings. No answer, then, "This call is being automatically forwarded to voice mail." Daniel disconnects and throws the phone on the passenger seat.

7:15 AM

Daniel opens the car door and gets out, heading toward the other car. He gets no more than a step or two when the red car pulls away. Cursing again Daniel jumps back in his car, starts the engine and drives after them. At the village square the car turns north, toward the highway rather than toward Chichen Itza.

"Where are they going?" Daniel yells and pounds the steering wheel. Then he thinks, had Kate hidden the tile somewhere out of town? Were she and Adam going to get it? And why would she trust Adam and not him? He is angry now and speeds after the red Mazda as it turns onto the highway, north toward Merida.

7:25 AM

Daniel follows, several cars behind. The road is crowded, so he can follow without fear of being seen and identified. After ten minutes driving, he realizes that this all does not make much sense. Why would Kate leave an errand like this, involving a trip this distance from Chichen Itza, until the morning she knew she had to be at the site early?

"No", he thought, this isn't Kate's idea. And if it is not Kate's idea, then whose idea is it and why?

7:40 AM

Daniel looks at his watch. How much further could they possibly be going? All the way to Merida? He realizes that everyone at the site would be wondering where they are and why they are late. He picks up his cell and dials Brian's cell phone. Better fill them in on what is happening, tell them they may have to take over for Kate, if she doesn't get back in time. The phone rings then goes to voice-mail. Daniel leaves a message. Then he calls Calvin. No answer there either. "Damn!"

8:10 AM

Fifty-five minutes from the hotel, Adam's car slows and turns off the highway onto a secondary road. Daniel suddenly realizes where he is and where they are going. The dig site. He slows the car and falls back. A following car will be seen on this little used, rural road. He can just catch a glimpse of the other car from time to time, but there isn't anywhere else they can go. He is sure he can't lose them.

Daniel can just see the red car ahead of him as it turns into the camp. The track is deeply rutted and the car needs to slow considerably. Too great a chance of his being seen, he thinks. Better leave the car here and go the rest of the way on foot. It isn't far, especially if he goes cross country through the shorn corn field between here and the camp.

He pulls the car off the road and gets out. Daniel heads across the field at a run, but finds that his progress is slowed by the dry, foot high corn stalks that remain. His light soled loafers don't give much support on the rutted, uneven ground. He feels a nagging fear for Kate. Why has Adam brought her here?

Back at the Hotel

7:20 AM

As Brian and Calvin leave the hotel for the short walk to the archeological site, they are approached by two men in dark suits. "Senor Conway? Senor Otis?" the older of the two says. "I am Detective Federo of the Yucatan State Policia and this is my partner, Detective Rejos. You will accompany us to the comisaria de policia, por favor."

"W . . . what's t . . . this all about?" asks Brian, fearing something has happened to Kate or Daniel.

"You will come with us," the younger man says gruffly and grabs Brian by the arm. Brian begins to resist, fearing a replay of the attack the day before, but he is clearly outmatched.

"Cool it, Brian," cautions Calvin. "Let's just see the credentials of these nice officers first. If they are the real deal, the least we can do is go have a talk with them." He's been smiling, but here his voice grows threatening and the smile vanishes. "But if they aren't who they say they are, I'm sure all these nice people, here on the sidewalk, will come to our rescue if we scream loud enough."

Detective Federo withdraws a wallet from his inside jacket pocket and shows it to Calvin. The other detective lets go of Brian and does the same. Federo says flatly, "We do not want to create a scene, but you will accompany us to the comisaria, now. We wish to ask you a few questions, that is all."

"These look official," Calvin says, indicating the credentials. "I guess we'll have to go along with them. I assume we get the traditional one phone call?" he says to the detective, as they are hustled to a police car parked at the curb.

7:38 AM

They are relieved of their cell phones, passports and keys as soon as they enter the police station. It is a tiny office on the ground floor of an office building off the village square. Behind the reception area a door leads to a hallway containing several other doors, all of them closed. Detective Rejos pushes open the first door on the right and ushers them into a 6 X 6 foot, windowless room. It is bare, except for a small table and four chairs. "Have a seat," the officer says roughly and leaves the room, slamming the door on his way out.

"W . . . what do you think t . . . this is all about?" asks Brian, almost incoherent with panic.

"I don't know," replies Calvin. "But I don't think it can be good." And they both lapse into silence

The Ball Court Chichen Itza

8:10 AM

Enrice` paces back and forth at the edge of the folding chairs placed for the expected dignitaries. Kate and Daniel are late. They are supposed to have arrived at 7:30. Here it was 10 after 8 and still no sign of them. He has no idea what their exact plans are, what it is they plan to announce. He hates to go into an interview blind, but going in deaf and dumb, as well, is ridiculous. The sound and video equipment are all in place. The hook-up for live feed and the telephone lines are in working order. The show will go on the air, live, in under two hours.

The spectator portion of the Ball Court is already beginning to fill with anxious onlookers and the media section with TV crews and the press. Only the VIP seating remains empty.

Enrice` calls the hotel for the fifth time. Still no answers in any of their rooms. He gets the front desk. "Si, Senor. Senor Keith left very early this morning and the Senorita shortly after that. The other two hombre, I do not know. So sorry. Si, if I see the Senor and Senorita I will tell them to call Senor Enrice`."

The dig site

8:25 AM

Daniel reaches the far edge of the corn field and kneels to catch his breath. He can see the camp buildings fifty feet in front of him. The red car is parked in front of the camp office and Adam is leaning against its hood, talking into a cell phone. Kate is nowhere in sight.

8:32 AM

Daniel watches for several minutes, surveying the area to see if there is anyone else around. There are no other cars and the rest of the camp appears to be deserted. Adam continues to talk on the phone, his back to Daniel. Where is Kate? In the office? Somewhere else in the camp?

Daniel assumes that Kate is here against her will. Gut instinct, nothing more. That makes Adam the bad guy. If that is so, what is he going to do about it?

Daniel creeps slowly closer, trying to be as quiet as possible, so as not to alert Adam to his presence. But Adam's attention seems to be fully focused on whomever he is arguing with on the phone. Daniel gets to within 6 feet of the other man and still hasn't been spotted. "So far, so good", he thinks.

8:42 AM

Daniel realizes that Adam is not only younger by at least 20 years, but he is also in better shape. He certainly has the advantage in any fight. Daniel looks around for some sort of weapon. All he can see nearby is a short wooded slat about 3 feet long and 2 inches by ½ inch. Not a heavy duty weapon, but better than nothing. He picks it up, holding it like a baseball bat, and moves forward. His foot hits some loose gravel and makes a crunching sound, just as he gets within striking distance.

Adam begins to turn at the sound and Daniel, forced to swing before he was ready, hits the younger man a glancing blow across his left shoulder, knocking him against the car. Adam gives an astonished howl and begins to right himself. Seeing who it is, he gives a short laugh, "If it isn't Sir Galahad to the rescue." He reaches into his jacket pocket and pulls out a small 22 caliber pistol. He slowly raises the gun, still laughing.

Daniel anticipates the weapon, when Adam reaches into his pocket. Getting his timing just right this time, he swings away as if for a home run. He catches Adam's gun hand squarely, before the other man has a chance to take aim. The gun goes off as it flies out of Adam's hand, putting a hole through the passenger window of the flashy, red car. Adam is off-balanced and in obvious pain. He falls to the ground, cradling his hand that is probably broken.

8:53 AM

"Where's Kate?" growls Daniel, standing over the fallen man. Adam ignores him. "Where is Kate?" He still gets no answer. Adam stirs and then in a flash reaches out to grab Daniel's leg and pull him down to the ground. Daniel, still holding the slab of wood, responds automatically and hits Adam on the back of the head. Adam collapses in the dirt and doesn't move.

Daniel looks around. He has to find Kate without Adam's help. The most probable place is the office. He tries the door, but it's locked. He isn't about to go looking through Adam's pockets for the key, so he moves back a few paces and kicks the door in.

II

The camp office

8:32 AM

I hear Adam talking to someone. Only Adam's voice, so I assume he is talking to someone on the phone. He seems to be arguing with someone, refusing to do something they want him to do. The arguing goes on for a while.

8:42 AM

I hear a laugh and Adam seems to be talking to someone else. Sir Galahad? There is a cry of pain, the sound of a gunshot, then silence, except for the soft sound of someone moaning. Then the commotion starts again; the sound of a scuffle and then a loud thud. Then silence.

8:56 AM

I hold my breath. Who's out there? Friend or foe? The door knob moves and the door shakes. I grab up the lamp again, happy for anything that might give me an advantage. Before I can cross the room, the door explodes inward.

There stands Daniel, disheveled and looking wild. At first, I think he might be an accomplice of Adam's. But no, he is clearly relieved to see me safe. And then I can see Adam's still body, lying on the ground, just outside the door.

"Is he dead?" I ask, unsure whether I want him dead or not? No, not dead, just hurt enough he'd wish he was dead. I step over his body, not giving him another thought. "Where's your car?" I yell at Daniel. "We need to get back." My voice rises in panic, as I realize just how late it is getting.

When Daniel tells me he left the car at the end of the drive into the camp, I screech frantically. "Too far, let's take Adam's," I rummage in the unconscious man's pockets for the keys.

"What should we do with him?" asks Daniel, nodding at the man on the ground.

"Leave him there, I suppose," I respond, heading toward the car.

Daniel looks at me in surprise. "Cold," he says. "We need to at least get him out of the sun. We'll put him in the office. Or maybe we should take him with us."

"No way," I say emphatically. "He kidnapped me and tried to kill you. I don't trust him, even if he is out cold. Put him in the office, if you must, but hurry." Daniel drags Adam into the office just as he begins to stir.

I go back into the little building to retrieve my bag, then pull the door shut behind me. No way of locking it, Daniel has broken the lock beyond repair. I walk to the car and grab my cell phone from the back seat, but as I begin to get into the driver's side of the sporty little car, Daniel grabs the keys out of my hand.

"No way," he says with authority. "You're not driving, I am."

I acquiesce, not wanting to take the time to argue and realizing I'm probably not in the best frame of mind to be behind the wheel. "Okay," I say, letting go of the keys, "but remember we're in a hurry." I run around to the other side of the car and clamber in.

9:12 AM

Minutes later we're flying down the road 45 minutes or more from where we need to be.

IV

The police station

9:05 AM

Brian and Calvin have been sitting in the small, uncomfortable room for over an hour, without anyone so much as peeking a head in the door to see if they are still alive. At first Brian jabbers on and on, trying to make some kind of sense out of what is happening to them. What do the police want? What have they done? When will they come back to question them? Will they get their one phone call or is it just in TV cop shows where that is the rule?

He finally asks Calvin, a note of panic in his voice, "D . . . do you t . . . think this m . . . might have something to do with the artifacts w . . . we took last summer?"

Calvin turns to him and hisses at him, in just above a whisper, "Shut up! They probably have the place bugged. Don't say anything." He looked directly into Brian's face. "Don't say another word." He turns away and slouches back into his chair. "What's more," he grumbles, "you're driving me crazy."

10:02 AM

For the next hour Calvin and Brian continue to cool their heels. Several times Detective Rejos comes to the door but says nothing, refusing to answer their questions or indicate if a telephone call is a possibility. During that time Calvin sits slumped in the uncomfortable metal chair, his eyes closed, his breathing even and relaxed. Brian isn't sure if he is asleep or not, but doesn't talk to him. Instead, Brian paces the room in an agitated near frenzy, muttering to himself incoherently.

The Ball Court

9:00 AM

Enrice` paces the area in front of the Lower Jaguar Temple, checking and rechecking the equipment that is all in working order and doesn't need checking. He has heard nothing from Kate and Daniel. He's getting more worried by the minute.

The general clamor of the media technicians suddenly quiets. Enrice` looks up to see Senor Tierro and a small entourage of assistants wending their way through the throng of men and equipment. The Antiquities Director comes over to him, thrusts out a hand and introduces himself needlessly. "Menos Tierro, Director of the Office of Antiquities, Senor Sanchez. You seem to have everything under control, I see. The broadcast is set to begin at 10, I believe?" He smiles broadly.

"Yes, the broadcast is set for 10, but we do have a problem," Enrice` responds, his concern obvious, but Senor Tierro fails to notice.

"A problem?" he says, smiling even more broadly, if possible. "I'm sure it's nothing we cannot solve. Tell me." And he waits for the other man to answer, smirking with an air of superiority.

Enrice` realizes that he doesn't like this supercilious bureaucrat. Tierro reminds him of something . . . something unpleasant, but he isn't exactly sure of what. The man has influence though and might be of some help, so Enrice` decides to confide in him. "Professor O'Hara and Dr. Keith aren't here yet," he moans. "They were supposed to be here an hour ago."

"Not to worry," Senor Tierro says smoothly. "I am sure between us, we can handle it until they arrive." He turns away as something on the other side of the field catches his attention.

"You don't understand," Enrice` entreats. "Professor O'Hara didn't clue me in on what she plans to announce," his frustration audible in his voice.

9:30 AM

Menos Tierro turns back to him, clearly distracted. "Not to worry. I know as much as either of the professors about the Prophecy and the Maya legend. I am sure I can fill in if they fail to arrive." His attention is attracted again by what is going on across the way. "It appears that the television networks are beginning their coverage. I think I might be of some use to them." And he strides away toward the cameras and microphones without another word to Enrice`.

II

On the road to Chichen Itza

9:20 AM

Daniel drives as fast as he can, without losing an axel on the rut ridden, back country road, but it isn't fast enough for me. I complain, but his only comment is, "If we break down out here in the middle of nowhere, we'll never get to Chichen Itza in time." He's right, of course, and I shut up, twisting my hands nervously in my lap.

When we finally get to the highway, Daniel picks up the pace. Still not as fast as I want him to go. Over the speed limit, but not fast enough to attract the attention of the gendarmes. Daniel looks over at me and asks in a clearly, angry growl, "What the hell happened this morning? I thought you agreed not to leave your room until I called to tell you I was waiting in the car out in front of the hotel?"

"Well, yes," I stammer, realizing once again, just how stupid I had been that morning. "But, you see . . ."

"No, I don't see," he says loudly. "We all agreed, and I thought you understood, how dangerous this has gotten. But no, first chance you get, you do just what you were told not to do." He seems to run out of steam here, and lapses into silent frustration.

"But," I begin again, "Adam rang my room; said you had to go speak with the police or the security people, and told him to pick me up."

"And you believed him?" His voice is quieter and some of the anger seems to have dissipated.

"Yes," I answer meekly. "Why shouldn't I? It didn't occur to me, until I got into the car, that it didn't seem right. I started to call you and that's when things started to turn ugly. Adam pulled the phone out of my hand and threw it into the back seat and then . . ." I stop and gulp, remembering the moment. Daniel waits while I compose myself. "And then, when I tried to get out of the car, he handcuffed me to the seat belt."

Daniel glances over at me again, his expression one of concern, not anger this time. "Did he hurt you?"

"No," I say definitively. "No, in fact, he was his usual pleasant, cheery self."

"Did he say why he was doing it?" Daniel asks, obviously perplexed. "Or who he was working for?"

"All he said was that he was doing it for the money. He tried to convince me that it doesn't make any difference if I am at Chichen Itza today. That it is all a preposterous hoax and nothing is going to happen. He didn't tell me who was paying him or why. The only time he got upset was when I asked him how he could work with the people who killed Eduardo. He denied this. Said the 'people' had nothing to do with Eduardo's death. That it was just an accident."

"Right," Daniel says with disbelief. "And why kidnap you and leave the rest of us free to interfere with today's proceedings?"

"Adam said that the three of you were being taken care of. Something about being detained by the police."

"So that's why I can't raise Calvin and Brian on their cells or at the hotel," he muses. "We'll have to check on that, but if they are with the police they should be safe, for the present." He thinks for a few moments and then adds, "Whoever hired Adam must have some significant influence."

'The Order, 'El Sociedad,'" I whisper. A chill runs through me, someone walking over my grave again. I hope that isn't a premonition.

9:44 AM

We reach the edge of the village quicker than I expect, but that is where our progress comes to a virtual halt. We hit a massive traffic jam at the village square. Everyone in the world seems to be trying to go to the same place we are.

"Do you think we should get out and walk it from here?" I ask dubiously.

"Look at the sidewalks and walkways," Daniel replies and points. They're crowded with pedestrians, shoulder to shoulder, making no more headway than we are. "I don't think we'd get there any faster on foot. I do have an idea though." Daniel, always ready in a crisis, I think. "If we continue to the other side of the square and make the right-hand turn, then take the country road out of town, the way we did the other morning, toward the café where we had breakfast, we should be able to circumvent the traffic, and get to the parking area outside the visitors' center from the back. Should be less traffic that way."

"Marvelous," I sing with a laugh and we crawl toward the intersection.

IV

The Police Station

10:05 AM

When Brian is just about convinced that they have been totally forgotten, Detective Feeder comes into the room and sits down in the chair facing Calvin. Calvin opens his eyes languidly and smiles. "Thought you had forgotten us," he says matter-of-factly.

"We have other things to do that are of more importance today. It is all chaos out there. More people than I have ever seen in my life."

"Since you have better things to do, perhaps you might ask your questions and then we can be out of your hair," Calvin remarks. Brian comes over and sits down at the table, relieved to have someone paying attention to them finally.

"I am sorry, but I fear I cannot do as you ask," the police officer says politely.

"And why is that, might I ask?" says Calvin with equal politeness.

"It is not my jurisdiction. I received a call this morning from the Office of Antiquities," Brian gives a start and opens his mouth as if to speak. Calvin shoots him a look, stomps on his foot, and he's quiet. Detective Federo doesn't seem to have noticed and continues uninterrupted. "They asked that we pick you up and hold you for questioning. I do not know to what it is in relation. Then, of course, the Office is closed today, because of the proceedings here, and I can get no response from anyone. So I am afraid you must remain here, until someone from that department is available. So sorry."

"But you, you can't k . . . keep us here," Brian sputters indignantly.

Calvin breaks in, "I think I have a solution, Detective. It just so happens we are acquainted with Senor Tierro, the director of the Office of Antiquities. I'm sure he will vouch for us. I have his private number in my cell phone and you can reach him directly."

The police office agrees willingly; anything to get one problem off his plate. He smiles and leaves the room.

The Ball Court

10:00 AM

Enrice` looks around helplessly; still no sign of Kate and Daniel. He can see Senor Tierro holding court in front of the TV crews. No help there, though the bigwig has promised to take up the slack. The show must go on, as the saying goes, and he is a showman, if nothing else. He gives the high sign to his sound man, smiles, speaks cheerfully into the microphone and begins his spiel.

10:10 AM

On the other side of the court, Senor Tierro is enjoying himself immensely, holding forth on the many treasures of ancient Mexico and the Maya in particular. He is careful not to give any definite answer to the questions regarding the Maya Prophecy and the supposed end of the world. He doesn't want a panic of any kind. One has to remember this is being broadcast to the entire world. His demeanor is calm and self assured. He emits no evidence of concern.

One of his aides comes up, taps him on the shoulder and hands him a cell phone. "The Policia," the aide whispers.

"Hola," Tierro says into the phone with a show of irritation at being interrupted. "El Policia? Que` es eso?" he says gruffly. "No se los conozco. I know no one of that name." He hung up and handed the phone back to the aide with a scowl, but he smiles as he turns away.

378

10:15 AM

Jorge watches from the edge of the Ball Court, taking in the quickly swelling crowd in the stadium. Kate is supposed to have met him hours ago in the parking area. He has been unable to reach her by phone. This is his fourth trip back to the court to see if she had arrived by a different route, but she still isn't here and no one that he asks has seen or heard from her. He is worried and at a loss as to what to do.

He turns and makes his way back to the parking lot.

10:20 AM

Senor Tierro watches as Jorge leaves the Ball Court. Even from a distance he can see the worried look on the older man's face. Tierro disengages himself from the TV commentators, smiling graciously, and walks over to the columned entryway to the Jaguar Temple. Here Enrice` is doing his best to keep his radio talk show going without any of his guest authorities. Senor Tierro waves at him to get his attention.

Enrice` finishes thanking a call-in listener and, without missing a beat, said, "We are in luck fans. Senor Tierro, director of the Office of Antiquities, has just joined us. Director, could you tell us about the history of the Maya Prophecy and the legends that surround it?"

Senor Tierro takes the microphone and launches into a long and intellectual explanation of the Maya calendars and the fact that they end on this exact date. He then, to Enrice`'s surprise, begins to tell the listening audience about the Codex that had been found in the Yucatan last summer. He speaks as if the Codex is authentic and the radio host realizes this is the first time any authority has done so. What a scoop, he thinks. Then he has a second, nearly paralyzing, thought. If the Codex is the real deal and the end of the world is eminent, and if Kate doesn't get here in time with the shield, whatever that is, what difference will a scoop make, no matter how big?

Police Station

10:30 AM

Detective Federo returns to the room a short time later. His expression is grim. "I am sorry," he says mournfully. "I got in touch with Senor, the director, Tierro."

"G . . . great!" cried Brian excitedly.

379

The detective raises his hand to forestall his excitement. "He denied knowing you," he says bleakly. "He said he never heard of you. He was most indignant."

"B . . . but t . . . that's a . . . a lie. He . . . he knows us. We m . . . met him on, on several occasions." He was clearly losing control. Calvin reaches over and puts his hand on Brian's arm. "D . . . did you mention P . . . professor O'Hara?"

"Yes sir, I did. That is when he hung up on me." Federo looks embarrassed. "Of course, he is very busy right now. We will just have to wait until all the . . . excitement is over. In the meantime, I am afraid I must keep you here."

"N . . . no," wails Brian, jumping up from his chair. "W . . . we can't s . . . stay here. We, we have to b . . . be at the Ball Court b . . . by eleven . . . eleven." He collapses back into his chair, exhausted by the emotional outpouring.

"Please, sir, calm yourself," placates Detective Federo. He is alarmed by Brian's distress.

Calvin has said nothing, not responding at all to the policeman's news, as if it comes as no surprise. Now he leans forward toward the other man across the table and says quietly, with complete control, "I have a suggestion." He has the officer's attention. "Our presence in your facility is, I am sure, an inconvenience, during this time particularly. I believe the call from the Office of Antiquities mentioned only a wish to question us. Am I right?" He looked earnestly at Detective Federo.

The policeman nods thoughtfully. "Si. Si."

"They made no accusations of any kind, correct?" Again Federo nods. "We have nothing to hide and will be pleased to answer any questions they might have, when they have the time to ask them." The policeman smiles, seeing where the young man is headed. "Since there are no charges, perhaps we can come to a compromise." He pauses and smiles broadly. "We really do not want to miss the festivities at Chichen Itza. After all, that's why we're here." He pauses again, playing the other man expertly. "What I suggest is . . . . We will surrender our passports to you and promise to present ourselves back here for questioning as soon as the event is over."

Brian is about to protest at the thought of giving up his passport, but Calvin stomps on his foot again, under the table.

Detective Federo rubs his chin thoughtfully, but Calvin knows he has a deal. "Well," the officer says slowly, "since there have been no charges mentioned, I see no reason I should not agree to your suggestion. I see you are men of honor and I cannot spare the manpower to keep an eye on you here." He stands and thrusts out his hand to shake Calvin's. "I have your word that you will return this afternoon? In the meantime, I will keep your passports as security."

Calvin shakes the other man's hand earnestly. "Until this afternoon."

"Of course," the older man says with a laugh, as he leads them from the room, "if the prophecy of the Maya comes to pass, we will not have to be concerned about that eventuality." And he laughs heartily. Brian shivers.

II

Parking lot at the Visitors'Center

10:35 AM

I look at my watch as Daniel pulls into the parking area near the visitors' center at the archeological site. "My God," I gasp, "we have barely a half hour."

"We have enough time," says Daniel, so calmly I feel like hitting him in frustration.

I get out of the car and run toward the turnstile at the visitors' gate. Two large security guards are standing in our way. They are not any of the guards I have seen on my previous visits. What is more, they are armed, which is not at all the norm. As we attempt to enter, they do not move aside.

"Boleto?" the one on the left says in a bored monotone. Then he adds as an afterthought, "por favor."

Both Daniel and I pull out our identification, passports and driver's licenses. The guard barely glances at the documents and shakes his head. "Pasaje. Boleto." He demands harshly.

"I think he's trying to tell us there is some kind of special pass required to enter," Daniel explains to me as if I am a two year old.

"I know, I know," I snap at him. I turn back to the guards and speak to the one on the right, who appears to be less hostile. With a coy smile, I tell him just who we are and why we need to get to the Ball Court. I tell him, "We are expected. Ask Senor Tierro. He is a man of great authority and will vouch for us." The guard just stares at me impassively, while his cohort continues to shake his head no. I'm not even sure he speaks English or understands a word I'm saying. I don't trust my halting Spanish, I might miss-say something, and get us into more trouble. We can't afford to be arrested at this juncture. I turn to Daniel and demand, "You tell him."

Daniel repeats what I have just said in his flawless Spanish. Neither of the guards seems to be listening.

When he finishes, the man on the left says flatly, "No pasaje, no entrada." He points authoritatively away from the gate, his affect inviting no argument.

Daniel turns and begins to walk away, pulling me with him. I resist, but he drags me along. "What are you doing?" I scream at him, trying to pull my arm away.

"Be quiet," he hisses. "Don't make a fuss or they'll arrest us for sure. We need to get in, but are not going to get in that way," he says as he continues walking. "There has to be another way in." We head back across the parking lot and around the corner of a large utility building. At the far side of the building there is a high chain link fence. The fence has a gate. I run over to it, excitedly, only to find it padlocked shut.

"Damn, damn, damn," I scream in a panic and shake the gate like a mad woman.

10:45 AM

I look over at Daniel who stomps his feet angrily in the dirt. For only the second time, since he found me locked in the camp office, he seems to have lost his cool. Now what are we going to do? I always rely on Daniel to come up with the answer in a crisis. If he doesn't have an answer now, what are we going to do? I look at my watch again. We have only 26 minutes left.

"Señorita. Señorita Kate," comes a voice from behind us. I turn to see Jorge coming quickly around the corner of the utility building. He rushes toward us, clearly alarmed. "Where have you been? You are so late. It is almost time."

"It's a long story," says Daniel, having regained his composure. "That can wait. We'll tell you all about it later. Right now we need to get in there. Can you get us past the guards at the gate?"

"Sí, sí. But this will be quicker," he says as he pulls a large ring of keys from his pocket. Walking over to the gate, he inserts a small key into the padlock and turns it. The padlock opens immediately and Jorge swings the gate open to let us through.

I look around to see just where we are. As I get my bearings, I realize we are just south of the Ball Court.

"Prisa, prisa. Hurry. Run. Go," Jorge exclaims anxiously. "I cannot keep up. Go, go without me."

I smile back at him and take off running, Daniel close behind me. Luckily I am in pretty good shape, but the sandals I'm wearing aren't meant for a marathon.

Only 21 minutes left

IV

The Ball Court

10:50 AM

Señor Tierro has taken over the broadcast, answering the phone and responding to the listeners' questions. Enrice` has been unable to stop him. The radio talk show host looks up at the sky. The sun, in the last hour, has risen above the eastern wall of the Jaguar Temple. The shadow cast by the wall is slowly receding. Very soon the area between the two columns will be in open sunlight. Enrice` looks at his watch and, seeing how short the time is, reaches over and unceremoniously takes the microphone out of Señor Tierro's hand.

"Thank you so much for your expertise and your time, Señor Tierro. That was Señor Menos Tierro, director of the Office of Antiquities here in Mexico. It was great to have him here with us and to share with us the history of the Maya prophecy."

He pauses to catch his breath and collect his thoughts. He then continues, his voice taking on a somber note. "I am sitting here under the massive Plumed Serpent columns, at the entrance to the Jaguar Temple in the great Ball Court at Chichen Itza. At ground zero, you might say. It is here, in barely 20 minutes, that the fate of the world . . . . no, the universe, will be determined. Today, as the Maya predicted, ages ago, there will be an event which takes place only once every 5000 or so years. Today there will be a grand convergence, an alignment of our Sun, the planet Venus, the galactic center, and the Earth. The Codex, recently found in the Yucatán Peninsula and attributed to Chan Bahlum II and translated by Professor Kate O'Hara and Dr. Daniel Keith, tells us that when this convergence occurs the world will end."

Enrice` hears a commotion from the other end of the field and sees a swarm of TV personalities headed in his direction. Obviously someone, over there, has been listening to his broadcast and they are coming to get in on the limelight.

He smiles, reveling in his 15 minutes of fame, for that was about all he has, whatever the outcome of the prophecy. He continues, "But the Codex had one more secret to reveal, according to Professor O'Hara." He pauses here for effect and then continues, "The Codex also contains a message for us, the men of the future. Professor O'Hara told me, just a few days ago, that the Codex gives a clue to how we can prevent the destruction of the world. But she did not share that secret with me."

He stops here, unsure of how to go on. "Professor O'Hara was supposed to be here this morning. She is overdue. We can only hope she makes it in time. The countdown has started. It is 10:53 AM on December 21, 2012. Do we have only 18 minutes until the end of the world?"

Cameras roll, the TV microphones pick up every word, and the entire world waits with breath held.

II

10:54 AM

We run a short distance across open ground and then come to the ruins of what had been a small temple at the southern end of the great Ball Court. Veering left we enter the Ball Court at the corner near the Western Wall. The stadium is packed with crowds of people standing and sitting on the grass. Ropes have been placed along both sides of the court, about 3 feet from the outer walls in order to protect the ruins from the crush of humanity. I slow and point out to Daniel the area inside the ropes, trying to indicate it is the only open corridor through the crowds. He nods and we run north, along the Western Wall. I can see, out of the corner of my eye, security guards waving and shouting at us, obviously wanting us out of the restricted area. We ignore them and keep running. They follow in our wake, yelling all the time.

Ahead of me, in the center of the field, is the area filled with folding chairs occupied by the VIPs. To the right of the seating area, I can see the paraphernalia of the media: satellite dishes, electrical cords, and technical equipment. I can make out the two tall Plumed Serpent columns, in front of which there is a milling mass of what I assume are the TV media. Beyond this crowd I can't see, but that is our destination.

I am rapidly tiring. My breath is coming in ragged gasps. My legs feel like bags of sand. I have a sharp pain in my side. I look over at Daniel. He's breathing hard, but he looks to be in better shape than I feel. What time is it I wonder, but I can't take the time to look at my watch. I can still hear the security guards screaming at us from behind, but can't turn my head to see how close they are.

IV

The Ball Court

10:58 AM

Enrice` continues the countdown, calling off the minutes as they expire. He is in a panic. What if he gets to zero, to 11:11 and nothing happens? And where the devil is Professor O'Hara. Senor Tierro, seated beside him, becomes more and more agitated as the minutes pass. Finally the Director grabs the microphone from Enrice`'s hand and begins speaking excitedly into it. His voice is high pitched and he speaks in a rapid rhythmic cadence, almost manic in his presentation.

"The Maya prophecy will come to pass. The will of the ancient gods of the Maya people will prevail. As they have ordained since the beginning of creation, the world will come to an end this day. The cycle will be completed, as previous ones have been, permitting a new cycle to begin. It is ordained by the gods. The fifth creation of the world will come to an end, today, and so the sixth creation will begin."

Enrice `grabs the microphone back from the other man. "Thank you again Señor Tierro for reviewing the wording of the Maya prophecy." The man is crazy, he thinks, and completely out of control. "It is now 11 o'clock; 11 minutes remain.

11:01 A.M

The sun continues to rise over the eastern wall, the shadow receding stealthily from the Ball Court. Enrice` can feel the tension mounting in the assembled multitude, but the crowd is entirely silent. Then he hears yelling from across the field. Some kind of commotion is going on, but he can't see what is happening. Some kind of altercation? Is the crowd

385

about to riot? Is this the way this small corner of the world will come to an end?

II

11:02 A.M.

Daniel and I reach the seating area. I can't get through the seats. I have to make my way around them. More people are screaming at me. Others reach out to grab me, but I push them off. I reach an open area past the seats. I can see the cluster of TV cameras and commentators not far in front of me. With my goal in sight, I get a burst of a renewed energy and pick up my pace. Daniel is right behind me.

I can hear Enrice`'s voice. They are obviously transmitting his broadcast over loudspeakers into the stadium. "11:02; nine minutes to go."

IV

11:02 AM

Señor Tierro has gotten up from his seat and is pacing excitedly back and forth between the two stone pillars, muttering to himself. He looks up as he hears the commotion from the center of the field. He can't believe his eyes. There in front of him is that redheaded witch, Kate O'Hara. He raises his hand and makes a gesture, as if signaling someone on the other side of the Ball Court.

11:03 A.M

Señor Tierro throws himself to the ground at the exact center of the area between the two Plumed Serpent columns. He takes a trowel from his coat pocket and begins digging. He works feverishly, refusing to stop, even when some of the reporters try to pull him off.

Several of his aides push their way into the fracas and form a protective barrier around him, to keep the reporters at bay.

II

11:04 A.M.

Daniel is very close behind me, almost on my heels. Suddenly, he screams in my ear, "Look out!" I feel him push me. I stumble to my left and fall to my knees. At that moment there is a sound, like a crack, and I can see Daniel fall.

I crawl over to where he is lying "Oh, my God. Oh, my God. Oh, my God." There is blood all over. His right shoulder and side are soaked with the precious fluid. He is panting and in obvious pain, but conscious.

"Go on," he gasps. "I'm alright. Go on. We don't have much time." And he manages a weak smile.

I get up, his blood all over my hands, and I run.

11:05 A.M

I push my way through the crowd of TV cameras and reporters, well aware of my disheveled appearance: red hair sticking out in all directions and blood all over my clothes. In front of me is my goal, a small patch of earth between the two stone pillars. What I see there shocks me. Señor Tierro, as disheveled and frantic as I am, his hands covered in dirt. He has removed the square of sod and is reaching into the hole with both hands.

The Sun is high. The area between the columns is still in shadow, but barely. What time is it? How many minutes, how many seconds, do we have left?

11:06 A.M.

Just as I reach the spot, Señor Tierro lifts the tile from the hole. He lifts it above his head, showing it to the crowd and watching cameras. A look of ecstasy comes over his face. He looks insane.

"He is our enemy," I think. "He is the one who killed Eduardo. I never suspected him."

The tile is still raised above his head and with a maniacal laugh, he raises it higher. I realize he is going to throw it to the ground and shatter it, and with it, all our hopes.

"No," I scream. "No. You can't do that." I throw myself at him and grab at the tile as he brings it forward toward the ground. I just get my hands on it and I hold on for dear life, trying to wrest it away from him. He is strong, stronger than I am. I am losing ground. I can't hold on. My hands are wet with sweat and Daniel's blood.

11:07 A.M.

The tile is slipping away. It slips from my fingers. I've lost it. My heart sinks. Senor Tierro looks down at me, gloating. He raises the tile again and is about to dash it to the ground. I watch in horror.

Suddenly someone else is there. Another set of hands grabs the precious shield and pushes Señor Tierro roughly out of the way.

11:09 A.M.

I look to see Brian grinning at me. And there, off to the side, I can see Calvin, sitting on top of a ranting Señor Tierro, smiling insolently.

Brian hands the tile to me and whispers, "Y . . . you have two minutes."

I take the stone tablet, gratefully, into my hands, kneel and place it reverently into the hole.

11:10 A.M.

The sun inches up to its zenith. The shadow recedes even further. It creeps over the edge of the hole. The crowd is hushed, silent.

Something's wrong. Something nags at me. I'm forgetting something. But what? But what?

And then the passage from the Codex comes back to me. I can see the words on the page. They go through my mind. I can hear them as if they are spoken by the old woman, the Shaman.

> He who finds the stone, the shield, must
> place the image of the sun god,
> K'ul kul'kan, upon sacred ground.

A picture comes into my head. The image of how Jorge and I found the tile. Not like this, with the image of the Plumed Serpent staring up at me, but with the glossy reflective surface shining up. Shiny, to reflect the rays of the sun.

"The sun," I gasp. Where was it? I look up. It is almost directly overhead. The shadow has bisected the hole in which the tile rests. "What time is it?"

I don't realize I have said it out loud, until Brian answers "Almost t . . . time, s . . . seconds."

I reach into the hole, lift the stone shield, and turn it over, so that the black shining surface reflects the sunlight, just as the Sun reaches its zenith.

11:11 A.M. December 21, 2012
13.0.0.0.0, 4 Ahau, 3 Kankin
Doomsday

The End

GLOSSARY

Ah Kin	Mayan priest
Ah Kin Mai	the Mayan High Priest
Ah Puch	god of Xibalbal, the underworld
ah waay	a witch
Ahau	a nobleman
Ahauab	a nobleman of the court
Abuela	grandmother
aj k'uh hun	head dresses
Aj K'uhn	a priestly scribe
Aloe	used to treat burns and skin rashes
b'ak' keeh	Venison
b'u'ul	Beans
Bahlamka	the Mayan name for Palenque
Ceiba tree	sacred Tree of Life
Cenote	natural well
cha'ah	Celebration
Chac Chel	goddess of the earth, goddess of childbirth, divine
chak	corn
Chaya	herb helps heal broken bones
Chum Tuum Bahlim	Jaguar throne of the Maya
esin of the Ek' Balam shrub	used to stop bleeding
Haab	Mayan solar calendar = 365 days made up of 18 cycles 0f 20 days plus 5 Wayeb' or nameless days

Huipil	a blouse usually made of two panels of cotton fabric
hun p'iit	little one
ix lu	Fish
K'in	Sun
K'inich	King
K'u ix tz'it	the god of the maize
K'ubul K'ik'	Blood
K'ubul Luuch	the sacred obsidian bowl
Kab	Honey
k'ak' kuch	burning ritual
kalawala	used to treat infection
Kamul	sweet potatoes
kib'	a candle made of bee's wax
Kin	Day
K'inich Ahau	the sun god
Kutz	wild turkey
lavender	used as perfume for body and linens
Long Count Calendar	a count of days since a mythological creation approximately 5213 years
Luuch	serving bowls
Milpa	a garden area forged out of the surrounding jungle for the agricultural use of the nearby villages
Museo Mexicana de Arqueologia	Mexican Museum of archeology
Naah	house
Noh Ek'	the Great Star, Venus as the morning star
Oficina de Antiguedad	office of antiquaties
Osole	pork stew
Otoch	Home
Paayla	pottery vessel

Petaca	small leather pouch
Pwes	well
Quetzal	sacred bird revered by the Maya
stalky cornsilk flower	mixed with cacao for fever
tunich tzam	stone throne
Tzolkin	Mayan lunar calandar = 260 days made up of 13 cycles of 20 days each
ul atole	an intoxicating beverage made of fermented corn and honey.
Wah	flat bread, made of corn
warab'alja	literally sleeping place, forest shrines whereshamans' souls accumulate
xchuu paal	little girls
xu'ux	a basket
Xux Ek'	the Wasp Star t, Venus as he evening star
Yax Cheel Cab	the first tree of this world, the Tree of Life midwife and guardian of fertility

All English words have been translated into the Yucatec Mayan dialect using the following website: http://www.mostlymaya.com/EnglishMayan. html

READERS' NOTES

1) The Maya are the best-known civilization of Mesoamerica. They originated in the Yucatán around 2600 B.C. They rose to prominence around A.D. 250 in southern Mexico, Guatemala, northern Belize and western Honduras. Building on the ideas of earlier civilizations, such as the Olmec, the Maya developed astronomy, calendar systems and hieroglyphic writing. The Maya were known as well for elaborate ceremonial architecture, including temple-pyramids, palaces and observatories, all built without metal tools. They were skilled farmers, clearing large sections of tropical rain forest where groundwater was scarce. They built large underground reservoirs for the storage of rainwater. The Maya were skilled weavers and potters, and had extensive trade networks with distant peoples.

About 300 B.C., the Maya developed a hierarchical system of government ruled by nobles and kings. The society was made up of independent states, each with a rural farming communities and large urban cities acting as ceremonial centers. The civilization began to decline around A.D. 900 for reasons which are still largely unknown. The northern Maya were integrated into the Toltec society by A.D. 1200, although some peripheral centers continued to thrive until the Spanish Conquest in the early sixteenth century.

Maya history was cyclical: city-states rose and fell into decline, only to be replaced by others. But it could also be described as one continuous civilization guided by religion as the foundation of their culture even into the present day. For those who still follow the ancient Maya traditions, the belief in the influence of the cosmos on human lives and the need to pay homage to the gods through rituals continues as a modern hybrid of Christian-Maya faith.

2) The Mayan long-count calendar, which spans roughly 5,125 years starting in 3114 B.C., reaches the end of a cycle on December 21, 2012. That day brings to a close the 13th Bak'tun of the fifth creation according to Mayan myth. Rather than moving to the next Bak'tun, the calendar will reset at the end of the 13th cycle and begin with the 1st Bak'tun of the next or sixth creation

For the Maya, the end of the long count represents the end of an old cycle and the beginning of a new one. Did this Maya Prophecy foretell the end of the world? http://news. nationalgeographic.com/news/2011/12/111220-end-of-world-2012-maya-calendar-explained-ancient-science#

3) Mayan calendars and dating system-The Maya used three different dating systems in combination: the Long Count, the Tzolkin (divine calendar), and the Haab (civil calendar). So in our Mayan date of 12.19.19.17.7, 4 Manik, 10 Mac: 12.19.19.17. 7 is the Long Count date; 4 Manik is the Tzolkin date; 10 Mac is the Haab date.

The Long Count represents the number of days since the start of the Mayan era, since the beginning of the fifth creation of the world. The basic unit is the kin (day), which is the last component of the Long Count date.

Going from right to left the remaining components are:

Uinal   1 uinal = 20 kin = 20 days)
Tun   1 tun = 18 uinal = 360 days = approx. 1 year
Katun   1 katun = 20 tun = 7,200 days = approx. 20 years
Baktun   1 baktun = 20 katun = 144,000 days = approx. 394 years

The kin, tun, and katun are numbered from 0 to 19
The uinal are numbered from 0 to 17.
The baktun are numbered from 1 to 13.
http://www.webexhibits.org/calendars/calendar-mayan.html

4) Chan Bahlum II (Serpent Jaguar), (aka K'nich Kan B'alam); May 23, 635-February 20, 702, was king of the pre-Columbian Maya

polity of Baakal (Palenque) in the Classic period of Mesoamerican chronology. Chan Bahlum II took the throne on January 10, 684, several months after the death of his father and predecessor, Pacal the Great. He continued the ambitious project of adorning Palenque with fine art and architecture begun by his father. He was succeeded by his younger brother, K'inich K'an Joy Chitam II.

He was known as the Prophet King and a seer. He was reported to be well versed in astronomy. And that he linked the fortunes of the Maya people to the movement of the stars. http://ancienttreasures.com/lrgtext.php3?product=P-2&CA=11

5) 13.0.0.0.0, 4 Ahau, 3 Kankin—The day on which all the Mayan calendars end. Cooresponds to Decwmber 21, 2012 by the Gregorian calendar. According to Mayan myth it is the end of the fifth creation of the world and the beginning of the sixth. It is these factors which have lead many to invent what has become known as the Mayan Doomsday Prophecy. http://en.wikipedia.org/wiki/2012_phenomenon

6) The Maya name "Chich'en Itza" means "at the mouth of the well of the Itza." This comes from the words: chi', meaning "mouth" or "edge", and ch'e'en, meaning "well."

Itzá is the name of an ethnic group in the northern Yucatan Peninsula in the 10th and 11th centuries. Their name is believed to derive from the Maya itz, meaning "magic," and (h)á, meaning "water." http://en.wikipedia.org/wiki/Chichen_Itza

7) Ah Chinche K'an is Ahkan's full name Translation from the Maya language mean yellow butterfly—literally yellow flying insect. http://www.mostlymaya.com/EnglishMayan.html

8) Chan Took Pakal, Took Pak's full name meaning small flint shield
http://www.mostlymaya.com/EnglishMayan.html

9) All English words have been translated into the Yucatec Mayan dialect using the following website http://www.mostlymaya.com/EnglishMayan.html

10) The Mayan Creation myth appears in several written forms, primarily in the Popul Vu and on various structures in murals and

stelae. It appears in various forms. This account is a compilation of these stories.

11) Maya codices (singular <u>codex</u>) are folding <u>books</u> from the <u>pre-Columbian</u> <u>Maya civilization</u>. They were written in <u>Maya hieroglyphic script</u> on bark cloth, made from the inner bark of certain trees, usually the wild fig tree (<u>Ficus glabrata</u>). The paper was called by the Mayas huun. The folding books were made by professional scribes. Long sheets of the paper were fan folded and placed between wooden covers. The Maya developed their huun-paper around the 5th century. Only four partial codices survived the Spanish Inquisition in Mexico. These codices have been named for the cities where they eventually settled. The <u>Dresden codex</u> is generally considered the most important of the few that survive. <u>http://en.wikipedia.org/wiki/Maya_codices</u>

12) Diego de Landa was the Catholic Bishop of the Yucatan during the latter part of the 16th Century. His writings about the culture of the Maya of the Yucatan provide us with much of what we know about the culture and oral traditions of the Maya in the Yucatan. He is also considered the man responsible for the burning of the Maya codices and records. The Indians were devastated by the wanton destruction of records that contained their history, rituals, and customs. The Maya of the Yucatan, for the most part, had accepted, or had been forced to accept, the covenants of the Catholic Church. Landa considered these writings to be heresy and the work of the devil. He believed that their continued existence would draw the natives back to their evil ways. Landa redeemed himself to a degree, as he wrote a history of the traditions and culture of the Maya of the Yucatan. He was also one of a handful of Catholic priests who put forth the effort to learn the language of the Maya. Landa wrote, to the best of his ability, the sounds and alphabet of the Maya language, as they related to Spanish. It is this alphabet that has proved to be invaluable in the present-day deciphering of the Maya hieroglyphs.
<u>http://www.ancientamerica.org/library/media/384chapter13.htm</u>

13) Foundation for the Maya doomsday prophecy:

Written references to the end of Bak'tun 13 are few. In fact, most Maya scholars cite only one: a stone tablet on Monument

6 at the Tortuguero. What exactly the tablet says, though, is a mystery, because the glyphs in question are partially damaged. In 1996 by Brown University's Stephen Houston and the University of Texas at Austin's David Stuart interpreted it to indicate that a god will descend at the end of Bak'tun 13. What would happen next is uncertain, although the scholars suggested this might have been a prophecy of some sort.

This 1996 analysis was picked up by many New Age websites as evidence that the Maya calendar had predicted the end of the world. The inscription may actually say, on the 21st of December 2012, the god is going to come down and start a new cycle and the old world is going to die and the new world is going to be reborn.

The only other inference to a doomsday prophecy and the end of the fifth creation is an illustration in the Dresden Codex that depicts Chac Chel the Earth Goddess pouring out the waters of the world onto the earth indicating the possible flooding of the Earth.

The hype around 2012 stems from Westerners looking to the ancients for guidance, hoping that peoples such as the Maya knew something then that could help us through difficult times now.

http://news.nationalgeographic.com/news/2011/12/111220-end-of-world-2012-maya-calendar-explained-ancient-science#

14) Bloodletting, the cutting of part of the body to release blood—is an ancient ritual used by many Mesoamerican societies. For the ancient Maya, bloodletting rituals constituted a way to communicate with the gods and royal ancestors. This practice was usually performed by nobles through the perforation of body parts, mainly, but not only, tongue, lips, and genitals.

http://archaeology.about.com/od/mayaarchaeology/a/Bloodletting-Rituals-Maya.htm

15) The Mayan myth of the twin gods, Hun Bstz and Hun Chuen.
16) The Mesoamerican ballgame may have originated with the Olmecs or perhaps earlier. Excavations by Michael Coe uncovered

a number of ballplayer figurines at San Lorenzo which were radiocarbon-dated as far back as 1250-1150 BC.

Much time and energy was spent building ball courts. Courts were considered to be portals to the Maya underworld. The Great Ball Court at Chichen Itza is the largest ball court in Mesoamerica. A six-panel carving at Chichen Itza depicts a scene from the Popul Vu (the Maya creation story). Players are depicted wearing padded belts and padded arm, knee, and leg bands The players are also often depicted wearing elaborate headdresses.

It is likely that all ages and classes of people played the ballgame. The mural relates the story of the ritual ballgames between the Maya Hero Twins and the demonic Lords of Xibalba. Solid rubber balls were used in the game and may have represented cosmological movement. Details of the games varied over time and place. Some versions were played between two individuals, others between 2 teams of players.

The games all were played with a hard rubber ball in a sunken or walled linear court, so that the field is shaped like a capital I. The goal was to knock the ball into the opponent's end of the court or to make the ball pass through one of two vertical stone rings placed on each side of the court. The ball game was extremely violent. Players wore heavy padding. Even so, there were often serious injuries, and occasionally death. Rituals of sacrifice and bloodletting often accompanied the ballgame. On some occasions post-game ceremonies featured the sacrifice of the captain and other players on the losing side. The guides at Chichen Itza assert that the prize for the winning team was to be deified by losing their heads, supposedly at the hands of the losing team.

Poc-ta-tok or pitzil was a Yucatec Maya name for the game. http://archaeology.about.com/od/mayaarchaeology/a/ Bloodletting-Rituals-Maya.htm

17) An equinox occurs twice a year, when the tilt of the Earth's axis is not inclined, but the center of the Sun is in the same plane as the Earth's equator. The term equinox means the date when the days and the nights are of equal length. An equinox happens each year at two specific dates when at certain locations on the Earth's

equator the center of the Sun can be observed to be directly overhead/ This occurs about March 20/21 and September 22/23 each year.

The Kukulkan pyramid is closely related to the equinoxes. The Mayans were extraordinary astronomers and mathematicians. The central Pyramid at Chichen Itza is designed so that with the arrival of either equinox, seven triangles of sunlight are projected down the north staircase. With the carving of the serpents head at the base of the stairway the impression is that the snake is crawling down from the sky.
http://en.wikipedia.org/wiki/Equinox

18) The Maya knew that the Galactic Center of our Milky Way galaxy, the plane of the galaxy and our Sun will align with the earth in an extraordinary and unique way on 12-21-2012 at 11:11 AM. They called this the crossing of the Sacred Tree of Life. This marks the end of a Great cycle or Long Count and the beginning of a new cycle in their calendar.

This convergence of astrological objects occurs only once every 5000 years. The Mayan Long Count or Great Cycle of about 5125 years ends on December 21st, 2012, and coincides roughly with this convergence. http://www.freehoroscopesastrology.com/2012-mayan-astrology.aspx

19) Radiocarbon dating is a radiometric dating method that uses the naturally occurring radioisotope carbon-14 (^{14}C) to estimate the age of carbonaceous materials. One of the most frequent uses of radiocarbon dating is to estimate the age of organic remains from archaeological sites. Comparing the remaining ^{14}C fraction of a sample to that expected from atmospheric ^{14}C allows the age of the sample to be estimated. The steady state radioactivity concentration of exchangeable carbon-14 is about 14 disintegrations per minute (dpm) per gram.

Carbon has two stable, nonradioactive isotopes: carbon-12 (^{12}C), and carbon-13 (^{13}C). In addition, there are trace amounts of the unstable isotope carbon-14 (^{14}C) on Earth. Carbon-14 has a half-life of 5730 years, meaning that the amount of carbon-14 in a sample is halved over the course of 5730 years due to <u>radioactive decay</u>.

The concentration of carbon-14 in the atmosphere varies with time and locality. For the most accurate work, these variations are compensated by means of <u>calibration curves</u>. Once a living organism dies, the amount of carbon-14 gradually decreases through radioactive <u>beta decay</u> with a half-life of 5,730 ± 40 years.

Measurements are traditionally made by counting the <u>radioactive decay</u> of individual carbon <u>atoms</u>. The sensitivity of the method has been greatly increased by the use of <u>accelerator mass spectrometry</u> (AMS). With this technique ^{14}C atoms can be detected and counted directly *vs.* only detecting those atoms that decay during the time interval allotted for an analysis. AMS allows dating samples containing only a few milligrams of carbon. Radiocarbon ages are usually reported in "years <u>Before Present</u>" (BP). This is the number of radiocarbon years before 1950.

Radiocarbon dating laboratories generally report an uncertainty for each date. For example, 3000 ± 30 BP indicates a <u>standard deviation</u> of 30 radiocarbon years. From the beginning of the <u>industrial revolution</u> in the 18th century to the 1950s, the fractional level of ^{14}C decreased. Atmospheric ^{14}C almost doubled during the 1950s and 1960s due to atmospheric <u>atomic bomb tests</u>. http://en.wikipedia.org/wiki/Nuclear_testing

20) Spanish Conquistadors: The Spanish conquest of Yucatán was the campaign undertaken by the Spanish conquistadores against the Late Post-classic Maya states particularly in the northern and central Yucatán Peninsula. The conquest and colonization of Mesoamerica began in the early 16th century. Spanish control over Yucatán itself was effectively in place by 1547.

21) Mayan concept of time: unlike our modern concept of linear time the Maya beliefs indicate that their view of time was cyclical. From their observations of nature and the heavens the Maya patterns and ever repeating cycles. Day follows night as the sun rises every morning. Seasons followed in the same sequence year after year. The cycle of the ages repeat as well. Man is born, ages, and dies to

make room for the next generation. The Maya believed that the world had been created five times. Each creation ended only to be reborn in a new creation. And so the fifth creation will end on 12-21-12 to usher in the new cycle of the sixth creation.

MAYAN TIMELINE

11,000 B.C.

The first hunter-gatherers settle in the Maya highlands and lowlands.

1313

The creation of the world takes place, according to the Maya Long Count calendar.

2600

Maya civilization begins.

2000

The rise of the Olmec civilization, from which many aspects of Maya culture are derived. Village farming becomes established throughout Maya regions.

700

Writing is developed in Mesoamerica.

400

The earliest known solar calendars carved in stone are in use among the Maya, although the solar calendar may have been known and used by the Maya before this date.

300

The Maya adopt the idea of a hierarchical society ruled by nobles and kings.

100

The city of Teotihuacan is founded and for centuries is the cultural, religious and trading centre of Mesoamerica.

40 A.D.

The Maya highlands fall under the domination of Teotihuacan, and the disintegration of Maya culture and language begins in some parts of the highlands

50

The Maya city of Cerros is built, with a complex of temples and ball courts. It is abandoned (for reasons unknown) a hundred years later and its people return to fishing and farming.

100

The decline of the Olmecs.

500

The Maya city of Tikal becomes the first great Maya city, as citizens from Teotihuacan make their way to Tikal, introducing new ideas involving weaponry, captives, ritual practices and human sacrifice.

600

An unknown event destroys the civilization at Teotihuacan, along with the empire it supported. Tikal becomes the largest city-state in Mesoamerica, with as many as 500,000 inhabitants within the city and its hinterland.

625

Chichen-Itza was first settled it was largely agricultural. Because of the many cenotes in the area, it would have been a good place to settle.

683

The Emperor Pacal dies at the age of 80 and is buried in the Temple of the Inscriptions at Palenque. His son Chan Bahlum II takes the throne.

751

Long-standing Maya alliances begin to break down. Trade between Maya city- states declines, and inter-state conflict increases.

800

Chichen-Itza became a religious center of increasing importance. Arts and sciences flourished here.

869

Construction ceases in Tikal, marking the beginning of the city's decline.

899

Tikal is abandoned.

900

The Classic Period of Maya history ends, with the collapse of the southern lowland cities. Maya cities in the northern Yucatán continue to thrive.

925

The foundations of this magnificent civilization weakened, and the Maya abandoned their religions centers and the rural land around them. New, smaller centers were built and the great cities like Chichen-Itza were visited only to perform religious rites or to bury the dead.

989

The Itza people by the 10th century A.D. returned to Chichen-Itza.

1000

The Toltecs conquered the city of Chichen Itza. Chichen-Itza expanded, the city added even more spectacular buildings: the Observatory, Kukulcan's Pyramid, the Temple of the Warriors, The Ball Court, and The Group of the Thousand Columns.

1194

Mayapan subdued Chichen. The city was gradually abandoned.

1518

Spaniards sailing from Cuba journey encounter local chiefs wearing colorful cotton capes, brilliant feather ornaments, and gold jewelry.
They barter European glass beads for gold and supplies.

1519

On August 16, 1519, Cortés and his small army set off for Tenochtitlan.

1522

Catholic churches and monasteries, as well as mansions for the new Spanish rulers, are built.

1530

Spanish plants and animals and a wide range of new materials and technologies are introduced. Metal tools and other implements replace stone tools.

1549

Diego de Landa Calderón (12 November 1524-1579) arrived in the YucTan.

1562

Father Landa conducted the infamous auto-da-fé of Maní, burning all Mayan writings condeming them as heresy and the work of the devil. His actions destroyed much of that civilization's history, literature, and traditions.

1571

Landa was appointed Bishop and he took the seat in 1573. Landa's period as Bishop was marked by continued campaigns against idolatry among the Maya. The Tribunal of the Inquisition was established. This institution resulted in mass imprisonment, torture, and execution of the indigenous Mayan population.

1590

About 900 churches and monasteries exist. The Spaniards have control over most of present-day Mexico.

1588

The Spanish crown later issued a land grant that included Chichen Itza and by 1588 it was a working cattle ranch.

1972

Mexico enacted federal law over Monuments and Archeological, Artistic and Historic Sites that put all the nation's pre-Columbian monuments, including those at Chichen Itza, under federal ownership.

2003

National Institute of Anthropology and History (INAH) have excavated and restored Chichen Itza's structures. It now administers the site and oversees tourism here.

BIBLIOGRAPHY

ANDA ALANÍS, GUILLERMO DE. (2007). "Sacrifice and Ritual Body Mutilation in Postclassical Maya Society: Taphonomy of the Human Remains from Chichén Itzá's Cenote Sagrado". In Vera Tiesler and Andrea Cucina (eds.). *New Perspectives on Human Sacrifice and Ritual Body Treatments in Ancient Maya Society.* New York: pp. 190-208.

Arnold, J. R.; Libby, W. F. (1949). "Age Determinations by Radiocarbon Content: Checks with Samples of Known Age". *Science* 110 (2869): 678-680. doi:10.1126/science.110.2869.678. PMID 15407879. http://hbar.phys.msu.ru/gorm/fomenko/libby.htm.

AVENI, ANTHONY F. (1997). *Stairways to the Stars: Skywatching in Three Great Ancient Cultures.* New York: John Wiley & Sons.

COE, MICHAEL D. (1987). *The Maya* (4th edition (revised) ed.). London; New York: Thames & Hudson.

Coe, Michael D. (2001). **Reading the Maya glyphs.** London; New York: Thames & Hudson.

Coe, Michael D. (2011). *The Maya: Ancient Peoples and Places (Eighth Edition).* London: Thames & Hudson

COLAS, PIERRE R. and VOSS, ALEXANDER. (2006). "A Game of Life and Death—The Maya Ball Game". In Grube, Nikolai (ed.). *Maya: Divine Kings of the Rain Forest.* Cologne, Germay: Könemann. pp. 186-191.

Finley, Michael. (2003). "The Correlation Question". In *The Real Maya Prophecies: Astronomy in the Inscriptions and Codices.* Maya Astronomy. Archived from the original on December 7, 2006. Retrieved 2007-05-11.

Godwin, H. (1962). "Half-life of Radiocarbon". *Nature* **195** (4845): 984.

JACOBS, JAMES Q. (1999). "Mesoamerican Archaeoastronomy: A Review of Contemporary Understandings of Prehispanic Astronomic Knowledge". *Mesoamerican Web Ring.* jqjacobs.net. http://www.jqjacobs.net/mesoamerica/meso_astro.html. Retrieved 2007-11-23

Jenkins, John Major. (2005). "The Mayan Calendar and the Transformation of Consciousness". alignement2012.com. http://alignment2012.com/mayancalendarbasics.htm. Retrieved 2010-01-26.Jenkins, John Major. "Introduction to Maya Cosmogenesis". http://alignment2012.com/mc-intro.html. Retrieved 2009-10-14.

Jenkins, John Major. "What is the Galactic Alignment?". http://alignment2012.com/whatisga.htm. Retrieved 2009-05-11.

Kelly, Joyce. (1982). *The Complete Visitor's Guide to Mesoamerican Ruins.* Norman: University of Oklahoma Press.

Kunow, Marianna. (2003) Maya Medicine. Albuquerque:University of New Mexico Press.

MacDonald, G. Jeffrey. (March 27, 2007). "Does Maya calendar predict 2012 apocalypse?". *USA Today.* http://www.usatoday.com/tech/science/2007-03-27-maya-2012_n.htm.Retrieved 2009-10-14.

Münnich, K.O., Östlund, H.G., de Vries, H. (1958). "Carbon-14 Activity during the past 5,000 Years". *Nature*:182 (4647),pp.1432-3.

NASA. "Precession". http://www-istp.gsfc.nasa.gov/stargaze/Sprecess.htm. Retrieved 2009-11-03.

Plastino, W., Kaihola, L.; Bartolomei, P.; Bella, F. (2001). "Cosmic Background Reduction In The Radiocarbon Measurement By Scintillation Spectrometry At The Underground Laboratory Of Gran Sasso". *Radiocarbon* 43 (2A): 157-161. https://digitalcommons.library.arizona.edu/objectviewer?o=http%3A%2F%2Fradiocarbon.library.arizona.edu%2Fvolume43%2Fnumber2A%2Fazu_radiocarbon_v43_n2a_157_161_v.pdf.

"Radiocarbon dating". Utrecht University. http://www1.phys.uu.nl/ams/Radiocarbon.htm. Retrieved 1 May 2008.

Roys, Ralph L. (1931) The Ethno-Botany of the Maya. New Orleans:Tulane University Press.

Roys, Ralph L. (1967), *The Book of Chilam Balam of Chumayel.* Norman, Okla.: University of Oklahoma Press.

Severin, Gregory M . . . "The Paris Codex: Decoding an Astronomical Ephemeris". In *Transactions of the American Philosophical Society,* New Series, Vol. 71, No. 5 (1981). p. 75.

Sharer, Robert. (2006) The Ancient Maya. Stanford: Stanford University Press.

SCHELE, LINDA and DAVID FREIDEL (1990). *A Forest of Kings: The Untold Story of the Ancient Maya* (Reprint ed.). New York: Harper Perennial.

Schele, Linda. (1998). *The code of kings : the language of seven sacred Maya temples and tombs.* New York : Scribner.

Stuiver M, Reimer PJ, Braziunas TF (1998). "High-precision radiocarbon age calibration for terrestrial and marine samples". *Radiocarbon* 40: 1127-51. http://depts.washington.edu/qil/datasets/uwten98_14c.txt

Tedlock, Dennis. (1996). *Popol Vuh: The Definitive Edition of The Mayan Book of The Dawn of Life and The Glories of Gods and Kings.* New York: Touchstone Publishing

Thompson, J. Eric S. (1966) *The Rise and Fall of Maya Civilization.* Norman, Okla.: University of Oklahoma Press.

Worcester-Makemson, Maud. (June 1957). "The miscellaneous dates of the Dresden codex". *Publications of the Vassar College Observatory* 6: 4. http://adsabs.harvard.edu/full/19: http://www.mostlymaya.com/EnglishMayan.html57PVasO . . . 6 . . . . 1M. Retrieved 2009-10-14.

Links:

Anthropology: http://www.anthropology.si.edu/maya/mayaprint.html

Archaeology of prehistoric native America: an encyclopedia. 1998. http://books.google.ca/books?id=_0u2y_SVnmoC&pg=RA1-PA682&lpg=RA1-PA682&dq=old+crow+caves+debate&source=bl&ots=OQs3QyVT5I&sig=4mAK2XUUV6dpJCa7I6hEwtQlQ&hl=en&ei=ul2gSqjjGqif8QaHo6zpDw&sa=X&oi=book_result&ct=result&resnum=4#v=onepage&q=old%20crow%20caves%20debate&f=false

Bloodletting: http://archaeology.about.com/od/mayaarchaeology/a/Bloodletting-Rituals-Maya.htm

Chan Bahlum II: http://ancienttreasures.com/lrgtext.php3?product=P-2&CA=11

Convergence: http://www.freehoroscopesastrology.com/2012-mayan-astrology.aspx

Diego de Landa: http://www.ancientamerica.org/library/media/384chapter13.htm

Doomsday Prophecy: http://news.nationalgeographic.com/news/2011/12/111220-end-of-world-2012-maya-calendar-explained-ancient-science

English to Mayan translation: http://www.mostlymaya.com/EnglishMayan.html

Mayan Calendars: http://www.pauahtun.org/Calendar/tools.html

Mayan Calendars: http://www.webexhibits.org/calendars/calendar-mayan.
html
Mayan códices: http://www.mayadiscovery.com/ing/history/codices.htm
Ritual ball game: http://archaeology.about.com/od/mayaarchaeology/a/
Bloodletting-Rituals-Maya.htm
Vernal equinox: http://www.world-mysteries.com/chichen_kukulcan.htm

Wikipedia,

http://en.wikipedia.org/wiki/Mayamedicine
http://en.wikipedia.org/wiki/Mayacivilization
http://en.wikipedia.org/wiki/Mayangods
http://en.wikipedia.org/wiki/Maya_script#Decipherment
http://en.wikipedia.org/wiki/Chan_Bahlum_II
http://en.wikipedia.org/wiki/2012_phenomenon
http://en.wikipedia.org/wiki/Chichen_Itza
http://en.wikipedia.org/wiki/Maya_codices
http://en.wikipedia.org/wiki/Radiocarbon_dating#mw-head
http://en.wikipedia.org/wiki/Nuclear_testing
http://en.wikipedia.org/wiki/Equinox